PRAISE FOR THE F

"Fans of the Expanse series will enj[illegible] engaging and fast-moving combination of corporate machinations, police procedural, and interstellar naval combat."

—*Booklist*

"A series you should start if you are a fan of grounded space opera with a military lean. The Palladium Wars comes at straight-up military fiction from an angle that keeps it interesting."

—*Locus* magazine

"I gulped down *Ballistic* in one long read, staying awake half the night, and now I want the next one!"

—George R.R. Martin

DESCENT

THE · PALLADIUM · WARS

ALSO BY MARKO KLOOS

Frontlines

Terms of Enlistment
Lines of Departure
Angles of Attack
Chains of Command
Fields of Fire
Points of Impact
Orders of Battle
Centers of Gravity
Measures of Absolution (A Frontlines Kindle novella)
"Lucky Thirteen" (A Frontlines Kindle short story)

The Palladium Wars

Aftershocks
Ballistic
Citadel

Frontlines: Evolution

Scorpio

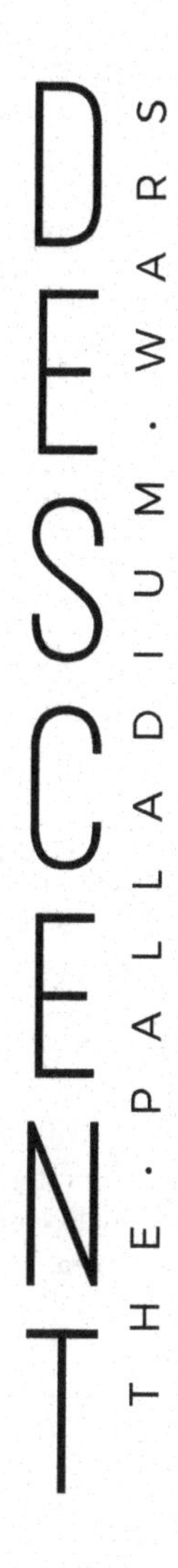

AUTHOR OF THE FRONTLINES SERIES

MARKO KLOOS

This is a work of fiction. Names, characters, organizations, places, events, and incidents are either products of the author's imagination or are used fictitiously. Otherwise, any resemblance to actual persons, living or dead, is purely coincidental.

Text copyright © 2024 by Marko Kloos
All rights reserved.

No part of this book may be reproduced, or stored in a retrieval system, or transmitted in any form or by any means, electronic, mechanical, photocopying, recording, or otherwise, without express written permission of the publisher.

Published by 47North, Seattle

www.apub.com

Amazon, the Amazon logo, and 47North are trademarks of Amazon.com, Inc., or its affiliates.

ISBN-13: 9781542036153 (paperback)
ISBN-13: 9781542036160 (digital)

Cover design by Shasti O'Leary Soudant
Cover image: © ZargonDesign / Getty; © MoinMoin, © Fred Fokkelman / Shutterstock

Printed in the United States of America

For Robin: Lucky 13 forever.

CHAPTER 1

ADEN

"Major Robertson, report to security lock five. I repeat, Major Robertson, report to security lock five."

Aden looked up from the vegetables he had been chopping and put the kitchen knife on the counter next to the pile of greens he was preparing for the dinner salad. He looked back at the kitchen boss, Sergeant Daly, who was ladling mashed potatoes from a large pot into one of the bins at the serving counter. Daly rested the pot on the edge of the counter and nodded at the kitchen door.

"Go ahead. We are just about done anyway. I can handle the rest."

"I haven't finished the salad yet," Aden replied.

"I don't know why you keep trying to get greens into these people," Daly said. "Most of them are going to skip the salad; you know that. Takes away tray space for carbs and fat. It's like Gretians are allergic to plant matter."

"Well, *I* wasn't going to skip it." Aden stepped over to the prep sink and washed his hands, then dried them with a clean towel.

"I'll finish it for you. What kind of base?"

"Oil and vinegar. I already mixed it. Over there, in the light-blue container," Aden said.

Sergeant Daly nodded at the kitchen door again in reply, and Aden put down the towel and walked off. The kitchen was empty except for the two of them, and Aden knew that one person could handle dinner without a problem. The detainment unit had space for 150 people, a full company of prisoners of war, but right now it only had a dozen residents, Aden included. All the POWs were long back on Gretia by now, even the Blackguards who got to serve double terms. The only ones who remained were a handful of reprobates and rule breakers who had violated their terms of release.

Aden stepped through the security arch that scanned him for sharp kitchen implements. It gave a green light and released the lock for the outer door, which slid open silently. Outside, the sound of his boot soles on the floor seemed too loud and harsh to his ears. This unit wasn't the one where he had served his original detainment after the war, but it was laid out the same way. Back when there were 150 people sharing the space, there was always some background noise—people talking in the communal spaces, working out on the running track, or listening to music in their rooms with the doors open. Now there was just an eerie silence, and the way Aden's footsteps echoed in the empty space made the place feel like a museum.

That's what we are after all, Aden thought. *Relics of the past, soldiers who served a cause that's dead, for a nation that no longer exists.*

In many ways, this imprisonment was easier than his last one had been. With so few people in such a large space, they all had their pick of rooms, and there was never a line for food or an argument over communal resources. Aden hardly ever saw all his fellow prisoners in one spot except for mealtimes and the mandatory morning orders. But sandwiched between those two terms had been half a standard year of freedom as a member of *Zephyr*'s crew, and that had rewired his brain somehow. Now the prison unit felt much more confining than before, the constant awareness that he couldn't just walk out of the arcology and join his friends on their next job.

The guard at the security lock opened the door and deactivated the stun arches, which switched their status lights from red to green. This was another change from the procedure he knew in the old prison unit. Before, the Rhodian jailers would come through the lock in pairs and escort him out instead of letting him walk across by himself and without a minder. But just as this prison unit was under capacity, the guard complement was far below the usual personnel count, and the quiet atmosphere had spread to the Rhodies as well. Aden's unit was at 10 percent occupancy, and there weren't enough of them to start trouble even if they had a mind for it.

And they know it, too, Aden thought as he walked through the security lock toward the sole guard standing on the other side. *They're just zookeepers at this point.*

"Good morning, Corporal Keeley," he said to the guard.

"Morning, Major," Keeley replied. "The CO wants to have a word."

"Bit early for the weekly status report, isn't it?"

"I don't know, Major. I am just fetching you as ordered. Follow me, please."

—

When Aden walked into the unit commander's office, he stopped short in the doorway. Instead of the warden, Captain Glynn, a tall officer in a Rhodian Navy uniform sat behind the CO's desk. There was another officer in the room as well, sitting in a chair she had moved next to the CO's desk and had turned to face the door.

"Good morning, Major Robertson," the Rhodian officer behind the desk said.

"Good morning," Aden replied, still recovering from the surprise of seeing two unexpected faces instead of the unit warden. "Lieutenant Commander Park, is it?"

"I wasn't sure if you'd remember me," Park said with a little smile. "I got a bump in rank after our business in deep space."

He folded his hands on the desk in front of him. Aden saw that he was wearing the three stripes of a commander, and the wreathed star above the stripes marked him as the CO of a ship.

"Commander," Aden corrected himself. "It's not a day I am likely to forget any time soon. We turned a nuke over to you. And you let me go even though you had me dead to rights with my fake ID pass."

"I had bigger fish to hook," Commander Park said and gestured at the chair in front of the desk. "Please, do sit down."

Aden walked into the room and took the offered chair.

"This is my XO, Lieutenant Hunter," Park said. "You've met her before as well, indirectly. She was with me on *Hecate* when we took out that Gretian gun cruiser together."

"I remember that, too. You gave us a tow to Rhodia One. And I was in a prison cell at the end of that trip. I know I already got one free pass from you before, but forgive me if I felt that was one hell of a way to pay me back."

"That was out of my hands," Dunstan said. "I'm not in charge of Rhodia One, just my own ship."

"You mean you didn't call ahead and tell them about my status?"

Dunstan shook his head. "I do believe I warned you when we parted ways that your pass would come up yellow again somewhere. But I didn't tell your little secret to Rhodia One security. They caught you all on their own."

"I guess you used up all your luck that day when your crew managed to evade three hundred tungsten slugs in that souped-up little racing yacht," Lieutenant Hunter contributed.

"What happened to that Gretian cruiser?"

Lieutenant Hunter and Commander Park exchanged a glance.

"That's classified information," the commander answered for his XO. "But you can probably figure out that there has been a change of management. Her raiding days are over. She'll be used for honest work from now on."

"And *Zephyr*?"

"She's still in dry dock, as far as I know. That shrapnel did more damage than they thought. The little racing yacht was not built for combat. You'd all be fine-grained stardust right now if someone hadn't spent a fortune on the permits and the hardware for military-grade point-defense emitters."

That someone was Tristan, of course. The ship's cook and medic had been the sole face behind *Zephyr's* ownership consortium, and when he died, he left them each a share of the title. Aden was the partial owner of a ship that he'd probably never set foot on again. He leaned back in his chair a little and glanced at the ceiling. Somewhere high above his head, Rhodia One orbited the planet, a city in space that saw hundreds of ships and thousands of people arriving and departing from its airlocks every day. His friends were up there right now, working on their ship and drinking and laughing together while he was locked up in this arcology.

His room down here was ten times the size of his bunk module on *Zephyr's* crew deck, but somehow the walls felt much closer together. His Mnemosyne access was curated and filtered and set to read-only mode: no messages out, no contacts with anyone except for approved family members and legal counsel. The comms restriction was a bit of a blessing in disguise to Aden. It meant that he wouldn't be tempted to contact his sister, Solveig, and jeopardize her safety. And without the option to get his friends on *Zephyr* on the approved contacts list, there was no chance for them to reject the comms request, no way for him to find out if none of his crewmates wanted to talk to him anymore. Only Captain Decker had known about his fake identity. She had given him a chance to prove his merits, but he wasn't sure the others would shrug off that he was a former Gretian Blackguard, not after he kept that fact a secret from them for six months.

"I'm sorry it went down for you the way it did," Commander Park said. "I mean that. How are you doing?"

"You mean in here?" Aden shrugged. "I'm fine, I guess. Bored to tears. When I was here after the war, I was the senior officer for my section. I had a whole company to run. I was accountable for discipline and order. You know the rules."

Commander Park nodded.

"Now I have nothing to do," Aden continued. "There are twelve POWs in this section. I can go days without seeing some of them. Not that I want to be in charge of anyone."

"How much time did they add?" Lieutenant Hunter asked. He had a good idea that she knew the answer already, but he played along and provided it anyway.

"Three years," he said. Saying the words out loud made his heart sink a little, as if acknowledging the sentence made it more real somehow. He had already lost a decade of his life to the war and the internment that followed, and having to give up three more years of it for the crime of not wanting to return home was a dry and bitter pill to have to swallow.

Commander Park shook his head slowly.

"That's a lot of extra time for a fake ID pass."

"It was a ten-minute hearing," Aden replied. "Level II parole violation, illegal reentry with intent. Mandatory sentence minimum."

"Mandatory sentencing is such horseshit," Park said. "You had a whole lot of extenuating circumstances on your side."

"Yeah, well, they weren't interested in hearing any of them."

"If I had known, I would have showed up at the hearing and made a case for leniency. But nobody told me about it. I only heard the news from your captain when I checked in on her a week later."

How are they? Aden almost asked, but he bit the question off before it could slip out of his mouth. He hoped they were well, but he would rather not hear that Maya and Tess wanted nothing more to do with him.

"Doesn't matter now," he said. "Not that I don't appreciate the sentiment. Why are you here anyway, Commander? I mean, I'm glad for the updates. But I don't think that's why you came down to this place. I'm sure you have better things to do than to check up on me."

Commander Park's curt smile made wrinkles appear in the corners of his light-blue eyes. Both Rhodian officers had eyes in the same shade of blue, ice floating on the clear surface of a deep mountain lake.

"No, Major Robertson," he said. "That's not the only reason we came down here."

Lieutenant Hunter cleared her throat.

"You've been here for three months. Do you really want to spend the next three *years* here?" she asked.

Aden shook his head with a thin smile that had no humor in it.

"Nobody in their right mind would want to spend three years of the rest of their life staring out of a window, Lieutenant," he said. "But that's not up to me."

"What if it *could* be up to you?" Commander Park said.

Aden leaned back in his chair and folded his arms across his chest.

"And here comes the reason for the rhetorical question."

"You're not obligated to listen to what we have to say," Lieutenant Hunter said. Aden could tell that she was mildly irritated because the slight Gretian accent in her otherwise fluent Rhodian became just a little bit more obvious. "We can head back to the spaceport, and you can return to lockup and serve out your time."

"It's entirely up to you," Commander Park added. "But we're not making this trip again. If you don't want to talk to us, you won't be able to change your mind later."

"You did me a favor once when you could have gone by the book. I figure I owe you more than just hearing you out for that. It wouldn't be grateful to have you come here for nothing."

"And you're curious about what I want from you," Commander Park said.

"And I'm curious about what you want from me," Aden confirmed.

"All right." Park nodded and straightened his posture in the CO's chair.

"Under normal circumstances, I'd take you to a secure facility to talk about what I am about to share with you," Commander Park said. "But taking you out of here would get more attention than I care to draw. Better to make it look like this is just another visit from navy intelligence."

"Now I'm curious *and* a little worried," Aden said.

"I'll get right to it and dispense with all the fluff and the preambles. Gretia is going to shit. There's an insurgency underway that is getting worse every month. Six months ago, the planet was quiet. The occupation forces had everything under control. Now it seems like they're filling body bags every other day. And no matter how many troops we pour into the mess, we can't seem to get ahead of these people."

Aden sat up straight.

"Any idea who they are and what they want?"

"The intel people think the hard core are military veterans. People who have small-unit special-operations training. They know their tactics. Worse, they know ours as well. And they have advanced weapons and gear. Stuff we didn't even see on the battlefield when the war was still going on. Whenever they hit us, they know what sort of hardware to bring and how to apply it to minimize our strengths and maximize theirs. And they are not concerned about civilian casualties. They've killed more of your people than ours."

"That's not a smart insurgency," Aden said. "Resistance movements are about winning hearts and minds as much as they are about fighting back. You need support from the population. Hard to get that when you're blowing them up."

"That's what the textbook says," Commander Park replied. "But they threw it out. At least the parts about not pissing off your own side. I think they're just causing as much chaos as possible. To let the whole planet know that the Alliance can't keep control."

"I haven't been a military intelligence officer in half a decade," Aden said. "If you're coming to me with this to get some special insight into the Gretian mind, I'll have to disappoint you, Commander."

"Remind me of your job in the Blackguard intelligence service," Park said.

"My specialty was counterintelligence. Force protection."

"And you were in the field."

"I was a company commander, but yes, I was in the field. I spent the whole war on Oceana."

"Mingling with the population. Keeping your eyes and ears open for any threats to the occupation forces. Gaining the trust of the locals. That sort of thing, right?"

"Correct," Aden said.

"If you spent five years snooping for the Blackguard among an unfriendly population without getting your cover blown, you must have been good at your job."

"Only because I could pass for a local. My mother is Oceanian. I spent a lot of time there as a child."

"It takes a little more than that to stay alive in a city full of people who'd drown you in the nearest canal if they found out your real identity. You seem to have a talent for convincing people you're someone else," Commander Park said.

He got out of his chair and walked over to the window on the back wall of the office, which overlooked the arcology's central atrium and its countless ledges and terraces overflowing with lush and colorful plant life. Aden watched as the Rhodian officer observed the scene silently for a few moments.

"The insurgency on the ground calls itself Odin's Wolves," he continued, still looking out into the atrium. "I'm not able to give them the same treatment we administered to Odin's Ravens because I am the commander of a warship, not a special operations officer. That's a job for other people."

Park turned around and slipped his hands into the pockets of his uniform trousers. He looked at Aden and frowned.

"The problem on the ground on Gretia is that the insurgency hasn't thrown out the entire textbook on resistance SOPs. They're still following the part about clandestine cell operations. We've managed to uncover a few of them, but never more than one or two individuals at once. And they are very good at sniffing out moles."

"You've tried to get people inside?" Aden asked.

"We did. Without much success. They are very careful with their recruiting. Whoever's in charge of Odin's Wolves is running a tight ship."

"And you need someone on the ground who can pass the smell test and get on the inside," Aden said, the realization making his stomach lurch a little.

Commander Park flashed his thin-lipped smile again.

"We have a handful of people with credentials that may pass muster with the Wolves," he said. "But none of them are trained military intelligence officers."

"You want to recruit me to go back to Gretia and infiltrate the insurgency for the Alliance," Aden summarized. "You must be out of your mind."

"You are the perfect candidate for that job, Major. You have experience with covert and clandestine operations. And you have already proven that you're willing to do the right thing. Even if it means going up against your own people."

"I helped you bag some pirate ships," Aden said. "There's a world of difference between that and going to ground in that place on your behalf. Do you have any idea what they'll do to me if they find out I am snooping for the Alliance?"

"They'll execute you as a traitor and send you to Alliance HQ in small pieces," Lieutenant Hunter offered.

"Then you realize that this isn't much of a sales pitch. I broke my parole terms to stay away from Gretia. That's why I am here in the first place. Why in all the worlds would I want to go back there and risk my neck for you?"

Commander Park leaned back in his chair and shrugged.

"I don't know, Major. If you could do anything you wanted right now, what would it be?"

Aden considered the question for a moment.

"I'd go find *Zephyr* and rejoin my crew. Hope they still want me around after I lied to them for months. And never set foot on Rhodia or Gretia again. No offense."

Commander Park nodded slowly.

"When they asked me to come out here and talk to you, I told them that they'd have to get creative if they wanted you to even consider their offer. They left the incentive up to me. Within reason, of course. I can't promise you a million ags and a pleasure yacht. But I can get you out of here and back into space with your friends."

"You'd be able to commute the rest of my sentence," Aden said.

"We can do better than that, I think. A full pardon, and they'd probably give you your choice of citizenship if you really don't ever want to go back to Gretia again after you're done. I'm sure they could make your fake identity official. And return all your credits to you, plus interest and hazard pay."

No way in all the hells, Aden wanted to reply. The sentence was already on the tip of his tongue. He swallowed it and took a deep breath to steady his mind. The thought of going back to Gretia wasn't appealing even without the prospect of violent death at the hands of his own people. But the alternative was to let the Rhodian commander walk out of this office dissatisfied, and somehow Aden knew that the offer wouldn't be extended to him again if he turned it down right now. He had been back in detention for three months now, long enough to be resigned to the inevitability of his extended sentence. Now there was a piece of bait dangling in front of him that could wipe the slate clean and let him pick up the new life he had chosen for himself.

"That's a lot of trust to put into someone who was your enemy until recently. What if I accept and then just disappear as soon as you let me loose on the planet?"

Commander Park shrugged again.

"You could do that. But you'd never be able to leave Gretia again, and you'd always have to look over your shoulder. I really don't think you want to live out the rest of your life in hiding there. As you said, that's why you're here in the first place."

"I don't want to go back there, with or without the insurgency. But I don't want to be here either. Not if I can't just walk free in three years instead of finding myself on a ship back to Gretia under guard," Aden said.

"Is that a *yes*, then?" Park asked.

"It's not a *no*. But I'll need some time to think about it."

"Of course," Commander Park said. "But bear in mind that there are people getting killed by this insurgency every day. Some of them are our soldiers. Most of them are *your* people. Civilians who walked across a public square at the wrong time, or who just made a convenient target. You don't seem like the kind of man who wouldn't help put a stop to it if he could."

"I assume there is an expiration date on that offer," Aden said.

Commander Park nodded.

"The offer expires as soon as Lieutenant Hunter and I walk out of this place and step into the skylift down in the atrium," he said. "If you agree to do this, we are taking you with us. If you decline, you may return to your confinement unit, and you won't see us again.

I realize that doesn't give you much time to consider the proposal. Unfortunately, we don't have a lot of time for a courtship dance where we try to maximize our respective leverage. No hard feelings if you decline. I just don't want to make this trip three more times while you make up your mind. The war isn't waiting for either of us."

Aden considered the proposal in silence for a few moments while the two Rhodian officers looked at him expectantly.

"You certainly know how to pitch a high-pressure sale," he said.

"It's not a clever negotiating tactic, Major Robertson. I think we're both getting a little too old for horseshit games. You know what I want from you. Now you can tell me what you ask in return, and we can shake on it and get the hells out of here. Otherwise I'll wish you the best of luck for the future and be on my way."

"Can I have fifteen minutes to consider?"

Commander Park got out of his chair and pulled on the bottom of his uniform tunic to straighten it.

"Certainly," he said. "I can let you have fifteen minutes. Lieutenant Hunter and I are going to go to the officers' mess upstairs for some coffee. The corporal of guards will be right outside."

Aden nodded. "Thank you, Commander. I'll not take up any more of your time than that."

"You've changed since the last time I saw you, Major. When I had you on *Minotaur*, I knew that you were a soldier the moment you walked in. You still had that military bearing. Now you look and act like a spacer. Your new friends rubbed off on you."

Park walked over to the door, and Lieutenant Hunter stood up and followed him. When she was at the door, Aden decided to address her in Gretian.

"Where were you born, Lieutenant?"

Hunter stopped in the doorway and turned around. If her expression had looked mildly irritated before, his words had turned it positively sour.

"I don't speak that anymore," she replied in Rhodian. "I don't even like hearing it anymore. But to answer your question, I was born and raised in Grund."

"Near Sandvik," he said, switching back to Rhodian as well. "I know the place."

She gave him a long look. Then she turned her head to address Commander Park, who was waiting for her outside.

"Go ahead, sir," she told him. "I'll be right there."

Park nodded and walked off. Lieutenant Hunter stepped back into the room and closed the door behind her.

"I was born and raised on Gretia," she said. "But I haven't been back there since I left. That was over ten years ago. Before the rest of you decided to set all the worlds on fire."

Aden wanted to voice a protest out of reflex, tell her the same thing he had told Park when they had first met—that he had joined before the war, and that he had been in field intelligence, not on the front lines. He had never fired a single round in anger in the four years of conflict, never touched a gun except on the firing range for the mandatory annual small-arms qualification. But the look on her face told him that she didn't care what he had done in the Blackguard, only that he had worn the uniform.

"I don't speak Gretian anymore," she repeated. "I don't even like to hear it spoken out loud. I'm a naval officer and proud citizen of Rhodia. So don't address me in that language again if you want to stay on my good side."

"I apologize for the offense," Aden said. "I should have known better."

Her glare softened a little at his expression of contrition.

"Maybe you didn't exactly deserve that," she said after a moment of awkward silence. "But without people like you, I'd still have a wife and a peaceful life, and I wouldn't need meds to sleep through the night."

"Maybe I *did* deserve it," he said. "I never killed anyone. But I went along with everything. Makes me just as guilty as the people who pulled the triggers."

She gave him another long look and shook her head slowly.

"I can't help my accent. I can't get rid of it. I don't have your ear for languages. But I picked my side a long time ago, without any doubts. Maybe you should pull your head out of your ass and do the same."

"Excuse me?" Aden said, taken aback.

"You gave up three years of your life because you didn't want to go back there. I know that you don't want to be Gretian anymore. But that's not an identity. That's just self-loathing. You don't even know who the hells you are at this point. And you may want to figure that out before they cut you loose again. Or you'll just keep drifting between all the worlds."

She turned and opened the door again. Outside, Corporal Keeley stood guard. He stepped back to make way for Lieutenant Hunter as she walked out of the room.

"Twelve minutes now, Major Robertson," she said over her shoulder. "Stop circling the chairs. Pick a side and commit yourself to it. The right one isn't hard to figure out here."

She closed the door behind her as she left, and the click of the locking mechanism echoed in the room like an exclamation point.

Chapter 2

Idina

The tunnel was as dark and silent as starless space. The air was warm and stale, and the walls of the concrete tube were dripping with moisture. It was the closest Idina had come to feeling at home since she had first set foot on Gretia.

She was at the front of her team's formation, quietly stepping through the puddles on the tunnel floor on the soft soles of her battle armor's boots. Wearing the old Palladian tunnel combat gear again felt like she had stepped back in time and space. Ahead, the darkness extended for a kilometer or more, the walls of the tunnel converging around a tiny black hole of a center far in the distance.

Idina held up her hand to signal a halt. Behind her, every member of her team silently crouched and took a knee, weapons at the ready. They had all been handpicked by Idina, Palladian commandos who had served in the war as enlisted and junior NCOs, battle-hardened and experienced in tunnel warfare. The hand signals weren't a necessity for silent communication because the helmets they were all wearing had soundproof comms sets. But old habits had been deeply ingrained over years of training and combat, and the motions were part of everyone's muscle memory.

The multi-spectrum sensor package in her armor's helmet scanned her field of vision a hundred times per second. It combined the information on the inside of her helmet visor, collating all the data and presenting it as a comprehensive overlay in front of her eyes—low light, infrared, thermal, electromagnetic, all synthesized into a view of the tunnel that could alert her to the movements of an insect's wings a hundred meters away. She still liked to cycle through all the modes manually to check the inputs, out of habit. The AI was good at crunching data, but it didn't parse things like gut feeling—or interpreting the sort of nuance that could make the difference between spotting a sophisticated trap or walking right into it.

"Shah, check my mark," she sent to the sergeant who was kneeling behind and to the right of her. "There's a temperature variation on the wall. Right side, sixty-three meters down."

Sergeant Shah moved up with swift and silent steps. He scanned the area she had indicated and studied the output on his own visor screen.

"It's a few degrees above ambient," Shah confirmed after a few seconds of analysis. "Little puddle on the floor that is blending in with the condensate. Splash pattern half a meter up the wall next to it. I'd say someone took a piss. Forty, forty-five minutes ago."

Idina chuckled softly.

"When you have to go, you have to go, I guess."

"Means we're definitely not alone down here," Shah said.

Far above their heads, a low rumble traveled through the bedrock, the sound of a commuter train passing through the transit tube that ran fifty meters above the defunct vactrain line they were patrolling. Idina could see the visualization of the infrasound waves moving outward from the source, marking the path of the train as it made its way along the magnetic track. She watched and waited until the train was out of range and the pulses on her visor subsided. They were a hundred meters below the outskirts of Sandvik, half a kilometer from the old vactrain terminal where they had entered the tunnel, and all the transit lines were stacked on top of each other this close to the city center. If she had to set up shop anywhere in this vactrain loop, it would be right here, where there was a lot of electromagnetic noise from the city above, and where it was easy to siphon power from the city's systems unnoticed.

None of the drones they had sent down the tunnels had found anything except disused infrastructure suffering the slow decay of neglect. But Idina had trusted her gut feeling and asked to take a team underground, and now they were here, retracing the path of the drones and clearing the large vacuum tube one quarter-kilometer segment at a time.

She checked the map of the vactrain system. *Three segments down, seven to go.*

"Let's hope it's not just some civvie on a treasure hunt," she said. "Move up to the next segment, nice and slow."

Idina underlined the order with the hand signal for "slow advance," a single pump of her fist. The staggered column of soldiers set itself in motion again behind her, following her down the tunnel in evenly spaced intervals, silent as ghosts. Even the weapons they carried were quiet, compact carbines with huge liquid-filled internal suppressors that made every shot sound like a weak spit from a breathless man. If they encountered trouble down here, they were able to dish out a great deal of violence very quickly and never get louder than a friendly conversation.

They passed the spot Idina had pointed out to Shah. The temperature difference between the stain and the concrete underneath it was minimal, but at close range it was obvious that someone had indeed relieved themself against the wall of the tunnel. She took the electronic swab she was carrying from its storage pocket and knelt to take a DNA sample. Even if they found nothing else down here, the Gretian cops with their impressively thorough data collection habits should be able to find out who had been wandering around in this tube.

At the end of the segment, there was an alcove set into the wall of the tunnel, a small vestibule with a heavy steel door. According to the schematics on Idina's screen, the door led to one of the maintenance areas and emergency shelters that were spaced out along the track in regular intervals. Every door down here had been welded shut by the Gretians under Alliance supervision years ago, along with every station entrance and service-access hatch along the thousand-kilometer vactrain loop. She glanced at the door as she moved past the vestibule. The edges of the steel slab were fused to the doorframe with thick and sloppy-looking welds that didn't appear at all like neat and precise Gretian handiwork. The outside of the frame was painted in alternating diagonal stripes of yellow and black, and there was a small emergency-lighting array mounted above the door that looked cloudy with mold and moisture.

Idina focused her attention on the tunnel in front of her again, but something she saw out of the corner of her eye made her return her gaze to the floor of the vestibule. There was an irregularity in the film of wet decay that covered everything down here. It was almost too faint even to her sensors to be noticeable, but it caught her eye just enough to warrant a closer inspection. She signaled a halt and crouched in front of the vestibule to look. Somewhere nearby, the water on the ground had been contaminated by a small amount of leaked lubricant or cooling liquid, and the surface of the puddle at her feet had a very faint rainbow sheen to it. Someone had stepped through the puddle and onto the dry concrete of the exit alcove, and their footwear had left a slightly damp imprint on the rough surface, transferring some of that iridescent slick into the grime on the floor of the raised vestibule. It was probably nothing—maybe whoever had taken a piss a few dozen meters back had stopped here to adjust themself or check to see if the door was still sealed—but Idina hadn't survived the war to become a seasoned color sergeant by ignoring her instincts.

She gestured for Sergeant Shah to join her and pointed out the footprint to him. Shah nodded and looked at the door in front of them. He took another step and carefully put his hand on it. The surface of the steel was grimy and flecked with little rust spots where the paint had worn off and succumbed to the humid environment.

"These welds look right to you?" she asked.

Shah slowly ran his fingertips over the surface of the sloppy weld lines. He extended his combat blade from its sheath in the armor on his forearm and poked at one welded edge, which gave way a little underneath the tip of the knife.

"I don't think this is a real weld," Shah said. He scraped away at the weld line with the blade. Big flakes of material fell with every stroke of the knife, pale gray chunks that rained down onto the concrete floor and bounced off in a way that seemed too light for pieces of welding alloy.

"It's a fake weld," Shah confirmed. He wedged the edge of the blade behind the tattered weld line and popped off a big piece with a quick turn of his wrist. "Looks like epoxy. They dressed up the mix to make it look like metal."

"That is in no way suspicious." Idina cycled through her visor's sensor filters until she reached the thermal imaging. In the spots where Shah had pried off the metal-colored epoxy, cooler air was seeping through the cracks. The color difference looked like light-blue wisps coming from the space behind the door and dissipating slowly in the warmer air of the tunnel.

She stepped back and pointed at the door. "Crack it open. Let's see what's in there that requires air conditioning."

"Go soft or hard?" Shah asked.

"Go soft. Let's stay sneaky as long as possible." She checked the schematic for the access doors on her visor's data projection.

"Inward opening. Hinges here, here, and here." She marked the spots with quick flashes from her rifle's infrared laser. "Lock's a triple-barrel magnetic dead bolt."

Shah nodded and moved his rifle around on its sling to free up his hands. He reached into one of his gear pouches and took out a small cylinder. Idina watched as he carefully sprayed thermal breaching compound into the cracks of the door by the lock. Behind her, the other members of the team were guarding their backs, alert for any movement or sound coming out of the tunnel beyond.

Shah finished his work, then stuck a detonator patch onto the compound.

"Ready for soft knock," he said.

"Do it," Idina ordered.

Shah triggered the patch and took a step back. The compound burned with a soft hiss. A moment later, a jet of flame shot out from the space between the door and the frame, washing out Idina's night vision briefly. Then the flame subsided, and a small cloud of smoke filled the vestibule and rose to the ceiling.

Sergeant Shah stepped forward again and gave the door a little push with one hand. It swung open slightly on its hinges, and more cool air came from the space inside to mingle with the smoke from the breaching compound. Idina aimed her rifle at the door and signaled the team behind her.

"Covering," she announced. "On three. *One, two, three.*"

At "three," Shah slowly pushed the door open. Idina followed the left edge of it with the muzzle of her weapon to cover the widening gap. Then the door was fully open. On the other side, a narrow maintenance tunnel went on in a straight line for ten meters before making a right turn at a ninety-degree angle. She quickly cycled through her sensor modes, but nothing in the dark tunnel segment indicated any traps or surveillance gear.

"Clear," she sent to the team.

They rushed past her into the dark tunnel, weapons at the ready. The last trooper in the formation took up position in the vestibule to cover their rear from any surprises coming down the main tunnel.

Shah advanced to the bend in the tunnel and stopped just before the turn. He pushed a spot on the back of his glove and released a micro-drone. It rose from its receptacle silently and hovered in the air in front of him. Then it flew around the bend and down the unseen part of the tunnel. A few moments later, it reappeared, and Shah grabbed it carefully and returned it to its spot on his armor. The video feed from the insect-sized device downloaded to his suit computer and appeared on the team's tactical screens. Idina watched the imagery carefully, the adrenaline of the unknown dangers jolting her nerves with the familiar sensation of something akin to an electric charge. The tunnel section around the bend terminated in a dead end twenty meters ahead. Another steel door was set into the wall at the end of the tunnel, this one without the camouflage of fake weld marks. The air here in the bend was only a few degrees cooler than in the tunnel, but Idina could tell by the thermal image that the source of the air-conditioned current was somewhere behind that door. On the ceiling above it, an optical surveillance module was watching the dark tunnel, barely visible against the concrete but obvious to the little recon drone by its faint electromagnetic signature. Idina studied the situation for a few heartbeats and made her decision.

"Shah, jam that sensor on my mark. We move up and do a hard knock on that door. Get ready."

Sergeant Shah activated the EM emitter mounted on the side of his rifle. He crouched by the corner and gave Idina a thumbs-up.

"Do it," Idina said.

Shah held his rifle around the corner and triggered the jamming emitter.

Idina gave the hand signal to advance and swiftly stepped past Shah and around the bend of the tunnel. Behind her, the team followed in precise formation, weapons aimed at the door in front of them.

When she was five meters from the door, she heard the soft metallic sound of a retracting dead bolt, and the door swung open in front of her. In the fraction of a second it took her to assess the man appearing in the opening, his eyes started to widen at the unexpected sight of half a dozen shadowy wraiths coming out of the darkness right in front of him.

Weapon, Idina registered.

He had a gun slung under his arm, a short-barreled little bullet hose with a long magazine cassette hanging off the bottom. Idina's hands moved on autopilot and pulled the trigger of her rifle three times in rapid succession: *chest, chest, head.* He dropped without a sound, carried forward a little from the momentum of the step he had just started to take, and crumpled to the grimy floor. From the way his limbs flopped when he hit the ground, she knew that he had been dead the millisecond her rifle round had lanced through his brain.

"Entry now, now, now," she barked into the comms.

She stepped over the dead body and rushed into the space beyond the door, adrenaline flooding her system and quickening her movement. Next to the door to her right, there was a solid wall, so she pivoted to the left as soon as she was through the door opening to let the rest of the team through. There were two more people in here, both caught in a state of surprise she knew would only last a second or two at best. The figure closest to her looked up from his hunched-over position in front of a waist-high table and yelled out a warning. He had a pistol in his waistband, and his hand made it halfway to the grip of the weapon before Idina shot him. Her suppressed rifle spat out three rounds again—*chest, chest, head.* The man coughed once and collapsed. On his way to the floor, he tried to grab the edge of the table, but his weight and momentum tipped it over and brought it down on him with a loud clattering sound.

Number three was in front of a desk in the corner of the room. He had been sitting with his back to the door, and now he scrambled to his feet and dashed toward a long gun that was leaning on the wall a meter from his sitting spot. Idina put her aiming marker on him, but two other suppressed guns thumped behind her and swept him off his feet in a flurry of bullet impacts that tore loose chunks from the military-style tunic he was wearing.

There was another door at the far end of the room, this one standing ajar. Idina advanced on the doorway from an angle, ready to engage. Close-quarters combat was a deadly dance, one that she had performed so often during the war that she had not forgotten any steps. She signaled for the trooper behind her to cover her advance and approached the door slowly, ready to pour ruin into the room beyond at the slightest sign of a threat. The safest way to clear the room would be to sanitize it with an anti-personnel grenade, but they were here for intel as much as for killing insurgents, and she didn't want to destroy whatever was in that room if it was important enough to be guarded by several armed men.

"Anyone in there, announce yourself and surrender, or die," she called out. The helmet computer's translator rendered her commands in Gretian with a half-second delay. "You have ten seconds to comply."

"Wait! Don't shoot," the reply to her challenge came a moment later, well before the ten-second deadline. The voice was female and high pitched with stress. Idina decided to take a risk and aim her rifle around the corner and through the open door. There was only one warm body in the room, mostly concealed by a large piece of furniture.

"I'm coming in," she said. "Put your hands up and remain where you are. If you move, I will shoot you."

"Okay. Okay." A pair of hands appeared above the edge of the furniture.

Idina signaled for cover and slowly stepped through the door with her weapon up and ready. The room was an armory of sorts, two workbenches on one end and a rack of small arms between them. The woman who had answered her challenge was crouched behind one of the workbenches. Idina aimed at the spot where she knew the bulk of the body would be.

"Are you armed?" she called out. "Tell me now before I shoot you full of holes out of reflex."

"I don't have a weapon on me. But there are guns all over this room."

"Don't try to grab any of them and we'll be fine," Idina said. "Now stand up slowly and keep your hands up so I can see them."

"I'm standing up now. Just don't shoot me," the woman said.

"That is entirely under your control. Make a move toward that gun rack and I'll drop you."

"I'm not an idiot," the woman replied. She stood up, slowly and carefully as Idina had instructed. Her face looked terrified, wide blue eyes in a pale heart-shaped face. Her hair was shorn military-style short on the sides and the back of her head and left longer on top, and a strand of it fell over her right eye as she straightened up. She made no effort to brush it out of her face.

"Step out from behind that thing and take three steps toward me, then get on your knees," Idina ordered. The woman did as she was told and knelt in the middle of the room with slow and deliberate movements, her hands still above her head. Behind Idina, two of her troopers had filed into the room on either side of her, and she signaled over her shoulder for one of them to restrain and secure the woman in front of them. Sergeant Shah stepped past Idina and cuffed their prisoner quickly and smoothly, then pulled her to her feet by the restraints before frisking her roughly and expertly.

"Name, rank, unit," Idina demanded in her inspection voice when Shah was done.

The woman blinked and shook her head a little, as if she had to stir the information loose in her brain.

"Corporal Anders," she supplied. "Birgit Anders. Second Company, Supply Battalion 226. Second Assault Brigade. Who are you?"

"We're the fucking monsters under your bed," Idina replied curtly. "What are you doing down here, Corporal Anders of Supply Battalion 226? The war's been over for five years now."

Anders nodded at the workbench and the weapons rack next to it. "I fix guns. I'm a unit armorer. *Was* a unit armorer," she corrected herself. "Specialty in small-arms repair."

"So you fix the guns that kill our people," Idina said. Corporal Anders's gaze flicked to the rifle in Idina's hand that was still roughly aimed in her direction.

"I've never killed anyone. I just repair broken hardware. It's what I know. There's nothing else for me to do. There's no more military. I need to eat somehow." She was talking a little faster now, pleading her case in front of someone she knew could kill her down here without any repercussions. Two kilos of pressure on the trigger of Idina's gun were all that it took to deprive the insurgency of a skilled expert in weapons repair, something no fighting force had in abundance. But as much as Idina's conscience didn't bother her about the armed men she had just killed, this woman was unarmed and no threat. The old, restrictive rules of engagement did not apply to her team, but even with the gloves off, cold-blooded murder was not part of the playbook.

"Shah, check that gun rack for traps and secure the room," she told her team's second-in-command. "I'll take her."

Shah nodded and walked the insurgent armorer over to Idina. She took the woman by the shoulder and pushed her toward the door, a little more roughly than necessary.

In the other room, Corporal Anders froze at the sight of her dead comrades sprawled out on the floor, and Idina could practically smell the renewed fear flaring up in the woman.

"You didn't have to kill them," she said. "They would have surrendered."

"Right. That's why that one went for his carbine." Idina nodded at the man lying motionless in front of the desk in the corner of the room. He had taken at least half a dozen rounds through his chest and head, and the pool of blood underneath his body was steadily spreading toward the middle of the room. "Now be quiet and thank your gods that I didn't just toss a fragmentation grenade into the room with you."

Idina handed off her prisoner to one of her troopers and looked around in the first room they had entered. Where the other room was clearly a workshop and armory, this one was a little operations center. The desk in the corner had a portable comdeck on it with a screen projected above the desk surface, and she stepped around the spreading pool of blood and over the dead body to check it out. One section of the screen showed the access corridor outside through the sensor lens they had briefly jammed when they made entry. The first man she had killed was barely in the frame of the sensor image, his head and shoulders in the bottom of the frame with another pool of blood slowly spreading outward. The other two-thirds of the screen showed various data screens, rows of Gretian writing that didn't make sense to her even with the automatic visual translation her helmet's visor provided. She closed the screen and picked up the comdeck.

"Gather and secure all the intel you can find," she told her team. "Scan the dead, swipe for DNA samples."

"What do you want to do with the bodies?" Sergeant Shah asked.

Under normal circumstances, Idina would have called in a military police team to secure the scene and comb through everything down here. But this wasn't a normal Pallas Brigade operation. This was off the books and outside the normal chain of command, and she had her orders as far as involvement of the regular Alliance military was concerned.

"Put a thermal charge on those guns once you've scanned them for serial numbers. Then get the three stiffs back into the armory and pile them up next to the rack. This safe room is permanently closed. We leave nothing but burnt carbon behind here."

"You got it," Shah said. It had taken a few weeks of training for everyone to lose their reflexive use of ranks and other military identifiers. Their combat armor was devoid of identifying patches, and their weapons were sterile, with no serial numbers or embedded security features. Only the automatic encrypted transmitters in their wrist computers would reveal to any regular Alliance troops that they were on the same side.

"Get her out of here," she told the trooper who was securing their prisoner. "If she tries anything, drop her and leave her. Link up with Dalit around the tunnel bend. We're right behind you."

She watched as her teammate led Corporal Anders out of the room and past the first man she had killed. The blood pooling underneath the corpse was covering the floor of the narrow access tunnel from side to side, forming a puddle that was just a little too big to avoid. Both her man and Anders stepped into the blood and disappeared in the darkness beyond, trailing bloody footsteps on the weathered concrete. Behind Idina, the rest of her team were busy frisking the dead bodies and collecting anything in the room that looked like it could yield some information. When they were done, they dragged the dead insurgents into the other room as she had ordered.

"Ready," Sergeant Shah said when he came out of the back room.

"We are leaving," Idina announced over the team comms. "Egress on the same route. Form up and head out."

The last one out was Shah. Before he stepped through the door, he took two thermal grenades from his harness, flipped the safeties, and pushed the timer buttons. He threw them through the doorway into the back room with the guns and the dead insurgents one after the other, with the precision of a weathered commando. Idina took a thermal charge off her own harness and readied it. When Shah trotted past her on his way into the tunnel, she activated her grenade and tossed it into the anteroom for good measure. She stepped out and closed the door. The thermal charges did not need oxygen to burn, and the three grenades would turn everything inside into glowing slag. When the insurgents came to check on their compatriots, they would have an interesting time trying to get the door open again, and they'd find nothing but ashes and globs of melted metal inside. She hoped it would send the message she wanted to convey.

Three fewer insurgents, one prisoner for interrogation, no friendly casualties, she thought as she followed her team back into the main tunnel. *Not a bad day's work at all.*

Chapter 3

Dunstan

"I feel a little dirty now," Dunstan said to Lieutenant Hunter when they stepped off the skylift on the arcology's spaceport level.

"Because you had to talk to a Gretian Blackguard?" Hunter asked with a little smile.

Dunstan shook his head. "Because I am doing the recruiting footwork for intelligence. You'd figure they'd send one of their own to do the job."

"You know why they picked us," Hunter said.

"Yeah, I know. It's just that every time I have to deal with the intel people, they manage to put something else onto the cart for me to pull. Last time they called me in, they gave me *Hecate* and sent us up against a rogue heavy cruiser. Now I get to recruit people for suicide missions."

"We didn't make him take the deal," Hunter said. "We told him about the risks. He decided that the rewards were worth it. I didn't even have to push."

Dunstan glanced at his first officer and smirked.

"You knew he'd go for it, didn't you?"

Hunter shrugged. "I don't know if you saw the light come on behind his eyes when you put the offer on the table. He walked in all gray and walked out in color."

"That's one way to put it," Dunstan said with a chuckle. He pulled out his issue comtab to look up the docking port for their assigned shuttle, a detail his synapses had already overwritten since their arrival here less than two hours ago. It seemed like a waste of time and fuel to send two navy officers on a half-day round trip for a half-hour conversation that could have happened over a secure video link, but the intel people were professionally paranoid, and this assignment had come with even stricter secrecy protocols than usual. Every conversation that could be had in person and in a secure facility would be had that way.

"Maybe he thinks he can pull the same trick again. Disappear on the way to Gretia, get a fake ID somewhere else, and sit us out somewhere on Oceana or Acheron. He has the skills," Hunter said.

Dunstan shook his head.

"I looked him up. The first time was a crime of opportunity. Lucky circumstances, if you can call them that. The freighter he was on when we sent him home got blotted out of space by Odin's Ravens. He barely made the escape pod. The only reason he got let loose on Oceana was the fact that their navy plucked the pod out of space and rescued him. He'd long be back on Gretia otherwise."

They were walking across the spaceport atrium, which was busy with midday travelers, soldiers and civil servants making their way to their gates or getting a quick lunch at one of the many food booths.

"Ever thought about the possibility that he's already a mole?" Hunter said. "For the Ravens and the Wolves, I mean. What if they put him in that pod on purpose and then blew up that freighter? They were in Alliance space. They knew one of ours would pick him up."

Dunstan let out a low whistle.

"That would be a very clever long game, wouldn't it?"

"They waited five years before they started blowing things up. Whoever's running the show clearly has patience," she said.

"You're starting to think like one of those intelligence people, Number One."

"It's not paranoia if they *are* really out there. With nuclear warheads."

"Point taken," Dunstan said. "But you can rest easy as far as that possibility goes. There were two other people in the pod with him when the Oceanians picked them up. The freighter's engineer and a civilian passenger. University girl, on the way home to Acheron. Intel combed through their records and found nothing. The engineer verified that the freighter got fired on without warning. They barely made it into the pod. Our Gretian major came within ten seconds of turning into stardust with the rest of the ship. Whoever shot at them wasn't concerned about his survival."

"So he's *probably* not a mole," Lieutenant Hunter said.

"Did he look like a sleeper agent for the insurgency to you?"

"I didn't realize they had a particular look," she replied dryly, and Dunstan chuckled.

"I'm willing to give him the benefit of the doubt," he said. "The man stuck his neck out for us and against these people when he didn't have to risk himself. All he wants is to go back to his new life and rejoin his crew. I think that's a convincing motivation."

"Hells, if he helps us take these people down, I'll be happy to sponsor him for any Alliance citizenship he wants."

They turned from the atrium into the concourse. A group of young Rhodian Navy cadets were walking out of the concourse at the same time, chatting and laughing until they saw Dunstan and Lieutenant Hunter, at which point they hastily parted to let the two officers pass between them unimpeded. Dunstan replied to their greetings with a nod. He looked at the faces of the new cadets as he made his way through the group. Some of them looked barely older than his daughters, too young to be wearing a uniform. He wondered if he'd be seeing any of these faces again on *Hecate* in a year, once their cadet class had passed their training and they were all freshly minted ensigns.

"Now I feel ancient," Dunstan said to Lieutenant Hunter when they were past the group and out of earshot. "I have boots in my locker that are older than any of these kids."

"The wheel keeps turning," she said. "We were fresh-faced cadets once, too. They'll do all right, just like we did."

May you all have long and quiet careers, he thought. *Patrol the transit lanes, arrest pirates, go on regular leaves, retire in twenty years without ever having fired a weapon in combat. We've had enough bloodletting for a few generations.*

—

The main civilian space dock on Rhodia One was even bigger than its military counterpart and twice as busy. The service bays that lined the walls of the dock were fifty meters high and twenty wide, tall and wide enough to fit a ship the size of *Hecate*. Every bay was occupied with ships in various states of disassembly and repair. This was the facility where smaller ships could be brought into the pressurized atmosphere and artificial gravity of the station to perform repairs or upgrades that required more extensive surgery than could be done in a vacuum on the outside docking arms.

Zephyr stood in the service bay on the far end of the dock, a five-minute walk along the central service catwalk that stretched the length of the dock suspended halfway between floor and ceiling. Dunstan hadn't seen her hull in person before, only on the sensor screens in *Hecate*'s Action Information Center, and he gave the ship a thorough look over as he approached her. The little courier looked out of place even in this civilian dry dock. The ships in the other bays were all rugged freighters and people haulers that showed the wear and tear of long, hard use on their hulls. *Zephyr* was smaller than any of them—she had at least fifteen meters of air between the ceiling and the tip of her chisel-shaped prow—and the little Acheroni-built racing yacht looked far more graceful, a slender hull built for speed instead of cargo volume. Dunstan had seen this ship hurtle through space at over twenty gravities of acceleration, outpacing anything in the Rhodian Navy arsenal that wasn't a missile. Even her paint job looked fast, a brilliant titanium white with two parallel blue strips of unequal width that ran the length of the ship from bow to drive cone. Her registration was stenciled on the lower hull in the same electric blue: OMV-2022, Oceanian Merchant Vessel number two thousand twenty-two. The recently patched sections of her hull were evident by the areas where the paint was a little brighter. Most of the ship was made from lightweight Acheroni composites. A ship like this wasn't built for standing up to bullets or shrapnel, and she had paid for her crew's bravery with a three-month space dock stay. Even so, it had been one of the luckiest possible outcomes for *Zephyr*. Dunstan knew just how close they had come to turning into a fine cloud of debris.

The ship's main airlock at the end of the service bay's catwalk extension stood open, but Dunstan followed navy protocol and stopped at the comms panel next to the airlock to announce himself.

"Commander Park, Rhodian Navy. Permission to come aboard?"

The reply came from the inside of the ship just a moment later.

"Permission granted, Commander."

On the other side of the airlock, the ship's captain appeared, wiping her hands with a rag. She had the top of her jumpsuit tied around her waist, and her hair was tied back. Captain Decker's face was shiny with sweat, and she gave it a quick rub with the rag she was holding.

"Need a hand?" Dunstan asked as he walked in.

She shook her head and folded the rag before putting it in the leg pocket of her jumpsuit.

"Just stowing some supplies for the trail," she said. "Nobody here to boss around, so I have to do all the muscle work by myself."

"Where's the rest of your crew?"

Captain Decker shrugged. "My engineer is somewhere between the inner and outer hulls right now with a laser welder. My pilot is on the way back from Acheron. And my first officer is waiting for us to pick him up on Oceana."

"I see. Doesn't that still leave you short a crew member?"

She shrugged again. "That's on your people. It's hard to replace a comms specialist who's fluent in three languages. And I'm kind of saving his spot for him."

"It may be a while before he gets out," Dunstan said.

"Yeah, well, I was growing fond of him. Ever since he saved our asses and yours. And he owns a fifth of this ship, so I feel a bit of an obligation to keep his chair warm."

"You mean his counterfeit persona owns a fifth of the ship."

Decker shook her head. "Doesn't matter what he was called or what he calls himself now. Oceanian law ties property to the physical person, not the legal identity. He's part owner of *Zephyr* as long as he can pass the biometric verification scan."

She looked at him with something like expectation. For a moment, they stood on the airlock deck in awkward silence. Then Captain Decker nodded at the ladderwell to her right.

"Would you like some coffee? I just finished restocking the galley. Got some good strong Palladian brew in the dispenser."

"I'll never turn down a good cup of coffee," Dunstan said.

She gestured toward the ladder. "After you, Commander. Galley deck is the one right below."

Dunstan looked around in the ship's galley while Captain Decker poured two mugs of coffee from the dispenser. It was a small but cozy space that had the individual touches of the crew all over it. Someone had decorated the walls and bulkheads with skilled and tasteful drawings, flowers and animals so intricate and detailed that they looked like they had come from a biology book. It resembled a living space in a way that no navy ship's common area ever managed. For a navy sailor, the ship was a temporary duty station, to be endured for a few months of patrol deployment every year. For spacers like the *Zephyr* crew, their ship was home, whether they were out on a courier run or sitting in a dry dock.

"Two tables, eight chairs," he said. "You ever have eight people on this ship to fill up all the seats in here?"

"Sometimes. We had six people on the crew before Tristan died and Aden got arrested. And we get passengers sometimes. There are two extra berth spots down on crew deck B for paying customers."

Captain Decker brought the two mugs over to the table where Dunstan was sitting. She put one in front of him and sat down across the table. He took a sip and nodded his approval.

"This is some coffee," he said.

"There's a mercantile on the yellow concourse that sells the roasted beans. You give them a large amount of money, and they give you a small amount of beans. Tristan didn't believe in that powdered shit. He got a coffee grinder for the galley. Takes a few extra steps to make some coffee if you grind the beans fresh every time. But once you're used to it, nothing else will do."

"I'm inclined to agree with that," Dunstan said.

"His philosophy was that you should always get the best you can afford when it comes to food, drink, or hotel rooms. Cheap out on everything else, just not on those."

"He was a smart man. I'm sorry about what happened to him. I hope you got some satisfaction out of taking down that cruiser with us."

Decker shrugged. "The bastard that killed our friend wasn't on that cruiser. He's still out there somewhere. If the gods are kind, we'll run into him again, and we'll get to call in the tab he owes us."

"I take it you're ready to get back out there," Dunstan said.

"This ship wasn't built to sit on its drive cone for months. And I am tired of sitting around. There's not much I've been able to do except watch other people work on her. Not that I'm ungrateful for the assist from the Rhodian Navy."

"I think we came out ahead on that trade," he replied. "A reactor overhaul and some upgrades in exchange for bagging a seventeen-thousand-ton heavy gun cruiser. If they had used that ship for commerce raiding—well. Just one ore freighter is worth a hundred times what the navy spent on repairing your ship."

"We haven't been making any money for the last three months. But at least we haven't been losing any, thanks to your people. That reactor replacement would have eaten up our operating budget and then some. As things stand, we're going to have to work some lucrative routes to claw our way back into the green."

Dunstan took a slow sip of coffee and put the mug on the table. He watched the little wisps of steam curling and rising from the surface of the hot beverage for a few moments. Captain Decker leaned back in her chair as far as the fixed furniture would allow and crossed her arms in front of her chest. She was still wearing the top of her jumpsuit around her waist, and her bare arms and the tight-fitting undershirt emphasized her lean and wiry build, the telltale physique of a career spacer.

"I came with a proposal on precisely that subject," he said.

Captain Decker raised an eyebrow and chuckled softly.

"Here it comes," she said. "The hook in the steak, as Aden calls it."

"There's no hook," Dunstan replied. "You can decline, and that will be the end of it. Nothing else will change. The navy won't be sending you a surprise bill or anything."

"Well." There was the hint of a smile playing in the corners of her mouth. "I suppose it would be rude to not hear you out. So let's hear your proposal."

Dunstan picked up his mug again and gestured toward the galley bulkhead with it before taking another sip.

"This is a fine little ship," he said. "I know our cooperation three months ago was a spur-of-the-moment thing, but it turned out exceptionally well. It made me think about what we could do if we had more time to work on our tactics."

"I've seen what your ship can do," Decker said. "We chased down that Tanaka for you. But this isn't a warship just because we have a decent point-defense system. You took down four ships simultaneously without firing a single shot of your own. We can pull a few more gravities than you, sure. But there's nothing else we can do that you can't do much better."

Dunstan shook his head.

"I've been out on piracy patrol with *Hecate* for the last few months. My command crew came up with a way to predict high-risk zones along the transfer lanes in real time. We spent the entire deployment hanging out in those zones and waiting for things to happen. The trouble is that even when you roughly know where they'll hit, even the high-risk zone is still a big patch of space. Too big for one ship alone to cover, no matter how good her systems are. We got lucky with one intercept because the acceleration math worked in our favor. But there were four more that got away from us because we couldn't get there in time. Not even at full burn."

"The navy can't be everywhere," Captain Decker said. "You know that fact is built into a lot of business models out here."

"Including yours," Dunstan replied, and she shrugged with a little smile. The first time they had met, she had turned over illegal cargo to him—not just any run-of-the-mill contraband but a thermonuclear warhead, the most restricted technology in the system. If he hadn't been convinced that they had acted in good faith, *Zephyr*'s crew would still be in Rhodian Navy custody right now, awaiting trial for an offense that carried decades of prison time in a high-security detention arcology. But he had decided to trust his instincts, and that trust had paid off in the end.

"There is one thing you can do much better than I can do with *Hecate*," he said. "You can go out onto the transit lanes and look like you belong. Nobody's going to avoid you. In fact, you may even draw the sort of attention we want."

Decker let out a throaty chuckle and shook her head slowly.

"You're counting on that, in fact."

"I am," he confirmed. "It worked very well the last time we tried."

"I'm sure you have access to any number of fast little ships you can send out as pirate bait," she said.

"I do. But none are as fast as yours. Or fitted with a military-grade point-defense system like yours. That little racing yacht is a tough nut to crack."

"Flattery won't win me over," Decker said, but her tone of voice told him that she wasn't displeased with his assessment. "So you want us to stick our necks out for you again."

"In a planned and orderly fashion. Not with spur-of-the-moment tactics like the last time."

"I assume you already worked that out," she said.

Dunstan nodded.

"You do what you usually do. Take contracts and make deliveries. Only this time we'll advise you which contracts to take. We can apply that predictive algorithm to the contract boards on every station in the system and filter out the ones that are most likely to draw interest. Once the Ravens notice that you're back in business, I don't think it will take long for them to come to you. And when they do, *Hecate* will be waiting for them."

Captain Decker leaned back and exhaled slowly.

"If we say no, what's to keep you from shadowing our ship anyway and using us as a lure without our consent?"

Now it was Dunstan's turn to shrug.

"Nothing at all," he said. "But I have no interest in playing hide-and-seek with your ship as well. This sneaky business is difficult enough even with coordination. It can't work if we're not pulling on the same rope. If you decline, I'll go back to lying in wait along the trade routes and hope I get lucky sooner or later. But consider that *Hecate* won't be nearby when these people find you again. You'll be all on your own."

"A few months ago, I would have told you that we can hold our own, and then I'd politely decline," Decker said. "But that was *before*. Before Tristan. Now I am feeling a lot better about the idea of having a Rhodian warship shadowing us. If these people are still looking for us, they'll find us sooner or later, whether you're around or not. And when they do, I'd just as soon have you around."

"Very good," Dunstan said. "To be honest, I was expecting a harder sell."

"Oh, I am not saying yet that we're going to do it. I'm just the first among equals. My opinion carries a lot of weight. But the others get a vote, too. I can't make that decision over their heads."

"I'm not above some light bribery. The navy won't let me transfer any military weaponry to your ship, not even small arms. But you can tell your engineer that if we team up, I'll be able to have my people upgrade your PDS with the latest software."

"I don't want any guns on *Zephyr* anyway," Decker said. "We've never flown armed. It's nothing but a hassle. Every time you dock somewhere, you need to declare everything. Arrival and departure inspections, unannounced checks of the armory. You know how it goes. Armed merchants make station managers twitchy."

There was a muffled banging sound somewhere inside the hull, and they both turned their heads reflexively to look in the direction of the noise. The sound repeated and settled into a rhythm, a slow and steady hammering.

"But I'm sure my engineer won't mind a PDS upgrade at all," Decker said. "That system is far more useful than any weapon we could fit into our hull. It has saved our asses more than once."

"I was there the last time," Dunstan replied. "And I agree with your assessment."

He maneuvered his legs out from the tight confines of the galley seating and stood up.

"I won't take up any more of your time, Captain. How soon will you be able to give me a definite answer?"

Decker stood up as well. She untied the sleeves of her flight suit from her waist and slipped her arms into them, then zipped the suit up with a smooth motion.

"I'll ask them over the 'Syne. Give me a few hours."

"You know my node address," Dunstan said. "Good luck, and thanks for the coffee. I hope your crew agrees with you about the value of having a shadow for a while. We make a pretty good hunter-killer team."

They walked over to the ladderwell and climbed up to the airlock deck. When he was at the open airlock, Decker called after him.

"Commander Park."

He stopped and turned around.

"Throw in a pardon or a commutation for Aden, and I am sure every member of my crew will vote to team up with you," she said. "We could really use him back on this ship."

He looked at her for a long moment while he decided how to calibrate his reply.

"I'm afraid that's out of my power," he said. "All I could do was put in a good word at the hearing. But I think it counted for something. He may be out sooner than you think."

If Captain Decker suspected that he was lying by omission, she didn't let it show on her face. She just pursed her lips and nodded.

"I figured it was worth a shot. Not that I don't appreciate everything you've already done for us," she said.

"I sincerely hope that your crew will still choose to accept my proposal," Dunstan said.

Decker flashed a grim smile.

"Oh, I am pretty sure they will. We all have unfinished business with Odin's Ravens. And we're really shit at letting go of grudges."

Chapter 4

Solveig

The sky above was all soggy clouds the color of dirty concrete, rushed along by chilly winds that were whipping the tops of the trees all around her. It was the sort of weather to match Solveig's mood.

It wasn't a great day for a run, especially not the first one after three months of convalescence, but it was a good alibi to get away from all the activity at the house, where dozens of her father's employees were preparing the estate for her father's solstice gathering. It had been an annual event until the last year of the war, and for some reason, her father had decided to resurrect the tradition this year.

She had tried running the track at her normal pace, but her body had protested this overconfidence in no uncertain terms, and she'd had to throttle back before she finished the first segment of the five-kilometer loop. Now, at the halfway point, she finally conceded defeat and slowed down to a walk to catch her breath again. Her lungs felt like they had lost half their capacity in the last three months, and the mended tissue of her gunshot wound was radiating a dull, throbbing pain that spiked a little with every step she took.

It'll take me a year to get back into my old shape, she thought. *But it could be worse. I could be in a walking frame like Stefan. Or dead like Cuthbert.*

The anguish she felt whenever she thought of her brave and devoted bodyguard had only recently begun to dull a little, three months after his death in the parking garage of the police headquarters. She had always known that it was the job of the security officers to shield their charges and even take a round for them if it came down to it. But that knowledge had been an abstraction in her mind until Cuthbert had shown her the reality of it, by standing in that door and trying to hold it against the odds so she would have a chance to get away. The company had paid out ample survivor benefits to his family—Solveig had made sure of that—but no amount of money seemed enough to her as compensation for someone who had willingly traded his own life for hers. Even if her body somehow healed itself to where not even the trace of her physical injuries remained, she knew she would never be able to forget the sight of Cuthbert on the ground as one of the insurgents stood over him and fired a burst into his body to finish him off.

Solveig saw a movement out of the corner of her eye and looked up and to her right. A security drone was hovering high above the nearby treetops on silent rotors, keeping an eye on her from a distance. The estate had been a safe place before, but her father had greatly beefed up the security measures while she was recovering at the medical center. Now there were drones everywhere, and Marten's security team were patrolling the outer perimeter in light armor instead of suits, armed with rifles instead of well-concealed sidearms. Solveig had no doubt that if she showed any indications of distress, there would be a heavily armed security gyrofoil overhead within minutes. She knew it was all security theater, intended to make her feel safe. The insurgent attack that almost killed her had happened three months ago, and she had only been a coincidental target, in that she'd put herself in the line of fire by accident when she had lunch with Stefan in the wrong place at the wrong time. But Falk Ragnar was who he was, and she knew that this was all as much for his own comfort as for hers—to make him feel like he was doing something, no matter how pointless and expensive it was.

You're trying to protect me from something you helped create, by throwing money at a problem that you helped cause.

Standing still made her cold in the chilly wind that was blowing through the trees, so she turned around and started trotting along again despite the burning in her lungs and the discomfort from the freshly healed wound. She didn't have to look over her shoulder to know that the security drone was following her again. Whatever small measure of privacy and solitude she had managed to carve out here with her morning runs before, it was all gone now, and she would never get it back.

The last segment of the running path snaked between the fishponds and up a little hill before leading back down to the main house. Solveig stopped at the crest of the hill to catch her breath. On the vast front lawn, the workers had finished erecting the party sphere. It was a large dome made of several hundred Alon segments, set into a gossamer of white carbon composite, fifty meters across and twenty-five high. As airy and fragile as it looked, it could easily shrug off the worst weather Gretia had to offer. Solveig didn't know when her father had commissioned it, but she had celebrated birthdays and attended solstice parties underneath the transparent canopy as long as she could remember. When she was much younger, the sight of the sphere on the front lawn would give her a warm tingle of joyous anticipation. Now it just made her feel anxious because she already visualized the hundreds of well-dressed people who would be milling around under that elegant latticework later today, sipping drinks and exchanging the latest gossip. The name Ragnar didn't quite have the power it had commanded before the war, but it was still that of a steadholder family, one of only a hundred and twenty-eight on the planet. At steadholder parties, billion-ag deals were signed with handshakes, political alliances were formed, and careers were launched or ended over appetizers. Whoever showed up today, Solveig knew that her father would be holding court with them, a smiling spider in the center of his social web, and that she would have to deal with a never-ending succession of tediously boring ass-kissers.

Down on the lawn, the lights of the sphere turned on and started cycling through their illumination patterns. A steady line of kitchen staff was crossing the lawn from the main building to the dome, carrying food trays and beverage dispensers. As Solveig watched, it started to rain, a light drizzle that turned into a full-on downpour within seconds, large and heavy drops that splashed down on her head and shoulders like tiny little punches. In the distance, the kitchen helpers were rushing toward the shelter of the party sphere as quickly as they dared with food trays in their hands.

Bad omen for the party, Solveig thought. It was a strangely comforting sight, evidence that even with all his money and power, not even Falk Ragnar could control everything around him and get his way all the time.

The security drone that had followed her soared high over her head and toward the house, unable to keep up its slow patrol pace with its small rotors in the heavy rain. Solveig pulled up the bottom of her shirt and wiped the rain out of her face with it. Then she followed the drone downhill at a more measured pace.

"Gods, you're completely soaked," Marten said. Her father's head of security shook his head with a little frown when he saw her walking into the atrium of the main house. "You picked a bad time for a run, Miss Solveig."

"You may be right about that," Solveig replied. She looked back at her own path into the atrium, where she had left small puddles on the marble floor with every step.

"Godrick, get a towel for Miss Ragnar," Marten said to a passing attendant, who immediately turned around and disappeared quickly in the direction of the laundry room before Solveig could object. He returned just a few seconds later with a folded towel that was still warm. She took it and nodded her thanks before drying herself off in a rudimentary fashion.

"It's a good thing I am not water-soluble," she said to Marten. "But I'm afraid Papa's little party is going to have a nautical theme."

Marten chuckled. "That would be something new. But it's just a quick-moving squall line. The weather scan says it'll clear up in about thirty-five minutes. We may even have sun again this evening."

"Very good. Then I'll have a smooth ride into the city. I'll get dried off and showered and changed, and then you can tell Hakan I am ready to go."

Marten shifted his weight a little and sighed.

"About that. Your father would like you to come and see him as soon as you can."

Solveig frowned. "Is this about the party?"

"I have no idea, miss. I'm just relaying what he told me."

"It's about the party," Solveig concluded. A few months ago, she would have had a knot in her stomach right now at the prospect of the impending discussion. Instead, all she felt was mild irritation.

"What time is it?"

Marten checked his comtab.

"It's 1328 hours."

"I'll be at the landing pad at 1500 hours to have Hakan take me back to Sandvik," she said. "I would like to see a flight-ready gyrofoil on the pad when I get there."

Marten looked at her with obvious discomfort.

"I'll have to wait for word from Mr. Ragnar," he said.

So that's how it's going to be, Solveig thought. *Very well.*

She twisted the towel around her head and tucked the ends in to keep it in place.

"You've let my father use you as a governess since I was old enough to run, Marten. I'm twenty-three now. I am not that little girl you pretended not to see on the security feed when she went into the kitchen at night to sneak ice cream. I'm vice president at large at Ragnar, and I run my own life now. Regardless of what my father says."

Marten gave her a curt smile that looked a little pained.

"He's still the boss, Miss Solveig."

Solveig nodded slightly to acknowledge the truth of the statement.

"But he won't be the boss forever," she said. "You may want to keep that in mind."

She walked past him, satisfied to see that his smile had faltered a little.

"Fifteen hundred hours, Marten," she said over her shoulder as she strode off, her walk rendered a little less assertive than she had intended by the wet little squishing noises her running shoes made with every step.

Marten had told her that her father was waiting in the library, but by the time she had showered and dressed and then made her way downstairs, the screens on the walls were playing news updates to an empty room. Solveig turned to go back upstairs. Her father had his favorite refuges when the house was busy, and she had a good idea where to find him.

"Solveig," Falk said when she walked into the gym. He was in the middle of the floor with his elegant two-handed cutting sword, and he interrupted whatever form he had been practicing and sheathed the blade. "How was your run?"

"Not great," she said. "It felt like I was running with a thirty-kilo backpack. And it started pouring before I was done."

Falk gestured to the sword rack by the wall. "It's dry in here. Want to go a few rounds? Let's put armor on. I'll trade the two-hander for a rapier."

Solveig shook her head. "Not today, Papa. I'm still not back to normal."

He flashed his white teeth. "Come on. I'll go easy on you. I haven't had anyone to spar with in a while."

"You can just tell Marten to send one of his people over," she said, and her father shook his head with a chuckle.

"There's no challenge to that. They're all crack shots with sidearms and rifles, but none of them know how to handle a sword," he said.

"They wouldn't fight you even if they knew. Nobody wants to hurt the boss by accident." *Or worse, beat him in a fair contest,* she added in her head. Papa would shrug off a slashed cheek or a bleeding forearm, but she knew he wouldn't tolerate getting bested by an underling. She was barely permitted to beat him every now and then, and every time she did, he would be surly for the rest of the day.

"That leaves only you, then," Falk said. "Three quick rounds."

Three months ago, she would have acquiesced rather than dealt with his irritation at being denied. But just like Marten's relaying of her father's order to come see him, this time she only felt annoyed by his insistence despite her firm no.

"I'm still not in the right space for violence," she said. "Even if it's only pretend violence."

There was the hint of a flicker in his smile. He had been acting as if nothing had changed between them, that things were the way they had always been. She had meant to remind him exactly why she wasn't back to form, and the brief silence that followed her words told her that it had worked as intended.

"Besides," she continued with a look at her clothes. "I'm not dressed for a workout. I'm heading out to Sandvik in an hour."

Falk stepped off the training mat and walked over to her.

"I want you to stay for the solstice party tonight, Solveig. It will be the first one since the war. It would be good to have you here with me."

"I can't deal with crowds right now, Papa. Just the sight of that sphere makes me anxious. The thought of being in there with hundreds of people."

"Security vetted all the visitors ahead of time," Falk said. "And everyone will go through the scanner. There's nothing to worry about. Marten has a small army out there."

"I know that. But I can't help what's going on in my brain. I've just now started sleeping through the night without meds. I'm sorry, Papa. I just can't. Not yet."

His jaw muscles flexed a little in the way they always did whenever he was irritated with something. Then he sighed and reached out to touch her face, and she only barely managed not to flinch at the unexpected gesture.

"All right," he said. "But you need to rejoin life at some point. You've been distant since you got home from the hospital. I barely see you around anymore."

I have been distant because I almost died, she thought. *I was shot by people you've paid to go out and murder.* When she had put him on the spot in the hospital after she had overheard his angry conversation, he had admitted giving money to the loyalists. He claimed that he'd had no idea about their plans for an insurrection, and that he'd stopped supporting them once he learned what they had planned. Everything just got out of hand, he had said. But she knew him too well to take him at his word, not when he had a vested interest in minimizing his involvement in front of her. She had pretended to accept his explanation, but she hadn't believed it for a second. Falk Ragnar never spent money blindly without knowing exactly how the expense would benefit him in the long term.

"I *am* rejoining life," she said. "I'm going back to work tomorrow."

"I still don't like the idea of you being by yourself in the city after all that has happened. I'd feel much better about it if I knew you had some Ragnar security around you."

"I'll be in a building full of Ragnar security most of the day. And the residential tower has its own security staff. I'm not worried about anything," she said.

She was prepared for him to bring up a fresh objection, tackle the issue from another angle until he got his way, just like he had always done. But something had changed between them since she had stood up to him about her relationship with Stefan, and that rift had only gotten wider since she had returned from the hospital. Instead of continuing the argument, he just sighed.

"I suppose you're right. That doesn't mean I'll stop worrying, though."

He doesn't want to tell me that I can't go, Solveig thought. *Because he knows I would do it anyway, and he's not prepared to deal with that.*

"I can't fault you for that, Papa," she said. On an impulse, she stood on the tips of her toes and stretched to give him a kiss on the cheek, and she felt him freeze in surprise for a moment at the unexpected touch.

"I'm sorry I'm such a mess that I can't stay for the party," she told him. "But I need to go and put myself back together. I think going back to work will help a great deal with that. I'll see you in a week or two."

"All right," Falk said. "But be careful. And don't ignore my vid requests, or I'll dispatch Marten and one of his strike teams to check on you."

"Of course."

Solveig walked out of the gym and headed back toward the family wing. The atrium was still a busy crossroads, but the kitchen staff and orderlies gave her some respectful space when she passed through. When she was on the steps to the private section, she turned around and watched the controlled chaos on the main floor for a few moments. She hadn't seen this many staff in the house in a long time. If she clapped her hands right now and told everyone to stop and stand on one leg, they'd do it without question—not because she had a commanding presence, but because they all feared her father, who had power over their livelihoods.

This house has always been a golden cage, she thought. *For me, for Aden, for Mama, for everyone but him. And I didn't realize that I've had the key ever since he put me into that corner office at Ragnar.*

She turned and walked up the steps to the family wing, and the prospect of getting on the gyrofoil and leaving all this gilded pageantry behind gave her the first real excitement she had felt in weeks.

Chapter 5

Aden

Being back on a spaceship after months in the prison arcology should have been a relief to Aden, but it wasn't. The ship wasn't *Zephyr*, the people traveling on it were not his friends, and it was heading for the last place in the system he wanted to be.

RMV *Kingsnorth* was an old, beat-to-shit Rhodian freighter with passenger accommodations that had been added to the ship seemingly as an afterthought. The cabins were in turn too hot or too cold, and the food they served in the ship's mess hall three times a day was obvious bottom-shelf bargain stuff bought in bulk from some place that wasn't too discriminating about what kind of protein went into the ready-to-heat meal trays. He had left his spices and Tristan's knife roll on *Zephyr* before they had all stepped off the ship on Rhodia One, so Aden had no way to improve the taste of the shipboard slop a little.

There were about thirty paying passengers on *Kingsnorth* with Aden, a motley group that was mostly made up of merchants, tourists, and other system drifters. Most of them spoke Rhodian, but Aden also heard occasional snippets of Oceanian and Hadean in the mess hall or out in the common spaces on the passenger deck. Two of his fellow passengers were Gretian, returning prisoners of war like himself, dressed in the same-issue jumpsuit he was wearing. He'd had no interest in socializing with them, but it would have looked strange for his old self to actively avoid his own people, so Aden had reciprocated their attempts at contact. At the very least, their company gave him a chance to practice being Aden Robertson again, the former Blackguard officer and newly released prisoner, an old version of himself for whom the six months of freedom as Aden Jansen had never happened.

I'm Major Aden Robertson. I am a proud Blackguard and a patriot of Gretia. I hate the boot of the Alliance on my neck, and I will do what it takes to pry it off. This was his mantra now, and he made himself recite it in the mirror every morning until he no longer felt disgust at the words.

—

"Good morning," Lieutenant Platt greeted Aden when he walked up to the mess table to take a seat. Platt and the other Gretian, Master Sergeant Vass, were sitting across from each other at the table as they had done for every meal Aden had seen them eat on this ship. It wasn't difficult for the Gretians to segregate themselves in the common spaces. None of the other passengers had been rude or hostile to the obvious former POWs, but the Rhodians were generally avoiding them, and most of the other nationalities kept to themselves as well.

"Good morning, *Major*," Aden corrected her with the grumpiest expression he could muster. It had the desired effect. Platt flinched and seemed to wilt a little in her chair.

"Yes, sir. Sorry, Major," she replied quickly. Platt was a decade younger than Aden and Vass, still a young woman even after five years of imprisonment. She had told them that she joined the Blackguard near the end of the war, a month before the cessation of hostilities. She'd been in uniform only long enough to get shipped out and assigned to a staff company before becoming a prisoner of war, and unlike almost every other POW Aden had known over the last five years, the little flame of zeal inside her hadn't been fully extinguished yet.

"They kept us locked up for five years, and they stripped the ranks and badges off our smocks," Aden said as he sat down next to Master Sergeant Vass. "Don't let them take your professional pride, too, Lieutenant. We are Blackguards. No matter what they claim."

"Yes, sir," Platt repeated and sat up straight. "It won't happen again."

Master Sergeant Vass exchanged an amused look with Aden. *Junior officers, am I right?*

"Less than eight hours to arrival," he said and nodded at the screen on the nearby bulkhead. It showed the image from the ship's bow sensors. Throughout their five-day journey from Rhodia One, there hadn't been anything to see except distant star fields, but now there was a small blue-and-green orb in the center of the screen, standing out in the blackness like a gemstone. The visual confirmation of their proximity to Gretia made Aden's stomach lurch a little. He hadn't set foot on his home planet in almost ten years. If the Rhodians hadn't plucked him off *Zephyr* and thrown him back into the detention arcology, he would have been fine with the thought of never returning again.

"What's the first thing you're going to do when we get home?" Platt asked. "I'm going to go to the park and dip my feet in the water."

"If it's still there," Vass replied. "Who knows what the Rhodies and their lackeys have done to the place since we left. They probably leveled it and turned it into a waste-storage facility just out of spite."

"What about you, Master Sergeant? What are you going to do when we're off the ship?"

"I'll spend some of the release money and eat my own weight in sausage rolls and deep-fried yam sticks," Vass said, and she nodded her approval.

Vass looked at Aden. "And you, sir?"

"I have no idea," Aden said with complete candor. "Haven't been back since my unit shipped out when the war started. I'm a stranger there by now."

"No family to go back to?" Vass pressed.

Aden slowly shook his head.

"I enlisted as a clean-slater. Let's just leave it at that, Master Sergeant."

A clean-slater was someone who joined the Blackguard with a new identity, an enlistment incentive for people who wanted to start fresh and make a full break with their past. Telling Vass and Platt that information was more than he wanted to share about himself, but he knew it would make them back off and stop trying to dig into his personal circumstances. It had the intended effect on Vass, who nodded deferentially.

"I guess I'll get some temporary lodging in Sandvik somewhere and take it from there," Aden said. "If I don't go too fancy, the release money is going to last me for a few months. After that—we'll see."

"The release money. Twenty thousand ags for five years of work," Sergeant Vass huffed. "That's three hundred fifty a month. All that time and labor, just stolen from us."

And what did we steal from them? Aden thought. *Tens of thousands of lives. And now they have to put back together everything we broke just because a few of us wanted to build an empire.*

"It could be worse," he said to Vass, keeping the irritation out of his voice only with some effort. "They could have sent us back with nothing at all."

"I suppose." Sergeant Vass stirred the food on his tray with his fork. "Still. Five years out of the world, with nothing but busy work to do and nothing to show for it. Feels like my life's been on hold. And I'm still five years closer to kicking it."

But you're alive, Aden wanted to tell him. All of them had received more grace from the Alliance than they deserved, especially the

Blackguards. But that sentiment belonged to Aden Jansen, not Major Robertson, so he left it unsaid and made a sound of vague agreement instead.

"At least we'll be home again," Platt said. "I'll take a bad day on my own planet over a great day on theirs, every time."

Home. Aden was grateful for the alibi for silence provided by the meal tray in front of him. The food was barely edible, but it was an excuse to fill his mouth. He didn't think of Gretia as home anymore. His home was the crew berth he had shared with Tess on *Zephyr*, not the planet a few hundred thousand kilometers ahead of *Kingsnorth*'s drive cone. But his way back to *Zephyr* had to go through Gretia first, and the success of his assignment depended on how well he could slip back into his old self. That meant he had to lock away the memories of the last nine months in a place where they couldn't trip him up. He was Major Aden Robertson again, company commander in the elite Blackguard, held by the Rhodians for over five years, and happy to be going back to his old life.

He finished his meal and got up from the table.

"Trees," he told the other two Gretians. "I'm looking forward to walking among trees again. Not the little scrubs they grow in the arboretums on Rhodia. Real trees. Ones that are too big to wrap your arms around. I'm going to take a long walk in a forest and listen to the leaves rustling in the wind."

That detail was specific and personal enough to get nods of approval. He hadn't had to make it up either. There were old forests on Gretia that were planted not too long after the first settlements had sprung up. Some of the Old Earth seeds hadn't taken to their new home, but others had—oaks, birches, elms, ash trees, and pines. There was a redwood forest out by the coast that had grown tall over most of a millennium. Walking among those trees felt like striding with the old gods. There were no trees like that anywhere else in the system. None of the other planets had seasons, or the sort of water cycle or soil that supported deep roots.

Aden looked at the bulkhead screen. The orb in the center hadn't gotten any bigger since he'd sat down for his meal, but he could still sense the gravity of the place drawing him in as they hurtled toward it tailfirst at ten kilometers per second.

"Eight hours to go. I guess I better get my stuff squared away and get in some rest before we dock," Aden said. "I'll see you both on the station."

They gave him respectful nods, and he walked over to the tray rack by the mess compartment's door to return his half-finished meal for recycling. On the way, he passed a table of Oceanians engrossed in conversation, and he pretended that he wasn't noticing the sidelong glances they gave him, dressed as he was in his obvious POW garb. Oceana had surrendered after a few hours of hopeless fighting, and their military casualties had been much lower than those suffered by the Rhodians or Palladians. But they had lived under occupation for the entire war, and their grudge against Gretians ran just as deep, especially when it came to members of the same military that had ruled them by force for four years.

Back to being the scum of the system, he thought as he walked out. *Not that we didn't earn it.*

The few things Aden had brought with him from the prison arcology weren't enough to cover even the narrow bunk in his berthing compartment.

It felt like a strange glitch in time and space to see the Blackguard uniform they had returned to him. He had discarded his own on Rhodia nine months ago when he was released for the first time. The new one was a replacement, probably sourced from another prisoner with the same height and build, but not even he could have told the difference, not with all the military identifiers removed. Without the unit patch and rank insignia, it was no longer a uniform, just a well-kept, used outfit in an unfashionable style.

None of the other things they had sent along with him were really his either. He had three sets of standard prison wear, olive-green undergarments and jumpsuits, and a small hygiene kit. The Rhodians had reissued the prisoner-of-war ID pass he had ditched in the canals of Adrasteia after buying his new identity on Oceana. Lastly, the intelligence officer who had given him a final briefing before they let him loose had handed him a comtab, with stern and specific instructions for its use. He was not allowed to contact anyone he had met as Aden Jansen because it put the mission and his friends at risk. Aden understood that requirement from an intelligence standpoint, of course. But it was a maddening kind of low-grade torture to have the tool for talking to his friends again and not being able to use it, and only the certainty that the Rhodians would know about it instantly kept his temptation in check.

Aden packed the things he had laid out on his bunk into the worn military shipboard bag they had given him for the transit. The clothes were not enough to fill it even halfway. He wondered how many of his fellow POWs had done as he did after his first release and dumped all the POW-issue clothing in the nearest recycling chute at the spaceport before spending a chunk of their release money on a few new outfits. This time, he had thought about it briefly and then decided against it. The expensive clothes he had bought that day had burned up with *Cloud Dancer*, the little Acheroni freighter he'd managed to book for passage, when the pirates had blown it out of space. It was an irrational impulse—if *Kingsnorth* suffered the same fate, it wouldn't matter in the slightest if he lost a thousand ags worth of unworn clothes in addition to his life—but he had resolved to not tempt fate and always buy at the destination from now on instead of at the point of departure.

I'm turning superstitious like a proper spacer, he mused with a smile when the thought crossed his mind. *Tristan would approve.*

He closed the bag and tucked the comtab and his ID pass into one of his jumpsuit's chest pockets. With his few possessions packed up and ready to go, there wasn't anything else to do for him, but he had no desire to return to the common space and be forced to make conversation with the other two Gretian ex-POWs or ignore sour looks from the other passengers. Aden lay down on his bunk and folded his hands behind his head. The berth had no networked view screen—he guessed the ship was too old or the management too stingy for such frivolous upgrades for bargain-rate passengers—so he couldn't see how close they were to Gretia by now. But he felt the proximity of the planet nonetheless, a vaguely malevolent presence on the other side of the aft bulkhead that grew larger in his mind with every passing minute.

Aden closed his eyes and listened to the thrumming of the ship's drive while he concentrated on his breathing. The deep, deliberate breaths Tess had taught him to slow his heart rate worked to calm his mind as usual. But even as he relaxed, he still couldn't shake the sudden feeling that he was in a cell instead of a berth, with no way out while he was waiting to hear the executioner's steps in the hallway outside.

Chapter 6

Idina

Tonight's safe house was an old warehouse near the Sandvik spaceport. Even with a hood on their head, an observant captive could probably figure out their general location by the regular nearby rumbling of shuttle engines at full throttle, but it didn't matter because the team never used any of the safe houses twice. The hood was mainly there for psychological effect.

"Talk to me about our catch of the day," Idina said to Sergeant Ansari, who was sitting at a makeshift desk with his comdeck.

"She checks out," Ansari said. "Corporal Birgit Anders, Supply Battalion 226, Second Assault Brigade. Qualified assistant unit armorer. She got discharged in the demobilization when her unit was dissolved, back in '19."

"Anything weird in her record?"

Ansari shook his head. "I went through her personnel file from front to back. Average scores, good evaluations. Never made a splash one way or the other."

"Just going with the flow," Idina said. "Not a true believer."

"Looks like it. She hasn't popped up anywhere in the civilian police records since then either. Not the kind of person you'd suspect to be an insurgent."

"Yeah, well, if there was a reliable way to tell the type, our work would be a lot easier," Idina replied. "I'm going to go talk to her and see what I can squeeze out. While she's still rattled from seeing us ice her friends."

The warehouse had an administrative section with a bunch of little office pods, and her team had appropriated one of them as a holding cell. Their prisoner was on a chair in the middle of the room, her arms and legs tied to the furniture with flexible restraints. Idina walked in and strode over to the chair, then pulled the hood off the head of their captive. The woman flinched and blinked at the sudden brightness from the ceiling lights. Idina dropped the hood and took a step back. There was another chair in the room, and she grabbed it by the backrest and placed it in front of the woman, who watched her as she sat down. Idina reached into her chest pocket and fished out a translator bud, which she put into her captive's left ear and seated it firmly. Then she unsheathed her kukri. The woman's eyes went wide when she saw the blade clearing its biometric sheath.

"Hold still," Idina said. "If you get cut by this, you won't stop bleeding for a very long time."

She cut the woman's wrist restraints with two quick movements of her blade. Using the kukri wasn't necessary, but it sent a not-so-subtle message that her little pocket utility blade wouldn't have conveyed. Idina sheathed her weapon again and sat back in her chair.

Time to channel Captain Dahl, she thought.

"Corporal Anders," Idina began. "I don't think I have to tell you how deep the shit is in which you find yourself at the moment."

Anders's gaze flitted around the room, then back to Idina. She took her lower arms off the armrests and rubbed her wrists.

"What are you going to do to me?" she asked.

Idina shrugged. "That depends entirely on you. But I am not going to murder you while your legs are tied to a chair, if that's what you're worried about."

The glance Anders gave the kukri on Idina's side told her that the other woman was very much concerned about that possibility. If she didn't entirely believe the assertion, it was fine with Idina because a genuine fear of death tended to encourage cooperation.

"I didn't *do* anything," Anders said. "I repair guns, that's all. I've never hurt or killed anyone. Not even when I was still serving, during the war."

"Maybe you've never killed anyone directly," Idina replied. "But I'd wager a fair amount that your friends have shot people with guns that you fixed. That puts you on the hook just as firmly in my book."

"I don't make anyone pull the trigger. And if I don't repair those guns, someone else will. What else was I supposed to do?"

"A few alternatives come to mind," Idina said. "The most obvious one is to find work that doesn't involve getting tied up in a terrorist insurgency."

"You call it terrorism. Some people call it armed resistance."

Idina shook her head.

"Your friends aren't too picky when it comes to target selection. I've had to clean up the mess after they've done their armed resistance. They splattered more Gretian brains than Alliance ones. If that's not terrorism, then the word has lost its meaning."

"Look, I didn't have an abundance of options when they dissolved the military. All I know how to do is to fix small arms. They offered good pay, and I needed the money."

"Who is paying you, and how?" Idina asked.

Anders glanced at the door again.

"If I tell you, are you going to let me go?"

Idina pursed her lips and shook her head slowly.

"That isn't an option, I'm afraid. We caught you in a clandestine armory with three armed insurgents and enough weapons to equip a platoon of infantry. There is nothing you can tell me that will result in you walking out of here and returning to your life as if nothing happened."

Idina leaned forward and put her hands on her knees for emphasis.

"What you tell me, however, is going to determine where you get to enjoy our hospitality. On one end of the scale, you can get transferred to Gretian custody. They'll put you in the corrections center outside of Sandvik. Middle of the scale, they'll ship you out to that penal colony in the frozen wastelands up north. I hear that's not so much fun."

She smiled grimly.

"On the other end of the scale, we can send you up into orbit, to the prison ship we set up for terrorist hard cases. A few years up there, and you'll lose so much muscle mass that you'll need an exoskeleton to walk around when you get back. If you get back. I hear it's no fun spending your days in a frozen shoebox surrounded by hard vacuum. It messes with the mind after a while."

Corporal Anders chuckled without humor.

"I think I'd rather you shoot me on the spot."

"I assure you that option isn't entirely off the table yet," Idina said. "Keep that in mind when you think about how to answer my questions."

Anders looked past Idina and glanced at the door again with the panicked gaze of a trapped animal looking for an avenue of escape.

"Even if you make it past me—which you will not—there is no way you'll get through that door and past my team," Idina told her. "Nobody knows you're here. Nobody will know you're gone. The only way for you to control your fate right now is to tell me what you know."

"I don't really know much. I told you; I just fix weapons. They bring them to me, I repair them, and they pay me."

"I'm sure you know a few things. Like the names of the people who were in that little armory with you. Or the people who bring the guns.

But if you aren't ready to talk yet, I can come back tomorrow or the day after. And if you don't want to talk at all, let me know now so we don't all waste our time here." Idina sat back and put her left hand on her upper thigh near the handle of her kukri.

"I'll tell you what I know," Corporal Anders said. The hint of urgency in her voice told Idina that her implied threat had worked as intended. Bladed weapons often intimidated people far better than guns because they were a better way to emphasize that human bodies were not much more than squishy bags of blood, easily punctured and quickly drained. Getting shot was an abstract concept to most, but virtually everyone knew how much a cut from a sharp blade would hurt.

"Your comrades," Idina prompted.

"Jesson, Herr, and Alpin," Anders supplied. "Sergeant Jesson, Officer Candidate Herr, and Lieutenant Alpin."

"All Gretian veterans," Idina said, and Anders nodded.

"Herr was in command school. Jesson was in the infantry. First Assault Brigade. Alpin was in the fleet. Served on a frigate, but I forgot which one. He was weapons officer, though."

Idina gave her an encouraging nod. "Go on. What about the people who bring the guns?"

"I don't know any of them by name. Last names, I mean. And they were never around for long. I only caught a few first names here and there. Someone drops off a gun; someone else picks it up when I'm done with it. I hardly ever see the same faces twice."

"How long have you been a part of this?" Idina asked.

"Since early last year. I knew Sergeant Jesson from the veteran association. He got me in with the group."

"A year and a half and you only know three people by name?"

"That's the way they work," Anders said in a slightly pleading tone. "You don't know who else is with the Wolves. You just know the people in your group, that's all."

"So you don't know who gives the orders or pulls those triggers."

Anders shook her head emphatically. "No, I don't. I know—I knew—those three. And the first names of maybe five or six others that would drop off or pick up."

"Who pays you?" Idina asked.

Anders shrugged. "I don't know *who* pays me. The money just shows up in my ledger now and then. Always different amounts. I don't know the senders, but they're never the same either. If you give me my comtab, I can show you the entries."

Idina shook her head with a grim smile.

"I am not about to hand you a two-way quantum comms device right now, Corporal Anders. But you can tell me everything else you know. What kind of weapons you fixed, and how many. How often they get delivered and picked up. Where the handovers happen. First names, faces, identifying features, mannerisms. Anything you may have overheard when your comrades were talking to each other. If you're thorough enough—and if what you're telling me matches up with what we know already—I'll be in a mood for concessions."

Corporal Anders nodded, relief evident on her face.

"But you need to keep one thing in mind," Idina continued. "If I find that you're telling me a bunch of made-up stories, I am going to leave you sitting here in the dark for a few days before I tell them to put you on a transport to the prison barge. And if you lie to me outright—if you tell me something I already know to be untrue—you get to see how sharp a kukri really is. It can slice very precisely for such a large blade. Are we on the same frequency?"

Even in the semidarkness of the empty office pod, Idina could see Anders's face blanch a little. The insurgent armorer nodded slowly and deliberately.

"Yes, we are," she replied.

"Good." Idina leaned forward again and drummed a quick little beat on top of her thighs. "Then let's begin."

When Idina returned to her team over two hours later, she was tired, and her knees and back were aching from sitting in a chair for too long. She walked over to the cooler pack they had brought along and pulled out a water bottle, which she opened and drained in one long, noisy gulp.

"What do you think?" Sergeant Shah asked when she was finished. The team had listened in on the entire interrogation, and Shah and Ansari had used their comdecks to analyze the information in real time.

"I think it's a delight to finally get someone who isn't a true believer," Idina said. "I barely had to threaten her with violence."

"A lot of what she said seems to check out," Ansari said from his spot at the makeshift desk. "Her friends are in the files. Names and units matched up. Nothing off about the records. The logs don't show any access or alteration since the end of the war. DNA profiles are a match as well."

"How is her comtab looking?"

"Going through everything right now. I'm backtracking all her comms and ledger deposits for the last few months."

Idina walked over to Ansari and looked over his shoulder. His comdeck was hardwired into an EM-shielded box that contained their captive's comtab, isolated to keep it from sending or receiving any data over the Mnemosyne while the sergeant copied and analyzed every scrap of data from the device. Ansari looked up at her and nodded at the screen of his comdeck, where various data fields were scrolling information.

"Just like she said. Random deposits to her ledger, all varying amounts between five hundred and two thousand-odd ags. None from the same transfer ID twice. *But*."

He isolated a few deposit records and flipped them side by side.

"Most of the ones I can track? They're not all from the same node. But a lot of them are coming from companies on Hades."

"Hades," Idina repeated. "The Gretians are going to be very interested in that, I think. Are you positive?"

Sergeant Ansari clicked his tongue and nodded. "Unless it's misdirection. But the Wolves would have to have their paws very deep in the system-wide financial networks to be able to fake originator node IDs. There's half a dozen separate Hades nodes that have sent money to her ledger. All tagged with codes for either gambling winnings or energy dividends."

"Not a bad cover," Idina said. "Lots of people have shares in Hades energy. Lots more gamble. And the amounts aren't anywhere near high or frequent enough to trigger automatic audits."

"I wonder how many other insurgents get paid like that under the radar," Ansari said.

"We'll take this back to the intel people and let them find out. This was a fine day, people. Three put on ice and one with lots of juice to squeeze out." Idina straightened up with a little groan and stifled a yawn.

"All right," she said. "As soon as the data dump is finished, we're packing up and heading out."

"What about the gunsmith?" Sergeant Shah asked.

"We hand her over to the Gretians," Idina decided. "She's a small fish. And she cooperated. But we'll keep her in the base brig for a few days before we hand her over. Maybe her memory will get jogged a little more if she thinks we're still considering the prison barge for her."

"Got it." Shah grabbed a pair of flexcuffs off the table in front of him and strolled off toward the hallway leading to the office pods.

"Hades," Sergeant Ansari mused. "Why the hells would *Hadeans* bankroll insurgents on Gretia?"

Idina shrugged.

"That's a job for intel to figure out. We just hunt them and stack them, Ansari. Let someone else worry about who bankrolls them and how. Once there's no one left to pay, it won't matter anyway."

Chapter 7

Dunstan

Dunstan was watching a video on the screen of his terminal when the intercom chirped. He paused the recording—his younger daughter, Kendra, playing in a socaball match—and tapped the intercom's sensor pad.

"Go ahead," he said.

"Commander, you may want to come to Ops," the voice of Lieutenant Hunter said. *"Looks like we may have a trail on the lure."*

"Finally," Dunstan replied. "I was starting to think there's some kind of pirate holiday week or something. I'll be right up."

"Understood."

He tapped the pad again to end the comm. On the screen in front of him, Kendra was frozen in midstride, running toward an opposing striker who had control of the ball. The pinched expression of focus on her face made her look very much like her mother, who scrunched her face in the same way when she was concentrating hard. This game was the latest in a long chain of school assemblies, sporting events, and recitals he'd had to miss over the years.

One more year, he thought. *Maybe two. Until Odin's Ravens are all plucked and cooked.* But even as the thought crossed his mind, it felt dishonest, like the comforting half-truths he told Mairi to placate her whenever he left for another deployment.

Now I am starting to lie to myself, he thought.

He touched his daughter's image on the screen with his fingertips and traced her silhouette for a moment. Then he turned off the terminal and stood up to leave his cabin.

—

Ops, the ship's operations center, was all calm business. *Hecate* wasn't strictly a stealth ship, but in the few months they had been out on patrols with *Hecate*, everyone had internalized the shipboard culture of stealth life. Everyone walked and talked softly when they were underway, nobody slammed hatches or locker doors, and even the coffee mugs were set down gently. Another part of stealth-ship service they had adopted was the informal atmosphere between enlisted, noncoms, and officers. Nobody called Ops to attention when Dunstan entered, as would be the custom on a larger warship. He stepped through the hatch and walked over to the tactical plot where Lieutenant Hunter was standing with crossed arms and watching the display.

"Fill me in, Number One," Dunstan said.

Hunter nodded at the display. *Hecate*'s icon sat in the middle of a three-dimensional grid pattern like a spider in the center of an orb-shaped web. A few ten thousand kilometers off their port side, a long chain of green icons tagged with ship IDs curved across the projection, merchant vessels in the transfer lane to Oceana, all plodding along at one g of acceleration and keeping regular intervals of a thousand kilometers. *Hecate* was coasting between occasional brief burns of her main drive to keep the IR signature from her already stealthy fusion drive cone to a minimum. They were keeping pace with one of the ships in the transit lane. Its green icon bore the transponder ID RMV-2606 SHANNON. In the database, *Shannon* was a Mercury-class fast courier on a delivery run from Rhodia to Oceana, carrying three and a half tons of medical equipment. In reality, *Shannon* didn't exist, and the ship broadcasting her transponder ID was their hunter-killer partner *Zephyr*, loaded with nothing but her current crew of three and an ample supply of decoys for her brand-new military-grade countermeasures launcher, courtesy of the Rhodian Navy. On the other side of the transfer lane, offset from the stream of merchant traffic, a single gray icon stood out, the tactical mark for a ship that hasn't been identified conclusively enough for a target classification.

"They started popping in and out of passive sensors a little while ago," Hunter said. "Running parallel to the merchie lane at first. About five minutes ago, they did a quick little acceleration burn and went on an intercept trajectory for *Zephyr*."

"Took the bait, did they?" Dunstan analyzed the plot. The unknown ship was coasting on a trajectory that would intersect with *Zephyr*'s path in a little over thirty minutes.

"Looks that way. Unless it's a merchie gone astray who's just trying to get back to the transfer lane."

"With a broken transponder and malfunctioning comms," Dunstan said. "And a course that just happens to take them across the bow of the only high-value courier within half a million klicks. One of these days it'll really be just a civvie with a busted transponder, and I'll be so shocked I'll drop my favorite coffee mug on the deck."

"I don't think this is that day," Lieutenant Hunter said.

"I really hope not. It's the first bite we've had on this patrol," Dunstan replied. "Who's the nearest Alliance unit?"

"ONS *Bora*. They're a little over five hundred K out, coming the other way on the reciprocal lane."

"Lieutenant Robson, send them a message on tight-beam. Tell them what we're up to so they don't waste their time and fuel trying for an intercept once the show begins."

"Aye, sir," Robson said and turned back toward the comms console.

"And give me a tight-beam connection to *Zephyr*, please."

"Aye, sir." Robson's fingers flew over the input fields of the control screen. "You're on for *Zephyr*."

"*Zephyr*, this is *Hecate* Actual. Do you read?"

"Hecate *Actual,* Zephyr. *Go ahead, Commander,"* Captain Decker's voice replied.

"It looks like you have a stalker. We picked up a contact on passive. They're on an intercept trajectory. Current position relative to yours is bearing 212, distance thirty-five thousand kilometers and closing. They'll be in showtime range in twenty-three minutes."

"Understood. We'll warm up the point defense and get ready to dance."

"Don't take any chances, Captain Decker. Something goes sideways, you drop the masquerade and get out of there at a full burn."

"Don't worry about us. We have a very acute sense of self-preservation. And I just got this ship fixed. I'll be damned if I let anyone put fresh dents into the hull."

Dunstan smiled to himself. He had taken a liking to the Oceanian captain of *Zephyr* since they had first met on his old frigate six months ago. Decker was competent, pragmatic, and loyal to her crew. Most importantly to Dunstan, she had proven her moral core. So many of the privateer captains who tap-danced on the line of legality were thoroughly mercenary at heart, with the bottom line as their only navigational reference out in the scrum. Captain Decker had delivered a nuclear warhead to the Rhodian Navy, a weapon of mass destruction whose mere possession could have seen her locked up in a prison arcology for the next twenty years. She hadn't dumped it in deep space to get rid of it, and she hadn't sold it on the black market, where it would have fetched her enough to allow for a very comfortable retirement for her and her entire crew. And she was still pestering him regularly about her crewmember, the man she knew as Aden Jansen, even though she knew he was a former Gretian Blackguard who had been part of the military that had occupied her home world for four years. But he was on her crew, and he had proven himself to them, and if that wasn't all that mattered to her, it was most of it.

"Use your new countermeasures liberally," he told Decker. "We can get reloads for those dispensers. But I don't think the navy will pay for another reactor so soon after dry dock."

"Don't worry, Commander. My pilot can't wait for a chance to start dumping those decoys into space. She's not too wild about the mass they added to the hull. Zephyr *out."*

"Ungrateful clods," Lieutenant Hunter huffed when the tight-beam connection dropped. "That was a two million ag upgrade. No other civvie out there has anything like it. Hells, there are ships in our own navy that don't."

"Now, now, Lieutenant. They'll appreciate the hardware upgrade the first time they have modern antiship ordnance coming their way," Dunstan said. He turned to Lieutenant Armer at the tactical station.

"On that note, warm up the antiship ordnance, Lieutenant. I want a firing solution on that contact as soon as they get into weapons range."

"I've been running one as soon as they popped up, sir," Lieutenant Armer said.

"Of course you have," Dunstan said with a little smile. "Very well. Let's see what we can shake loose out here today. Steady as she goes, helm."

For the next fifteen minutes, Dunstan sipped coffee from his command mug while he watched the icon for the unknown contact creep closer to the transfer lane where *Zephyr* was still plodding along at one gravity and pretending to be deaf and blind to the ship sneaking up on it. Whoever was at the helm on the rogue vessel knew their business. They didn't get hasty or careless with their intercept. They were burning their main drive in short, irregular intervals to keep their IR signature to a minimum, and the vector of their approach never strayed out of the blind spot generated by *Zephyr's* own drive plume. It was, Dunstan concluded, precisely the way his own crew would shoot the approach if they wanted to jump an unaware ship and get into weapons range before their quarry could throttle up and accelerate out of reach.

"Crossing into weapons range," Lieutenant Armer reported from the tactical station when the edge of the red sphere surrounding *Hecate's* ship symbol crept across the icon representing the unidentified ship. *Zephyr* was lightly armed for a ship of her small size, but the weapons she carried gave her a nasty bite. She didn't have the space or energy budget for a rail-gun mount, but she carried a retractable gun turret with a twin 35 mm autocannon mount. Chemically propelled grenades were nowhere near as fast as rail-gun slugs—the armor of a capital ship like a battlecruiser would shrug them off like pebbles—but the system's pirate ships were usually converted civilian designs, and the rapid-fire autocannons would tear a souped-up freighter to pieces at short range. The rotary launcher in her ordnance bay only held small antiship missiles, but the ones they had loaded were the navy's brand-new Tridents. They were fast, very difficult to intercept even for modern point-defense arrays, and fitted with warheads that contained three independently homing penetrator darts that punched through armor and burrowed deeply inside the target vessel before exploding. *Hecate* could not stand up to a capital warship in a firepower contest, but she could more than hold her own against the sort of quarry she was designed to hunt. Her best weapon, of course, wasn't a gun or a missile, but the AI core at her heart, which had more computing power than the rest of the Rhodian Navy combined. They couldn't disable a battlecruiser with gunfire or missiles, but they could shut its systems down remotely after plowing through the enemy ship's AI firewalls. It was a new and barely tested evolution of warfare, but there was a Gretian heavy-gun cruiser docked at a military fleet yard above Rhodia that was seventeen thousand tons of proof that the concept had merit. *Hecate* had captured the flagship of Odin's Ravens three months ago, a ship over ten times its own size and far better armed and armored, and they had done it without scratching her hull or killing a single member of her crew.

"Do we have preliminary ID on the bogey yet?" Dunstan asked.

At the electronic warfare station, Lieutenant Robson turned around in her chair.

"Negative. Nothing conclusive yet. They're not lighting their drive enough for a profile, and they're too far out for a good visual ID. From their acceleration curve, I'd say it's a thousand-ton hull, maybe fifteen hundred."

"We'll get a better look in a few minutes," Dunstan said. "They'll have to make their play soon."

"Tight-beam comms from *Zephyr*, sir," Lieutenant Armer called out.

Dunstan picked up his handset. "On speaker."

"Aye, sir."

"*Zephyr*, *Hecate* Actual. Go ahead."

"We just got a tight-beam from astern," Captain Decker said. *"Relaying it to you now."*

There was a moment of static, and then another voice came through the speakers in the Ops, a slightly nasal male timbre that sounded confident and arrogant, as if the speaker was used to giving orders and having them obeyed.

"Merchant vessel Shannon, *this is the Rhodian Navy. Maintain your current heading and shut down your drive. We are coming alongside shortly for an inspection."*

Dunstan raised an eyebrow and exchanged a look with Lieutenant Armer.

"That's a new one," he said. "You sure there aren't any of ours in the neighborhood?"

"Positive, sir. Nothing on the official board, anyway."

Dunstan straightened up in his chair. There was a possibility that some other Rhodian Navy unit was out on clandestine antipiracy patrol under the cloak of black operations, much like *Hecate* was doing now.

"Unidentified Rhodian Navy vessel, this is RMV Shannon. *We do not see your transponder ID,"* Captain Decker sent back. *"Why are you running dark and sending your challenge on tight-beam instead of an open channel?"*

"Shannon, *forgive me if I don't lay out our piracy countermeasures for you in detail. We will activate our beacon shortly. Stand by for inspection. Do not deviate from your course or accelerate or we are authorized to use lethal force."*

"Understood, Navy. We're cutting acceleration," Captain Decker replied, with just the right note of concern in her voice.

A few moments later, a new icon appeared on *Hecate*'s plot as the rogue vessel activated its ID beacon. Dunstan chuckled when he read the label next to the ship's blue symbol: RNS-892 Delphi.

"That's definitely a new approach," he said. "He sure sounds legit. Any chance that's the real *Delphi*?"

Lieutenant Robson consulted her console screens and shook her head after a few moments of scrolling through data fields.

"*Delphi*'s laid up in the reserve yard and scheduled for decommissioning, sir. Unless they dusted her off and sent her out here without telling anyone about it."

Dunstan walked over to Robson's station and looked at her screens.

"Leander class. I very much doubt they'd reactivate a forty-year-old hull for covert operations. But stranger things have happened."

"Their IFF code is ancient but it checks out," Lieutenant Robson said.

"If we have pirates out here squawking valid navy IDs, we're about to have a whole new dimension of problems." Dunstan returned to his command chair and sat down with a little groan. "Let's see where this goes. I don't want to light up a friendly by accident because someone in Fleet Ops forgot to update the mission roster for the sector. But we still need to assume we'll have a fight. Call to Action Stations, Number One."

"Aye, sir." Lieutenant Hunter picked up the handset for the ship-wide announcement system. A low-key tone sounded, only slightly more intrusive than a skylift bell.

"Action stations, action stations. All hands to battle positions. Assume vacsuit state alpha. Set EMCON condition one. Ship-to-ship action imminent. This is not a drill."

The Ops personnel suited up with practiced efficiency. Thirty seconds after Hunter's call to action stations, they were all at their stations in lightweight vacsuits, helmets on their heads and sealed to the suits, with only the visors open for easier communication. Dunstan connected the oxygen and data lines of his suit to the command chair and flexed his hands inside the ballistic gloves to stretch the material out.

On the plot, *Shannon-Zephyr* had stopped accelerating. They were now coasting in the transfer lane as instructed by the ship that was chasing them down, and the rogue vessel had cut the distance to its quarry to under five thousand kilometers, unaware that they were being stalked in turn by *Hecate.*

There's always a bigger fish in the sea, Dunstan thought. *Of course, that applies to us as well.*

"Helm, spin us around for a wake check, please," he ordered.

"Wake check, aye," the helmsman said. The tactical plot spun around as the ship turned with its maneuvering thrusters to point the bow and its sensor array behind them.

"Nothing on passive," Lieutenant Armer announced. "We're clear out to at least a hundred thousand klicks."

"Very well. Turn us back around and reacquire the bogey."

"Turning through one eighty, aye," the helmsman acknowledged.

The tactical plot continued its spin until *Hecate*'s nose was once again pointed toward *Zephyr* and her pursuer.

"Bogey now at 288 over 14, distance eight thousand five hundred klicks," Armer called out. "Bogey's distance to *Zephyr* is down to three thousand klicks."

Even knowing *Zephyr*'s capabilities, Dunstan knew it was a bit of a gamble to let the presumed pirate get too close to its intended victim. The technical sophistication of the ships they had busted so far had ranged from crudely converted old freighters with improvised antiship ordnance to genuine warships with serious weaponry. From the skill evident in their approach and their ability to keep stealth, Dunstan suspected that the unknown rogue vessel was situated near the sophisticated end of that spectrum. But the next move was up to *Zephyr*, and he had confidence that her captain knew how far to stick her hand into the trap before she yanked it out.

Several more minutes ticked by on the mission clock. The unknown ship was in no hurry to get into position. Finally, there was a change in their speed and acceleration reading, and Lieutenant Robson let out a satisfied little vocalization.

"They're doing a corrective burn," she said from her station, her eyes firmly fixed on her displays. "There they are."

She isolated a section of her screen and sent it to the main tactical display, where it hovered above the plot in a little window. Dunstan expanded it for a better look. The ship chasing *Zephyr* was counterburning their main drive to slow down their approach and match the speed of their target, and the hull was briefly outlined against the hot plume from their drive cone. It was an indistinct image, diluted by the distance and the sensor array's infrared filter, but it was enough for the AI to serve up a preliminary identification.

"Huh," Lieutenant Robson said. "It's a warship, all right. Just not one of ours. Computer says it's a sixty-three percent match for a Cerberus-class corvette. They're Oceanian. The ship is, anyway."

"Cerberus class," Dunstan repeated. "Any of those still active?"

Robson called up another screen and ran a brief query. She looked at Dunstan and shook her head.

"They had four. One was destroyed early in the war. The other three were seized by the Gretian Navy. Two of those were lost before the armistice. Unknown disposition for the last hull."

"What kind of weapons does that class carry?" Dunstan asked.

"Two twin antiship launchers and an automatic gun turret," Robson replied immediately. "Fifty-seven-millimeter rapid fire. Not a bad punch for a hull that size."

"Not at all," Dunstan said. "Comms, tight-beam to *Zephyr*."

"Aye, sir. You are on for *Zephyr*."

"*Zephyr*, *Hecate* Actual. We think we have an ID on your tail. They're not Rhodian."

"What a surprise," Captain Decker replied dryly. *"What are we dealing with?"*

"It's a missile corvette. You don't want to let them get too close. If they retained their stock armament, they have four medium-range ASMs loaded."

"Appreciate the heads-up, Commander. We'll go evasive shortly."

"Understood." Dunstan dropped the connection and turned his attention back to the tactical plot. They had the rogue ship dead to rights, flying with a forged transponder ID and pretending to be a Rhodian Navy vessel. But if *Hecate* made her presence known and sprang her own trap now, the only options would be to either blow the other ship out of space or disable and capture it. Taking a stolen warship off the board would be a respectable short-term mission success. But taking out individual ships one by one was a time-consuming task in this vast system, and it didn't solve the problem of Odin's Ravens at the root.

It's a warship, he thought. *They can't dock at any civilian space station anywhere in the system without drawing instant attention. But they have to refuel and rearm somewhere.*

Zephyr's captain cut down his options for him. On the plot, the acceleration and speed values next to the icon labeled RMV-2606 SHANNON changed rapidly as the ship burned its main drive again.

"*Zephyr* is taking off," Lieutenant Armer said. "Look at her go. Four g. Five g. Six. Seven. Bogey is accelerating as well. They're giving chase. Burning through five g."

"That's right, keep that throttle wide open," Robson said. "That's a beautiful drive plume. ID probability just went up to ninety-eight percent. It's definitely a Cerberus."

Dunstan had been out in the void protecting merchant traffic for so long that standing by and allowing a pirate ship in range of his own weapons to chase down a merchant without instant retribution felt all wrong, like seeing a mugging right in front of him and not intervening.

"Bandit, Bandit," Lieutenant Hunter called out. "The bogey just launched at *Zephyr*. One thousand klicks, forty-five seconds to impact."

On the plot, a small red V shape detached from the Cerberus corvette's ship icon and hurtled toward *Zephyr* at one hundred gravities of acceleration, a modern antiship missile homing in on its target. *Zephyr's* own acceleration jumped again, this time just beyond ten g. It was fast for a merchant vessel but only half of what Dunstan knew *Zephyr* could do.

She's keeping up the charade even with ordnance coming her way, he thought. By accelerating at half throttle, *Zephyr's* point-defense AI would have less time to calculate the intercept and jam the enemy missile's warhead, but they also wouldn't give the ruse away.

"They must have launched right at the edge of their engagement envelope," Lieutenant Hunter said. "No way they'll score a hit from this far out. Not with the point defenses on that little rocket sled."

Dunstan knew that his XO was almost certainly right. The PDS AI on *Zephyr* had received the latest upgrades when she was in dry dock. They had replaced the directed-energy emitters with the newest version, which used half the energy of the old ones and had almost twice the range. Combined with the new countermeasures dispensers, *Zephyr* now had a point-defense system that was equal to that on any warship. But space combat had a lot of unpredictable variables, and he still felt an uncomfortable knot in his stomach as he watched the red V race up *Zephyr's* wake relentlessly. For all her new hardware, she was still a lightly built speed yacht that achieved her stupendous acceleration at the cost of systems redundancy and damage resilience. Even a near miss from a modern warhead could shred her, and a direct hit would blow her to pieces.

"Fifteen seconds," Armer said. "Bogey is now at eleven g and still on intercept. Missile is still tracking *Zephyr*. Twelve. Eleven. Ten."

The red V symbol on the plot rushed toward the green icon for SHANNON. At the display's scale, they began to overlap as the missile closed to within a hundred kilometers of its target. Dunstan held his breath as the two symbols merged. Then both of them blinked out of existence.

"Intercept," Lieutenant Armer said with poorly suppressed anger in his voice.

"Confirm that," Dunstan said immediately. "Get me a visual and a passive EM scan of the area. Whatever you can see at this range. And don't lose sight of that corvette."

"He's not going anywhere unnoticed," Lieutenant Robson said. "Bandit is turning away and coasting again. Bearing 299 over 11, distance twenty-eight thousand klicks."

An alert chirped on her display, and she glanced at it and did a little double take.

"Sir, incoming tight-beam from *Zephyr*."

There was a general exhalation in Ops at her announcement. Dunstan grinned and puffed out a breath in relief.

"On speaker."

"Hecate, Zephyr. *We're still here, so don't plan our heroic funerals just yet, please.*"

Dunstan shook his head with a grin.

"Understood, *Zephyr*. Whatever you did convinced everyone. Including the bad guys. They cut their drive and changed course."

"They're not even stopping to sift through our wreckage. How rude," Decker said. *"My pilot says that she spoke too soon and too poorly of the countermeasure dispensers, and that she doesn't mind the extra weight after all."*

"So they worked," Dunstan said. *Thank the navy techs.*

"They did. We dumped a pair of decoys in our wake and shut down our drive and the transponder when the missile went for them. Didn't have any time to practice that move, but I have a great pilot."

"That you do. Tell her I can get her a job with the navy if she ever wants secure employment."

"She says 'not in this lifetime,'" Decker replied after a moment, and Lieutenant Hunter chuckled.

"*Zephyr*, I suggest you keep your transponder off and your drive cold for a few hours, until we've had time to clear the area. Then change your transponder ID back and head for Oceana. We will catch up with you there once we've concluded our business with this stolen corvette."

"Understood, Hecate. *I take it you're not going to run them down?"*

"They don't know we are here. And they're assuming their prize just went up in stardust. I think I want to tail them for a while and see where they are headed."

"Copy that. Happy hunting, Commander, and watch your wake. We'll see you at Oceana One when you're done. Zephyr *out."*

"She didn't sound like she just barely missed getting half a ton of high explosives up her drive cone," Lieutenant Hunter said. "I'd have to change my flight suit right now in her place."

"I'm sure the shakes will set in once the adrenaline wears off," Dunstan said. "They always do."

He leaned back in his command chair and let out his own tension in a long, slow exhalation. His coffee mug was still in the holder in front of the armrest. He took it out and sipped from it. The rest of his coffee was lukewarm now, but he emptied the mug anyway. Then he turned back toward the tactical plot, where the icon for the rogue corvette had turned from the gray of an unidentified contact to the scarlet red of a hostile one. Their new course took them away from the transfer lane at a perpendicular angle, off into deep space.

"Helm, set a pursuit course," he ordered. "Standard burn-and-coast profile."

"Aye, sir. Coming to new heading 299, burn and coast."

The ship slowly turned its nose toward its quarry until the red icon was right in front of *Hecate*'s bow.

Let's see where this raven has its nest, Dunstan thought.

CHAPTER 8

SOLVEIG

The noise started before the skylift's doors were halfway open, a swell of applause that sounded like a fierce rainstorm. Solveig had suspected there would be some sort of welcoming committee to greet her on her first day back at work after almost getting killed, but she wasn't prepared to see what looked like the entire executive floor lined up in the sky lobby, clapping and cheering as she walked out of the lift. Magnus Pettar, the company director and proxy for her father, was front and center, a broad smile on his face that she knew was as fake as the color of his hair.

"Miss Ragnar," he said over the applause and extended a hand. "Welcome home. It's so very good to see you up here again. We have missed you greatly."

I very much doubt that, Solveig thought. Magnus was her father's lackey, a placeholder to keep the big chair warm until she could claim it in a few years. To him, her face would always be an unwelcome reminder of that fact. She knew that he wouldn't have spilled any tears if she had died in the police headquarters attack three months ago.

She shook the offered hand and returned his smile.

"Thank you," she said, then looked at all the faces staring at her behind Magnus and repeated herself, raising her voice a little. "Thank you all. I appreciate the welcome back."

Solveig could tell that Magnus was expecting her to say a few more words than that, maybe give a little speech, but the overwrought attention and cheerfulness irritated her. She had been on the job for just six months before the insurgent attack on the police headquarters sent her to the hospital and rehabilitation for another three. But she was Falk Ragnar's daughter, the only person in the building whose last name was prominently displayed on the outside of it, so all these executives and their staff made a show to celebrate her return as if she was the patron deity of the business.

Solveig made her way through the crowd, which parted for her as she crossed the sky lobby. The applause followed her all the way to the door of her office, where her assistant, Anja, stood ready as she had every morning for the six months of Solveig's presence in the office, dressed in conservative business attire and clutching a compad to her chest.

"Good morning, Miss Solveig," Anja said. "It's so good to have you back."

"Thank you, Anja," Solveig replied. "Any calls for me while I was gone?"

Anja chuckled at the joke and followed Solveig into the office.

"Would you close the door behind you, please?" Solveig asked. "I think I need a bit of quiet for a little while."

"Certainly," Anja replied and touched the control panel on her way in. Behind her, the office door slid closed on silent tracks, and the noise from the floor and the sky lobby cut off instantly, kept on the other side of the soundproof glass. Outside, the crowd that had greeted Solveig was already dispersing, people returning to their own workspaces alone or in small groups.

None of that was for me, of course, she thought. *It was all for Papa.*

She had barely gotten used to her oversized desk and enormous office by the time she'd ended up in the hospital. After three months of absence, recovering from her injuries in small hospital and rehabilitation rooms and then in her old suite back at the estate, her office here on the executive floor seemed foreign to her all over again. It was too much space for someone her size, far too nice a view for someone with her lack of professional accomplishments. None of it felt earned, and neither did the fact that she had a personal assistant standing by to see to her needs.

"What did they have you do while I was gone, Anja?" she asked.

"I took turns with the assistant for the VP of operations," Anja replied. Her assistant always made sure to put on a professional face, but Solveig could see the nucleus of a frown in the corner of her mouth.

"They made you look after Gisbert?" Solveig shook her head. "I'm sorry I was gone so long. You didn't do anything to deserve that kind of punishment."

"That's quite all right," Anja replied. "You couldn't help it, after all. I'm just glad they didn't assign me somewhere else permanently. I rather like where I am right now."

"Believe me, I would have preferred to be here instead." Solveig sat down in her chair and winced a little as the change in muscle tension sent a dull ache through her that radiated out from the spot where an armor-piercing rifle sabot had pierced her back, missing her spine by a finger's width as it tore through her body.

"Are you all right, Miss Solveig?" Anja asked with concern on her face. "Do you need me to fetch you anything?"

Solveig took her briefcase off her shoulder and shook her head as she settled in behind the expanse of her polished wood desk.

"I'm fine, Anja. On second thought, I'll have a cup of tea if you wouldn't mind."

"Would you like your usual?"

Solveig shook her head again. "I'm supposed to lay off the strong brews for a while. Could you see if you can find me something mild? Maybe an herbal from Oceana."

"Of course. I'll be right back with that, Miss Solveig."

Anja seemed glad for the immediate task because she left the office with a focused stride that looked like Solveig had asked her to retrieve a lifesaving medication. When the door closed behind her assistant, Solveig got out of her chair with a little groan. She could see the glances people were giving her as they walked by on the floor behind the large ceiling-to-floor windows of her office. The windows had a privacy function that turned them opaque on request. Before, she had considered it a little rude to shield herself from view outside of private meetings, but somewhere along her way back into life from that bloody garage floor in the police headquarters, that sentiment had disappeared without a trace. She tapped the window controls on her desk, and the glass brightened until the panels were as white as the walls of her office.

Anja returned a few moments later, a cup of tea on a saucer in one hand and her compad in the other. She placed the cup on Solveig's desk with practiced precision.

"They didn't have any Oceanian herbals, but I am told this Acheroni green is very similar," she said with a hint of apology.

"Thank you, Anja. I'm sure it is." Solveig opened her weekly calendar summary and frowned.

"There's nothing on my schedule for today. Or tomorrow. The first thing on there is a midweek board meeting."

"I suppose they didn't want to throw a lot at you on your first day back," Anja replied. "Ease you into the flow of things, maybe. I can check with the director if you'd like."

"Don't worry about it," Solveig said. "I'll go see him myself in a little while."

"Yes, Miss Solveig. Is there anything else you need right now?" Anja asked.

"I think I am fine for the moment. Thank you, Anja. I'll call you in if something comes to mind."

"Of course." Anja walked out and closed the door behind her.

Solveig turned her chair toward the windows that faced Principal Square. It was cool and overcast, with heavy gray clouds that hung so low in the sky they seemed to skim the top of the buildings in downtown Sandvik. Gyrofoils were flitting around above the city, their position lights glowing like gems against the drab background of the clouds. Down in the streets converging on the square, the automated transport pods were ferrying passengers through the city in long, precisely spaced lines. The roads and squares were wet from the rain that had passed across Sandvik a little while ago, and the reflections of hundreds of traffic signals and advertising holograms painted colored streaks of light onto the streets that re-formed in ever-changing patterns as the wheels of the transport pods disturbed them in regular intervals.

Solveig took a sip of the tea Anja had brought. It wasn't like an Oceanian herbal at all, but it wasn't terrible either. Her schedule screen was still up, the projection floating above the surface of her desk. She added another screen and called up her message queue, which was almost empty. Few missives had reached her work stack since the day of her near death, and none had been added in the past month.

None of this would be different if I had died, Solveig thought. The city on the other side of the windows would still look the same as it did now. The executive floor would go about its business the same way it was doing now. Almost everyone here would have mostly forgotten about her by now, a brief footnote in the history of the company, elevated to her position by privilege and gone again before she could make a mark on anything. She knew her father would have been heartbroken, and he would have grieved for her for the rest of his life. But even he would have found a substitute to take her place, another proxy to install in this office as a placeholder.

She reached into the briefcase by her chair and pulled out her notebook to put it on the desk next to her teacup. It looked a little lost on the mostly empty polished wood surface. Solveig flipped open the cover flap and leafed through the pages.

Solveig was a diligent notetaker. A long time ago, she had acquired the habit from her Acheroni language tutor, who had explained that writing down information by hand made the brain retain information better than entering it into a compad or recording it for later. Something about the act of putting a pen to paper required her to synthesize and distill what she heard and streamline it to the essentials. Her instructors and fellow students at the university had poked gentle and sometimes not-so-gentle fun at her quaint Old Earth habit of getting out a paper notebook and making physical marks on it with liquid graphite clay while everyone else let their comtabs transcribe the lectures for them. In the end, it had been her turn to chuckle when she had been at the top of her class in most of her subjects. By then, she had long internalized the habit, and she found that it helped her think much better when she could do it on paper. It was far easier for her to spot connections, similarities, and disparities between different data sets.

Paradoxically, paper notebooks were also more secure than digital records, especially growing up in a house with its own network security department. Anything that connected to the Mnemosyne or the corporate network could be hacked by data thieves or inspected by corporate security. Her paper notebooks were secure as long as she kept possession of them.

The first dozen pages were filled with notes on Acheroni grammar and syntax, something that would be deeply uninteresting to anyone who glanced at it. Past that, the actual notes began, each subject with its own section. This was a notebook she had started when she came out of her medication fog a week or two after her emergency surgery, and she had filled it most of the way during her long convalescence with thoughts, observations, and suspicions. The headers she had written at the top of each page in capital letters jumped out at her as she leafed through the notebook: PRINCIPAL SQUARE BOMBING. POLICE STATION ATTACK. BRIDGE MASSACRE. PAPA CONTRIBUTES—HOW? DEFUNCT RAGNAR SUBSIDIARIES (LAGERTHA LAND SYSTEMS—OTHERS?). WHO IS ON THE PAYROLLS?

The first page had the words "Lagertha Land Systems" circled, with a question mark scribbled next to them. She trusted nothing her father had told her about his involvement, and most of what she had written down so far was conjecture, but this was one of the few verified facts she had on her list. It was the name of the contractor that manufactured the combat glove found at the scene of the first insurgent attack nine months ago. It wasn't much, but it was something, the end of a thread she could pull. She knew she'd have to move with caution—her father would not harm her because she was his heir, and because he needed her where she was. She was sure that Odin's Wolves would not extend her the same leniency, and she had no idea just how much pull he had with them, how deep his involvement ran. But if she was going to undo whatever hooks her father still had in this place, she had to know just where they were and which way to twist them out without killing the company with it.

Maybe Aden had it right all along. But if the Ragnar name can be redeemed, it'll be up to me to do that. And if I can't redeem it, maybe I can keep Papa from taking it over a cliff.

Solveig opened another data screen and authenticated herself on the company network. She took a sip of her tea, pulled her notebook closer to the input projection on her desk, and started to look for data points to connect.

It didn't take long for Solveig to run into her first obstacle. Lagertha Land Systems had been one of the many Ragnar subsidiaries, a smaller defense contractor that had been bought out by Ragnar well before the war. They had been sanctioned by the Alliance just like most other military suppliers, and Ragnar had shut down Lagertha's main production facilities shortly after the war. The company still existed as a legal entity in the roster of subsidiaries, with a caretaker director and a budget, even though nothing had been produced in a Lagertha factory in over five years. The data bank entries for the company looked like those of any other inactive subsidiary Ragnar had parked for legal reasons. But when Solveig tried to access the financial records, a notice popped up on her screen projection: INSUFFICIENT ACCESS LEVEL.

She raised an eyebrow and repeated the request, only to get the message again. When the third try yielded the same result, she sat back and tapped the assistance option on the screen that would summon the attention of an administrator in Ragnar's neural networks department. It only took a few seconds for another screen projection to pop into existence above her desk, this one flashing a connection request. She approved it and leaned back in her chair. The network engineer who appeared on the screen was young and handsome and dressed as well as anyone on the executive floor.

"Good morning, Miss Ragnar. My name is Ulrich. How may I assist you today?"

"Good morning, Ulrich," Solveig replied. "Has my access level been downgraded for some reason while I was gone?"

Ulrich consulted one of his own screens.

"No, ma'am. You have director-level access throughout the system. It hasn't been changed since you were established in the data bank."

"That's puzzling," Solveig said. "Because I am trying to access some data, and I keep getting denied."

"I am sorry to hear that, and I will look into it for you. Can you tell me which data node you are requesting to access?"

"Second- and third-level operational data at one of the subsidiaries. Lagertha Systems, manufacturer key 'byf.'"

This time, it took Ulrich a little longer to trace the request. When he looked at his comms window again, he had an apologetic expression on his face.

"The data you are trying to access requires elevated rights that your level does not grant. I am sorry."

"You're saying there's a security lock on that node that won't let someone with director-level credentials through?"

Ulrich looked over to his data screen again. "Yes, ma'am. It's a Tier One restriction. Director levels are Tier Two through Four. Yours is Tier Two."

"Who's Tier One?" Solveig asked.

"That's the chief executive and chief financial officer, and the head of corporate network security. The restriction has been on there for a while. It may just be a remnant from an audit. But I can't lift it without permission."

"Override it and grant me access, please," Solveig said.

Ulrich's professional smile didn't falter as he shook his head.

"I'm terribly sorry, but that isn't something I can do without authorization. I suggest requesting permission from one of the Tier One parties. They can add you to the access list or downgrade the restriction."

Permission, Solveig thought, and she felt the spark of the familiar Ragnar temper she had inherited from her father. *I am not going to Magnus to request permission for anything.*

"*I* am authorizing you," she replied. "I'm vice president at large. Add me to the list or drop the restriction. And be quick about it, please. I have a lot of work to do."

Ulrich's discomfort was evident even behind his professional demeanor.

"As I have already said, the CEO—"

"The CEO's name is not on the side of the building," Solveig said curtly. "How long have you been with Ragnar?"

"Three years, ma'am. I got hired right out of university."

"You are lucky you haven't met my father, then. Nobody who ever told him no twice was still in the employee database ten minutes later."

Solveig pushed her chair back and stood up.

"I'm going to go to the bathroom to wash my hands," she told Ulrich. "When I come back and sit down at my desk again, I don't want to see that message on my screen anymore. I am not asking you; I am telling you. And keep quiet about it. I am conducting an internal audit. Not a word to anyone unless you want to be included in it."

She closed the call window without waiting for his reply. There was no real need for her to wash her hands, but she walked over to the bathroom and did it anyway. The brief exchange with Ulrich had stoked her temper from a spark into a hot little flame, and it took her a little while to extinguish it again.

Back at her desk, the screen she had opened earlier came to life once more. The warning about the access level was no longer flashing across the projection.

I bullied him, she thought. *I acted like the rules don't apply to me because of who I am, and he caved and did what I told him. And the strange thing is that I don't feel bad about it, not even a little bit. What has happened to me?*

That's power, she heard her father's voice in her head, one of the countless conversations they'd had in his den back home over the years. *Power is control over external events. Power is when people do what you say. Either because they want something from you or because they're afraid of you.*

Solveig continued her excursion into the financial records of Lagertha Land Systems, and she was fifteen minutes into reading transaction entries when she realized that she was humming softly to herself despite the dry and uninteresting material in front of her. She was feeling *good.* Flexing her inherited authority successfully had given her a strange little rush that had boosted her mood.

If that's what power feels like, it's no wonder Papa is addicted to it, she thought.

Chapter 9

Aden

The Sandvik spaceport on Gretia looked almost exactly like Aden remembered it from when he was young, when his mother had taken him on trips to Oceana every summer. He couldn't precisely recall the last time he had walked through the huge, airy main terminal with its glass-and-steel framework and the enormous transparent dome in the middle of the roof, but the sight of it triggered the memories of the trips, the anticipation at the prospect of three months alone with his mother under the Oceanian sun, swimming in the warm waters and eating fresh seafood with almost every meal.

Even back then I couldn't wait to leave this place behind, he thought when he recalled the joy he had felt whenever they had walked through the terminal on the way to their departure gate.

The arrivals area was separated from the main part of the terminal by a section of floor-to-ceiling Alon windows. He spent a little while in front of the transparent barrier, taking in the sight of the busy terminal on the other side, while the passengers that had just disembarked the shuttle with him made their way to the end of the arrivals concourse, where the automatic entry inspection gates were marked with signs in all five system languages. The two other former POWs from *Kingsnorth,*

Master Sergeant Vass and Lieutenant Platt, hadn't been on the shuttle down from the spin station with him, and he was glad he wouldn't have to make excuses for not wanting to tag along with them.

Aden stood and watched the traffic in the terminal, people setting out on interplanetary trips or returning home, the typical spaceport variety of life in transit. When he decided that he had delayed the inevitable for as long as he could without starting to look suspicious, he picked up his bag and walked toward the security gates.

Time to be Aden Robertson again.

The inspection locks were a row of clear doors with scanner pads in front of them. Aden stepped up to one of them and placed his ID pass on the pad as instructed by the pictogram next to the device. Instead of flashing green, the light on the scanner pulsed yellow.

"Please follow the lighted yellow path on the floor to the security station for a secondary inspection," an announcement sounded. In front of Aden, the next set of doors opened, and the clear barriers beyond reconfigured themselves to form a passageway that led off to the right instead of straight ahead into the main terminal. On the floor, a yellow guideline appeared and began to pulse slowly. Aden sighed and stepped through the lock to follow the indicated path.

This again, he thought. *Welcome home, I guess.*

He had almost expected to see a Rhodian or Palladian soldier behind the ballistic Alon screen of the security booth, but the officer waiting for him was a Gretian policeman. The uniform was the same green-and-silver jumpsuit he knew from before the war, and when Aden stepped up to the booth, he could see that the officer was wearing a sidearm. It felt strangely offensive to see that the police uniform had all its proper identifiers on it—shoulder boards with rank insignia, police star on the chest pocket, and the Gretian flag on the upper right sleeve—while the military uniform in his bag had been plucked clean of everything.

"Good afternoon," the officer said. "Your ID pass, please."

Aden returned the greeting and handed over the pass, and the officer inserted it into his document scanner. He looked up from the screen and did a little double take.

"A returnee," he said. "I didn't know there were any left. The last group came through over three months ago."

"I managed to get my stay extended," Aden replied.

"Oh, yeah? What did you do to get on their bad side?"

"I got myself in trouble a few times. They said I had an attitude problem."

"And did you?" the officer asked with a little smile.

"I spent five years in lockup," Aden said. "Of course I had an attitude."

"I'm not surprised. I can't even imagine being away from home for that long. The Alliance really took it out on you soldiers." He looked at his screen, and Aden saw his eyes move across the data fields as he verified the information on the pass. Then he took the ID out of the scanner and handed it back across the counter to Aden.

"You're cleared for entry," he said. "Welcome home."

"Is there anywhere I have to report in?" Aden asked. "I've been in the military for seventeen years. And I haven't been back to Gretia in a long time. I'm pretty sure my old base doesn't exist anymore."

"If it does, it's been taken over by the Rhodies or the Palladians. Do you know where you'll be staying?"

Aden shook his head. "I was planning to get a hotel room somewhere until I figure out what to do next."

"You'll have to register with the community within thirty days to establish residence. And you'll need a new ID pass. If you're going to stay here in Sandvik, you'll want to take the loop train down to Civic Square and go to the registry office there."

"Thank you," Aden said. He tucked his ID back into the pocket of his jumpsuit and picked up his bag.

"They used to have a welcoming booth in the arrivals hall for the returning soldiers," the officer said. "They did all the initial paperwork there on the spot. But they closed it down a few months ago, after the last big group came home. They should have left someone on station for late arrivals like you."

"It's all right," Aden replied. "I grew up in Sandvik. I can find my way around. It's still the same city, after all."

The policeman gave him a look that wasn't unlike the ones his mother had given him whenever he had said something charmingly ignorant as a child.

"It is, and it isn't," he said. "It probably looks the way you remember it. But it doesn't feel like it did. You know, before. You'll see."

Aden nodded slowly and shouldered his bag.

"Thank you for the help, Officer," he said.

"Of course. Welcome home again. And best of luck to you."

The police officer had been right. Standing in the middle of the arrivals hall, the place looked and felt the same, but there were obvious little differences that felt like his memories of the spaceport, spliced in with a few details from an alternate reality. The most jarring one was the sight of Alliance soldiers patrolling the terminal. A pair of Rhodian marines were walking down the concourse in light battle armor and with carbines slung across their chests, observing their surroundings with no-nonsense expressions behind their helmet visors. They gave Aden a long look when they walked past. One of them said something to the other in a low voice, and the second marine chuckled. He watched them as they moved through the arrivals hall with the confidence of elite soldiers in control of their environment.

The transit station for the loop train was below the arrivals hall. He resisted the pull of the food stalls on the way to the skylift platforms even though the smells were amazing after a week of cheap shipboard meals. There would be plenty of places to eat in the city, after his body had adjusted to the planetary gravity again.

The trains were more modern and the ride into Sandvik faster than he remembered. Fifteen minutes after he had set foot into the spaceport's arrivals hall, he was standing in the Civic Square loop train station. It was late afternoon, and the station was busy—steady streams of people heading for the various platforms or the exits, the din of hundreds of simultaneous conversations punctuated by announcements and the rushing sound of trains coming out of the loop tubes. At the exit to the square, a small group of Alliance soldiers and Gretian police officers stood next to the doors and watched the flow of people going in and out. Once again, his detention-issue clothing made him stand out, and he could see the eyes of some of the soldiers homing in on him. But nobody challenged him as he walked past the cluster of uniforms, and he stepped out of the station and onto the expanse of Civic Square.

The initial sensation he felt when he was under an open Gretian sky again for the first time in almost a decade was a cold breeze that carried a light mist of rain with it. The center of Sandvik was not the overwhelming assault on the senses that Coriolis City on Acheron had been, but Civic Square was still the second-largest public square in the biggest city on Gretia, and it took Aden a few minutes to acclimate to the sights and sounds after months in detention and a week in the cramped confines of a small freighter. Most of the square was a park, carefully manicured lawns and tall Old Earth trees that rivaled the height of some of the buildings surrounding the square. There were footpaths leading toward the center of the park from each side and corner, coming together in the middle like the spokes of a wheel meeting at the hub. The center was a smaller square with a tall monument, a white obelisk that commemorated the founding of the city over nine hundred years ago, with the names of the original settlers memorialized on the plinth that surrounded the structure. It was a short walk to the nearest tree, and Aden wandered over to put his hand on the trunk to feel the rough bark of it under his palms. It seemed more real than the trees in the Rhodian arcology somehow.

He had forgotten the location of the registry office on the square, so he consulted his comtab, which brought up a screen that overlaid the route on the park in front of him. The office was all the way on the other side of the square from where he was standing, a ten-minute walk away, but he didn't mind the idea of a little walk in the park. He put away his comtab and set off along the nearest footpath without hurry.

When he reached the memorial obelisk at the center of the park a little while later, the light drizzle and the water dripping from the tree branches arcing above the path had combined to soak the top of his jumpsuit, and the wind did its part to make him uncomfortably cold. He paused next to the memorial and put his bag down on one of the marble benches that were surrounding the inner square. There was nothing in his small pile of prison clothes that was suitable for this weather. The only substantial overgarment in the bag was the tunic of the Blackguard dress uniform, made from a thick fabric blend that was designed for the variable Gretian climate. His old, trained habits made him hesitate for a moment—mixing uniform items with civilian clothes had been a major faux pas in the service—but the fabric felt invitingly warm under his clammy hands, and he pulled the tunic out of the bag and put it on. It wasn't designed to be worn over a jumpsuit, so it felt too snug when he closed the front, but the wind no longer made him shiver, and he was glad he hadn't disposed of this one at the spaceport like he had done with his original dress uniform on Rhodia months ago. He closed his bag and continued his walk across the square.

There was an indistinct commotion at the end of Civic Square, amplified voices that sounded like they were dueling with each other against the background din of a large crowd. As Aden got closer, he saw that the space between the edge of the green and the buildings lining that side of the square was packed with hundreds of people. Someone was speaking in the middle of the crowd, amplified by a voice enhancer, but a few people in the crowd had their own, and they seemed intent on drowning out the speaker. There was an angry energy to the scene, and Aden stopped at the tree line and pulled out his comtab to check his directions, unwilling to get closer than necessary. The building that contained the registry office was on the other side of the crowd, but there were so many people gathered on this side of the square that Aden couldn't see a way around them. There was a loose line of police officers in front of the door, all dressed in light armor and standing with their hands on their riot sticks. Between the amplified voices trying to talk over each other, he couldn't make out much of the argument, but it was a political rally of some kind, and it was clear that the speakers had irreconcilably opposed positions on whatever matter was under discussion. Overhead, a military gyrofoil hovered above the scene at high altitude, its position lights flashing in brilliant bursts of red and green against the background of the dark clouds.

I guess I am not checking in with the registry office today, Aden thought.

He turned to his left and started walking along the tree line. The geometry of the square and its surroundings was the same as it had been when he lived here, but he was sure that a lot of the eateries and clothing shops he knew from his time no longer existed. He still had the comtab out and in his hand, so he checked it for nearby stores and mercantiles.

"Hey," a loud voice said to his right. "Hey, what the *fuck*."

He looked up from his comtab to see that a group of rally attendants had spilled out onto the green, and some of them were walking toward him at a quick pace. The one who had called out to him was a young man with an angry frown on his face. Aden looked at his comtab again and quickened his pace a little.

"I'm *talking* to you, man. Hold up." The young man rushed in and blocked Aden's way. His friends gathered next to him and fixed Aden with equally unfriendly looks.

"Excuse me," Aden said and tried to walk around his interlocutor, who took two quick steps to the side to stand in his way again.

"What the *fuck* are you doing, coming here dressed like that," he said to Aden. "A fucking Blackguard smock. You gotta be out of your fucking mind."

Aden slipped his comtab back into his pocket.

"Just trying to stay warm, that's all," he replied. "You want to step out of my way? I don't have any business with you."

"You come to our protest wearing that butcher coat and I'll *make* you my business," the young man said. He looked like he was in his early twenties, midtwenties at best, which rankled Aden. In a spacer bar on a spin station somewhere, a challenge like that to the wrong person would have seen this kid on the floor already, with a busted lip if he was lucky and a skull fracture if he wasn't.

"I have no idea what the fuck you are protesting," Aden told him. "I've been on the planet for less than an hour. Leave me alone with your political shit."

He glanced past the angry young protester and saw that their interaction had drawn the attention of more people who had started to walk over from the main crowd. Aden was already halfway surrounded by his accuser's four friends, and things were not in his favor if they had violence on their minds. If more of their angry and worked-up compatriots decided to join in on the fun, this had the potential to end up badly in a hurry.

"Take that fucking thing off and hand it over," the kid demanded.

I'm not Aden Jansen right now, he reminded himself. That Aden would talk this group down, take off the tunic to give them a win, walk away. *But that's not who they sent back here. They sent back Major Robertson.*

"The hells I will," he said in his command voice. "I earned the right to wear this when you snot noses were still learning how to spell your names. I just spent five years in lockup and now I want to have a drink in peace. Go back to your little event and leave me alone. Before I decide to go to war with you."

The young protester recoiled just a little, enough to tell Aden that he had rocked the kid's confidence. He gave him a hard glare to underline the message and took a step forward to force him to get out of the way.

From his right, a glob of spit flew at him and splashed against the standing collar of his uniform tunic, deflecting some of it onto his neck.

"Warmonger," one of the other protesters said. "You Blackguard piece of shit."

Some long-dormant circuit tripped in Aden's brain. Before he could catch himself, he was lashing out almost reflexively, flinging his elbow to the right and driving it into the spitter's face, where it crashed into his nose with a dull cracking sound that satisfied him beyond measure. He took a half step and kicked the man in front of him in the groin, and the kid went down with a strangled cry. Then he was swept off his feet as several people tackled him and brought him to the ground as well. For the next few seconds, the fight was a wild exchange of kicks and punches. Aden got hold of someone's leg and dug his fingers into their calf muscle, but his grip broke when the other man pulled back his leg and kicked him in the side. He blocked a punch aimed at his head and failed to block another one that hit him in the chest. Someone tried to wrap their arms around his legs to keep him from kicking, and he jerked them loose and lashed out with both feet to an angry shout of pain from his attacker. Then a punch from an unseen angle hit him in the side of his head and glanced off his cheekbone, and his vision dissolved into bright white spots. Several pairs of hands pulled on his tunic from different angles and tore the front closure while they jerked him around. Another kick to his ribs took his breath away and sent a sharp stab of pain through the right side of his body.

There was a sudden burst of activity around him, more angry yells and shouts of pain, and the flurry of kicks and punches raining down on him lessened and then stopped altogether. He rolled over and got to his knees, anticipating another knockdown blow that didn't come. Instead, someone grabbed his arm and tried to pull him up. A moment later, someone else did the same with his other arm, and their joint effort yanked him back on his feet.

"Police are moving in," someone said next to him. "Time to go. Get him the hells out of here."

His unknown helpers took him between them and hauled him along with them at a quick trot. All around them, Aden heard people brawling. He tried to regain his breath and look around, but his vision was still blurred from the strike to his head and his rescuers rushed him along relentlessly. Behind them, an amplified voice shouted commands, and the noises of discontent and protest from the crowd on the square got louder. He heard his helpers huffing with exertion as they ran with him.

At least I hope *they're helpers,* he thought, and the idea of getting carried off to be killed in a less public location gave him another surge of adrenaline that cleared his head.

"Hold on," he said and tried to free his arms from the deadlock the people on either side of him were exerting. "Just a second."

"Don't have one to spare right now," one of them said in an out-of-breath voice. "Keep running, talk later. Unless you want to get arrested."

It seemed like good advice for the moment, and Aden decided to go along with it. The pain in his side flared up with every step, but his legs were working normally again, and he felt the grip on his arms lighten and then disappear altogether as he kept pace with the others on his own. There were three of them, one on each side of him and someone else bringing up the rear, their presence only evident from the sound of quick steps behind him.

They were running together for a few minutes when one of his new companions nudged him toward a building on their right. When they turned toward it, Aden saw that it wasn't really a building at all but an indoor shopping passage that connected this city block to the next one.

"In here," someone said. "Out of sight of those fucking drones."

Once inside, they slowed their pace to a walk. The passage had two levels surrounding an atrium with a high ceiling, and it reminded Aden of the main concourse on a space station. There were benches in the atrium, and his rescuers steered him toward one of them. He sat down with a little groan, and one of them joined him. The other two remained standing, trying to catch their breath after the dash away from the square. One of them was a woman who looked to be in her thirties. She had dark blonde hair that was gathered into a loose tail, and there were a few strands of it hanging into her face. The man next to her looked like he was lifted straight from a recruiting poster, a handsome face with high cheekbones and a sharp jawline, and short hair that was so blond it looked almost white. Aden turned to look at the man sitting next to him, who had a mop of dark hair and a full beard that was neatly trimmed.

"Well," the woman said. "That was a bit of excitement." Her eyes were a piercing shade of light blue, and they narrowed slightly as she looked at him with reproach.

"You're either very brave or really dumb," she said. "Take that tunic off. Before you draw any more attention."

Aden looked down the front of his uniform jacket. The fastener had been ripped open, and the black fabric was specked with grass and dirt. He peeled off the tunic and rolled it up in his arms.

"Shit. My bag's gone," he said.

"You won't get that back," the woman said. "Unless you want to give them another shot at breaking your face."

"You a Blackguard?" the man next to her asked. Aden guessed that answering in the affirmative wouldn't hurt him with this group, so he nodded.

"Did you *want* to get a rise out of those reformers on purpose with that? Because that wasn't the best idea, if you haven't realized that already," the handsome recruiting-poster model said.

"It was raining and I wanted to stay dry," Aden said. "I didn't have anything else to put on. Didn't know I was going to run across a few hundred soldier haters."

The two in front of him exchanged a look.

"Have you been locked away until today or something?" the woman asked.

"As a matter of fact, I have," Aden replied. "I just got here from Rhodia. Spent over five years enjoying their hospitality."

"The Blackguard came home seven months ago," her companion said. "Why'd they hold on to you for this long? You some kind of hard case?"

A hard case. The notion amused Aden, but he had a persona to play, so he just shrugged.

The woman glanced up at the second level of the passage. Aden followed her gaze and saw a pair of security officers making the rounds upstairs.

"Take his tunic and put it in your pack, Helge," she said to her white-blond companion.

Helge took off the backpack he was wearing and held out his hand. Aden gave him the rolled-up Blackguard uniform, and he opened his pack and quickly stuffed it inside.

"What's your name?" the woman asked him.

"I'm Aden," he replied. "Aden Robertson. *Major* Aden Robertson."

Helge looked at her and chuckled softly.

"*Major*. A major of Blackguards. You're outranked," he told her.

"I'm Bryn," she said to Aden, ignoring her friend. "Captain Bryn Bakke." She nodded at Helge. "This is Senior Lieutenant Helge Lind. And the fellow sitting to your right is Corporal Lars Holm."

Aden nodded his acknowledgment at the other two.

"Now that we have the exchange of credentials out of the way, we should get moving," Helge said. "He absolutely looks like he's been in a fight. Once those security people come around, they'll start asking questions."

"You do look rough," Bryn said. "Do you have a place to stay yet?"

Aden shook his head.

"I told you; I just got here. I walked out of the spaceport half an hour ago."

She exchanged looks with her friends again. Then she nodded at the other end of the shopping passage.

"Come on, Major. We'll take you to our place for now. Lars is a combat medic. He can patch you up a little. And we can bring you up to speed on everything that's changed since the war. So you don't offer yourself up to those fuckers for an ass kicking again. Or worse."

"Thank you, Captain," Aden said and stood up. "And thanks for getting me out of that mess."

"Don't mention it," Bryn said as they set off for the far exit together. "We veterans need to look out for each other. Because nobody else will."

Chapter 10

Idina

It was a gloomy and rainy day, and the cloud cover was so low that it shrouded the tops of the tallest buildings in Sandvik. Captain Dahl kept the police gyrofoil just underneath the clouds, but the lightweight two-seater still got buffeted by the winds despite its automatic flight-stabilization system, and Idina regretted having eaten a full lunch before she set out on patrol with her Gretian partner.

"You are unusually quiet today," Dahl commented with a sidelong glance at her. "Is something bothering you?"

Idina yawned and shook her head.

"Sorry. I had a long evening at work yesterday." She stretched in her seat with a little groan. "I just don't bounce back from a night of too little sleep the way I used to."

Dahl chuckled. "When I was much younger and spending time in questionable company, I used to be able to go an entire weekend without sleep. Now my idea of a good evening is going to bed on time."

"I can't picture you in *questionable company*," Idina said.

"It may be hard to believe, but I did have my wild and irresponsible phase once."

"I'm going to want to see some photographic evidence for that claim."

"Oh, I made sure to destroy all of that," Dahl said with a little smile. After all this time working with the Gretian police captain, Idina had picked up enough of the language to understand much of what Dahl was saying to her even before the automatic translation from her earbuds chimed in half a second later, and she knew that the other woman had picked up more than a few words of Palladian the same way.

An alert popped up with a notification sound on the comms screen in front of them, and Dahl reached over and tapped on it to check the details.

"That rally on Civic Square," she read. "They had permission for five hundred people to gather. Now the crowd is beyond the limit. The units on the ground are requesting more overhead coverage to keep an eye on things."

Dahl turned off the gyrofoil's autopilot and took the flight controls. She turned the craft around and accelerated toward the square, which was two kilometers north of their position according to the map on the screen.

"All airborne units, this is the patrol supervisor," Dahl said into the comms. "Anyone not on an active call, proceed to Civic Square for active dispatch notice and establish overwatch for the ground units."

Less than a minute later, they were over Civic Square. It was the prettiest of the open spaces in the inner city as far as Idina was concerned, a large open swath of green dotted with tall trees and sectioned by neat walkways that fanned out from the center in a star shape. Dahl dipped the nose of the gyrofoil down when they had cleared the surrounding buildings until the craft was barely above the tallest of the treetops. Ahead and above them, an Alliance combat gyrofoil was already on station over the scene of the rally. The sight of the armored war machine with its gun turret put Idina a little more at ease. More than half of the attacks since the beginning of the armed insurgency eight months ago had happened at mass gatherings like this one, and having visible firepower overhead could be the difference between another successful terrorist strike and one that was foiled in the act or aborted at the last minute.

"There they are," Dahl said and pulled up the gyrofoil at the north end of the square. There was a strip of open ground between the manicured green and the nearest row of buildings, and the rally crowd was taking up a patch of it that was at least a hundred meters wide. After many hours in the passenger seats of Gretian police gyrofoils, Idina had become skilled at operating the sensors of the surveillance pods despite the Gretian labels on the control fields. She brought up a wide-angle view of the scene below to get a full picture of the situation while Dahl put the craft in a stationary hover high above the crowd. Several people looked up at hearing the noise from the gyrofoil's rotors and some made rude gestures in their direction.

"Don't be rude now," Idina admonished the unfriendly faces on her screen. "We're just here to keep you from getting blown up."

"Some people will never like the police no matter what we do," Dahl said. "Sometimes I feel they should get their wish and see what it is like to live without us for a little while. Just a few weeks."

The crowd seemed lively, but there was no sign of imminent trouble. They were gathered in several large groups that looked to be engaging each other in a contest of chants and counterchants. In front of the closest building, a line of officers in riot gear kept an eye on the rally, but the focus of the attendants was on each other and not the police.

"We have thirty on the ground in armor, three flying units overhead, and a gunship on overwatch," Idina said. "That should be plenty unless things start to get rowdy. Computer says the head count down there is six hundred fifty."

"That is not a terrible ratio," Dahl replied. "If they remain peaceful, we will let them be and fine the organizer later. If they do not remain peaceful, we have the numbers to deal with it."

Idina stifled another yawn. The patrols with Dahl were much less exciting than the missions she ran with her team of covert operatives, but they were important nonetheless. With Dahl, she had access to intelligence they wouldn't have otherwise. The covert team had to work in darkness and below the official radars of both the Alliance and the Gretian police, but the joint patrols kept Idina aware of what was happening in the city, and Dahl was keeping her in the loop on the Gretian side. The trauma of the police headquarters massacre was still running deep after three months. Over a hundred police officers had lost their lives, most of them seasoned investigators and senior leadership personnel. Two of Idina's troops and the Alliance deputy high commissioner had died as well. Even with all the joint investigations and professions of solidarity that had followed the attack, the hard-earned trust between the Alliance and the Gretian police had been clouded with a general mood of suspicion. From the beginning of the inquiry, it had been clear that the attackers had inside information. They had known the layout of the place intimately, even the restricted sections of the headquarters, and they had known where and when to strike to inflict the most damage, both to the building and the institution it represented. The obvious conclusion—that the insurgency had moles deep inside the Gretian police force—had been a slow poison that had crept into most aspects of their cooperation over the last three months. Idina hadn't been exempt from the effects of it. Her trust in Dahl was unshaken, but she didn't fully trust anyone else in a Gretian uniform, including the people who had access to the cockpit recordings of the patrol gyrofoil.

"What do you have planned after work?" Idina asked Dahl. It was the code phrase they had established for the need to talk outside of the gyrofoil, away from the camera lenses and microphones that kept track of everything that was said and done in the craft whenever it was occupied.

"I think I will have a good glass of wine and go to bed early," Dahl replied, a response that told Idina she had received the coded message and was going to oblige the request. If she had said that she was looking forward to a long shower, it would have told Idina that Dahl was waving her off, that she couldn't talk freely now.

"That sounds like a good evening," Idina said. They were careful to keep the subject of the insurgency out of their conversations now whenever they were in the cockpit, and she shuddered at the thought of the information they had exchanged before the attack on the headquarters. They had shared names of suspects, locations, and investigative strategies. If any of the moles had access to all that data in real time, they could have made sure their compatriots were one step ahead of the police by informing them of impending arrests or passing on the times and locations for raids to the insurgency. In her darker moments, Idina imagined that the disastrous Quick Reaction Force raid on the capsule hotel near the spaceport had been the fault of her or one of the other Alliance troops riding with the Gretians in their own vehicles, unwittingly revealing mission details to the terrorists through the cockpit recordings. It was far from certain that the insurgency did have access to those streams, but it was prudent to act as if they did. That was the corrosive quality of distrust—it bred paranoia and dissolved the glue that held organizations and alliances together.

Dahl had set the gyrofoil into motion again, and now they were making slow loops of the north end of the square to keep an eye on the crowd from all angles. Two more police craft had appeared at Dahl's direction to take up overhead positions above the southern end of the square and the main intersection closest to the rally. The rain had picked up again, a light but steady drizzle that drifted across the plaza in quick-moving bands.

"They must be either really dedicated or really bored to be out there in this weather," Idina said.

"Some are one, some the other. A lot of them are both," Dahl replied. "Everyone feels as though the other side is out to either plunge them into war again or destroy the foundations of our society. The only thing they have in common is that both sides resent being governed by outsiders."

"They should resent the insurgency for killing its own people. When I was picking up body parts on that bridge, it didn't look like that cannon made any distinction between loyalists and reformers."

"Some of them argue that this is the fault of the Alliance because you are here, and that the problem will go away again once you leave. It is not an uncommon viewpoint."

"People are entitled to their misconceptions," Idina replied. "But we both know that if the Alliance packed up and left tomorrow, those people wouldn't just hand over their guns."

"They would keep using them," Dahl agreed. "First to get rid of people they consider traitors and collaborators. Then to gain control over everyone else. We have no military left. They know that if you all go home tomorrow, they will be the only people with guns. Except for the police."

And if they have already infiltrated the police, then there'll be no opposition at all. Idina didn't voice the thought because she was mindful of the fact that every word they spoke in the gyrofoil was recorded, but she knew that Dahl was aware of that implication as well.

"You would certainly be on that list," she said.

Dahl shrugged. "I have been on it since I went on my first patrol with an Alliance soldier."

They were at the far end of their little patrol loop around the north section of the square, and Idina had to turn the surveillance pod's sensor array to keep the crowd fully in view. As she did, some movement caught her eye. There was a certain typical flow to how the bodies in a crowd moved, and once someone had seen enough gatherings from a high angle, it was easy to spot trouble because of the disruption to that flow. At the periphery of the rally, a handful of people were moving away from the center with quick and urgent steps. Idina put the central marker of the optical sensor on the little group and watched, her finger on the transmit button for the comms link to the Alliance gunship overhead.

"Something's happening," she said to Dahl. "Just inside the green, over by the tree line. Fifty meters to the left of the central path."

A small group of people were rushing toward someone walking on the green. When they reached him, they formed a semicircle around the solitary person. Whatever words were exchanged, Idina could tell from the body language of the group that this was not a friendly conversation.

"I see it," Dahl said. "It looks like a disagreement."

"Someone is about to get punched," Idina predicted.

The exchange escalated into violence almost as soon as the words were out of her mouth. The man the little group had surrounded threw a punch at one of them and a kick at another, and then the scene devolved into a small-scale brawl as the group piled onto their attacker and began punching and kicking him in turn.

"Ground units, this is the patrol supervisor. There is a physical altercation on the north side of the green, fifty meters to the west of the central footpath," Dahl sent on the comms. "First group, see if you can reach them and sort things out before they get out of hand."

Someone sent their acknowledgment back, and Idina watched as several of the armored officers left the line in front of the building they were guarding and moved toward the crowd. They were on the other side of the disturbance, with hundreds of bodies between them and the brawl, and the rally goers were slow to get out of the way of the officers as they started wading through the crowd. In the group of people that stood closest to the fight, some had noticed the commotion and were rushing out onto the green to either watch or participate. It was the sort of thing that could set a match to an already worked-up crowd and spark a riot.

Dahl turned the gyrofoil and flew diagonally across the square toward the assembly. Idina turned the sensor pod to keep sight of the fighting group, but the canopies of the trees they passed obscured the brawlers for a few moments. When she had a clear line of sight to the spot again, more rally goers had joined the disagreement, and now at least a dozen people were punching and kicking each other on the manicured lawn of the green, with more moving toward the trouble.

"Oh, no, you will *not*," Dahl said in a conversational tone. She swooped in and pulled the gyrofoil into a hover between the main crowd and the green, descending to a spot just a few meters above the ground with flashing exterior lights. The downwash from the gyrofoil's four rotors blew across the square like a small but intense storm, whipping up leaves and spraying rainwater outward in a fifty-meter circle. The people who had been moving toward the green covered their heads and faces with their arms and turned away, obviously receiving the message Dahl was sending. She held the craft in its blocking position for a few moments, then ascended again and swung the nose around toward the original source of trouble. The gyrofoil's sudden nearby descent had gotten the attention of most of the pugilists, but a few hotheads were still taking swings at each other. Dahl gave them a quick blast of sound from the gyrofoil's emergency siren.

"Stop the fighting. Rejoin the event peacefully or leave the area," she ordered over the PA system when she had their attention. When they obeyed and dispersed, Dahl looked over at Idina with a satisfied little smile.

"The wonderful power of a little bit of well-directed intimidation," she said.

"It's one of my very favorite persuasion strategies," Idina replied.

To her right, she saw hurried movement out of the corner of her eye through the gap between two of the nearby trees, and she turned her head to see a small group of people rushing from the scene. Before she could get a head count or make out any details, they disappeared again behind the foliage of another tree.

"Go above the treetops again," she told Dahl. "I want to take a look at something."

Dahl complied and pulled up the craft until they were well above the tops of the trees that were lining the edge of the green. Idina didn't have to look for long to reacquire the group she had just spotted. They were moving in a hurried trot, two people supporting a third one between them, and a fourth just a few steps behind. Their path took them away from the rally and toward the west edge of the square. Idina tracked them with the optical sensor and waited for one of them to turn their head so she could get a good image of a face, but none did. They were moving with a sort of purpose and well-coordinated effort that reminded Idina of an infantry team evacuating a wounded soldier from the battlefield. The group reached the western side and turned to move south along the storefronts there.

"Do you want me to follow them?" Dahl asked. She had looked over at the surveillance screen to see what Idina was tracking.

"Don't follow," she replied. "I don't want to make it obvious that I'm watching them. In fact, turn the nose the other way. I can rotate the pod to keep them in sight."

Dahl turned the craft around on its dorsal axis until they were facing away from Idina's quarry. She swiveled the pod sensors in the opposite direction of the gyrofoil's rotation to keep the optics trained on the little group.

"What are you thinking?" Dahl asked.

"I don't know for sure," Idina replied. "It's just an instinct, I guess. They're in a hurry to get away from the police. But they're oddly disciplined about it."

The people in the middle of her screen moved up the west side of the square. They were all dressed in unremarkable civilian clothing except for the person in the middle, who wore a strangely formal-looking jacket with his utilitarian pants. She tapped the screen to point it out to Dahl.

"Does that look like a piece of uniform to you? Police or military?"

Dahl looked at the screen. "Dark blue, with a standing collar. That looks like a military dress uniform."

"That's what I thought."

Idina tracked them for another hundred meters, until the group took a right turn and strode into a shopping passage. Just before they disappeared inside, the last person in the group quickly looked over his shoulder in what seemed like a reflexive move, and she saw his face for the fraction of a second. Then they were gone, blended into the foot traffic in the busy passage.

"What is that place?" Idina asked.

Dahl glanced at the screen again. "That is the Arkaden mercantile. Shops and food stalls."

"Does it go all the way through that building?"

Dahl tapped the navigation screen and changed the overlay to a three-dimensional view that showed her the structure of the building Idina had pointed out.

"It does," Dahl confirmed. "It connects the square with the street on the other side of the block. Do you want me to fly across and get us line of sight to the other exit?"

Idina thought about it briefly and shook her head. "If they see a gyrofoil overhead when they pop out of that exit, they'll know we were keeping an eye on them. Let them think they're in the clear."

She reversed the recording stream and slowed it down until the group seemingly walked backward out of the passage in slow motion. When she had reached the spot where one of them had looked up, she froze the image. For the brief instant when he had looked back over his shoulder, his face had been turned toward the sensors of the surveillance pod, and the freeze-frame showed it at an angle that was halfway between a profile and a portrait.

Good enough for facial recognition, Idina thought. *Maybe you're nobody. But if you aren't, I'll see you again soon.*

"I got what I need already," she told Dahl.

"Very well," Dahl replied with a glance at Idina's surveillance screen, where the suspect's face was still frozen in the middle of the frame, his blue eyes looking almost directly at the camera lens that was recording him from two hundred meters away.

They landed on the gyrofoil pad at Joint Base Sandvik just as night was setting in. In the warm season, it stayed light outside until late in the evening, but the sunset had moved backward on the clock a few minutes every day during the planetary autumn, and now they ended every daytime patrol with the setting sun. When Idina climbed out of the cockpit, a cold breeze greeted her, but she welcomed it because it made her feel a little more awake and alert. She walked a few meters away from the craft and stretched her limbs and back while Dahl shut down the gyrofoil and secured the machine for the night.

"What is it that you wanted to talk about?" Dahl asked when she had joined Idina and they were walking away from the long row of parked police craft and toward the briefing building.

Idina took a folded-up piece of paper out of the chest pocket of her flight suit and handed it to Dahl.

"There are a few names on this list. We ran them through the system already, but we only have access to the military files up to the demobilization. I would like to double-check them against the police and civil data banks."

Dahl eyed the paper for a moment before taking it. She unfolded it and read what Idina had written down.

"I am assuming this has to do with your latest extracurricular activities."

"You can assume," Idina said, and Dahl smirked at the reply.

"Are these people alive or dead?"

"One alive, three dead," Idina said. "All confirmed insurgents. All four have military records. We have those, but I need to know more about these people. Prior convictions. Civil penalties. Known associates. Prior residences. Financial ties. You know the scope."

Dahl nodded.

"That may take a while, and I do not know how deeply I can dig right now. All data access is logged and monitored in the police data bank system. I can look up whatever I need if I have an investigative justification. But people upstairs will know that I have searched out that information."

"And you can't get around those file logs?"

Dahl shrugged with an expression of mild discomfort on her face.

"The only way to do it properly would be for someone at the director level to grant me unlogged access. But I would have to take all the details of the investigation to them and make my case. And we do not know how high up the trunk the tree has already rotted."

"How about ways to do it improperly?" Idina asked.

Dahl gave her a long sideways look.

"You know I am not someone who condones breaking the law," she said. "Once we start to pick and choose which ones to follow and which ones to ignore for convenience, the laws cease to be laws, and they become mere suggestions."

They walked across the gyrofoil pad in silence for a few moments. Then Dahl spoke up again.

"The people on that list who are dead now," she said. "They were armed when you found them?"

"They were," Idina confirmed. "They had the chance to drop their weapons and surrender. They chose to fight instead."

Dahl looked at the piece of paper in her hand again. She folded it, but instead of handing it back like Idina expected, she sighed and slipped it into one of the many pockets of her green-and-silver police suit.

"A hundred and nine of my friends and colleagues are dead because of these people. I do not want to lose anyone else to them. Gretian or Alliance. And if that requires some flexibility with the rules, I suppose that is the way it will have to be. I will find a way to get access."

Chapter 11

Dunstan

Dunstan had chased a lot of suspicious ships through the system during his career, but this current tail was easily his most difficult pursuit.

The Oceanian Cerberus-class corvette that had tried to intercept *Zephyr* was commanded by someone who was very skilled at staying hidden. They had chased their quarry for several days now, and whoever was in charge on the corvette acted like there were Alliance patrols everywhere even though they were in the deepest of deep space, far beyond any planets, moons, or current transfer lanes. They changed course in irregular intervals and employed the same burn-and-coast technique as *Hecate*, briefly lighting up the main drive for acceleration and then riding the momentum for equally irregular periods of time. Whenever the corvette fired up its drive for another dash, *Hecate* had used the other ship's temporary blindness to the rear to do likewise and keep pace, but even with their state-of-the-art passive sensors, they had almost lost the trail several times. Dunstan's crew knew their business as well, however, and they were still in dogged pursuit despite their target's skill at stealthy movement.

—

Lieutenant Hunter floated through the Ops hatch and pushed off toward her station. She sailed over to her chair and grabbed the backrest, then used it as an anchor to flip herself around and into the seat.

"Seven days in zero g," she grumbled as she buckled herself in. "When we catch these people, I'll make sure they get an extra year or two tacked on to their sentence for that."

"Remember the first few weeks in advanced training?" Dunstan asked. "Everyone is always excited about weightlessness exercises."

"It's fun for the first ten or twenty times. In the training chamber. Before you have to spend a few days strapping in for everything."

"Including using the head," Dunstan replied.

"*Especially* using the head." Hunter settled in at her station and activated the control screen layout. "There's always one in the group of new trainees who thinks the handlebars on the sidewalls are enough. It usually ends in a cloud of piss bubbles."

She looked over at the tactical plot and frowned.

"No change. Still out in the middle of a whole lot of nothing," Dunstan said.

"I'm starting to wonder whether this fellow really has a destination. Maybe he noticed us five days ago and just decided to take us on a grand tour of the ass end of the system."

They were far out in deep space, farther than Dunstan had ever gone on regular patrols. The other ship's course had led them well beyond the orbit of Pallas, the planet most distant from the sun. Nobody but the occasional science expedition ever came this way because there was nothing of interest to justify the fuel expenditure—no stations or outposts to visit, no asteroid belt to mine for resources, no satellite relays to maintain.

"It's times like this when I miss the old cruiser," he said. "She was old and creaky, but by the gods, she had space. If I had an ag for every time I've bumped my head on this boat, it would pay for a very posh dinner with the wife back home."

The past week had been an exhausting mix of boredom and tension as they followed the rogue ship. It took concentration and care for the Ops personnel to keep *Hecate*'s distance from the other vessel while timing the acceleration burns to theirs. But the monotony of the task combined with the unchanging environment generated a pernicious sort of stress that was cumulative. The Ops crew had done nothing but stare at the tactical plot and mirror the other ship's booster burns and course changes, and Dunstan could see that everyone was getting more tired by the day. Fatigue lengthened reaction times and introduced errors, even among well-trained and experienced crews. This team hadn't hit their limits yet, but he could tell some of them weren't far away from that line.

"You look like you are well overdue for some rack time, Commander," Lieutenant Hunter said.

"That bad, huh?" he replied. At the unfortunate mention of rest, Dunstan felt an unwelcome yawn coming on, and he failed to stifle it. Hunter watched him with a little smile as he decided to go all-out with it and turn the yawn into an upper-body stretch.

"All right. You have the conn, Number One."

"XO has the conn," Hunter confirmed. "You should stop by the galley on the way to your bunk. The kitchen managed to turn out some egg cakes for Chief Philips's birthday."

"In zero g?" Dunstan unbuckled his harness and pushed himself out of the command chair. "That's pretty impressive."

"It's bad luck to break birthday traditions. Gravity or not."

Dunstan floated down past the airlock deck and into the galley deck. There was nobody in the cooking nook, but two of the dispenser drawers on the bulkhead were labeled as full and marked with their contents. Under zero g, it was standard procedure to serve packaged rations instead of fresh food because cooking was nearly impossible without gravity, but fresh food was good for crew morale, and Dunstan was glad to see that Petty Officer Blunt, *Hecate*'s cook, had found a way to put together a large batch of individual-sized egg cakes. They didn't hold together as well as properly made ones, and their shapes wouldn't win any cooking contests, but they tasted amazing after a few days of zero-g rations, and Dunstan scarfed his cake down in just a few big bites. He suppressed the impulse to claim a second and pushed off from the dispenser drawer to put the treats safely out of his reach.

In the ladderwell, he looked down toward the medical deck and considered stopping there for a shower before rack time. After a moment of contemplation, he decided against it and pulled himself upstairs on the ladder rungs to head to his berth. On his last few ships, he'd had a day berth near the CIC in addition to his regular quarters, but *Hecate* wasn't big enough for that convenience.

He was about to unlock his berthing space on the command quarters deck when the announcement alert chirped.

"Commander to Ops."

Dunstan sighed and turned back toward the ladderwell.

My magic powers grow stronger, he thought. *Now I can make things happen just by thinking about taking a shower.*

Back in Ops, Lieutenant Hunter gave him an apologetic look as he returned to his command chair and strapped himself in again.

"Sorry to cut into your rack time, Commander. I think we're close to the end of the trail. The bogey is counterburning for deceleration."

On the tactical screen, the velocity reading of the rogue ship was on a sharp downward trajectory. The visual from the bow sensors showed the blurry outline of the corvette in the middle of a drive plume that blossomed bright and clear on infrared.

“They’re putting on the brakes pretty hard,” Dunstan said. “Call to action stations and prepare for a cold counterburn.”

“Aye, sir.” Hunter picked up the announcement handset.

“Action stations, action stations. All hands to battle positions. Assume vacsuit state alpha. This is not a drill. Engineering, rig for cold counterburn.”

The palladium in *Hecate*’s AI cores had been the main budget-destroying item on her design sheet, but the new stealth features had added their own hefty price tags. Her hull was clad in radiation-absorbing material, and the nozzles of her fusion drive were a stealth design that reduced her infrared signature. But the core of her propulsion system’s black ops modifications was an intercooler and heat diffuser unit that cooled down the exhaust gases from her fusion drive to just a few dozen degrees. The excess heat was stored in a battery of internal heat sinks that could be ejected one by one once they reached their thermal thresholds. It was an innovative and very expensive way to all but eliminate the usual massive IR signature from a fusion drive’s exhaust plume and store the generated heat inside the ship in an insulated and shielded location. *Hecate*’s cold counterburn system diverted the exhaust gases through conduits where they were cooled further with hydrogen and ejected at the front of the ship. It only allowed for a modest low-g burn, and it wasn’t a guarantee for complete invisibility, but it let *Hecate* perform a stealthy deceleration without having to flip around and expose her drive cone.

“Engineering reports ready for cold counterburn,” Lieutenant Hunter relayed. “All decks secured and ready for action.”

“Very well. Let’s throw out the anchor before we rear-end these people. Counterburn at one g on my mark. Three, two, one, *mark*.”

In just a few seconds, the sensation of floaty lightness Dunstan had been accustomed to for days now was replaced by a pull that made his shoulders lurch forward a little until they were held by the safety harness of his chair. As *Hecate* began her counterburn, there was gravity again, but it was in the wrong direction, turning the bow bulkhead above their heads into down and the floor of the Ops deck into up. It was a slightly disconcerting sensation, as if they were all hanging in their chairs upside down. Dunstan adjusted his chair into the reclined high-g position, which made the feeling less pronounced, and Lieutenant Hunter and the rest of the Ops crew did likewise.

On the plot, the distance between *Hecate* and her quarry decreased steadily over the next twenty minutes. The other ship was burning her drive at full throttle, ten g of acceleration to quickly scrub the speed she had built up coasting between her sporadic burns. Dunstan felt his anxiety slowly increasing as the range readout ticked down rapidly with every passing second. They had built enough distance into their pursuit to avoid overshooting the rogue corvette, but the noses of the two vessels were now pointed at each other, each ship with an unobstructed field of view for their bow sensors. This was the point in the pursuit where *Hecate* was at the greatest risk of being discovered.

"Well, I'm sure they're not slowing down in the middle of nowhere for no reason," Dunstan said.

"There's nothing else on the sensors so far," Lieutenant Armer said. "Of course, they're making a lot of IR noise with that drive plume. I've got a twenty-degree blind spot you could hide a small moon behind. Not that there's one charted out here."

"Maybe it's a rendezvous spot and they have company coming," Hunter suggested.

"That's a very long trip to a very remote spot. Even for a private meeting," Dunstan said.

"And that's what makes me think we're on the right trail. There's no way anyone would spend a week zigzagging through the outer system if they didn't want to hide something big," Dunstan replied.

"Or they're setting one bitch of a trap for us." Lieutenant Hunter shrugged to shift the straps of her harness. "Like that other ship tried with *Zephyr* a few months back, the one that led them right into firing range of that gun cruiser."

"I guess we'll find out shortly. The bogey is throttling back on the burn," Armer said. "They're down to seven g. Five. Three."

Dunstan watched the optical feed as the heat plume outlining the other ship shrank rapidly, then went out altogether.

"They've cut their main drive," Armer said.

"Keep up the counterburn for a few more minutes," Dunstan ordered. "Let's keep that gap as wide as we can."

"Aye, sir."

The distance between the blue icon and the red icon on the tactical display was still shrinking, but at a much slower rate than before. They were still closing with a bow-on hostile, however, and with every kilometer that ticked down on the readout, the sensors on the pirate ship had a better shot at sniffing out *Hecate*'s presence.

"How good is the sensor suite on that thing, Lieutenant Robson?"

"If it's a stock Cerberus, it's just okay," Robson replied. "It's an escort corvette, not a deep-space combatant. They're not optimized for long-range passive detection."

"Bogey is turning around," Armer said.

Without the background illumination from their counterburn flare, the other ship was just a vague low-resolution outline on the optical sensors again, but Dunstan could see the shape change briefly as the rogue corvette flipped around its dorsal axis to return its nose to the direction of travel. He allowed himself a small sigh of relief.

"All right. I want a clean passive sweep. Prepare to cut the cold counterburn."

"Prepare to cut counterburn, aye." Lieutenant Hunter reached for her handset. "All hands, prepare for zero g."

"Throttle down on my mark. Three, two, one, *mark*."

The sensation of getting pulled up in his chair went away, and the familiar feeling of weightlessness replaced it as *Hecate*'s fusion rocket shut down and stopped redirecting its thrust to the ship's bow. Dunstan readjusted his harness and ignored the brief swell of mild nausea that usually followed a zero-g transition.

"Shutdown complete," Hunter announced. "We are coasting ballistic again."

Now that the bow sensors had a clear view of the space in front of *Hecate* once more, the red icon on the plot shifted slightly as the system AI refined the position of the corvette they were chasing. The other ship was coasting as well, gliding through the void without a noise from her comms or radiation from her active sensors. The rest of the tactical plot was as empty as before, revealing no threats but offering no clues either.

"Where the hells are you going?" Dunstan wondered out loud in a low voice.

The answer to his question revealed itself thirty minutes later, when the tactical plot chirped a new alert.

"Contact," Lieutenant Robson called out at the same moment. "Passive contact bearing 357 degrees over 9, distance eighteen thousand."

On the plot display, a new icon appeared for the first time in days, the gray symbol of an unidentified passive contact, surrounded by a lozenge-shaped outline that represented the AI's uncertainty zone. Dunstan felt the old hunter's rush surging up his spine, the instinctive adrenaline spike that came with finally laying eyes on prey after a long and tense wait.

"Get me an ID," Dunstan ordered.

"Working on it, sir." Robson was fully focused on the screen projections that curved around her in a ninety-degree arc, each segmented into multiple data fields. "The AI is still trying to find a match. But whatever it is, it's not small."

"Another surprise battlecruiser?" Lieutenant Hunter asked. "That would be just our luck."

"We already got the only one that was missing," Dunstan replied. "Not that I would mind adding another capital warship to our score."

"I don't think it's a cruiser, sir," Robson said. "It looks—weird."

"*Weird*," Hunter repeated.

"Put the visual on tactical, please," Dunstan said.

Lieutenant Robson flicked the image window from her screen to the plot display, where it opened above the tactical grid.

"Yeah," Lieutenant Hunter agreed after a moment of silence. "That *does* look weird."

The image was a composite long-range scan combining the inputs from all the sensors in *Hecate*'s bow array. It was pixelated and indistinct, but the geometry of the blurry shape indicated a human-engineered object. If it was a spaceship, Dunstan had never seen anything that looked even remotely similar.

"The AI says it's roughly seven hundred by two hundred meters. Still no ID on the infrared signature or hull shape."

"Seven *hundred* meters?" Dunstan repeated in disbelief.

"Affirmative. Plus or minus twenty-five meters," Robson returned.

"Gods. That's bigger than the navy's largest hull."

"Sir, our current trajectory is taking us pretty close past—whatever *that* is," Lieutenant Armer warned. "If we don't do a corrective burn, we're going to pass within two thousand klicks of it."

Dunstan considered the weapons officer's warning. He looked over at the plot display to study the projected trajectories. The ship they were chasing was headed straight for the new contact. *Hecate*'s dotted course line curved just past the outer edge of the uncertainty zone, close enough that he wouldn't have dared a flyby with any of his old ships.

"I want to get as close as I can and get a very good look at whatever that is," he said. "Let's get inside of five thousand and evaluate from there. We can do another cold burn to swing us around wide if needed.

And if they spot us, anything they launch at us at that range is just going to be wasted ordnance. Steady as she goes for now."

"Aye, sir," Armer replied.

"But do put the point defense on standby once we cross inside of ten thousand," Dunstan added. "Just in case."

The grainy and blurry image of the strange object gradually resolved into finer detail as *Hecate* got closer. The largest part of it was roughly cylindrical, a third as wide as it was long. There were multiple appendages and extensions cluttering up the shape and breaking up the outline, none of them in a configuration that made any sense to Dunstan yet.

"Picking up the tiniest bit of EM noise from the bogey," Lieutenant Robson reported.

The ship they had been chasing for a week was now almost thirty degrees off *Hecate*'s port bow. Without corrective burns, their trajectories had been diverging steadily since Robson had spotted the new object, and the change in aspects gave *Hecate*'s sensor suite a closer look at the other ship's profile. It was a handsome little corvette, even if its new owners had downgraded its appearance by replacing the standard silver-and-blue Oceanian Navy paint job with a dull and nonreflective dark-gray coating. Despite her small size and her modest armament, she was still a genuine warship instead of a battle-rigged civilian design, and as such she was much more dangerous to civilian shipping than a converted freighter with a makeshift weapons suite. Dunstan had gambled that leaving the corvette on a long leash would pay off, despite the risk of seeing her slip away and losing her altogether. Right now, it looked like they had bet on the right set of numbers.

"Are they using comms?" Dunstan asked.

"Nothing on broadwave. I'm getting quick little bursts of EM spikes. Probably low-power tight-beam transmissions."

"Knocking on the door, no doubt."

"Their EMCON has been really solid ever since we started chasing them," Robson said with what sounded like a shade of grudging respect in her voice. "This is the first time they so much as made the EM readout twitch. If they weren't so close and presenting their side aspect, we probably wouldn't have picked it up."

"Maybe we've busted all the sloppy crews and the bad ships," Dunstan replied. "Makes sense that whatever's left is their best gear and their smartest captains."

On the viewscreen that displayed the optical feed above the tactical plot, the large object ahead slowly changed angles with every passing minute of their approach. The slow rotation of the image revealed more structural strangeness. The large cylinder-shaped center of it was connected to another, smaller shape that ran parallel to the main section. A small forest of appendages protruded from both sections, and now the resolution was good enough that Dunstan could see they were outriggers.

"Docking extensions," he said. "Those are docking arms. That's not a ship. It's a damn space station."

"It's a ship, all right," Lieutenant Robson said from her station. She flipped one of her screens around for him to see the schematic that was displayed on it. "The AI just got a likely match. Ultralarge Bison-class ore hauler. Two hundred and fifty thousand tons empty, five million tons of deadweight at full load."

Lieutenant Hunter let out a low whistle. "That's a big hull."

"They don't come any bigger than that," Dunstan said. The massive ships that shuttled billions of tons of ore from Pallas to the other planets in the system were the largest anyone had put into space since the generational ships that had settled Gretia and Rhodia a thousand years ago from Old Earth. The ore haulers were safe from pirates because they were too large and slow to steal, and because their cargo loads were cumbersome to handle and difficult to turn into money.

Now that he knew what he was looking at, the image on the screen became obvious to Dunstan despite the fuzziness from the long-range optics laboring at high magnification: command section at the front, propulsion section with a ring of massive drive cones at the rear, and rows of modular cargo elements in between. The outriggers he had spotted earlier extended from some of the cargo pods at right angles, and now he could see smaller ships attached to them in irregular intervals.

"There is zero radio chatter," Lieutenant Robson said. "Not even short-range stuff inside those hulls. No live Mnemosyne nodes. If they're running internal comms, they're using hardwired gear."

"Coming up on five thousand klicks," Armer announced from the tactical station. "If we want to adjust our trajectory, now's the time."

Dunstan assessed the situation on the plot. If they didn't change their course with another cold burn, they'd be closing to within nine hundred kilometers. It was a risky move, even for a ship as stealthy as *Hecate*. But picking up the presence of a ship with passive sensors was a tricky thing to do even when one knew where to look. Neither the rogue ship nor the ore hauler gave any indication they had noticed their uninvited company.

"Steady as she goes," Dunstan said. "But use the cold thrusters to turn our nose toward that thing. I want to keep a bow-on aspect as much as possible."

If I only had Minotaur *right now,* he thought. His light cruiser had been old and borderline obsolete, but she'd packed a much bigger offensive punch than *Hecate*, with eight heavy antiship missiles and a pair of rail-gun mounts. He could have waited until the corvette finished docking, wrecked every ship on the ore hauler's outriggers before they could cut themselves loose and get underway, and then blown up the big ship's drive section. But he knew that he wouldn't have gotten this close to the prize without *Hecate*, and there was no telling what other surprises were stashed away in the hull of that beast.

Charging in with guns blazing is Dreadnought thinking, he reminded himself. *No need to rush in before getting the full picture.*

"Distance eight hundred ninety klicks," Armer said.

They were at the perigee of their flyby, the point of their closest approach to the cluster of pirate ships. The bulk of the ore hauler had hidden much of what was on the other side of the enormous hull, and the full extent of the installation had revealed itself gradually as *Hecate*'s ballistic trajectory had carried her past the other ship's bow. There was another large vessel next to the ore carrier, a sleek ship that was too graceful to be either a commercial freighter or a warship. Unlike the smaller ships docked on the outriggers, this one looked like it was connected to the ore hauler by a dense latticework of struts and scaffolds.

"Another Oceanian," Lieutenant Robson said when the AI had matched the sensor image with another entry in the ship database. "Looks like a Sunrise-class cruise ship."

"I've been on one of those," Dunstan mused. "Went on an interplanetary cruise with the wife. That was the year before the war."

"That's not really an ideal hull for pirate raids," Lieutenant Armer said.

"I don't think they're using it for that. Look at all this rigging. They've lashed those two hulls together." Dunstan pointed out the multitude of connections between the cruise ship and the ore hauler. The cruise ship only looked small in relation to the other vessel, but it was still eighty thousand tons of deadweight, more than twice the mass of a battlecruiser and half again as long.

"I think you're right after all, Commander," Robson said. "It *is* a space station."

"One they can move around at will. That's why we've been playing hide-and-seek with them for so long. Their home base is mobile. They can adjust to the transfer lanes as they change and pick their sweet spots for commerce raiding."

"I count nine individual ships in anchorage, not counting that passenger liner," Robson said.

"Tactical," Dunstan said in Lieutenant Armer's direction. "Give me an assessment for offensive action."

Armer cleared his throat and studied the plot for a few heartbeats. "We're not in a great spot for going offensive. They have more ships than we have missiles, and the ones we have loaded aren't going to do much to those two large hulls. I'd double or triple up on the corvette because they've got point defenses. Then I'd work my way down the priority list based on threat assessments and hope I get lucky with my hits. But there's no way we can take out everything they have at anchor and disable those monster hulls as well. Someone's going to get away."

Dunstan nodded in unhappy agreement. *Hecate*'s weakness was her light armament, intended for self-defense and precision strikes rather than head-on engagements with multiple opponents.

"And we'd have to violate the rules of engagement," Lieutenant Hunter added.

According to current procedure, navy ships were required to issue a warning before they opened fire on a pirate vessel, to give the enemy crew a chance to surrender and minimize bloodshed. They were only allowed to skip the warning if they had to act in immediate defense of themselves or others, and the only way that circumstance could apply right now would be to let the other side shoot at them first.

"I'm not going to kill a few thousand people without warning, Number One," Dunstan said. "Not even pirates."

Hunter nodded curtly, and there was a moment of tense silence in Ops.

"As Lieutenant Armer said, we can't get them all. Even if we throw out the rules and shoot first. That means brute force is off the table for now."

He looked at the tactical plot again, where *Hecate* was past the point of perigee and slowly opening the distance to the tight cluster of red icons again.

"But we're better at the sneaky stuff anyway. Helm, let her coast out to five thousand klicks. We're going to use the cold thrusters to slow us down and find a cozy spot. One with a good view of the whole neighborhood."

He looked at Hunter and flashed a curt smile.

"There'll be an opening for us sooner or later. And while we wait for that, we can use our time wisely. We found the nest. Now let's watch and see who's coming or going before we start smashing eggs."

CHAPTER 12

SOLVEIG

Waiting for the door signal to sound felt like a new, perfidious sort of torture to Solveig.

She had busied herself with putting together a meal and cleaning up the little kitchen of her studio, but there was nothing left to do once the poke bowls were finished. The place was new and clean, and she hadn't been in it long enough for anything to get messy, but she paced the studio anyway to scour it for imperfections that failed to materialize. It was a new building, and she had just moved in yesterday, so everything was as sterile and devoid of character as an upscale hotel suite.

When the door alarm finally chirped, she almost jumped despite having anticipated the sound for the last twenty minutes. The screen projection on the living room wall switched from its standby display of scenic images to a view of the atrium outside of her door, where Stefan Berg was standing and flashing a tired-looking little smile at the security sensors.

Solveig took a slow breath and walked over to the door.

"Hello," he said when she opened it. "Sorry I'm a little late. Work stuff, as always."

They had a moment when neither of them seemed to be able to decide what kind of physical greeting was appropriate. Then Solveig broke the awkward little stalemate by hugging Stefan carefully, and he reciprocated the hug in an equally gentle manner.

"No worries," she said. "I got in a little late myself. Come in, please."

She hadn't seen him in person since the day of the attack they had both barely survived. Stefan had lost nothing of his handsomeness, but he had dropped some weight he couldn't afford to lose, and there were lines in the corners of his eyes that hadn't been there before. The most jarring change to his appearance was the mobility exoskeleton he was wearing. The titanium frame of the device enveloped his lower body from his hips down to his feet, giving him balance and stability while artificial nanofiber strands supplied the muscle power his legs could no longer provide on their own. It was a sleek device, the very best her father's money could buy, but it was still a foreign object that looked immediately out of place on his body.

He noticed her glance at the device and shrugged.

"Yeah, that's going to be my second set of trousers for a few more months. Until my spinal nerves have learned how to do their job properly again."

"But you will be able to get rid of it," Solveig said.

"That's what the neurosurgeon said. There was just a lot of stuff to fuse back together."

She closed the door behind him and led him into her living room, where he looked around with an approving nod.

"So you finally have your own place in the city," he said. "It's very nice. Not what I was expecting, though."

"What *were* you expecting?" she asked.

"I don't know. Maybe one of those penthouse places overlooking the park. Some place with a gyrofoil pad on the roof."

She laughed. "I can't afford one of those on my salary yet. And I don't think I'd want to spend that sort of money even if I could."

"I figured you of all people wouldn't have to worry about a budget."

Her smile faltered a little.

"I pay my own way," she said. "Now that I can. My father's money never comes without strings. If he pays, he gets to set the conditions. And I didn't want any."

"I understand," Stefan replied. "For mine, it's favors. You accept something from him, you owe him one. I'm pretty sure he keeps a ledger."

"Let me take your jacket," Solveig said.

He took it off and handed it to her. Underneath, he was wearing a shoulder harness that held a handgun on one side and several ammunition cassettes on the other. When he saw that she was looking at the weapon, he gave an apologetic shrug.

"New directive from upstairs," he explained. "We are under orders to always carry our service weapons now, even off duty. I used to leave mine in the locker after work. Never saw the need to bring it home, and I live in one of the sketchy districts near the spaceport. Now it's no longer optional. Not even for people on desk duty."

She brought his jacket over to the wardrobe niche by the door and draped it over a holder. When she returned to Stefan, he had shrugged off the gun harness as well.

"Can I put that down somewhere?" he asked. "It gets uncomfortable at the end of the day."

"Of course." Solveig nodded at the counter between the kitchen and the living space. He walked over to it and carefully put the harness with the weapon on the spotless surface.

"It should make me feel safer to have that with me," Stefan said. "But it doesn't. I had one when they attacked our building. It didn't do me much good."

"At least you had some way to fight back," Solveig said. "All I could do was to run and hide."

"And yet we both got shot in the end."

She walked over to the counter as well and looked at the gun. It seemed as out of place in her studio as the mobility exoskeleton did on Stefan's body.

"Can I see it?" she asked.

Stefan looked at her with mild surprise.

"Sure." He reached for the harness and pulled the gun out of its holster. Then he ejected the ammunition cassette from the bottom of the grip and placed it on the counter.

"It's unloaded now," he said and handed her the weapon. She took it carefully and looked at it in her hand. It was lighter than she had expected, and there was a certain utilitarian beauty to its sleek and streamlined form. When she closed her hand around the grip fully, a little strip of light at the back of the gun started to glow red.

"It's locked to my DNA," Stefan said. "Nobody else can fire it. Still, don't aim it at anything you don't want to put a hole into."

She raised the weapon and pointed it past him at the sky through the window on the far side of the room. It felt far too comfortable in her hand for a device that was designed to kill people. She had never been interested in weapons beyond the blades in her father's gym. But she remembered the utter helplessness she had felt in the police station, when all she could do was to run away while Stefan and Cuthbert tried to protect her, and the paralyzing terror of being cornered without a way to fight back was something she never wanted to experience again.

"Straighten your wrist," Stefan said. "Don't lock your elbow. Use the other hand for support. But wrap it around the grip, don't put it underneath."

She corrected her posture the way he had told her, and he nodded his approval.

"Now you look like a professional," he said.

Solveig held her aim for a few moments, pleased with the reassuring heft of the gun. Then she lowered it and handed it back to him.

"In the end, it's just one of the tools of the trade," he said as he replaced the ammunition cassette and returned the weapon to its holster. "And it's the one I use least. I'd never even fired a live round outside of the practice range until—well, you know."

"I don't think I'll ever be able to forget anything about that day. And I've tried," Solveig said.

She had set the table earlier, taking her time to calibrate the setting so it would look neither too formal nor too casual. They sat down together, and Solveig poured water for them both while Stefan looked at the artwork on the walls.

"Those graphics were here when I moved in," she said. "I haven't had time to redecorate yet."

"When did you move in?" he asked.

"Yesterday," she said, and he smiled.

"I'm your first houseguest, then. I feel honored."

"You may want to wait with feeling honored until you've tried dinner," Solveig said. "I haven't had time to go out and buy some kitchen stuff either, so I had to work with the basics."

She got up and walked over to the kitchen to fetch the dinner she had prepared.

"Acheroni cold noodle bowls," she announced when she brought the bowls to the table and set them down. "It's a really simple recipe. I made it a lot when I was at university."

Even before the attack on the police headquarters, they hadn't seen each other more than once a week, and their covert meetings had mostly been limited to quick, shared lunches on Savory Row or slightly longer dinners. Her relationship with Stefan had just been out in the open when they had sat down together in the police canteen, and everything had blown up around them fifteen minutes into their first official lunch date.

"This is the first time we've met in a private place," Solveig said while they were both plucking away at their noodles with their sticks.

"I guess it is," Stefan replied. "It's nice to be able to talk without having to speak over the noise of a hundred other people."

"I didn't know you were already back at work."

"I made myself a nuisance until they let me come back to active duty," he said. "I was going a bit crazy. Nothing to do except go to the medical center for rehabilitation twice a week. Of course, they put me on administrative desk duty, so the joke is on me. But most investigative work is done sitting in a chair anyway."

"They haven't caught them yet," she said, a statement of fact rather than a question. "The people who did that."

"The Alliance troops killed them all. None of the insurgents made it out of there alive."

"I mean the ones who were behind it. The people who sent them."

He shook his head slowly. "We've run into nothing but dead ends. Whoever is running their operations knows how to set up an airtight outfit. Every time we catch one of them alive, we get maybe two or three of their friends. But never any of the higher-ups."

The higher-ups, Solveig thought, and her mind immediately went to Papa. He'd told her that he had given the insurgency money, but that he had cut his ties with them once things got too violent. She weighed his assurances against the fact that he never told anyone more than he thought they should know. Whenever he was in a bind, he only admitted to whatever was sufficient to get him out of it. She had meant to tell Stefan about the irregularities she had found at Ragnar, to see if his trained detective eyes could see something that she had overlooked. But if there was a trail there that led back to her father, she would be the one who'd set the investigators on it. Whatever else Stefan was to her, he was a criminal police detective, and she was sure that he had a duty to report whatever she shared with him if it pointed to the insurgency.

"I'm sorry," she said. "I'm having you talk about work. I should have led with a more pleasant subject."

"No, that's all right," Stefan said with a smile. The new little wrinkles in the corners of his green eyes made him look a little more seasoned than before, and she liked it.

"So much has changed since the last time I saw you in person. It kind of feels like this is our first date all over again," Solveig said.

"It does, doesn't it?" Stefan wiped his mouth with his napkin and smiled again. "So let's pretend it is. Tell me something about yourself."

She laughed when she realized that he was serious.

"All right," she said. "I'm Solveig. I'm twenty-three years old, and I'm from a very rich and very dysfunctional family. I'm vice president at the company my great-great-grandfather founded. I like spicy foods, and I have a thing for Acheroni culture even though I've never been to Acheron until this year."

"Tell me something I don't know yet," Stefan prompted. "Do you have any middle names?"

She was almost certain that he had seen that information in the police data bank already, but she humored him anyway.

"Vigdis," she said. "After my mother."

"Is there a reason why you never talk about her? Or am I being insensitive?"

"She divorced my father when I was very young," Solveig said. "I have an older brother. He had a falling out with my father when he became an adult. He left and joined the military, and my mother left us not too long after that. I haven't seen either of them since. Now it's your turn. Tell me something about yourself."

He put down his eating sticks and folded his hands over the noodle bowl.

"Let's see. I'm Stefan. No middle name. I like to joke that my parents couldn't afford one, but it's not too far from the truth. I come from a poor and also very dysfunctional family. First one to go to university in three generations. Joined the police force because the government paid for my degree, and because I liked the idea of helping people for a living."

"That's the tidy biography for a job interview. Or running for public office," she said. "Now tell me something I don't know."

He thought about it for a moment.

"I have an older brother as well. He volunteered for the military the day he came of age. That was in the middle of the war. He went off to training, then they sent his unit to Pallas, and I never saw him again. He's still listed as missing. I want to believe he really is still out there somewhere. And who knows? I still think of him first whenever I get a message on my comtab."

Solveig thought of Aden, and the way she had felt when she had seen his first message to her, two words coded in a way that told her right away it was him. The sudden swell of empathy and sorrow she felt for Stefan almost brought tears to her eyes.

"There's always hope," she said, and her own voice sounded thick to her. "I never stopped believing. And I know I'll see him again someday." She felt a little guilty about lying by omission, but there was no way she would risk disclosing to anyone that Aden had returned, no matter how much she wanted to make Stefan feel better.

"Sorry I managed to bring the conversation back to painful subjects," he said. "I really know how to set the mood on a first date, don't I?"

She laughed and wiped her eyes. "We feel what we feel. No need to apologize for that. I love my brother. I know what it's like to be left not knowing."

"That was one of the reasons why I left home as soon as I could. They were so overprotective after Holger went missing. I couldn't leave the house for fifteen minutes without one of them checking on me. It was like they wanted to wrap me in safety foam for the rest of my life."

"It was the same for me," Solveig said. "Until I went to university, I don't think I was ever out in public without one or two of our security people nearby."

"I'm surprised your father finally let you move into your own place in the city. Especially after what happened."

"It wasn't up to him anymore," she said. "But we both made concessions in the end. He pretends that he is fine with it. And I pretend I don't notice that he stationed a protective detail in the other studio on this floor."

Stefan chuckled. "How did you figure *that* out?"

"Just a feeling. He didn't send anyone I know, but I've been around bodyguards all my life. You pick up on certain things."

"What kind of things?" he asked.

"They're too discreet. You can be so inconspicuous that it makes you stand out, if that makes sense. I've been sneaking around my father's restrictions since I was a teenager. I know when I am being followed."

"If that corporate career doesn't work out, you should consider going into intelligence," Stefan said.

"You said the same thing about the police once. I want to keep my paranoia a private activity, not turn it into a professional pursuit," Solveig replied, and he laughed.

"Fair enough. I'll stop with the career advice. You seem to be doing just fine without my input."

As halting and awkward as their first face-to-face exchange in three months had begun, their conversation soon settled into the easy flow it had been before their separation. Solveig was glad she had decided to make noodle bowls for their dinner because the nature of the dish allowed them to stretch out the meal. They were still talking long after the bowls were empty, and she had lost count how many times she had refilled their glasses of sparkling water. Neither she nor Stefan had so much as glanced at the time display on the living room wall projection, and the first indicator of the advanced progression of the evening was the room lighting as it switched to the bedtime routine Solveig had set just yesterday.

"There is no way it's already 2200," Solveig said as she glanced at the ceiling that was dimming its light emitters gradually.

Stefan pulled his comtab from a pocket and glanced at it. "It is in fact 2200 hours. And as much as I have enjoyed this, I think it's time for me to make my way back home."

"Room, turn the lights back up," she told the AI, and the ceiling lighting returned to its original brightness.

They both got up from the table reluctantly. Solveig started to collect the dishes, but he picked up his own before she could take it, and they both walked over to the kitchen nook to clean up. She watched as he took the harness with his service weapon off the counter and put it on again, wrinkling the fabric of his tunic where the straps bunched it up a little. Solveig fetched his jacket from the wardrobe niche, and he slipped into it with a little groan.

"Those fused nerves pinch a bit whenever I'm getting up after sitting too long," he explained. "But the sacrifice was worth it. Thank you for the lovely dinner. I haven't enjoyed myself like this since before."

"I feel the same way," Solveig said. "Thank you for the company."

She opened the door for him, and he stepped out into the hall. When he turned around to say his goodbye, she walked out as well until they were both standing in front of her door.

"As long as we are pretending that this is our first date, I would argue that first-date rules are in effect. We can pretend you just dropped me off at home."

It took him a moment to catch on. Then he smiled and took a step closer, and she reached up and put her hand on his shoulder to make her consent obvious. Their kiss was careful and tender and entirely too short for Solveig's taste. When he pulled back, he looked almost bashful.

"I had a great time," she said. "Maybe we can do this again sometime soon."

"Are you saying there may be a second date?" Stefan asked with a smile.

"I'm feeling pretty good about it," she said.

"Still got it," he said and did a little fist pump, and she laughed.

"Have a good night," he said and took two steps backward before he turned around to walk toward the skylift ledge.

"You, too," Solveig said.

She walked back into her studio, but she turned and watched Stefan from the door until he had stepped onto the skylift platform and started his trip down to the lobby. When he had dropped out of sight, Solveig let out a slow breath and closed the door with a smile.

Chapter 13

Aden

"No offense, Major. But that wasn't a good fight to pick. You're lucky you didn't end up on a stretcher. Or worse."

They had taken him to an apartment somewhere in the old city. Aden was sitting at the kitchen table with the top of his jumpsuit pulled down to his waist. Lars, the former combat medic, was treating his various scrapes and bruises with ingredients from a military medical kit on the table in front of them. At first, he hadn't noticed much pain from the punches and kicks he had received, but now that the adrenaline had worn off, he felt like he had fallen out of a second-floor window and landed in a garbage container full of construction debris.

"I didn't pick the fight," Aden said. "They did."

"You did walk right past them while wearing a Blackguard dress smock," Captain Bryn Bakke said from the kitchen, where she was filling a glass with water from the dispenser nozzle. "That was a surefire way to work them up. Not that that crowd ever needs much of an excuse to get violent."

She walked to the table and put the glass in front of Aden. Then she took one of the empty chairs, turned it around, and sat down on it backward, hugging the backrest with both arms.

"I didn't know who they were or what they were doing. I tried to walk away. But then one of them spit on me. On my uniform. Couldn't let that go." Aden winced a little as Lars was dabbing something on the cut on his eyebrow that made the wound sting sharply. "In hindsight, it may have been a bad call."

"That would have been a really terrible epitaph," Bryn said. "He survived the war and made it through captivity, only to get beaten to death by a bunch of snot-nosed reefos."

"Reefos," Aden repeated.

"Reformers," Bryn said. "That's the name of their movement."

"What is it they want to see reformed?"

"Gods, what *don't* they want reformed? That would be a much shorter list. Let's see." She started counting off with her fingers. "The government. The courts. The civil service. The police. Everything is rotten, you see. And if you disagree with them, you're an irredentist and a warmonger."

"I guess I really am out of the loop," Aden said. "I mean, I wasn't hoping for flowers and a parade. But I wasn't expecting a beating either."

"Patriotism is a crime now, you know," Lars contributed. He was a soft-spoken man in his late twenties whose voice sounded like he was never too far from the verge of tears.

The third member of the group, the tall, blond senior lieutenant named Helge, walked into the kitchen with Aden's dress uniform in his hands. He placed it on the table next to the medkit, and Aden saw that it was neatly folded to military standards.

"I ran it through the cleaner," Helge said. "The blood and the spit came out, but the ripped seams will need some serious mending."

"That's all right. I don't intend to wear that again. But thank you for cleaning it up for me," Aden replied.

Helge ran his fingers along the red trim on the collar.

"You Blackguards got the best dress uniforms. The other ones didn't look half as sharp."

"Helge is a subject-matter expert," Bryn said. "He was in the protocol battalion at the defense ministry. They had the dress uniforms of all the branches in their lockers."

"You were a protocol soldier, huh?" Aden asked. "That is a hard slot to get into." The protocol battalion were the soldiers that served in the government quarter, standing ceremonial guard duty and performing military honors for visiting dignitaries.

"I was," Helge confirmed. "I had a platoon in the Fifth Company."

"What about you, Major?" Bryn asked. "What was your unit in the Blackguard?"

"Signals Intelligence Company 300," Aden replied. "I was the commanding officer at the end of the war."

Helge and Bryn exchanged a look.

"An intelligence officer," Bryn said. "No wonder they kept you for as long as they did. Where were you stationed?"

"We were on Oceana. Got on the ground with the follow-up wave during the invasion and didn't leave again for four years. Until the planetary garrison surrendered."

Bryn nodded. Aden was certain that the question hadn't been mere idle curiosity, and he expected them to verify his claims as soon as they could because he would do the same in their place. But he knew that his high rank and uncommon branch would all but rule out the possibility that he was an impostor. Nobody pretending to be a veteran would be able to get away with claiming to be a company commander in signals intelligence.

"I wouldn't have guessed intelligence, but I knew you weren't a grunt," Helge said.

"And how did you figure that?"

"Your hand-to-hand skills aren't so hot. No offense."

Aden chuckled. "None taken, Lieutenant."

"All right, that's as much as I can do for you right now with what I have in this ouch box." Lars got up from the chair next to Aden and took off his purple medical gloves. "You're going to be black-and-blue for a week. But nothing is broken, and I don't see any sign of head trauma. Still, if you get a headache that won't go away, or you feel confused or start throwing up, you need to go to a medical center right away."

"I've been feeling nothing *but* confused ever since I stepped off the damn shuttle," Aden said, and the others chuckled.

Aden got out of his chair and carefully put on his undershirt. The upper part of his flight suit proved a little trickier in his banged-up state, and Lars helped him get his arms back into the sleeves.

"Thank you for patching me up, Corporal," Aden said.

"Yes, sir. Just doing my duty. I'm glad I could help."

Aden walked over into the living space, where a pair of large floor-to-ceiling windows looked out over a busy street that was lined with shops and eating nooks. He had grown up in the city, but he didn't recognize this part of it at first sight.

Bryn walked up and stood next to him.

"When was the last time you saw this place?" she asked.

"Just before we got mobilized for deployment. So—nine years."

"You didn't come home on leave in *four* years of war?"

Aden shook his head.

"Oceana wasn't a combat zone. We were low priority on the transport list. I would have spent most of my leaves on spaceships. I decided to stay on the planet instead."

"It was like a slap in the face," Bryn said. "Coming back home and walking out of that spaceport only to see Alliance patrols on the street corners. That was the moment for me when it really sank in that we'd lost the war. And five years later, they're still here."

"They won't be around forever," Aden said. "Occupations are a pain in the ass to keep up. The logistics chain is millions of kilometers long. Troop rotations, resupply, all that stuff needs to be planned months in advance. And it costs a fortune to maintain."

"They've been squeezing us for reparations for half a decade now. I'm sure they're not running a loss. They'll keep mining that lode until it's exhausted."

And we brought it upon ourselves, Aden thought. But that was an Aden Jansen sentiment, not one that Major Robertson would voice, so he kept silent and pretended to be in thought as he looked out of the window.

"What are you going to do now?" Bryn asked.

He shrugged.

"I'll do what I was going to do before they jumped me, I guess. Get some proper clothes, find something to eat, then look for a place to stay. In that order, more or less."

She pointed at the street beyond the window.

"There are some decent clothing shops down that way about a quarter klick. And Savory Row is just beyond that on the left. You can't miss it. Two hundred meters of nothing but eateries and food stalls. I don't know how your tastes run, but you're bound to find something there."

She got out her comtab and opened a screen projection with her thumb and forefinger.

"There's a social assistance office on Civic Square, but you may want to wait to go back there until that rally has cleared. You're a returning veteran, so you have priority for benefits. They'll be able to put you up in transitional housing for a while."

"Thank you, Captain," Aden said. "I'll go see them in the morning. I'm sure I can find some place to stay for the night."

"Get out your comtab," she said.

He pulled the device out of his pocket, and she tapped her comtab against his.

"That's my node information. Just in case. If you can't find anything, let me know. We can put you up for the night if you don't mind sleeping on an inflatable bedroll."

"I've slept on worse," Aden said. "I appreciate the offer."

When he passed the kitchen table on the way to the door, Helge handed him a cloth bag. Aden looked inside and saw his uniform jacket.

"Better to keep that covered up," Helge said, and Aden nodded.

"Major," Bryn said when he was at the door, and he turned around.

"Be careful out there," she said. "It may look like the place you remember. But a lot has changed since you left. Most of it for the worse."

—

Outside, the gloomy day had settled into a drab late afternoon, and the streets were flecked with puddles that reflected a darkening gray sky. Once Aden had walked a few blocks to get his bearings, the geography of the city came back to him, and he only needed to consult his comtab occasionally to find his way around again.

The old city had no shortage of shops and mercantiles, and he walked into the first clothing place he saw. The incident on Civic Square had caused him to be self-conscious about the jumpsuit he was wearing, which made him stick out on the street despite lacking any markings identifying him as a prisoner of war. To his relief, it was an automated shop without an attendant in sight. He stepped into one of the service booths and used the screen inside to look at the variety of available styles. After all this time in uniform and then prison clothing, he had no idea anymore what was fashionable, so he activated the virtual assistant and let it curate the selection for him. He chose a few outfits that looked like they struck a good balance between formal and casual. When he had finished his selection and verified the total charge, the booth took his measurements with a quick series of scans from a rotating laser wand.

"Your purchase is now being tailored," the virtual assistant informed him in an upbeat voice. *"Please make yourself comfortable in the lounge area. Your items will be delivered to you in nine minutes."*

Aden left the booth and sat down in one of the lounge chairs to wait. On the walls of the store, screen projections were cycling through an unending parade of ridiculously attractive people showcasing the latest styles. A service robot rolled up to his chair and offered refreshments on a little tray, and he helped himself to some water.

Halfway through his wait, his comtab hummed an alert. He took it out and glanced at the screen, expecting to see a ledger notification of the purchase he just made.

CURRY 56 ON SAVORY ROW HAS THE BEST SAUSAGE IN SANDVIK, the notification read. YOU SHOULD TRY IT FOR DINNER.

He sat up straight and read the alert again. A few seconds later, it faded from the screen. When he checked the device to see the comms stub that had triggered the notification, the message queue was as empty as it had been since he had received the comtab on Rhodia over a week ago.

Aden resisted the impulse to look around. He put the comtab away again and took another sip from the cup of water the robot had delivered.

Well, that didn't take long, he thought. He had known the Rhodians would have ways to keep a close eye on him even down here. Having swift confirmation of that fact was a little jarring, but it felt oddly comforting as well to know that they were on top of things already, that he hadn't just been let loose to fend for himself with nothing but a comtab and an ambitious assignment.

The service robot came back around a few minutes later and presented a bag with his purchases. He took it and went into one of the changing cabins in the back of the store.

It felt good to take off the POW jumpsuit, and it felt even better to step out of the cabin in comfortable civilian clothes and throw the prison garb into the store's refuse chute.

That's the last time I'll wear one of those, he resolved as the jumpsuit slid down the stainless fixture and toward oblivion.

Savory Row was just a few minutes away, and Aden chose to take a walk instead of hailing a surface pod. The sun had begun to set, and the lights of the Sandvik skyline illuminated the clouds from below. Slightly to his right and half a kilometer up the road, the office buildings at Principal Square loomed above the city center like a tall, ragged cliff made of glass and steel. Ragnar Tower was in the center of the row, an unsubtle slab-sided monument to his father's ambitions, the family name glowing in tall letters near the top like a wordless shout across the city. He thought of Solveig, who was probably somewhere in the building right now, unaware that he was less than a kilometer away. As much as he wanted to see her, to wrap his arms around her again and show her that he was all right, he knew that she was only safe if he kept away from her. She had enough skill at subterfuge to duck under the radar of Marten and the corporate security division, but he was under no illusion that she could stay unnoticed by the Rhodian intelligence service.

Savory Row had been around since Aden was a child. It was a long side street between two main thoroughfares that was dedicated to food stalls, little hole-in-the-wall eateries, and shops selling culinary ingredients and specialized cooking gadgets. He didn't remember many of the places that lined the street on both sides, but the smells wafting from the stalls were just like he remembered them from his university days, a wide variety of foods cooking in dozens of small kitchens.

Curry 56 was halfway down the street, nestled between a bakery and a spice shop. The menu on the screen projection next to the door advertised a small variety of Gretian comfort foods. Aden walked in and got in line to order from the serving window. It was one of the bigger eateries on Savory Row, and it was busy with diners at this hour. He ordered the house special—curried sausage and yam sticks—and went to the back of the place where there was still some open seating along the counter that stretched across the rear wall.

He was halfway through his meal when someone sat down at the counter next to him with the same dish Aden was eating. The other man mumbled a greeting and turned his attention to his food.

They were eating side by side in silence for a few minutes before Aden's neighbor spoke again.

"Don't take this as an attempt to pick you up, but that's a sharp outfit. You have a good eye for matching colors."

"Thanks," Aden said. The other man hadn't turned his head toward him when he spoke. Instead, he was looking at the comtab he had placed on the little soffit between the counter and the back wall, and he was talking into the device as if he was in a vid conversation with someone. He spoke in a low voice that Aden had to strain to hear in the general din of conversations in the dining room.

"You look like a different person. It suits you much better than that prison jumpsuit. Not that those things are flattering on anyone."

Aden speared another slice of curry sausage with his fork and dipped it into the sauce before putting it in his mouth.

"You people don't waste any time," he replied without turning his head.

"Neither do you, Major. It's only your first day back, and you're already mixing it up at political rallies. I'm pretty impressed."

"I kind of walked into that one by accident."

"I'm not saying it was a bad thing. I figured you'd need a few days to make new friends."

"Your Gretian is flawless," Aden said. "You're either a local, or you went to a very good language school."

"We all have our talents," the other man replied. "I hear you're not bad at languages yourself."

"I get by. But I'm sure you didn't want to meet to discuss the finer points of regional dialects."

The other man chuckled softly.

"You *are* a trained intelligence officer," he said with a hint of mockery.

"I'm on the ground. I've made contact with a few fellow veterans. There's nothing else to report yet. As you have pointed out already, it's my first day back."

"You're doing just fine. I'm only here to establish first contact. And to remind you to tread very softly. We've lost several operatives and informers in the last few months. If you come across the people we're after, and they have even the slightest suspicion that you're working for us, they'll shoot you in the back of the head without hesitation."

"I know," Aden said. "I already got a variation of that speech before I left."

"Whoever briefed you back home hasn't spent the last year walking these streets," the man said. From the glimpses Aden had been able to sneak out of the corner of his right eye, his handler was an older man with short gray hair and a closely cropped full beard. "They may not have fully conveyed the risk you're taking."

"I was covert on Oceana for four years," Aden replied. "During wartime, among an unfriendly population. If any of my local contacts had made me for an occupation agent, I would have ended up as crab food in the canals. I know how to watch my step."

"I don't doubt that you know your business, Major. But getting made isn't the only risk. The Alliance forces are out for blood right now. You could get shot at by people who have no idea they're aiming at a friendly."

"My plan is to avoid situations that would give them a reason to shoot at me," Aden said.

The older man chuckled again. "You're trying to infiltrate a violent insurgency. You may find yourself in a spot where you don't get that choice."

"And that would be a very bad day at the office," Aden said. "But I can't let the possibility scare me off. If I start thinking through all the what-ifs, I'll spend the next three months huddled under a blanket in a hotel somewhere until my money runs out."

The answer seemed to satisfy the other man, and they both ate in silence for a little while. When his neighbor was finished, he got up from his stool and gathered his things.

"Good luck," he said without looking at Aden. "I came to show you that you aren't on your own down here, and that we're keeping an eye on things. But watch yourself, Major. This has turned into a war, and a dirty one at that."

His handler walked away, and someone else came to claim the empty stool a few moments later. Aden finished the rest of his meal and got up to leave as well. Outside, it had started to rain again, and he released the weather cowl from the collar of his new jacket and pulled it onto his head.

His comtab showed several hotels in easy walking range. He had plenty of money on his ledger, and after a week in the passenger berth of a freighter, the idea of spending a few nights in a plush private suite and decompressing a little was more than just a little tempting. But spending the time and the money would be an indulgence, and a day or two of doing nothing wouldn't do anything to get him closer to finishing this mission and getting back into space with a Rhodian pardon in his pocket.

An inflatable bedroll instead of a comfortable hotel bed, he thought. But the bedroll was free, and it gave him the chance to get to know the little group of soldiers he had met and start earning their trust. And if he was entirely honest with himself, Bryn was an attractive woman, and the prospect of spending some more time in her proximity was more appealing than being by himself in a hotel suite.

He looked up the node stub she had left on his device. After a moment of hesitation, he tapped on it to request a connection. The reply came in the form of a screen projection that opened up in front of him like a small window into the apartment he had left over an hour ago.

"I see you found the clothing place," Bryn said with a little smile. The way the screen framed her face emphasized the color of her eyes, which were a stunning pale blue that bordered on gray.

"I did," Aden replied. "That Rhodian refuse bag is on the way to the recyclers."

"That outfit suits you much better. Now you look like a local. A well-dressed local."

"Listen, I was about to look for a place to stay for the night, but I think I could use some company. I've been holed up by myself far too long. If your offer to put me up at your place still stands, I'd like to accept it. I'll buy everyone dinner in exchange."

"Of course, Major," Bryn said. "Come on over. Dinner won't be expensive. Helge went out, and Lars may be gone as well by the time you get here. But I could stand a lamb pocket if you pass a place on the way back. With extra garlic yogurt."

"Extra garlic yogurt, aye," Aden said. Bryn smiled at his reply.

"I think that's the first time a major acknowledged a directive of mine," she said. "I'll see you when you get here."

The screen projection blinked out of existence. Another one popped up a second later, this one showing a navigation overlay on the street in front of Aden, blue arrows directing him toward his destination.

The honey trap is one of the oldest tricks in the spy manual, he thought. Maybe there was an attractive woman with an appetite for lamb from a grill spit waiting for him when he got back, and maybe there'd be a welcoming committee of suspicious veterans ready to tie him to a chair and squeeze him for information. Either way, he stood to gain something from it, and he had to be prepared for both possibilities.

Not that I'm unwilling to make sacrifices for the mission, but I sure hope it's option one, he thought as he set out on his walk back to the apartment.

Chapter 14

Idina

The morning air was cold, and there was a stiffness in Idina's finger joints that made her hand slip on the charging knob of her sidearm as she tried to load it. The unexpected jolt from the release of the weapon's main spring almost made her lose her grip and drop the pistol into the bulletproof funnel of the sand-filled safety box. She mouthed a silent curse and seized the gun tightly, then looked around. The troopers of the midday watch were all on the way to the briefing room or checking their assigned gyrofoils on the landing pad nearby, and nobody had seen her handling her weapon like a green recruit three weeks into basic training. Last night had brought the first ground frost of the season, and some of the soldiers were scraping thin layers of rime ice from the cockpit windows of their patrol craft.

Sweltering summers, freezing winters, she thought. *But the three weeks in between sure are lovely.*

She flexed her fingers until the stiff feeling was mostly gone and repeated the loading process, which went smoothly this time. She slid the gun into the holster on her thigh and snapped the safety hood over the weapon, then stretched her back while stifling a yawn. The wolf hunter team hadn't been out on raids for the last few nights, but she still felt a lingering fatigue that even uninterrupted sleep hadn't been able to erase.

In the briefing room, her patrol partner was already at the lectern. Idina took a chair in the back of the room and observed the Alliance soldiers and Gretian police officers as Captain Dahl began her briefing. It was a daily routine—calling roll, assigning patrol sectors, listing the special events for the day—but everybody paid close attention despite the repetitive nature of the process. The attack on the police headquarters had been costly for the insurgency, but the Gretian police had paid the biggest share of the butcher's bill by far, and the surviving officers were determined to get justice and retribution for their friends and colleagues. Their Alliance counterparts had their own scores to settle with the insurgency, and in the three months since the HQ attack, everyone had been showing up for patrol duty with focus and grim determination despite the relative calm in the wake of the massacre, as if they had all taken the Palladian proverb to heart: *Be wary of the storm, but be most wary when there is no storm in sight.*

When Dahl had finished the briefing and sent the teams off to their gyrofoils, Idina stood up and remained in the room until everyone but her partner had left. Dahl gathered her compad and handful of hard copies from the lectern and walked over to her.

"Good morning," Idina said. "You look well rested."

"You do not," Dahl remarked. "Have you been engaging in extracurricular activities again?"

"Not in a while. I guess I am just getting too old for this operational pace."

"You have a *little* bit of life left in you," Dahl said. "I did not start feeling my age until I crested fifty. But then I *really* started to feel it."

"Fantastic," Idina said, and Dahl smiled. She handed Idina the hard-copy sheets she was carrying with her compad.

"I got you the data you requested. The four people you encountered on your last activity. This is everything I could find in the data banks

I could access without attracting attention. Or breaking the rules *too* much."

"Thank you," Idina said. She took the hard-copy stack and leafed through it. The collage of records Dahl had assembled was a mix of data from various sources—police, civil administration, financial ledgers. She felt a flash of guilt when she saw the ID pass pictures of the people they had neutralized in the clandestine armory. Three of them were now just roughly body-shaped piles of carbon, reduced to ash by her team's thermal grenades. The fourth was in a special access-restricted cell in the Sandvik detention center right now, awaiting an expedited trial and likely transport to the high-security penal colony on Gretia's frigid northern continent.

"There is something else I found," Dahl said. "This one did not require any rule breaking. The identity of the person whose face we recorded with the gyrofoil sensors at the protest on Civic Square the other day."

She opened a screen above her comtab and flipped it around for Idina to see. It was a standard Gretian police records page. The picture at the top showed a handsome man with high cheekbones, a very defined jawline, and a razor-sharp haircut that made him look like he was fresh out of boot camp.

"His name is Helge Lind," Dahl said. "Twenty-nine years old. He was a senior lieutenant in the Gretian Army. He served in the ceremonial battalion at the Ministry of Defense."

"He has the look for it. That ideal Gretian warrior face for propaganda. No offense."

"None taken. He does look annoyingly perfect," Dahl replied.

"I am guessing you found out something noteworthy about Lieutenant Perfect. I mean, other than the fact that he served directly in the nerve center of the war effort."

"As a protocol troop. They picked good-looking people like him to make an impressive show for visitors. Standing in a row and presenting arms, that sort of thing."

"So he was a clothes rack, not an orderly for anyone important."

"That is correct. As far as we know, anyway. What is interesting about him is the company he keeps," Dahl said. She nodded at the hard-copy sheets in Idina's hand. "He is an associate of one of the people in those files, one Lieutenant Dirk Alpin. They were detained for civil disturbance offenses together twice in the last six months."

"Now *that* is interesting," Idina replied. She leafed through the stack of printouts again until she found Alpin's civil record.

This was the guy I shot when he reached for the gun in his waistband, she thought.

"Maybe they were unit mates in the service," she guessed. "Was the other guy a protocol troop as well?"

Dahl shook her head. "Alpin was in the navy. But the veteran benefits data bank says they were both in the same prison company on Rhodia. And they are in the same rank bracket, so they would have socialized there."

"Prison buddies," Idina mused. "What are the chances that one of them joined the insurgency but the other one didn't?"

"Considering their joint arrest records, I would say the odds are low."

"I agree. I mean, it's not out of the question that he doesn't know his friend was a terrorist in his spare time. It's not exactly the sort of thing you advertise. But I certainly want to talk to Lieutenant Helge Lind before I give him the benefit of the doubt. What does he do for a living?"

Dahl turned the screen projection around again and flipped through the data grid.

"He works as a cargo handler at the Sandvik spaceport."

"The *spaceport*," Idina repeated. "Well then."

She folded the printouts and slipped them into one of her leg pockets. "I guess we're going out to the spaceport on this fine, frosty morning."

After nine months of aerial patrols with Dahl, Idina knew the landmarks and roads of Sandvik from above as well as any place back home, especially the stretch from the joint base to the city center where their shifts usually took place. Overnight, the weather had turned completely from a solid cloud cover and steady rain to a clear blue sky. Idina watched the morning traffic on the streets into the city, long lines of surface pods gliding over the pale green roadway solar panels that powered much of the traffic infrastructure. From five hundred meters up, it looked quiet and peaceful, not like a place where Idina had come close to death more often than on the battlefields of Pallas during the war. Dahl was flying the craft manually, changing altitude and direction a little in irregular intervals, and following the main streets into the city center instead of letting the autopilot fly them in a straight line. At first, Idina had assumed it was some kind of counterterrorism measure, to make it harder to shoot the gyrofoil down, but now she knew that Dahl simply did it because she enjoyed flying.

The Sandvik spaceport was across the city from the joint military base, and Dahl increased their altitude as they crossed the city center to obey the airspace restrictions on the craft's navigation screen. The sky above Sandvik was busy with private craft, corporate gyrofoils, police patrols, and military traffic. Idina watched the flow of traffic from above, red and green position lights blinking and flitting about in aerial corridors that were as defined as the stream of pod traffic on the streets.

"Sandvik Control, this is JSP Air Unit 011, five kilometers south-southeast at one thousand, inbound to land at Sandvik

Spaceport," Dahl sent when they were approaching the spaceport's restricted airspace.

"JSP 011, Sandvik Control. Maintain current heading and altitude and stand by for cross-check and verification," the reply came over comms.

"Sandvik Control, JSP 011, maintaining heading and altitude for cross-check and verification," Dahl acknowledged. A red warning light popped up on the navigation screen, signaling that an air-defense system had locked on to their gyrofoil and was tracking their movements. The spaceport was a high-priority security zone, and the defensive systems dedicated to its protection were almost as numerous and sophisticated as the ones around the government quarter's Green Zone. Idina was certain that if Dahl diverged from her assigned approach and started to dive toward a sensitive location, a point-defense battery would blast their little craft out of the sky and turn them into a cloud of composites and body parts without further warning. After two insurgent bombings with gyrofoils as delivery systems, the Alliance did not take any chances with stray aerial traffic.

While they waited for their approach clearance, Idina watched one of the large orbital shuttles lining up in the launch pattern, then firing its main engines and soaring into the blue sky on a bright exhaust plume. Behind it, on the far periphery of the spaceport's restricted airspace, an armored Alliance combat gyrofoil was patrolling the perimeter, missiles and gun pods loaded on its ordnance pylons in a highly visible show of force.

"JSP 011, Sandvik Control. You are cleared to land on pad 121 via approach vector Delta Five," the controller sent on comms in a curt voice.

"Sandvik Control, JSP 011. Cleared to land, pad 121," Dahl replied. She selected the assigned approach vector on the navigation screen and let the computer take over. Immediately, the gyrofoil turned to the left and descended to line up in the approach path. The on-screen warning that let them know the local point-defense system was still tracking them didn't disappear until the craft's landing gear had touched the ground.

Outside, the air smelled faintly of ozone and rocket exhaust. The vertical landing pads had their own terminal, which was a good distance away from the freight and cargo section, and Dahl requested a surface pod from ground control rather than make the kilometer-long walk across the apron between the terminals.

The shift supervisor in the cargo section was a tall and burly man who looked like he worked out by lifting fully packed freight pallets. The cargo hall was a hive of noisy activity, dozens of power loaders moving containers between fast-moving transport bands and whirring lifting arms. Idina could sense the supervisor's dislike of her Alliance uniform in the same way the gyrofoil's systems had sensed the fire control lock from the ground battery, but Dahl took charge as usual, and it was a little amusing to see the burly Gretian's attitude shift from bristly to respectful as soon as Dahl started speaking in her no-nonsense police officer voice.

"We are looking for someone who works here in the cargo section," Dahl told him. She pulled out her comtab and flicked open a screen with a picture of their suspect. "His name is Helge Lind."

The supervisor nodded. "He is one of my power-loader drivers. Is he in trouble?"

"Not as of yet," Dahl replied. "But we need to talk to him about a police matter. Please tell us where to find him. And do not let him know that we are coming."

Idina lightly tapped her fingers on the sheath of her kukri. The supervisor's gaze flicked to the weapon and then back to Dahl, who had closed the screen projection with the picture.

"I will have to take you to him. This is a secure area, and it is not safe for people to walk around without an escort."

Dahl nodded. "Lead the way, please."

The shift supervisor led them on a long trek through the cargo section along a succession of pathways that were marked on the floor with orange paint. It was as big a space as Idina had seen on Gretia under a single roof, but the numerous transport and sorting machines and the stacks of cargo containers made it feel like a crowded maze. Idina knew that all the nonmilitary freight that arrived from orbit or departed into space passed through this spaceport, but it was one thing to know the fact and another to see what that sort of cargo volume looked like when it was processed. The automatic systems were augmented by dozens of workers in power loaders, heavy-lifting exoskeletons that looked like upscaled versions of military power armor. Idina followed Dahl and the supervisor through the labyrinth of equipment on the marked paths. Every worker she saw on the way who wasn't operating a loader kept to the orange pathways, which were flanked by safety warnings stenciled onto the floor in regular intervals.

They crossed into a section of the hall that looked like it was dedicated to the staging of freight for surface transport. Idina saw a long row of numbered gates on the far wall where more workers on power loaders were busy stacking containers and moving them into waiting cargo haulers. The supervisor walked to the end of the marked pathway and tapped the comms bud in his ear.

"Lind, this is Karstein. Come over to transit zone seventy-one, please. There is someone here to see you."

He listened to the reply in his ear and nodded at Dahl.

"He is on the way, Officer."

"Thank you," Dahl replied. "This is official police business. Once he arrives, you may return to your own duties. We will go back the way we came once we are finished here." Even through Idina's translator earbud, the captain's tone left little doubt that she wasn't merely making a suggestion.

They didn't have to wait long. A minute or two later, a power loader turned the corner of a tall container stack fifty meters away and stomped toward them. Idina immediately recognized the loader's driver from his file picture even from a distance. He saw them waiting for him in the safety zone, and she thought she saw the tiniest bit of hesitation in his next step, a loader leg lifting just a fraction of a second out of tune with his stride. Next to them, Supervisor Karstein waved once, and the man in the loader returned the wave with a brief lifting of the loader's arm. There was a row of recharging pads for the power loaders nearby, and Lind walked his machine over to one of them and backed into it, then powered it down. He unlocked his safety harness and jumped down from the loader. He glanced over at them again, and something about his body language told Idina exactly what was going to happen next. Before she could open her mouth for a warning to Dahl, Lind turned around and started running, a full-bore sprint toward the open receiving gates on the other side of the hall.

"Shit," she exclaimed and took off after him. Behind her, Dahl and the supervisor exchanged a few quick and loud words, and then Dahl followed in Idina's wake at a run.

"Halt! Police!" Dahl's amplified voice boomed behind her. "Stop right now!"

Lind paid no mind. He raced across the hall, arms pumping, propelled by the emergency adrenaline dump that came with the knowledge of being chased. Idina was a fair sprinter in the relative low-g environment of Gretia, but her quarry had longer legs and a strong motivation to get away, and the gap between them widened as they dashed across the floor. Ahead, another power loader came out of a container aisle, and Lind dodged its stride before it could punt him across the hall by accident. The near miss seemed to give him an extra boost of speed, and he reached the cargo gate with a fifty-meter lead on Idina. He ran through the gate and dropped out of her line of sight on the other side.

The loading ramp beyond the cargo gates had bays for the freight crawlers that were a meter and a half below the level of the ramp, and Idina had to slow down to avoid launching herself off the edge at a full sprint. She looked around for Lind, who was already halfway across the loading apron toward another staging area where the containers were stacked in rows that towered ten meters high. She jumped down onto the apron and resumed her pursuit. Just as he reached the nearest row, he looked over his shoulder and locked eyes with her for the fraction of a second. Then he disappeared around the corner, and she mouthed a curse.

If I had my battlefield boosters, you'd be in restraints already, Idina thought. She reached down with her right hand to retract the safety hood on her holster, but the push-and-pull motion it required was difficult to do at a full run, and she was still struggling with it when she reached the end of the container row and turned the corner.

Lind had stopped running. He was standing in the space between the containers and facing her, and his hands were steadying a gun that was pointed right at her.

Idina tried to stop and draw her sidearm at the same time and failed to do either. The pistol in Lind's hand boomed, a sharp crack that echoed from the walls of the containers. The projectile punched Idina in the chest just below the edge of her armor's collar, high up on the sternum. It knocked the remaining air out of her lungs and sent her stumbling, and she lost her balance and crashed to the ground with a loud clatter of belt-mounted equipment. Lind shifted his aim to follow her movement with the muzzle of his gun. Still on her back, Idina managed to get her duty holster's safety hood out of the way, and she closed her hand around the grip of her sidearm to pull it out. It felt like she was moving at a quarter of her usual speed, as if time was slowing down for her but not for the man about to kill her. Even as her gun cleared its holster, she knew she wasn't going to stop him from pulling his trigger again.

The shot that rang out was so loud that it made her unprotected left ear go deaf. In front of her, Lind dropped his gun. He did a little half turn and took two steps before his legs gave out and he dropped to his hands and knees. Then he slowly fell over sideways and curled into a fetal position with a loud and drawn-out groan.

"Do not move," Dahl shouted somewhere behind her. Idina rolled over and turned around to see her Gretian police partner in a wide two-handed shooting stance that looked like she was at the firing range. She was breathing hard, but the pistol in her hands didn't move. Dahl stepped forward past Idina, her gun still aimed at Lind, who was groaning and slowly writhing on the ground. When she reached his weapon, she kicked it aside and out of his reach.

"Are you all right?" she called out over her shoulder without taking her eyes off Lind.

"I'm okay," Idina replied. "He hit me in my armor. I just need to catch my breath for a second."

She sat up and looked down at her chest. The projectile from Lind's gun had shattered against the ballistic panel of her soft armor, leaving behind an irregular smudge of singed spidersilk flecked with bullet fragments.

"Explosive round," she said. "Son of a bitch."

There was a wet sensation on the underside of her chin, and she reached up to touch it with her fingertips. When she looked at them, they were smeared with her blood. She carefully probed the spot that hurt the most and touched something small and sharp in the center of the wetness. Some of the round's shrapnel had sprayed up from the impact and burrowed itself in her skin.

Dahl was by Lind's side now. She holstered her weapon and quickly locked his wrists behind his back with a flexible restraint, then rolled him over onto his stomach, and he groaned again.

"Do you have any other weapons on you?" she asked as she patted him down. He responded with another groan.

Idina got up and walked over to them, securing her pistol again as she went.

"I rounded the corner and he was right there. Shot me as soon as I came in sight. I got caught up in hunting fever. Should have had the gun out before I took off after him. Stupid mistake."

"It happens," Dahl said. "I am glad I came around that corner when I did." She looked up at Idina from her crouched position. "You are bleeding."

"It's just a scratch. I'm lucky he didn't have armor-piercing rounds in that thing." Idina walked over to the pistol Dahl had kicked away and picked it up. It looked identical to the gun in Dahl's holster. She took out the ammunition block and worked the action to eject the live round from the weapon's firing chamber.

"This looks familiar," she said and held up the pistol for Dahl to see.

"Standard police issue," Dahl confirmed. She turned back to the man lying prone on the ground. "Where did you get that weapon, friend?"

When she finished searching Lind, Dahl carefully rolled him back onto his side in a stabilizing position. He was no longer groaning. His eyes were half-open and unfocused, and his handsome face now looked ashen and pale. Dahl's shot had hit him high in the chest, right underneath his collarbone on the left side of his body.

"You do not get out of this the easy way," Dahl said to him. She unfastened the top of his jumpsuit, then took out a knife and cut it open at an angle. The entry wound looked tidy, only as big as the circumference of Idina's little finger. The blood seeping from it ran down the front of his chest and made a little pool on the ground. Dahl pulled a medpack from her leg pocket and ripped it open, then stuck it on top of the wound.

"Patrol lead to all available air and ground units in the vicinity of the spaceport," she said into her comms set. "Shots fired. One suspect is down. I need medical assistance at my location immediately."

Idina's heart was still thumping in her chest. She forced herself to take a few deep breaths to slow her pulse and calm herself, which was a difficult thing to do right after getting shot. She looked on as Dahl put her hand on Lind's neck to check his pulse with the tips of her fingers.

"He is still with us," she said. "But his pulse is fast and weak. I wish I did not have to shoot him."

"You saved my life," Idina replied. "He had a choice when he drew his gun. You didn't."

"I know. But it is still no small thing for me to use deadly force."

"I wonder what drove him to do that. He bolted as soon as he was off that power loader. Like all the hells were chasing him. That was quite the overreaction to seeing a pair of uniforms."

"I do not know. Hopefully he will survive so we can hear the answer to that question from his own mouth. And so I do not have to remember his face for the rest of my life," Dahl said.

Behind them, a power loader came around the corner, and Idina put her hands on her gun again reflexively. The loader's operator got wide-eyed when he saw the scene in front of him and stopped his machine.

"You cannot come through here," Dahl said in a loud and authoritative voice.

"I have to get twenty tons of freight from this stack," the driver said. His gaze flitted from Dahl to Idina and to the motionless Lind on the ground in turn. "There is a pickup in fifteen minutes."

"They will have to wait a while for their cargo," Dahl replied. "This is a police crime scene now. Move along. No discussion," she added when the driver opened his mouth for a protest. He stared at Dahl for a moment as if to gauge her resolve. Then he shrugged, turned his power loader around, and stomped back the way he had come to the sound of softly whining hydraulics.

"There may be a dead man on the ground for all he knows, and he expects us to drag the body out of the way so he can go about his business," Dahl mused. "Some people truly believe they are the only real humans in all the worlds. The rest of us are just entertainment holograms."

A loud rumbling sound came from behind them, and the ground underneath their feet shook a little with the vibrations. Idina turned around to see one of the orbital shuttles take off from the launch zone, accelerating skyward on a drive plume that was twice as long as the craft itself. In the sky beyond, two gyrofoils were descending toward them with flashing emergency lights.

"Here is our backup," Dahl said. "Finally. This man already has one leg in whatever paradise he believes in."

In the open space beyond the mouth of the container alley, Idina saw more freight workers gathering and looking on with curiosity. They were keeping their distance, but she knew they were in the space the gyrofoils would need to land. She fished a small handful of emergency flares out of her jumpsuit's leg pocket and strode toward the group.

"Clear the area," she shouted in Gretian. It was one of the phrases she had picked up from Dahl during their time on patrol together. Her accent was probably terrible, but the workers seemed to get the message. They dispersed slowly while she lit the flares one by one and laid out a triangle-shaped landing zone for the approaching gyrofoils.

The pair of police craft came in low over the cargo sector and circled the landing area once before extending their landing skids and descending onto the space Idina had marked for them. She waved at them and turned back toward Dahl.

High above the spaceport, a thunderclap ripped the clear blue sky in half.

Idina looked up at the source of the sound and saw a bright fireball that quickly expanded against the background of the blue sky. It took her a few seconds to comprehend what she was seeing. Out of the roiling center of the explosion, white smoke trails expanded in every direction and began arcing toward the ground like billowing tentacles. A wordless sound of dismay escaped her mouth as she watched.

A point-defense intercept, she thought. *They shot down another insurgency gyrofoil loaded with explosives.* But the large chunks of debris that had continued their upward trajectory out of the explosion told her that the destroyed craft had been on a rapid ascent when it blew up, not a descent. She recognized the shape of a wing among the pieces that were now tumbling across the sky in a wide arc, its white-paint coating reflecting the light of the sun in brilliant little flashes as it rotated in the airflow.

Gods. That's the military shuttle that just took off. There's going to be debris and bodies raining down all over this city.

She tapped into her comms and switched to the emergency channel.

"Code Black, Code Black. All Alliance units, this is JSP Day Lead. We have a Code Black at the spaceport. Send out the QRF and mobilize all personnel for lockdown protocol. I repeat, Code Black at the spaceport."

Thirty meters ahead of her, Dahl was busy issuing her own commands on the police guard frequency. Over by the main terminal, an alarm klaxon started to wail, followed by more of its kind all over the spaceport until the noise seemed to come from every direction.

A Gretian police officer ran past her toward Dahl, followed by a JSP trooper who stopped next to her.

"Where do you need me, Color Sergeant?" he shouted.

She gestured in Dahl's direction.

"Help the Gretians and get that piece of shit into your gyrofoil and to the med center," she said. "Do not go to the Gretian one. Take him to the Alliance base. And have them put him under guard as soon as you get there. Whether he's dead or alive."

"Yes, ma'am," the trooper said and rushed off to follow her orders. Up in the sky, the smoke and debris cloud from the explosion had expanded in all directions. The larger wreckage pieces were still trailing smoke as they fell out of the sky. From the direction of the city center,

Idina could hear the two-tone wailing of the civil alert sirens now over the din of the spaceport's alarm klaxons.

The JSP trooper and his Gretian partner had brought their gyrofoil's medevac stretcher, and now they loaded the motionless Lind onto it and carried him toward their patrol craft. Idina looked at him as the stretcher passed her. Lind's face was slack and drained of all color. There was a large, irregular pool of dark blood in the spot where he had lain on the ground, more than Idina knew someone could lose without shaking hands with death.

The military gyrofoil Idina had spotted earlier at the edge of the airspace was now circling overhead, its gun turret swiveling from side to side as the sensors were searching for hostile targets. Over by the freight doors to Idina's right, workers had come out of the cargo hall to look at the devastation in the sky, and some retreated into the building at the sight of the low-flying war machine and its array of automatic cannons.

"Clear the area," Idina shouted in their direction and waved her hand in a corresponding gesture, but her voice got lost in the overall din of alarms and gyrofoil engines, and she gave up on the effort and went to join Dahl again, who was still talking on her comms and looking at the sky with dismay.

"I called in everybody," Idina said to her when Dahl had finished her comms.

"So did I," Dahl replied. "We will need them all. The entire city got to watch what just happened."

"That debris field is going to be ten kilometers wide. Please tell me that wasn't a passenger shuttle."

"I do not know the answer to that yet. But we need to get back in the air either way. All those burning pieces are going to cause damage and hurt people all over the city. And if there are bodies, we will have many crime scenes to secure in the next few hours."

"Let's go, then," Idina replied.

They took off across the spaceport apron toward the vertical landing pads together. All around them, people were running among the nerve-grating sounds of alarms, and surface pods were speeding across the apron without paying any heed to the traffic markings.

Please let it be a cargo shuttle, Idina thought as she ran after Dahl. *Let it be just three dead crew and fifty tons of spare parts.* But even as her lungs started to burn with the exertion, she couldn't rid her mind of the image of people falling out of the sky, still strapped into their acceleration couches, smashing through rooftops or splattering on the streets like overripe fruit.

Chapter 15

Dunstan

"You have to hand it to them, they're running some tight ops over there. That's as smooth an in-space replenishing as I've ever seen in the fleet," Lieutenant Hunter said.

Five thousand kilometers in front of *Hecate*'s bow, the impressive feat of patchwork engineering that was the pirate deep-space station was coasting along on the same heading, still unaware of the stealth ship that had been shadowing them for days now. Another ship had arrived less than an hour ago, a commercial deuterium tanker that had maneuvered alongside the ore-hauler section of the station and swiftly started replenishment operations once they had matched course and speed.

"They have some marketable skills," Dunstan conceded. "Too bad they chose to use them for this."

"Oh, I'm sure they get paid much better than navy deckhands. Nobody in their right mind would be spending their days in the outer rim without some serious compensation. I know I wouldn't."

"And yet here you are," Dunstan said with a smile.

Since *Hecate* had started to track the ore hauler and its small fleet of docked ships, they had fallen into a steady routine, tracking departing and arriving ships and letting the AI soak up all the electronic intelligence it could gather. The only real excitement happened whenever the cobbled-together makeshift structure repositioned itself, which they had done three times in the last five days by firing the synchronized drives of the ore hauler and its passenger-liner adjunct for a few hours of one-g acceleration. The intervals between burns had been as random as their new headings, but it was clear they were zigzagging along the system's outer rim to evade long-range detection.

"Do we have a definite ID on that deuterium tanker yet?" Dunstan asked.

Lieutenant Robson looked up from her station. "Negative, sir. Nothing conclusive. It's Acheron built. Edo 750-class medium bulk tanker. Could be any of a dozen hulls in that class. We'll know better once they leave and we get a full profile of their drive plume from astern."

"They're running regular task-force operations right in front of our nose, and all we can do right now is to record IDs and take pictures of hull markings," Hunter said.

"We'll get our window," Dunstan replied.

Lieutenant Hunter nodded at the screen projection above the tactical plot.

"Respectfully, sir—that's our window, right there. They're refueling right now. Once that tanker is gone, they'll be topped off again. We can keep following them for a few more days. But we'll run out of fuel long before they will."

"What do you propose, Lieutenant?" Dunstan asked.

His first officer leaned forward in her chair and looked at the pirate vessels performing their slow-motion replenishment choreography thousands of kilometers away.

"This ship isn't built for a long-duration patrol," she said. "We can keep tracking them until we have to break off the chase and head home for lack of supplies. Or we can use what we have and take out what we can. And right now they're as vulnerable as they're going to be. They're in tight formation with that tanker. They've got a bunch of high-volume fuel hoses running between them. It wouldn't take a lot of ordnance to really ruin their day."

Dunstan looked at the tactical plot. All the red icons on the display were in a tight cluster, huddled together around the bulk of the station, a dream scenario for a cruiser commander who could launch thirty antiship missiles or a pair of low-yield nukes at the bunched-up formation. Even *Hecate's* light missile load would probably wreak havoc on the unprepared pirate fleet, tethered as they were to their mothership. He knew that it wouldn't take much damage to knock most of those ships out of action. But he also knew that once he ordered Lieutenant Armer to punch the launch buttons on the weapons console, all the options they had right now would narrow down to one. With that button press, they'd be betting the ship that whatever they had in their magazines would be enough to overwhelm that group or shock them into surrender.

"I can't say I love the odds, Number One," he said. "We'd be doing the one thing this ship isn't designed to do well."

"Respectfully, sir—except for that corvette, those aren't warships. They're a bunch of old junkers with some black-market weaponry bolted on. They're not built for a fight; they're built for raiding unarmed merchants. And they aren't prepared right now."

Dunstan looked around in the Ops center. Every officer on the deck was following their conversation and waiting for his reaction. He reached for the buckle on his seat harness and turned the lock.

"Lieutenant Armer, you have the conn. A quick word in private, Number One?"

They floated down the ladder to the airlock deck, which was empty except for tied-down storage crates. Dunstan seized one of the grab bars by the arms locker to steady himself. Lieutenant Hunter pushed off from the ladder and floated to the grab bar on the other side of the locker. She swung herself around and looked at him expectantly.

"What's on your mind, sir?"

"I understand the instinct, Lieutenant," he said. "I have it, too. We've been hunting these people for months and chasing them down one by one. And now there's a whole group of them right in our crosshairs."

"We can end this in five minutes, sir."

"*If* we shoot first. They won't have time to surrender or get into their pods. Are you at peace with the idea of violating the rules of engagement and killing hundreds of people without warning?"

"*These* people? Absolutely," Lieutenant Hunter replied without hesitation. "None of them would give us any warning either."

"But we're not pirates, Number One. We're the Rhodian Navy."

"Precisely, Commander." Hunter gestured around the airlock deck and tapped the Alon pane of the weapons locker between them, where the ship's small arms were lined up neatly in locked racks. "This is a *warship*, sir. And we're at war. Any of the ships leaving from that station could be the one that drops the next nuke on Rhodia."

Dunstan thought of his wife and daughters, going about their daily business back home right now. For a moment, he pictured them in his mind—Mairi preparing dinner in the kitchen at home, his daughters hunched over their compads at school—as another thermonuclear warhead streaked out of the sky high above their heads and turned the arcology into a white-hot fireball of vaporized glass, steel, and human bodies.

We didn't start this, he reminded himself. *They did. And even if they have no nukes left, they're still killing people on the trade routes almost every day. How many merchant vessels have they blown out of space in the last few months?*

"We can't stay on station out here forever," Hunter pressed on. "We can't call for backup. And if we leave, we may not find them again before the next big attack happens."

"All right, Lieutenant. You've made your point," Dunstan said. "I guess we're about to take a billion-ag warship into a knife fight."

"Aye, sir," Hunter said with satisfaction in her voice. She pushed off toward the ladderwell, and Dunstan watched her grab one of the rungs and use it to change her trajectory upward.

Gods-damn it, he thought. *This is one of those days when I hate wearing these stripes.*

—

"Lieutenant Armer, work out a battle plan for engaging the enemy," Dunstan said when he floated back into the Ops deck. "Number One, call to action stations."

"Aye, sir." Lieutenant Hunter was already strapped into her seat and wearing her vacsuit helmet. She picked up the wired comms handset next to her station and spoke into it in her crisp command voice.

"Action stations, action stations. All hands to battle positions. Assume vacsuit state alpha. Set EMCON condition one. Ship-to-ship action imminent. This is not a drill."

"Command crew, listen up," Dunstan said when everybody was fully suited up. "I intend to commit an intentional violation of our rules of engagement and open fire on a suspected pirate without the required lethal-force warning. Anyone who wants to voice their dissent can do so now without fear of reprisal. I will log your objection for the record in case of future disciplinary proceedings."

He waited a few heartbeats for someone to speak up, then nodded when everyone in Ops carried on with their tasks as if they hadn't heard him.

"Very well," he said. "Let's get down to business. Tactical, let's hear an updated assessment."

"My earlier assessment mostly holds, sir. That corvette should be the priority target," Lieutenant Armer said immediately. "It's the only warship at anchor. If they left it stock in Block II configuration, they have a decent point-defense system but nothing that can handle two or three of our Tridents."

"Agreed," Dunstan said. "Who's next on the list?"

"That ore-hauler hull will just soak up whatever we throw at it. But the tanker next to it is a deuterium-filled egg. We launch two at the corvette and two at the tanker. One each into the drive sections of the two big hulls to clip their wings. And we'll allocate the rest of the missiles to the ships at anchorage. They're all converted civilian hulls. One hit from a Trident will wreck their day."

"And we'll hope for some fireworks when that tanker goes up," Dunstan said. "Set the launchers to standby and allocate your ordnance as proposed, Mr. Armer."

"Aye, sir."

Dunstan looked at the cluster of connected ships on the sensor screen, three large hulls lashed together and a cluster of smaller ones hanging off the docking outriggers like grapes on a vine. There was no way to know exactly how many people were in those ships right now, sleeping in their bunks or stowing cargo, unaware of the antiship missiles that were being assigned to kill them in a few minutes. There would be dozens of people even on a small freighter, and the ore hauler and passenger liner together likely had crews numbering in the many hundreds, maybe thousands.

They're just hulls, he reminded himself. In battle, warships launched missiles at other ships, not people. The enemy units were red icons on the tactical plot, and a commander's task was to extinguish those symbols from the display. The ships Lieutenant Armer was targeting right now had been raiding trade routes, destroying merchant vessels and killing survivors in their life pods, atrocities that not even the Gretians had dared to commit during the war for fear of inviting the same treatment from Alliance ships. Still, the sorts of deaths to which he had just consigned the crews on those ships were any spacer's nightmare, and he could not help feeling a spark of pity for them even as he was giving the orders to kill them.

"Prepare for burn," he ordered. "One g, steady as she goes. We'll close to under a thousand klicks before we launch."

"Prepare for burn, aye." Lieutenant Hunter picked up the comms set again. "All hands, prepare for gravity."

"Throttle up on my mark. Three, two, one, *mark*."

Dunstan's body weight returned as *Hecate*'s drive fired up and produced the one g of acceleration he had ordered. The tactical plot, which had been static since the tanker arrived and docked with the pirate station, came to life again and started to count down the range to their target by just under ten meters squared per second.

"One g acceleration, steady as she goes," Lieutenant Armer confirmed. "Time to launch is fourteen minutes and forty-five seconds."

"Steady as she goes," Dunstan said. "Let's go deliver the goods."

The elasticity of time perception was never more obvious to Dunstan than when the ship was at action stations and the mission clock on the Ops bulkhead was ticking toward imminent violence. Fifteen minutes of waiting for the shooting to start felt both like forever and no time at all. *Hecate* was a silent assassin in the dark, sneaking up on her targets to stab them from the shadows. If everything went right, it wouldn't be a fair fight. But if Dunstan had learned anything during the war, it was that notions like chivalry had no place in battle.

"Five hundred klicks," Lieutenant Armer announced when *Hecate*'s icon on the tactical plot was almost touching the red line that marked the optimal engagement range for the Trident missiles. "Two minutes until launch."

"Stand by on ordnance bay doors," Dunstan ordered. "Energize the point-defense grid."

"Aye, sir. PDS is energized and ready."

"Let's hope we won't need it. Prepare to open outer bay doors."

He focused on his breathing as he watched the seconds count down on the bulkhead display. Ninety seconds shrunk down to sixty, then thirty. When the counter reached ten, Dunstan took one more deep breath and let it out slowly.

"One thousand klicks," Lieutenant Armer called out when *Hecate* passed the invisible line in space that marked the launch spot.

"Open outer bay doors," Dunstan ordered. "Weapons free. Flush those launchers."

"Weapons free, weapons free. Cycling launcher one. Cycling launcher two."

Hecate didn't have missile silos in her hull like the larger warships in the fleet. Instead, she carried her ordnance in two rotary launchers, each loaded with six Trident missiles. The ship's hull vibrated slightly as each launcher began spitting out missiles in staggered two-second intervals. Lieutenant Armer counted out loud as each pair of weapons shot out of the launch bay doors and hurtled toward the pirate station.

"One, two, three, four, five, and six. Birds away, birds away. Launcher one is empty. Launcher two is empty."

On the tactical screen, a line of blue Vs raced ahead in front of *Hecate* at two hundred gravities of acceleration.

That's it, Dunstan thought. *All our cards are in play, and we're betting the house on it.*

"I have all twelve birds tracking in passive mode," Armer reported. "Time to target, twenty-five seconds."

"EM scope is clear. No new contacts, no active radiation from the targets. They won't know what hit them," Lieutenant Robson said.

With ten seconds to go, the line of V shapes in front of *Hecate* shifted formation ever so slightly as each individual missile nudged itself toward its target. Five seconds before impact, the tactical screen lit up with a dozen different active radar signatures, and the electronic warfare screen at Lieutenant Robson's station chirped a string of alerts.

"Birds went active," Lieutenant Armer said. "Three, two, one. *Target.*"

The first of the Tridents hit its mark, the massive stern section of the ore hauler. The fireballs from the warheads looked almost inconsequential against the bulk of the ship at this distance. Then the other missiles arrived in one-second intervals, and the sensor display erupted in a rapid succession of thermal blooms as warhead after warhead found its target.

"Good hits, good hits," Armer narrated. "We have some secondaries. Looks like the—*whoa.*"

Another fireball lit up the screen and pushed the optical sensors past their limit. For a few moments, it washed out the image, a sphere of light that was as bright as a small sun, and Dunstan's first thought was that one of the pirate ships at anchorage had been carrying a nuke that just got set off by a secondary explosion.

"Direct hit on the tanker, sir. She just went up like a grenade. They must have had more than just deuterium matrix in their tanks," Armer said.

Everyone in Ops was staring at the optical feed in silence for a few moments. Dunstan was glad that nobody expressed any glee or satisfaction at the image they saw when the fireball had begun to dissipate in the vacuum of space. What had been a tight formation before was now a mess of damaged ships spinning out of control amid clouds of debris and escaping air. The ore hauler that made up more than half of the station's bulk was slowly rotating bow over stern, its aft section tattered and aglow with hundreds of small internal fires. The tanker that had been tied up to the ore carrier just a minute ago was gone, blotted from existence by the explosion that had temporarily blinded *Hecate*'s optical gear. The cruise liner that was connected to the ore hauler had been shielded from the worst of the blast by the hull of its much bigger neighbor, but it was far from unscathed. High-speed shrapnel and debris had peppered the ship and torn away large sections of its hull plating, exposing some of the decks underneath. Dunstan was glad the resolution of the optical sensors was too low to distinguish human bodies at this distance, but he knew even without the visual verification that there were corpses drifting out of those ragged holes, pushed along by the air rushing out of the hull.

"Anything on active?" he asked.

"Negative," Lieutenant Robson replied. "Lots of EM noise but no active radiation."

"Not even pod beacons?"

Robson shook her head with a grim expression. "No distress signals. If anyone is launching escape pods, they're not sending."

"As tight as they've been locking down their EMCON, they may have disabled the beacons," Lieutenant Hunter said.

Dunstan tried to get a count of damaged hulls, but the image on the sensor screen was one of complete chaos and destruction, too much stuff swirling around at too far a distance to make out details. They had struck the station a fatal blow, but the large ships had only been part of the equation, and there was no way to get an accurate picture from where they were right now.

"Take us closer for a post-strike assessment," he ordered. "Plot a good angle for a pass, but don't get too close. A hundred klicks should be enough to get the full picture."

"Laying in new heading for flyby at one hundred klicks, aye," Hunter acknowledged.

As *Hecate* closed the distance, the full extent of the carnage they had caused gradually unfolded on the sensor display. The ships that had been moored on the station's docking outriggers closest to the tanker were simply gone, converted into clouds of debris along with the outriggers themselves. The docking arms on the far side of the ore hauler, the ones shielded by the bulk of the hull, were still intact, but most of the docked ships were venting air and trailing debris as well, evidence that the Trident warheads had found most of their marks.

That was for Danae *and* Cloud Dancer, *and all the other ships that got no warnings either before you bastards shot them to pieces,* Dunstan thought. *You brought the war back to the system. We just returned it to you with interest.*

There was some noise on comms now, people on low-power handsets transmitting panicked and frantic orders or calls for help, their confusion and fear obvious in their voices. Some of the crippled ships had managed to launch life pods, which were now drifting in the debris field and illuminating the nearby hulls with the orange light flashing from their beacons. *Hecate* was close enough now for Dunstan to see more pods launching from the mauled passenger ship that made up a third of the station construct. Soon, the space around the station was dotted with blinking orange lights.

"If we'd had six more missiles, we could have finished the job," Lieutenant Armer said with a hint of regret.

"We had enough," Dunstan replied.

"That tanker certainly amplified our investment," Lieutenant Hunter said. "That was a few kilotons of free explosives for us to put to good use. It really tore the guts out of that drive section."

From close range, the damage the tanker explosion had done to the ore hauler looked catastrophic. Ore tugs were all built around the same design, a command section at the front and a drive section aft, connected by a long spine with attachment points for the cargo modules that held the raw ore. This ship's drive section had been ripped open along most of its length, creating a massive wound that was bleeding frozen air and fluids from the exposed and shattered decks underneath. The blast had ripped several of the cargo modules from the central spine and visibly damaged most of the rest. What had been an aging but fully operational bulk ore hauler an hour ago was now a broken hull that no shipyard could fix, and only its immense size and mass had saved it from getting obliterated outright.

"That's a lot of life pods out there," Robson said in a low voice.

"We'll send an update to the fleet once we are in the clear again," Dunstan said. "They have a week of power and supplies in those pods. Plenty of time for the navy to send a few frigates to pick them up. That station is never going to move under its own power again."

Over at Lieutenant Robson's station, an alarm blared. At the same time, the tactical display flashed and updated the plot with a threat vector.

"Fire control radar," Robson called out. "Someone's got a lock on us, sir."

"Energize the PDS. Go active on the sensors and do a sweep," Dunstan ordered. "Helm, all ahead flank. Get us some distance."

"Vampire, vampire," Lieutenant Armer shouted. "We have incoming from the station. Bearing 280 over 9, distance twelve hundred."

On the tactical display, two red Vs appeared in the middle of the cluster of enemy ship icons and raced toward *Hecate*.

"PDS is online and in AI control mode. Tracking incoming ordnance. Time to intercept, twenty-five seconds." Robson's fingers were a blur on the control fields of her console. "Sir, that fire control radar is Oceanian. So are the missiles. They're Osprey-As."

"That didn't come from the station," Dunstan concluded. "It's that damn corvette."

"How the hells did they survive our Tridents?" Lieutenant Armer asked.

"Maybe they had their PDS on standby," Robson offered without looking up from her screens. "Maybe our birds went off target at the last moment."

Hecate was accelerating at over ten gravities now, and Dunstan started to feel the heaviness that came whenever the ship was approaching the limit of the gravmag system's compensators. They were racing away from the incoming missiles but not in the hope of outrunning them. Every fraction of a second they could add to the flight time of the Ospreys gave the AI more time to take over the guidance systems of the warheads or calculate the intercept timing for the point-defense emitters.

"Ten seconds. AI override on Vampire-1," Robson said. "Splash one." Her voice sounded as calm as if she had just called out a socaball goal in an uninteresting match.

One of the red V icons disappeared from the tactical plot as *Hecate*'s AI brute-forced its electronic brain and ordered it to self-immolate. The other one kept up its mindless pursuit, following in their wake at one-hundred-plus g and closing the remaining distance rapidly.

"Five seconds," Robson called out. "Four. Three."

A low hum reverberated through the ship. On the tactical display, the other red V blinked out of existence.

"Splash two. PDS intercepted Vampire-2 at two seconds and seventy-five klicks out," Robson announced, this time with satisfaction in her voice.

"Cut the throttle and bring the bow sensors to bear," Dunstan ordered. "Active sweep as soon as she comes about. They know where we are. No sense staying blind on purpose."

Lieutenant Hunter shut down the main drive and flipped *Hecate* around with her lateral thrusters until they were coasting backward, carried along by their brief burst of acceleration.

"Active sweep commencing," Lieutenant Armer said. "New contact, bearing 355 under 35, distance thirty-five hundred. Constant bearing, bogey is coming after us hard at twelve-and-a-half g."

"How many missile tubes does a Cerberus-class corvette have again?" Dunstan asked.

"Four, sir," Robson replied.

"They just launched two at us. We know they fired one at *Zephyr* last week."

"Those launchers need to be reloaded externally," Armer said. "And we didn't see an ordnance tender when they were docked."

"So they have one bird left at the most," Dunstan summarized.

"I think they're dry, sir. They would have launched a triple if they had the shots. I would have," Armer said.

"Three thousand and closing fast," Lieutenant Hunter warned. "Are we running or jousting?"

"They have the acceleration advantage. We can take them on a long stern chase, but they'll catch up with us eventually."

"Whatever they have left, they need to turn on their fire-control radar again to take a shot," Lieutenant Robson said. "If we're close enough when they do, I can shut them down."

Dunstan looked at the tactical display. The enemy corvette was closing the distance quickly, a move that made little sense if they still had long-range ordnance to launch. He tried to put himself into the head of the corvette's captain.

They're betting we have no missiles left either because we haven't returned fire even though we have them locked up on active sensors. They know we're stealthy but smaller and slower than they are. There's only one reason for them to want to get into knife-fight range.

"Turn us around," Dunstan ordered. "Throttle up to eight g."

"We won't outrun them at eight g," Hunter cautioned.

"I don't want to outrun them, Number One. I want them to catch up."

"Aye, sir. Turning to match headings. Throttling up to eight g," she said.

He turned to Lieutenant Robson.

"You said the Cerberus class has a fifty-seven-millimeter gun mount?"

"Yes, sir," she replied. "Standard caseless, not a rail gun."

"Those are slow rounds. They can't send them up our drive cone at eight g. They'll try to pass us and shoot into our path from ahead," Dunstan said. "That's going to be your window, Lieutenant. The moment that fire-control radar lights up, you take them over and shut them down."

"Aye, sir," Robson said. "Child's play."

Dunstan watched the tactical grid as the pirate corvette steadily chewed up the distance between them. The captain of the enemy ship was displaying respectable fighting spirit by charging after an unknown attacker to get into gun range. Most of the pirates Dunstan had encountered only fought from ambush, and they avoided engaging Alliance warships unless they had no other choice. This captain could have kept his ship hidden behind the bigger hulls floating in the debris field and waited until the coast was clear. Instead, they were in an aggressive pursuit, forcing *Hecate* to take countermeasures that kept them from being able to slip back into the shadows. It was, Dunstan concluded, almost exactly what he would have done in the other captain's place.

At over four g of acceleration advantage, it didn't take long for the pirate corvette to catch up to *Hecate*. Dunstan kept his eyes on the red icon jumping a little closer to the center with every one-second refresh of the plot display. The enemy captain was using the speed margin to dogleg his course in random intervals by a few degrees to avoid flying straight up *Hecate*'s wake.

"Sultan-1 is now at bearing 169 under 19, distance five hundred fifteen," Armer reported. "Heading thirty-five degrees relative."

The corvette was clear of *Hecate*'s drive-plume blind spot now, and the distance was short enough for the sensor optics to get a good image of their pursuer. It was a handsome design for a warship, flowing lines and sleek proportions, a far more elegant and efficient machine than the converted civilian designs they usually encountered. Escort corvettes like this one were built to protect merchants. Using it to ambush and kill them instead felt like a particularly offensive sort of sacrilege.

"They're booking it," Lieutenant Hunter said. "Passing through 120 degrees under 16."

"They'll turn into us a few degrees when they're at our three o'clock," Dunstan said. "Any moment now. And—there they go."

The red icon on the plot pulled ahead of *Hecate* and started to close the distance at a steep approach angle. At twelve g of acceleration, the corvette's drive plume was a tail of bright fusion fire as long as the ship itself. The trajectories of the two ships on the tactical grid had gradually diverged as the corvette was performing its high-speed pass, and now they began to converge again to form the third side of a long, stretched-out triangle.

"Sultan-1 is crossing our trajectory in fifteen seconds," Armer called out.

"Here it comes," Dunstan said. "Go active on the bow array. Full sensor sweep."

"Aye, sir. Full sweep commencing."

Hecate's front sensor array lashed the space ahead of the ship with megawatts of energy, turning on the equivalent of a high-powered flashlight in a dark cellar. The red icon on the tactical screen shifted slightly as the computer updated the position of the corvette with the precise feedback from the active sensors.

"Five seconds," Armer said. "Three. Two. One."

By the time Armer had reached two, the radar-warning receiver chirped its sharp alarm again.

"Active fire-control radar," Robson called out. "Commencing AI override now."

"Incoming ordnance," Lieutenant Armer shouted.

On the plot, a small red triangle appeared in the wake of the corvette. A second later, another followed, then a third and a fourth.

"Lieutenant Robson," Dunstan said.

"Working on it, sir." She followed up on her reply with a satisfied little shout. "Yes. AI override commencing."

"Shut them down *now.* Whatever you can unplug."

The point-defense emitters hummed again. Two of the red triangles in front of *Hecate* disappeared from the plot. The third one blew up into a cloud of debris, so close to *Hecate* that Dunstan could see the flash on the sensor screen. Then something hit the bow hard, and alarms started trilling at Lieutenant Hunter's station.

"We took one on the chin," Hunter said matter-of-factly.

Ahead of them, the corvette's gun mount had stopped firing. The pirate ship was pulling away quickly, still burning hard at over twelve g on a trajectory that opened the angle between their headings again. The screen projection above the tactical plot that had shown the view from the optical array on *Hecate*'s bow was dark except for an error message flashing in the center: Feed Offline.

"They cut their burn," Lieutenant Armer said. "Bogey has stopped accelerating."

"Turning around for round two?" Dunstan asked.

"Negative. They're not maneuvering, just coasting ballistic."

Lieutenant Robson cleared her throat.

"They didn't cut their burn. I did that."

"You shut down their drive?"

Robson nodded. She looked over at Dunstan and let out a breath that sounded like she had been holding it for a minute. "But that's not all I turned off."

She reached into the opening of her helmet and wiped her face with her gloved hand. "Oh, gods."

"What did you do, Lieutenant?"

"You ordered me to unplug whatever I could, sir. I got access to the engineering network and initiated a reactor shutdown. But that takes thirty seconds to complete."

She looked from Dunstan to Lieutenant Hunter and the other officers in Ops.

"So I overrode the fail-safe and shut down their gravmag circuit. It was the only other important plug I could pull in a hurry."

"Gods." Lieutenant Hunter turned her head and looked at the tactical plot. The pirate corvette was still coasting on the same heading, steadily increasing the distance between the two ships. "How hard were they burning when you turned off their compensator?"

"Twelve point seven g," Lieutenant Armer answered in her stead.

There was a moment of silence in Ops as everyone realized the implications of Armer's words.

"They ran at over twelve g without a gravmag for thirty seconds," Hunter said.

"Affirmative," Armer replied.

Hecate's first officer exchanged a look with Dunstan.

"Who needs missiles?" she said.

Dunstan cleared his throat. "Lay in an intercept course for that corvette. Have all decks report in and get me a damage report."

"Aye, sir. Laying in intercept trajectory for Sultan-1," Hunter replied.

The lozenge shape on the plot in front of *Hecate* was still red because it represented an enemy warship, but Dunstan knew that the classification was no longer strictly correct. Everyone on that corvette was dead now, killed by rupturing blood vessels and gravity-induced brain hypoxia. The people they had just blown up with the station were just as dead, and many of them had suffered far worse deaths than falling unconscious and not waking up again. But the idea of the enemy corvette, coasting through space outwardly intact but crewed only by corpses, somehow horrified him more than the thought of getting blown up by a missile.

They chose their fates, he reminded himself. But even as the thought came into his head, it felt a little self-serving, a reflexive mantra for absolution.

Chapter 16

Solveig

The deep, low booming sound that rolled over the city made the windows of Solveig's office rattle in their frames. It reverberated among the tall buildings of the city center before dissipating in the clear blue morning sky. Solveig flinched and turned away from the window, adrenaline jolting her nervous system into alertness. When nothing else followed and the noise had faded, she looked over at the windowpanes, which were undamaged. On the floor outside her office, she could hear the commotion of shifting chairs and surprised exclamations.

She turned back toward her array of open screens and took slow, deep breaths until the shock from the unwelcome spike of stress hormones had started to subside. Solveig got out of her chair and walked over to the window to check for the source of the sound that had triggered her fight-or-flight response. Her first instinct was to look down at Principal Square, where the insurgency had set off a pair of bombs in the middle of a political rally many months ago. The second blast had been so powerful that it sent a chunk of shrapnel forty floors up Ragnar Tower and into one of the Alon panes in front of her. This new boom had sounded just as potent but more distant to her ears. Down on the square, everything looked calm. People were going about their business just like every day, and surface pods were gliding along the periphery of the plaza in their assigned travel lanes.

Behind Solveig, Anja entered the office and walked over to the window where she was standing.

"What in the gods' names was that?" Anja asked.

"Something blew up," Solveig replied. "Something big."

Anja joined her and looked out at the square below them. Far in the distance, emergency sirens had started to wail somewhere to their right, out of the field of vision the office windows afforded. She shot Solveig a worried look.

"Another bomb?"

"I have no idea," Solveig said. "But whatever it was, I'm sure we'll find out soon."

A pair of police gyrofoils flew above the square at low altitude, clearing the tallest buildings by just a few dozen meters. Solveig and Anja watched the craft in silence as they crossed the vast plaza at high speed and disappeared again. A few moments later, the small patrol craft were followed by a much larger military combat gyrofoil with Alliance markings that thundered over the square at an even lower altitude and made the windows shake again in the wake of its passage. If the Alliance military was rushing to the scene, it was almost certainly an insurgent attack, but from their vantage point it was impossible to ascertain what happened.

"Are you all right? You're pale."

It was only when Anja touched her gently on the arm that Solveig realized that her breaths had turned fast and shallow. She forced herself to control her breathing to get the anxiety under control, which had flared up in the wake of the explosion. The tight feeling around her chest went away slowly, but the dread she felt did not go with it, the premonition that something awful was unfolding. She listened for unusual sounds on the floor behind her, but all she heard was the usual background noise of the day's business, comms screens chirping soft alerts and people talking in subdued voices. When Solveig looked at her hand, she could see that it was shaking a little, and she made a fist and pressed it to the side of her leg.

"I'm fine," Solveig said. "It's just that I've learned that nothing good ever follows loud booms like that."

They stood at the window for a little while before Solveig concluded that there was nothing more to see except gyrofoils flitting across the sky and transport pods continuing their programmed routes on the streets, and she returned to her desk to continue her work as Anja left the room again with a worried expression.

Explosions and sirens, Solveig thought. *Is that going to be the background sound of our lives for years to come?*

On the executive floor, people were opening new screens above their desks to check the network feeds, but she had no desire to do the same. Whatever had happened, it was likely to mean more pointless deaths and misery, and trying to stay on top of the news in real time would just make her pointlessly anxious. She told the room to make the windows facing the executive floor opaque and returned her attention to her work, trying to ignore the distant sounds of emergency sirens reaching her ears through the Alon panels of her office windows.

Despite her repeated denials to Stefan, Solveig had concluded that she would make a good detective after all. The idea of embarking on that career path had never crossed her mind. Her father would be aghast at the prospect of his heir going into low-paid civil service, and she had no interest in the gorier aspects of the job, dealing with the aftermath of violence and picking through bloody crime scenes. But the nuts-and-bolts work of investigations, tracking data and figuring out discrepancies—that was something she enjoyed. She could bathe in data streams and connect virtual dots all day long.

"Is everything all right, Miss Solveig?" Anja asked.

Solveig moved one of her screen projections to the side to look at her assistant, who was standing in the door of her office with a concerned expression.

"I'm *fine*, Anja," she replied. "Why do you ask?"

"You have not called for food or tea all day. Are you not feeling well?"

Solveig glanced over at the windows to see that the daylight had begun to fade. She checked the time and saw that it was late afternoon. She had been in her office sifting through data screens all day without stopping to eat ever since the disruption and excitement this morning. Despite her best efforts, she hadn't been able to shield herself from the news of the day because everyone else in the office was preoccupied with it. A shuttle had blown up just after takeoff from the spaceport, and the police and Alliance military were all over the city to pick up wreckage and retrieve the bodies of the accident victims. It was terrible business, but she knew there was nothing she could do about it, no way to help make the situation better except by staying out of the way.

"I guess I got a little too caught up in my work," she said. "I'll make up for it at dinner, don't worry."

"Yes, Miss Solveig." Anja turned and walked away. Solveig moved her displaced screen back to its original position and looked at the data pages fanned out in front of her to get her head back into the material.

The tables and charts she had been studying all day were financial transaction records, her favorite subject when it came to forensic analysis. *People lie but numbers never do,* one of her business economics professors had told her once. After a little while out in the real world, she would qualify that statement a little: people lied, and they often lied *with* numbers, but when it came to finances, there was no way to cover up a truth or keep a lie going forever. She could reconstruct someone's entire existence just from the flow of money through their ledger, trace their movements by their daily transactions, learn their likes and preferences, their hobbies and their dirty little secrets. The lives of business entities were no different, just more complex and harder to unravel. But once she had access to the financial life of a person or a company, she had the tools to know more about them than even their spouses or closest partners did, maybe even know them better than they knew themselves.

From the numbers in front of her, she knew that something was not quite right, but it had taken her all day to figure out what had triggered her instincts.

Like any large corporation, Ragnar had dozens of subsidiaries. Some were parts suppliers or service providers, some merely paper companies established as legal entities for tax or trust purposes. Corporate bookkeeping was a complex shell game, and the university classes she had taken were not nearly in depth enough for Solveig to peel back every layer of the immense legal construct that was Ragnar Industries. There were, however, some things that did not require an advanced legal degree to analyze. Every company needed to pay bills and account for the expenditures, and that money flow could be plotted on trend lines and tracked. Ragnar's numbers were not quite adding up. The aggregate energy use across all facilities was within the average margin for a company of its size and composition, but the energy bills for some of the subsidiaries were not. There were several who used more power than they should. It wasn't a large amount per facility, just a few percent above the reference range, but it was consistent over time, with no seasonal fluctuations. And as small as the individual amounts were, they added up to a nontrivial pile of ags when Solveig combined all the statistical overages.

Someone was overprovisioning energy for half a dozen Ragnar facilities. When she went back in time through the records, Solveig saw that it wasn't a recent divergence. Whatever was going on had been happening for years, all the way back to the end of the war. A month or two of anomalous energy use were statistical blips. Six years of it was not just a trend; it was a system.

Solveig looked up the facilities in question. All were smaller subsidiaries, manufacturing plants mostly scattered all over the continent. Only one was in Sandvik, a company training center out in one of the commercial zones that surrounded the spaceport. She magnified the street-level image of the building. It looked unremarkable, an anonymous corporate office like hundreds of others in that part of the city.

Why does a training facility need as much power as a small factory? Solveig wondered. *What are they teaching in there, fusion reactor maintenance?*

She flicked the location data over to her comtab. A quick glance at the device told her that it was close to the end of business for the office day. Now that Anja had pointed out she hadn't eaten anything since breakfast, the thought of a bowl of stir-fry from Savory Row suddenly had an almost indecent appeal. Solveig opened a comtab screen and sent a comms request to Stefan.

"Gretian Police, Overworked Junior Detective Division," he said when he answered, and she smiled. His tousled hair and green eyes were a welcome sight, but his lips had reached a new level of appeal now that she knew what they felt like on hers.

"You're the first good thing happening to me today," he said. "Did you hear the news?"

"They say there was an accident at the spaceport," Solveig replied. "What happened?"

"One of the transports exploded. We've been out there all day to secure intersections and collect evidence. I just got back in a little while ago."

"That's terrible. I'm sorry."

"That's what I do," Stefan said. "Police detectives never get called out for pleasant business."

"I feel awful now. I was going to ask if you're free for dinner, but it sounds like you have your hands full."

"The evening shift just relieved us. To be perfectly honest, I could use a pleasant distraction right now. I'd love to meet up for dinner. As long as we talk about anything but work."

"I can handle that," Solveig said with a smile.

"It may take me a little while to get out of here. Everyone leaves the Green Zone at once at 1700. There's always a wait at the security checkpoint. And they still have a bunch of intersections closed to pod traffic right now."

"I'll give you a head start," she said. "Let me know when you clear security, and I'll leave here once you're out of there."

"If you're sure you want to wait for me."

"Of *course* I'm sure. See if you can cut in line at the checkpoint, though. I haven't had anything to eat since breakfast. And I honestly don't remember if I even *had* breakfast."

"So it's a life-or-death emergency," Stefan said with a smile. "You should have led with that. Now I can use a patrol pod and turn off the speed limiter. The usual place?"

"The usual place," she confirmed.

"See you there shortly," Stefan said. "I am looking forward to it."

He ended the connection, and Solveig smiled at the spot where the screen projection with his face had floated above her comtab just a second ago.

The little restaurant that was their go-to dinner spot was packed at this hour, but Solveig didn't mind the crowd even if they had to share their table with a pair of strangers. The anonymity afforded by the crowd felt comforting, and whenever she was out with Stefan like this, she felt like a normal person for a little while, not a coddled asset. If there were Ragnar security people tailing her, they were keeping their distance, and that was fine with her. As usual, the time dilation she experienced whenever she was with Stefan was in full effect, and she only realized they had spent over an hour eating and talking when he checked an incoming message on his comtab, and she saw the current time in the corner of the little screen projection.

"Do you have to be somewhere?" she asked. "I thought the evening shift relieved you."

Stefan shook his head. "Just a scheduling change for the weekend. I am the chump who can be counted on to trade shifts on short notice whenever someone has family business popping up."

"You're not a chump for that. You're a good colleague."

He shrugged, but his little smile told her that he was pleased with her assessment. "It's never a sacrifice for me, really. A shift is a shift. I don't have a spouse or kids waiting at home like most of the older detectives."

He looked at the plates on their table, which were thoroughly picked clean.

"I guess we need to bow to the inevitable and give them their table space back. I think we've gotten a few cranky looks from the serving counter already. Do you want to go for a drink?"

"I would love to," Solveig replied. "But I have a business errand to run this evening."

"Oh, really?" Stefan put his comtab away. "What's the errand? Unless that's a corporate secret."

"Nothing dramatic. I am running an audit at work, and there are a few things I need to check to make sure I'm not chasing ghosts. I need to stop by one of our facilities for a quick look around, that's all."

"Do you want some company? I could come along if you'd like. If there's a roadblock because of that crash, I can get us through."

"I'm sure you have far better things to do with your time," Solveig said.

"Not at all. I was just going to go home to my sad little rental capsule and have a solitary beer before bed. Where is this facility?"

Solveig pulled out her own comtab and looked at the location data she had sent herself earlier.

"Thirteenth District," she read off the screen and showed him the address.

"Then I should absolutely come with you. That's in the middle of the business zone. It's not a place to take evening walks all alone."

"You don't have to do that. I can handle myself," Solveig said.

"I know you can. But I'd feel better if you'd let me join you. Otherwise, I'll just spend the whole evening drowning my anxiety."

"Well," she said, "I can't have that on my conscience. But I must warn you. It's most likely going to be a very boring visit."

Stefan stood up and collected their trays.

"I'm *never* bored when I'm around you," he said and turned to bring the trays to the collection rack, and Solveig felt the warmth of a blush on her cheeks.

The spaceport was surrounded by commercial areas, businesses that catered to the operation of the orbital shuttles or the distribution of the cargo that moved through the place every day. Solveig didn't know what it looked like here in the daylight, but after hours, the streets in the commercial zone were eerily empty, devoid of people or surface pods. It was easy to imagine they were all alone in the city somehow, and only the occasional engine roar of shuttles taking off from the spaceport contradicted the illusion.

"Here we are," Stefan said when the pod came to a halt. He leaned forward to get a better look of their surroundings. "Is this it?"

Solveig compared the building in front of them with the image she had pulled from the database at work earlier.

"Yeah, this is it. Vegvisir Consulting."

They got out of the pod and stood in front of the building for a few moments to look at it. Nothing about its nondescript and sterile exterior gave any indication of the sort of business that was operating inside. There wasn't even a sign on the facade that told the name of the company. When Solveig pointed out that fact to Stefan, he looked at her and smiled.

"So inconspicuous that it stands out," he said. She smiled at hearing her own words from the other day repeated back to her.

The front doors were locked, the atrium behind them bathed in darkness. Stefan slowly paced behind her as she tried to make out more details through the glass.

"Are you *sure* this belongs to your company?" he asked. "Because it'll be very awkward if my colleagues from the patrol division show up and I have to explain what we're doing."

There was a security pad at the door, and Solveig walked up to it. On a hunch, she took out her company ID and tapped it against the pad, then placed the tips of her fingers on the biometric field. The little light on the pad turned from blinking red to a solid green, and the locking bolts of the door unlatched with a soft whirring sound. She pushed the door open with her palm and looked back at Stefan.

"Director-level access," she said. "Looks like it works on all the doors on the company network."

"That's a relief." Stefan looked up and down the street. "I still feel like we are breaking and entering."

They walked inside and let the door close behind them. The atrium was as generic as the outside of the building. There was bland artwork on the walls and a row of chairs lined up in a waiting area surrounded by tall plants in pots. A large reception counter stood directly across from the entrance, jutting into the atrium space like the bridge of a ship.

"Computer, turn on the lights," she said into the silence. A second later, the lighting in the atrium came on. The air had a stale sort of quality to it, and when she stepped closer to one of the synthetic plants by the waiting area, she saw that the leaves were coated in a thin layer of dust. To her left, Stefan walked over to the front desk and ran a finger across the top.

"I don't think anyone has used this place in quite a while," he said.

The data screen emitters behind the reception counter responded to Stefan's touch and brought up the standard Ragnar Industries network-authentication screen. Solveig turned the projectors off and looked around behind the desk. There was no sign that anyone had been sitting at this station recently—no family pictures or funny motivational sayings, no coffee rings on the table, no reminders or directives stuck to the low wall below the countertop. She turned around and walked down the hallway behind the front desk. There were offices on either side, all with empty desks and dusty chairs surrounded by bare walls. At the end of the hallway, a conference room stood open, two dozen high-backed chairs lined up around a desk that was large enough to serve as a gyrofoil landing pad. Everything she saw was in perfect working order, but there was no sign anyone had been in this office recently.

"Found the kitchen," Stefan said in the hallway behind her. She followed him through one of the side doors into a kitchen nook that had a row of beverage dispensers lined up along the back wall and racks of cups on another. He went to the dispensers and reached behind one of them. A few seconds of turning and pushing later, he pulled out a slender metal cylinder and held it up to look at it under the light from the ceiling strip.

"What's that?" Solveig asked.

"It's what goes for coffee in most large offices," he said. "Concentrate for the dispenser. It gets mixed with water, and the machine heats the mix and spits it out."

He showed her the bottom of the cylinder, which had a numeric code stamped on it.

"We have the same brand in our canteen. Had the same brand," he corrected himself. "Police detectives drink a lot of coffee. One of these will last us maybe two weeks. This one is over four years old."

"You are a detective," Solveig said. She took the cylinder from him and flipped it around in her hand. "Could there be a good reason why that dispenser has a really old coffee-syrup cartridge in it?"

"Could be they got a great deal on a huge lot of that stuff, and they still have a bunch of it in their supply closet. Or maybe there's just one person in the whole building who drinks coffee, and only one cup every other Monday. But looking at the rest of the place? I would bet that nobody has had coffee from that dispenser in a long time."

Solveig nodded slowly and nibbled on her lower lip.

This is one of our corporate assets, and it looks like it has been standing empty for years. And yet it's still on the network and getting provisioned with power. A lot *of power.*

"Let's go and see what's down in the basement," she said to Stefan.

The smell of stagnant water hit Solveig's nose the moment she opened the door to the basement level. The musty scent of slow decay was present down here as well, stronger than on the main floor, but it was overpowered by the wet, moldy odor coming from the open space at the end of the hallway. The first room they passed was a locker room, followed by another. The next room beyond was a health center, equipped with rows of exercise machines and weight racks. The space at the end of the hallway was a mirror image of the atrium directly above in size and layout. It contained a swimming pool that was still full of water. A layer of green scum covered most of the surface, and big blotches of black mold marred the walls of the pool room. Moisture was dripping from the ceiling and running down the mold-covered walls, leaving long black streaks that looked like the walls were weeping.

Stefan squatted by the edge of the pool and stuck two fingers through the green algae layer and into the water.

"It's warm," he said. "Body temperature. No wonder it's a fungal biotope down here."

"It's still heated?"

"Yeah. Kind of wasteful, isn't it?"

Solveig did a rough visual measure of the pool's dimensions. *Twelve meters by six meters, make it two meters deep; 144 cubic meters, that's 144,000 liters. Constantly kept at thirty-seven degrees for five years. That would certainly explain some of the power drain.*

"We shouldn't spend too much time down here," Stefan said. He stood up and wiped his fingers on his trousers. "All this mold is a health hazard. You don't want to breathe in too much of it."

Could it be that simple? Solveig thought. *Someone forgot to turn off the pool heaters, and we've been spending a small fortune every year for half a decade just to keep a hundred and forty thousand liters of algae stew warm?*

She looked over her shoulder at the scum-covered pool surface as they walked back into the hallway to leave. There was no movement on the surface of the water, and the layer of algae looked like a dirty green carpet. It felt like a letdown to have the mystery come to such a neat and easy solution. But as she followed Stefan to the stairwell, her brain was crunching data—rough cost of energy per kilowatt, multiplied by pool volume and time—and she knew that the numbers didn't add up even before they were back in the atrium upstairs. They explained some of the power drain, and certainly the consistent nature of it, but they couldn't come close to accounting for the total amount Ragnar had paid out over the years.

Besides, she thought as she walked out of the building and climbed back into the surface pod with Stefan, *that's just one out of six locations. What are the chances all the other ones have a forgotten pool in the basement as well?*

Chapter 17

Aden

It felt strangely comfortable to see that despite four years of war and half a decade of occupation, the Gretian bureaucracy had remained a steadfast and unmoving boulder in the stream of change that had swept away so much of the old ways. Aden had arrived at the registry office in Civic Square at nine o'clock, right at the start of their official business hours, and it had taken a long wait in a short line to turn in his temporary Rhodian ID pass and get a Gretian one. Now he was in a different office in the building, waiting for his turn to have the mandatory talk with a veteran-benefits caseworker. To his surprise, he was called in almost as soon as he had sat down in the waiting area.

"Good morning," the worker greeted him when he walked into the office. "Have a seat, please."

"Good morning," Aden replied. There was no name tag on the door or the desk, and the caseworker hadn't offered it, so Aden left it at that and sat down as directed. The other man turned toward the open screen projection on his desk, where Aden saw his own face looking back at him, the official picture from his long-gone military ID that was many years out of date.

"I thought I'd seen the last of the returnees," the worker said. "You're lucky. A few months ago, the crowd was wall to wall out there."

"I couldn't make it any earlier," Aden replied.

"Well, welcome home. I'm sure you're glad to be back." The words didn't carry any trace of genuine interest or concern, and Aden merely nodded in reply. The other man was balding and heavyset, and he looked like he was close to retirement and very much looking forward to it.

"Robertson, Aden," he read off his screen. "Former branch of service, Blackguard Corps. Rank at demobilization, major."

"That is correct," Aden confirmed.

"As a former member of the armed forces, you are entitled to returnee benefits. These include housing assistance, a transitional stipend, and medical care. Do you choose to claim these benefits?"

"I do," Aden said.

"Very well. Your stipend will be transferred to your ledger within twenty-four hours. This is a one-time payment to help you with your transition to civilian life. Be advised that this will be your only direct financial assistance. Do you have a place to stay yet?"

Aden shook his head.

"I slept at a friend's house last night after I got in. But I don't have anything permanent yet."

"I can get you a spot in a transitional housing unit for veterans. That will give you a place to acclimate while you get settled. It won't cost you anything, but there's a residency limit of twelve months."

After all the time he had spent in a communal living setting with other soldiers, Aden would much rather spend his own money on a mediocre rental than live rent free in yet another version of military housing. But his preferences had to take a back seat to the mission, and his task was to stay as close to his fellow veterans as possible. Once the job was done, he would be able to choose his true preference again, which was his cramped little berth on *Zephyr*'s bottom crew deck.

"Having a place to stay for now would be very helpful," Aden said. "Thank you."

The caseworker shrugged.

"They're your benefits. You might as well use them while you can. The gods know you earned them."

He typed up something on his input field and flicked it over to Aden, whose comtab chimed a confirmation in reply.

"Those are your directions and access credentials. I've assigned you a unit, but you can probably change it if you don't like the view or something. They're less than half-full at this point. If you have any more questions, just ask one of the staff. They have resident advisors to help you."

Aden knew what an implied dismissal felt like. He got out of his chair and nodded curtly.

"Thank you for your help."

"Of course," the other man replied, his attention focused on his screen again. Their business had obviously concluded. Aden walked out of the office, feeling irritated and amused in equal measure at the unconcealed bored disinterest of the government bureaucrat.

This could have been a thirty-second session at one of the service kiosks in the lobby, he thought as the door closed behind him on the way out.

The transitional housing unit wasn't as bad as Aden had anticipated. It was a generic-looking apartment tower on a quiet side street between the old city and the business district. From the location and the way the lobby was decorated—pots of synthetic plants and generic art on the walls—Aden guessed that it had been a corporate residential facility before the government had bought or requisitioned it for veteran housing, and he was darkly amused at the thought that it may well have been a Ragnar property. As he crossed the lobby on the way to the skylift bank, a small group of men sitting in a lounging corner shot him some curious glances, and he gave them a curt nod before he stepped onto the skylift platform.

The apartment was unadorned to the point of looking sterile, but it was clean, and the view from the living-space windows showed a slice of the financial district's skyline. The bathroom and kitchen nook were small but functional. Aden was pleased to find that the apartment was furnished and equipped with the basics, dishes in the cabinets and hygiene products in the bathroom. He unpacked his bag and put his few possessions away. There was a beverage dispenser with a small variety of instant capsules in the kitchen. He made himself a cup of coffee and sat down in the living room with it. The screen on the wall was already synchronized with the comtab in his pocket, and he looked at his comms queue, which was empty except for the stub left behind by his brief call with Bryn yesterday. Nothing had happened between them last night—they'd eaten dinner and talked for a few hours before she had retired to her bedroom, and he'd made himself comfortable on the lounging corner in the living room—but he still felt a little pang of guilt when he thought of Tess. *Zephyr*'s engineer had made it clear that they were merely crewmates with benefits for now, but if there was the potential for them to become something more, the budding attraction he felt for Bryn could put an end to that.

For the hundredth time since the Rhodians had let him loose with a comtab in his pocket, he thought about finding a stealthy way to send a message to her somehow, just to let her know that he was all right. But as strong as the temptation was, the thought of the *Zephyr* crew imprisoned or dead extinguished it quickly. The Rhodians had never explicitly stated that his friends were on probation as well, but it had been strongly implied, and Aden was certain that even something as innocuous as looking up *Zephyr*'s current location on the Mnemosyne would raise an eyebrow of whoever was currently monitoring his com tab. The door of this apartment wasn't locked for him, and he could leave anytime he wanted, but he'd always have someone watching over his shoulder, tracking his movement and monitoring his company.

I'm still in a cage, he thought. *I just carry it around with me now.*

The screen on the living room wall slowly cycled through various pages of information, presented against a soothing background of scattered clouds in a blue sky that looked nothing like the one he could see out of the window when he turned his head. Most of the news headlines held no interest for him, referencing people and events he didn't know. There was a personalized service page where he could request appointments for health care and employment counseling, and he reserved slots for both later in the week. When his coffee cup was empty, he carried it into the kitchen nook and rinsed it, then looked for the zero-g cup rack out of habit. There was none, of course—the designers of this unit hadn't made any provisions for the possibility of the building experiencing high-g maneuvers—and he returned the cup to the cupboard above the sink.

Back in the living room, Aden brought up his comms queue on the screen again and selected the only entry in it to send out a connection request. A few moments later, Bryn's face appeared on the screen.

"Hello," she said. "I didn't hear you leave this morning."

"I did not want to impose any further," Aden replied.

"Nonsense. You didn't impose at all. I had a pleasant time last night. I could have made breakfast to pay you back for the dinner, you know."

Aden made a pained face. "My ability to read social cues has really atrophied in detention, hasn't it?"

She shrugged with a smile.

"It'll come back to you. With some practice."

"Gods, I hope so. Five years away, and it almost feels like I am here for the first time."

"I felt the same way at first. And I was only gone for three years. But don't worry, it'll pass."

She peered past him and looked at his surroundings.

"I see they got you a place at the THU already. That was quick. I was expecting you'd have to stay at my place for a few more nights. It took them a week and a half to get me a unit when I came home."

"It'll do for now," Aden said. "But it feels an awful lot like the place I just left. Just without the stasis field at the door. I've been here for half an hour and I'm already bored."

Bryn chuckled softly.

"You just got in, you have some transition assistance on your ledger, and you have a private place for now. I seem to remember that most of us went out and got hammered for a week straight."

"Well, you got home with a bunch of people you know. I'm a lone straggler. And getting drunk by myself isn't really my thing."

She looked at him in thought for a moment.

"There's this thing I have to do today," she said. "If you're looking for some company, you could tag along. Can't promise anything, but it'll almost certainly be more exciting than sitting in that unit by yourself and watching the networks."

"What kind of *thing*?" Aden asked.

"It's a sort of community service," she said with a little smile that told Aden her categorization was probably facetious. "They're always looking for more people. And there's pay in it. Five hundred ags for the evening."

"It is not something that'll get me thrown into lockup again, is it?"

Bryn's smile got a little wider, and there was a sparkle of mischief in her eyes.

"I won't tell you the odds of that happening are zero. But what's a fun evening without the chance of arrest?"

Aden laughed.

"You see, there it is again. I think you're joking but I'm afraid you're not."

"I am joking. Mostly. But there's nothing illegal about it. There's a political rally out in Vigard this evening. The people who run it like to have veterans around. For security, in case the reefos try to disrupt it. And they will."

"Is that what you and the others were doing on Civic Square yesterday?" Aden asked.

Bryn shook her head.

"We were just there for numbers. Sandvik is full of police and Alliance troops. They don't like it when one side or the other shows up with their own security. Vigard's a different story. There's no Alliance base there. And they're doing the rally at the university. That's reefo turf. Full of overeducated kids who think they know everything."

"And you think it's going to get violent?"

"We'll be there to make sure it doesn't," Bryn said. "Those uni kids don't like dissenting viewpoints. Especially not on their home turf. But they don't know shit about fighting. They'll beat their chests and make noise. But if there's a line of vets between them and the rally, that's all they'll do. We stand in formation for an hour or two and look mean. Then the rally people feed us dinner and pay us, and everyone goes home."

"That simple, huh?" Aden asked.

"Ideally. We're not going there to make trouble. It's entirely up to the locals whether there'll be any. The more of us show up, the less likely it is."

Aden looked around in the apartment while he thought about Bryn's proposal. He didn't care for the prospect of being in the middle of the sort of violence again that had him bleeding on the ground yesterday. But this was an offer that no intelligence operative in their right mind would turn down. There would be more faces and names, and maybe an opportunity to get noticed by the right people.

"Come along," Bryn nudged him. "It won't be boring. And I won't have to ride out there all by myself."

"What about the others? Lars and Helge?"

"Lars is working tonight, and Helge is out of town. Come on. It'll be nice to have company. And I can introduce you to some more old comrades."

She gave him an encouraging smile. On the large screen, her light-blue eyes had an almost hypnotic quality to them.

If this really is a honey trap, I am about to stick myself to it with both hands, Aden thought.

"All right," he said. "I'll come along."

Bryn's smile widened. It looked like someone had bumped up the brightness of the screen by a few percent.

"That's the spirit," she said. "Be over at my place by ten hundred. We'll take a surface pod from here."

"Ten hundred," Aden confirmed. "I'll see you then."

"Oh, and just in case—wear something that won't get ruined if it gets some blood on it."

When Aden got to her place at 0955 hours, Bryn was already waiting outside. She was wearing a loose-fitting utilitarian outfit that looked like she was about to go on a nature hike, slate-colored baggy pants with what looked like a dozen pockets, and a weatherproof pullover jacket with a hood.

"Well," she said when he walked up to her. "At least you aren't wearing any Blackguard gear. But you're almost certainly going to be the most stylish person at that rally."

Aden shrugged. "I only have what I bought yesterday. I threw the jumpsuit out while I was still in the store. Don't care to ever wear one of those again."

On the street in front of them, a transport pod came rolling up. It stopped at the edge of the solar roadway and opened its side door.

"There's our ride," Bryn said. She got into the pod and dropped into one of the seats, which were arranged in two pairs that faced each other. Aden followed and sat down diagonally across from her. The door closed silently, and the pod set itself in motion again. A screen projection appeared between them, showing a map of their intended route and their time of arrival. Bryn dismissed it with a flick of her wrist.

"It's an hour and a half by pod," she said. "Vactrain would have gotten us there in ten minutes, but that one hasn't run since the end of the war. They keep talking about bringing it back online. I think it'll take another five years."

"What happened to it?" Aden asked.

"They had to shut it down when the navy blew up the energy relays at Hades. Most of the power to run the loop came from that link. And when the war was over, the Hadeans didn't renew the contract. They offered a new one, at triple the old rate. Even if we fixed all the damage, it's too expensive to run now, until the Hadeans come down on their rates. But they are holding a bit of a grudge."

"Just like the rest of the system," Aden said.

"Everyone is happy to finally have us over a barrel. Including Hades. They rebuilt those relays in six months. Now they want to make us pay for them for another ten years. But hey—the victors set the terms, right? They're the ones who get to write history. We would have done the same if we had won."

There was a small coldbox between the two seats of the front row, and Bryn leaned forward to open it. She took out a bottle and looked up at him.

"Want one, too?"

She handed him the bottle she had just retrieved and reached for another one. He took it and looked at the label to see that it was wheat beer.

"Are you sure it's a good idea to tie one on before we get there?"

"It's just one drink. Relax and enjoy it. It's ninety minutes to Vigard. I'd order you to loosen up a little, but unfortunately you outrank me."

Aden twisted the top of the bottle and watched the foam bubbling up through the neck. Before he joined *Zephyr*'s crew, he hadn't had any alcohol in five years, but Tristan had made sure to see him make up for lost time in the six months he was crisscrossing the system with his new friends. However, the version of him sitting in this pod right now was fresh off the shuttle after half a decade of enforced abstinence, so he made a proper show of taking his first sip and making appreciative noises.

"That's better," Bryn said and took a swig from her own bottle. "I think you're the first field-grade officer who has ever taken direction from me."

"I was barely field grade when the war was over," Aden said. "I got promoted to major three months before the war ended. I just had enough time in rank to get my dress smock back from the supply group with the new shoulder boards."

Bryn flashed a knowing smile. "Ah, the supply group. I know more than one private third class who got promoted to second class and asked for first-class bars when they turned their smock in for alteration because they knew it'd never get back to them before the next promotion in six months."

They both chuckled. Bryn looked out of the side window, where the city was gliding past at fifty kilometers per hour.

"All the nonsense and the little grievances. And still, I'd go back to it in a second if I could," she said. "The Alliance did a lot of dumb things when they took over. But the dumbest was to dissolve the military and put us all out on the streets. All these years we put in, and nothing to show for it. They fired tens of thousands of people who know how to fight, and now they're surprised there's a resistance movement. Dumb fucks."

"The reefos," Aden said. "The reformers. What is their grievance?"

"You mean what *isn't* their grievance." Bryn rolled her eyes a little. "They want to do away with whatever was before. No more High Council. Disown all the plot-holder families. No more military ever again. They want to turn us into a toothless version of Oceana. Because we're all warmongers, you see. The loyalists just want the Alliance out so we can run our own planet again. Not with the old leadership in charge, mind. But there's a way to fix that problem without scuttling a thousand years of tradition."

"I am going to guess you're not a reformer," Aden said, and she huffed.

"I was in the military for twelve years. My father and grandfather both served. I'm the sixth-generation descendant of a plot holder. And those people want to make all of that meaningless. No, I don't have much sympathy for the reformers. Bunch of young shitheads with utopian ideas. None of them could run a sausage stand."

She gave him an apologetic smile.

"Sorry. That's probably more politics talk than you want to hear on your second day back."

"Hey, I asked," Aden said. "Thanks for the primer."

She raised her bottle briefly in acknowledgment.

The viewscreen on the pod's front was silently cycling through a series of network feeds, interspersed with advertising and weather reports. Something on the screen caught Bryn's eye. She leaned forward and tapped on one of the feeds to expand it.

"What the hells," she said.

Bryn turned on the audio, and the pod filled with the noises of emergency sirens and somber narration.

". . . confirmed by the authorities. Sandvik Spaceport is under a ground stop and closed to all traffic. The situation on the ground is still in flux, but police and Alliance military units have deployed in the city. Residents are advised to clear the streets and remain indoors."

The image was a wide-angle shot of Sandvik's skyline. Several columns of smoke were rising from various spots in the city. Dozens of gyrofoils were flitting around in the air above and between the high rises of the business district. For a moment, Ragnar Tower came into view when the camera of the news drone panned over Principal Square before moving on to the financial district. Something had happened in the city they had just left, and the scrolling chyron at the bottom of the screen cycled through updates that made his stomach clench.

ORBITAL SHUTTLE EXPLODES OVER SANDVIK, the first summary read. MORE THAN A HUNDRED DEAD IN WORST SHUTTLE DISASTER IN TWENTY YEARS. Another one announced: 100+ ALLIANCE SOLDIERS DIE IN SHUTTLE CRASH. SANDVIK AIRSPACE CLOSED TO ALL TRAFFIC. MILITARY DEPLOYED IN THE STREETS.

They watched the stream in silence for a few minutes until the network had run out of new footage and started looping the older material. Bryn tapped the screen again and cycled through the feeds until she had found one that showed the shuttle explosion from a distance, likely recorded on a ground-based security camera that happened to be pointed in the right direction at the time of the disaster. The doomed shuttle was rising into the clear blue sky on a plume of engine exhaust, and then it disappeared in a bright flash and a rapidly expanding cloud of vapor and debris. Aden stared at the screen projection, horrified at the sight of a hundred people getting vaporized in the blink of an eye.

"Shuttle crash," Bryn said with mocking disbelief in her voice. "Right."

"What makes you think it wasn't?" he asked.

"I was in the ordnance corps. I know what a binary propellant explosion looks like."

"You're saying someone blew up that shuttle on purpose?"

She shrugged and sat back in her seat.

"I'm not a gambler. But I'd bet a fair amount that this wasn't just an unfortunate malfunction."

Aden reached out and muted the network feed, and the cabin was quiet again except for the sound of the electric drive propelling the pod along the solar pathway to Vigard. He still had the cold bottle of beer in his hands, and he took a sip from it while he processed what he had just seen. He looked at Bryn, who flashed a tiny smile.

"Whoever did this had some good timing," she said.

"Why is that?"

She looked out at the landscape scrolling past the window of the pod.

"Every police officer and Alliance trooper in the area will be busy in Sandvik for the next few days. Nobody's going to give the slightest shit about some political rally in Vigard."

"You said you were in the ordnance corps," he said. "What unit?"

"I was an ammunition stock control supervisor—184th Ordnance Company, Eighth Marines."

Interesting, Aden thought. *An ordnance officer. One who used to have the key card to the regiment's explosives storage.*

Chapter 18

Idina

"There's another one," Dahl said in a voice that sounded like gravel sliding down a rocky slope. Ahead and to the right of the gyrofoil, a thin smoke plume was rising from a piece of wreckage on the ground. Dahl put the gyrofoil into a slow right turn and orbited the site. A sizable chunk of shuttle hull had crashed into a street in the financial district, tearing a gash into an office building on the way down and littering the roadway with debris.

"See any bodies?" Idina asked. Her own voice seemed less substantial to herself, as if she was listening to a recording of it played through lousy headphones.

"Negative," Dahl replied. "Thank the gods."

For the last hour, they had been tracking down fallen bits and pieces of the exploded shuttle that had come down all over the city. Every time they found another one, Idina marked the location and called it in to the troops on the ground, who were racing to the sites in armored vehicles to secure them and recover the fragment. Whenever they spotted bodies, she added the observed casualty count to the marker so the ground teams would prioritize those locations and retrieve their dead comrades. The shuttle had been a military charter, ferrying a company of Alliance troops into orbit for the trip home to Rhodia, 149 soldiers on the way home at the end of their deployment rotation.

One hundred forty-nine lives, Idina thought. *Every one of them someone's child, parent, sibling, friend, partner.* Hundreds of families would be grieving soon, once the dead were all collected and the identities verified and official word of the disaster sent back home. There was no doubt that everyone in the system knew about the attack already. The explosion had happened above the Gretian capital in the middle of the morning, and thousands of people had witnessed it. Some network news gyrofoils had taken their time clearing the airspace above Sandvik in the aftermath to record the event as long as possible, and Idina was sure that high-resolution footage from their camera arrays was already playing on millions of screens. The white-hot anger she had felt earlier was gone now, but nothing had taken its place, leaving her with a deep sense of emptiness.

Dahl slowed down to a hover directly above the debris impact site. The gyrofoil was close enough to the damaged office building that Idina could see people staring at them from the windows. Some of them had the telltale glow of comtab screen projections in front of their faces.

This isn't a fucking air show, Idina thought. She gestured at them through the cockpit window to cut it out, but they ignored her. On the street below, people had started to gather to get a look at the debris field.

"*This is the police,*" Dahl said on the public address system. "*Clear the area and do not approach the accident site. It is not safe.*"

She looked over at Idina and shook her head.

"Idiots. I will never understand it. What do they hope to see here?"

On the tactical screen in front of Idina, an update flashed, and she tapped on the alert to read the full message.

"Recovery team is on the way," she said. "ETA is seven minutes. Are we waiting? You know those people are going to be taking close-ups of the pieces as soon as we're gone."

"I have done my part to protect them from themselves," Dahl replied. "There are many more sites left to mark."

The gyrofoil ascended until they were above the rooftops of the nearby office buildings again, and Idina resumed her lookout as Dahl started another slow loop above the area. On Idina's screen, it looked like every armored Alliance ground vehicle on the planet was converging on Sandvik's inner city, and the sky was swarming with combat gyrofoils and police patrol craft.

An alarm started to chirp on the avionics display in front of Dahl's flight controls and a warning flashed, alternating between orange and red. Dahl reached out to silence the alert and check its source.

"The temperature in the front right rotor hub is climbing," she said. "We may have a leaking bearing cassette. See if you can spot anything from your angle."

Idina leaned forward to look at the whirring rotor on the front of the gyrofoil's starboard side. The central hub of the assembly was splattered with thin streaks of black that ran down the curve of the hub and dispersed in the fast-spinning rotor disk.

"Looks like it's bleeding lubricant," she reported.

"That would be a leaking bearing cassette."

"Fantastic. Do we need to set this thing down?"

Dahl pursed her lips as she evaluated the situation for a moment before shaking her head.

"Not yet. We are above normal but it is not in the critical range yet. But we need to head back to base on the shortest route." She brought the craft around in a gentle left-hand turn.

"Well, shit," Idina said. "A hundred patrols without so much as a loose bolt. And our first failure comes in the middle of a major emergency."

"If you do not count that one time we crashed," Dahl said.

"That doesn't count. The gyro was fine right until the whole damn hotel exploded underneath it."

"All police air units, this is the Sector One patrol supervisor. I am returning to base with a technical defect," Dahl announced on the police guard channel. "As of this moment, Heimdall 91 is in command of all Sector One patrols."

"Sector One, Heimdall 91. I have command," the officer in the promoted craft acknowledged.

Dahl cut the comms and let out a sigh that sounded distinctly irritated.

"We may be able to get a new craft and resume the patrol," she said. "But there may not be any left on the ground. I think everything we have is up here already."

The sky above Sandvik was swarming with combat gyrofoils and police patrol craft now. It looked like they were in the middle of a large-scale airborne assault exercise. Idina watched an Alliance military gyro come to a hover above a nearby intersection and a squad of troops rappelling down to street level from the open tail ramp of the craft. Between the guns and missiles on the gyrofoil and the weapons in the hands of the troops, that squad of infantry had enough combat power to level an entire city block and kill everyone in it, but there was nothing for all that strength to go up against, just wreckage to collect and bodies to recover.

The insurgency could win, Idina thought. *All they need to do is to keep bleeding us like this. Hit us again and again, until enough people back home decide they've spent enough money on nothing but flag-draped burial capsules in return.*

On the landing pad back at the base, a Palladian trooper in battle armor was waiting for them. As he trotted across the pad toward the police gyrofoil, Idina recognized Sergeant Ansari. She unlatched her harness and climbed out of the cockpit to meet him.

"Colors Chaudhary," he said when he reached her. "Captain Shaw needs you at the aviation section right away. He sent me to get you. Only you," he added with a quick glance at Dahl.

Idina exchanged brief goodbyes with Dahl and followed Ansari to a waiting utility transport. A minute later, they were speeding down the central base artery toward the military airfield.

A combat gyrofoil was waiting for them on the apron, its engines running and position lights flashing. Ansari pulled up right in front of the open tail ramp, where Captain Shaw was standing with another trooper. The wolf hunter team was already in the cargo hold, all wearing battle armor. Shaw waved her over when she got out of the transport, and she followed him up the ramp.

"What's going on, sir?" she shouted against the din of the engines.

"When we're in the air," he said.

"I don't have my combat gear."

"Get some hardshell and a rifle out of the ship armory once we're at altitude," he said. "You'll have plenty of time to get suited up on the way."

She claimed one of the jump seats and strapped herself in. The tail ramp rose and locked into place, and the noise from the engines turned into a muffled droning. Then they were in the air and climbing into the blue sky at full throttle. Once they had transitioned to level flight at their cruising altitude, Captain Shaw unlatched his harness and got out of his seat. From the way her teammates were looking at him, Idina could tell that none of them had any idea where they were going either.

"Settle in and relax," he told the team. "Take a nap if you can. We'll be in the air for a few hours."

"Going where, sir?" Idina asked.

"The frozen ass end of this planet," he replied. "That big ice sheet they call the northern continent."

"What in the hells are we doing up there, sir?" Sergeant Shah asked.

"We're going to get an idea of the level of shit we're in. The shuttle that blew up this morning wasn't the main event. While we were all mobilized and committed, someone raided the penal colony on the northern continent. All those insurgents the Gretians moved up there in the last year or so? They've all been freed. Every last one of them."

There were muttered exclamations of anger and disbelief among the team.

"How the *fuck* did they manage that?" Sergeant Ansari demanded. "What were those fucking Gretians doing? Sitting on their hands?"

"The QRF got there an hour ago. They're still sorting out the mess. But it looks like the bad guys came in with multiple gyrofoils in police livery, with valid transponder IDs. Each with an assault squad in the back. Heavy weapons, breaching hardware, the whole arsenal."

"Shit," Shah said in a low voice, drawing the word out into three syllables.

"The Gretian police have moles on their force," Idina said. "We've known that for certain since the HQ bombing at least."

"That's why this is top secret for now. Not a word to anyone who isn't on this ship right now. They're trying to keep a lid on the whole thing," Captain Shaw continued. "That's supposed to be the most secure facility on the planet outside of the Green Zone. And the insurgents just rolled in with a whole flight of gyros with real credentials and shot the place to shit. If word of that gets around, nobody's going to trust any police uniform anymore."

"What are we going to do up there?" Sergeant Shah asked.

"We are going to get a picture of the situation on the ground. If they left any guards alive, we're going to interrogate them. Before the Gretians or our own intel people can show up and piss in the stew."

—

The Gretian high-security prison stood on a peninsula on the northern shore of the continent, at the end of a long stretch of barren landscape that didn't have a scrap of vegetation growing on it. When they descended for their final approach, Idina looked out of the windows of the gyrofoil and imagined being a prisoner trying to escape across this inhospitable wasteland, hundreds of square kilometers of gravel flats and lava fields that offered no shelter, concealment, or sustenance. The sky seemed to blend with the horizon in the distance, gray flowing into gray. Once someone got out of sight of the penal colony, they'd have no landmarks or terrain features to use for navigation. Anyone trying to make it south across the continent would get hopelessly lost and then freeze to death or starve within days. It was the perfect location for a prison, both physically and psychologically.

The penal facility was a cluster of low concrete buildings arranged in a star shape around a central hub, a large five-sided tower that was twice as tall as the structures around it. On the roof of the tower, Idina saw the remnants of an air-defense battery and its sensor cluster, demolished by heavy weapons fire. The wreckage of the battery was still smoldering, sending up a thin plume of black smoke that swirled around in the downwash from the gyrofoil's rotors as they passed directly overhead.

The Quick Reaction Force had set up operations in the cargo hold of their combat gyrofoil on the facility's landing pad. Several of the QRF troopers were nearby, watching Idina's craft as it approached to land, and she saw that two of them had portable air-defense missile launchers ready on their shoulders.

The new QRF commander was an Oceanian captain named Niel who had the size and build of a small armored vehicle. He greeted Idina and Captain Shaw with firm handshakes and led them over to the back of the QRF gyrofoil. Hardwire links snaked down the tail ramp and across the concrete to a nearby mobile antenna cluster.

"They fried all the comms before they left," Captain Niel explained. "Literally. Tossed thermal charges into the network room and turned all the gear into slag."

"These people really got caught with their pants down," Idina said. "Did they even put up a fight?"

Niel shook his head. "No casualties. On either side."

"Amazing." She shook her head in disgust.

"Don't be too hard on them. This wasn't a prison break. It was an airborne assault. And they had nothing to fight with anyway. Someone locked down the armory."

"They had inside help," Captain Shaw said. "That's just fucking wonderful."

"This was absolutely an inside job. They were in and out in under ten minutes. Whoever locked the armory also opened the security doors from the landing pad all the way to the central control room."

"Yeah, I wouldn't have fought back either," Shaw replied. "That's a hopeless scenario. At least we won't need to clean up a massacre. Small blessings on a shit day like this."

They went up into the prison complex with Captain Niel. The interior of the place was as gray and depressing as the outside and the landscape around the facility. The imprisoned insurgents had been held in their own section, and all the units in the block stood open now. Idina stepped into one of the cells to look around. It was a concrete box, maybe six meters by two, and almost everything in it was made from concrete as well—a desk, an immovable chair, and a bed. In the corner, there was a toilet and a small stainless sink the size of a soup bowl. She imagined being locked in here for any length of time, looking out at a gray sky through a window slit barely wider than the span of her hand, and it almost made her feel pity for the insurgents they had sent here over the last few months. After only thirty seconds in the cell, she already felt like the walls were closer together than they had been when she walked in.

It would be kinder to just shoot them outright, she thought. *I know I'd prefer a quick bullet over slowly going insane in here.*

The control room in the center of the prison was as quiet as the empty cells in the insurgent wing. Without a functional network, all the screens in the room were blank. Someone in a Gretian uniform sat at one of the consoles, flanked by armored QRF troopers. There was an acrid, chemical smell in the air from the fire suppressant that had doused the network room nearby.

"This is the supervisor," Niel said. "We've separated the rest of the staff and put them in empty cells for now."

"What's your name?" Idina asked the Gretian.

"Karst," he replied. "Captain Karst, Corrections Service. I am in charge here."

Captain Shaw chuckled without humor. "From where I am standing, I'm going to have to disagree with that assessment."

"How many prisoners just walked out of here?" Idina asked.

"Seventy-nine," Karst said. "They also took three of my staff."

"Seventy-nine," Shaw repeated. "That's two platoons of insurgents back in circulation. After we busted our asses for months to get them off the streets one by one."

"I wish that was not so, believe me. I am in charge here, and that makes me responsible. If I can help in any way, I will."

"You can start by telling me everything that just happened," Idina told him. "And every detail you can remember. What they looked like. How they communicated. What kind of weapons they had. Whether you recognized anyone, or someone else did. Leave out nothing. Even if you think the detail isn't important."

She pulled up one of the nearby empty chairs and sat down on it. The sheath of her kukri clacked against the backrest, and she adjusted it to get it out of the way.

"Begin," she said. "And maybe we can salvage something from the massive garbage fire that is this day."

When they were finished, the team gathered at the gyrofoil for the ride home. Two more craft had arrived on the landing pad. One was a Gretian police transport full of people wearing Corrections Service uniforms and dark expressions. The other, smaller craft was unmarked, and the few passengers were in civilian clothing and even more dour-looking than the first group.

"That warden is going to be scrubbing prison toilets with a toothbrush for the rest of his career," Captain Shaw said as they watched the civilians walk toward the building with grim purpose.

"If he's lucky," Idina replied. "They'll work him over for a while to find out if he's a mole."

"What do you think?"

"He was forthcoming. And it didn't feel like he was lying about anything. But who the hell knows? His own people know his pressure points better than we do," she said.

"As far as I am concerned, every one of them is a collaborator until proven otherwise," Shaw said.

Idina thought of Dahl. The idea that her Gretian patrol partner could be a secret insurgent was ludicrous to her. But they had been a team for almost a year now, built mutual trust through shared danger, and they'd had time to figure each other out. If she had just freshly arrived from Pallas for a deployment amid all this, Idina knew that she wouldn't trust any Gretian, not even Dahl.

It was only midafternoon, but they were so far north on the planet that the sun was already setting on the western horizon. The wind had picked up, a steady cold breeze that bit into her cheeks and fingertips. As she walked up the ramp of the gyrofoil, a few snowflakes drifted past her, the first of the season. She caught one on the back of her hand and watched as the crystalline filigree melted into a tiny drop of water. The engines of the gyrofoil came to life with a low whine that quickly turned into the steady whooshing roar of spinning rotors.

"Seventy-nine," Sergeant Ansari said when she strapped in next to him. "Six months of work down the shitter. What are we going to do now, Colors?"

Idina latched the buckle of her harness and stuck her fingers between her thighs to warm them up. To her left, the tail ramp slowly rose, narrowing her view of the distant sunset gradually until the ramp locked into place and the golden light inside the cargo hold was snuffed out.

"We are going to get back to work, Ansari. Our target pool just refilled itself. And I'll be damned if I turn any of those people over to the Gretians again."

CHAPTER 19

DUNSTAN

It was a deeply unnatural act to be flying in close formation with an enemy warship. Even the knowledge that its crew was dead and its shipboard systems under the control of *Hecate*'s AI didn't fully alleviate the instinctive discomfort Dunstan felt at the sight of the pirate corvette a few hundred meters to port, twice as long as *Hecate* and double her mass. They were so close that he could see the individual laser weld lines between the segments of the hull plating. The other ship's gun mount was still trained to the rear, frozen in the act of cycling armor-piercing shells when Lieutenant Robson took over their systems.

"Their reactor is back online," Robson said. She had been quiet and subdued since the intercept, and Dunstan resolved to have a talk with her as soon as their business here was concluded. "I restored power to all systems."

"That's not a bad-looking ship," Lieutenant Hunter observed. "I've always liked those Ocie corvettes. Fast, good sensors, decent mix of weapons."

"Outruns everything that can outgun it, and outguns everything that can catch it," Dunstan said. "That ship is a lot of trouble in the hands of a good crew. And that crew knew their business." *Until we turned their brains into pudding,* he thought.

"A lot of those smaller patrol units went unaccounted for after the war. I wonder just how many are out there again under new management," Hunter said.

"What's the crew complement of a Cerberus, Lieutenant Robson?" Dunstan asked.

"Checking now, sir." Robson flicked through her data screens for a few moments. "Sixty-five. Eleven officers, sixteen petty officers, thirty-eight enlisted."

"Must have been a task to train all those people to run that ship," Hunter said. "Those junkyard specials are one thing. But that is a modern warship. You can't just pick up a manual and learn how to operate the tech in a month or two."

"That's one of the mysteries we're going to solve, Lieutenant. Bring us alongside and match our velocity for docking," Dunstan said.

"You want to go over there, sir?"

"I don't *want* to, Number One. I don't enjoy the idea of poking around in a graveyard. But there are sixty-odd pirates on that ship who didn't have time to get rid of evidence. We'll never have an opportunity like this again."

—

With *Hecate*'s AI controlling the thrusters, the ship took up position next to the corvette with a swift precision that no human could match. They were coasting along at over thirty kilometers per second, but the AI lined them up so precisely that the docking collar extending from *Hecate* latched onto the airlock of the corvette on the first try.

"Ring is latched and secured. Hard lock confirmed," Lieutenant Hunter reported. The image from the port sensor array showed a wide-angle view of the hull next to *Hecate*'s airlock. The docking collar bridged the ten meters between the two ships, a flexible white tube made from ultrastrong ballistic material that would nonetheless pull apart like tissue if either ship suddenly accelerated or pulled away hard.

"I haven't done a free-floating transfer in a while," Dunstan said as he pulled up the top of his vacsuit and slipped his arms into the sleeves.

"Should be a cakewalk, sir," Lieutenant Robson said. "I've got the other side ready and waiting. Lights are on everywhere, and you can communicate through the shipboard audio."

"And you're sure they didn't rig something to trigger the scuttling charges once you open that airlock over there."

"Positive, sir. Nothing funny about those circuits. And even if they did, I disabled the scuttling charges as soon as I had full control," Robson said.

"Very good. I'm going to step outside for a little while, then. Lieutenant Armer, you're with me. Number One, you have the conn."

"I have the conn," Lieutenant Hunter confirmed.

Armer unbuckled his harness and floated out of his seat to join Dunstan at the ladderwell.

"If any surprises pop up on the plot while we are over there, do not wait for us to make it back through the collar. Close the airlock and cut yourself loose, and then get the hells out of here as fast as you can. That is an order."

"Aye, sir," Lieutenant Hunter said. "Nobody will be boarding *this* ship."

Dunstan exchanged a nod with his first officer and pushed off to descend to the airlock deck with Armer.

"Ready for a field trip, Mr. Armer?" he asked when they were in front of the airlock.

"Yes, sir," Armer replied. "Like Robson said—should be a cakewalk."

Dunstan turned toward the arms locker and entered his security credentials to open the door. He took two holstered sidearms from one of the racks and handed one to Armer, who took it and attached it to the outside of his vacsuit. Dunstan did the same with his weapon and checked the ammo cassette in the grip. It was almost certainly an unnecessary precaution—Robson had confirmed that there was no sign of life left on the corvette—but it was still an enemy ship, and there was no way he'd set foot on it without a weapon.

"All right, Lieutenant Robson," Dunstan said into his helmet comms. "Ready at the main airlock for ship-to-ship transfer."

"Affirmative. Opening inner airlock door."

The orange warning light above the airlock started blinking, and the inner door unlocked and rotated back into its frame. Dunstan and Armer stepped into the airlock and sealed their helmets. Behind them, the inner door rotated back into the closed position and locked into place. The warning light switched from orange to red.

"Cycling airlock," Robson sent. *"Airlock is now decompressed. Opening outer airlock door in three—two—one."*

The airlock door unlocked and slowly moved inward, then to the side. The lighting in the docking collar beyond turned on and illuminated the inside of the tube. On the other side of the collar, ten meters away, the scuffed-up gray laminate of the corvette's outer airlock hatch looked unwelcoming to Dunstan, like the door of a prison cell. A moment later, it started to open as well, gradually revealing the airlock beyond.

"Here we go," Dunstan said. "Nobody make any sudden left turns, please."

A corvette was a small warship, but it felt almost decadently spacious to Dunstan after all the time he had spent on *Hecate*. The airlock deck was roughly twice the size of the one on *Hecate*, and it had another airlock on the opposite side of the hull where his own ship only had one.

"We're in," Dunstan sent to Lieutenant Robson. "Lock up behind us."

"Copy that. Closing outer airlock door."

The corvette's hull sealed itself again, shutting out the vacuum beyond. Dunstan looked around on the corvette's airlock dock. The wall between the airlocks once had been decorated with a painting of the ship's seal, but the new owners had scrubbed most of the paint away, leaving only a pale outline of the crest.

"The command deck is three decks up from your position," Lieutenant Robson sent. *"I am opening all the ladderwell hatches now."*

The round hatch at the top of the ladder unlatched with a faint electric whine and slid open. Dunstan floated over to the ladder and looked up. The only sounds he could hear from his helmet mics were the background noises of the ship's systems and his own exhalations. He grabbed one of the rungs and pulled himself up through the opening in the deck to begin his ascent toward the command deck.

The first deck he passed on the way was a berthing compartment. The doors of the individual berths were closed, and the rest of the compartment was empty. The next deck was the ship's galley. The sudden extreme acceleration the ship had endured when Lieutenant Robson turned off their gravmag system had forced open some of the cabinets and lockers in the kitchen nook, and the utensils and containers that had been inside were now drifting across the galley. He raised his hand to deflect a fork that was tumbling through the air toward him end over end and pushed it away toward the compartment's far bulkhead.

"Watch the sharps," he cautioned Lieutenant Armer, who was coming up the ladderwell below him.

When he reached the hatch opening for the command deck, Dunstan took a deep breath before he stuck his head above the lip of the hatch collar.

Time to inspect our handiwork, he thought.

The command crew of the corvette were all suited up and strapped into their seats, but it was obvious to Dunstan at first glance that everyone was dead. Their limbs drifted without purpose or control in the zero-g environment. Everyone had kept their visors up for easier communication, and globules of blood floated in the air, shaped into spheres by surface tension. There were so many of them that it was impossible for Dunstan to avoid them all as he pushed off from the ladder and drifted through the CIC toward the captain's chair, and he closed his visor to avoid getting any blood orbs into his helmet and onto his face. When the gravmag rotor stopped, the crew had experienced a sudden acceleration from one g to over twelve in the fraction of a second, and their bodies had continued to suffer the effects of that gravity for half a minute before the reactor shut down and the main drive ceased to produce thrust. If that scenario held any consolation for Dunstan, it was the knowledge that all the crew had likely been knocked unconscious almost immediately, and that none of them would have felt their blood vessels rupture and their hearts give out under the sustained squeeze of the unsurvivable acceleration.

The bloodshot eyes of the man in the command chair were half-open, but there was no light in them. He had bled from his nose and mouth, and the blood had stained the liner of his helmet and the front of his vacsuit. He looked to be about Dunstan's age or maybe even a little older, a smooth-shaved but weathered face that was etched with lines and wrinkles not unlike the ones he saw in his own mirror every day. Some blood had pooled in the corner of one of the dead man's eyes, and as Dunstan looked at the slack and lifeless face, a drop of it detached and floated off into the space between them. Dunstan waved it aside with his glove, where it left a small red mark on the fabric on the back of his hand.

You fought your ship well, Dunstan thought. *Where did you go to command school?* It took a high caliber of confidence in one's own skills to go head-to-head against another warship like that, the sort that spoke of excellent training and a lot of experience.

There were six more people on the command deck, all strapped into their seats in front of their duty stations. Dunstan checked each of them in turn so his helmet optics could record their faces. None of the command crew looked younger than thirty. It felt odd to tilt up their helmets and look at each of them in turn, like he was performing some sort of final sacrament. He had destroyed his share of enemy ships during the war, but they'd been just that to him—icons on a tactical display, hull outlines on a sensor screen. This was the first time he got to look into the eyes of the people he had killed.

"They were out of missiles," Lieutenant Armer said behind him. The weapons officer was floating by the tactical station, holding himself in position with one hand on a safety handle while he opened control screens with the other. "Four launch silos, all empty. That's why they came charging in for a gunfight."

"That's what I figured," Dunstan replied. "Nobody in their right mind goes CQB unless it's the only option left on the menu."

"Hecate *to commander,*" Lieutenant Hunter's voice came over his helmet headset.

"Go ahead, *Hecate*," he replied.

"Don't rush to the airlock just yet, but we picked up a contact on passive. Deceleration burn signature, heading for the station we just wrecked. They're quite a way out yet, but we're right between where they are and where they want to go."

"Understood. How much time do we have?"

"I'd say thirty minutes at most. But if they start searching the area on active, all bets are off on that number."

Dunstan mouthed a silent curse. This ship could be the biggest intelligence haul anyone had reeled in since the beginning of the insurgency, but *Hecate* could neither fight nor run away while they were lashed together. And as valuable as the corvette would be to Alliance military intelligence, she wasn't worth risking the Rhodian Navy's most advanced ship.

"Thirty minutes," he repeated. "We'll gather what we can over here. Make sure you copy every scrap of data you can get from the data banks. Everything that's networked, right down to the galley dispensers."

"Already in progress, sir," Hunter replied.

"We'll be back at the airlock in twenty. But if they light you up on active before then, you cut *Hecate* loose and run. Do not take any chances. The navy has plenty more commanders to put in that chair."

"Affirmative. Hecate *out."*

Dunstan turned to Lieutenant Armer.

"Head down the ladderwell and check the decks below the airlock level. Take scans of every body you come across, and work quickly. I'll take the upper decks."

"Aye, sir." Armer pushed off toward the ladderwell without hesitation and disappeared below.

Dunstan looked around on the command deck again. Aside from the bodies of the senior crew, everything of interest here would be in the data banks that *Hecate*'s AI was currently copying and analyzing. There was no time to search the rest of the ship thoroughly, but if there was something important somewhere that hadn't been committed to digital memory, he had a pretty good idea where to look for it.

He floated back to the ladderwell and pulled himself upward.

"Robson, do you read?"

"Affirmative, sir," Lieutenant Robson's answer came without delay.

"Which deck is the command berth?"

"Second deck up from CIC," Robson said.

"I'm heading up there. Unlock all the individual berth doors, please."

"Unlocking them now."

Dunstan reached the command berth deck just as the lights on the security panels flipped from red to green. The deck only had four berths, and he opened them one by one. This was the space where the senior officers had their quarters, close to CIC and well separate from the decks for the lower-ranking crew members. Like everything else on the corvette, the senior berths were bigger than their counterparts on *Hecate*. The commanding officer's space was the biggest, two berths turned into one by removing the wall between them.

The captain's berth was as tidy as any navy quarters Dunstan had ever seen. There was a bunk with storage bins under it, a desk, and a foldaway sink and toilet. The only personal touches were some hard-copy pictures that had been stuck to the wall above the desk. Dunstan got closer to give his helmet optics a better look. One of them was an obvious family picture, a dark-haired woman and two small children, little boys with chubby cheeks and blue eyes. They were huddled together for the shot in a circular seating nook and smiling at the lens. Dunstan felt a stab of guilt at the sight of the happy faces looking back at him, the man who had given the order that had killed their loved one. Another picture showed a couple at the railing of a ship's deck—not a spaceship, but a watercraft, afloat under a blue sky on a sea so vast and calm that it could only be on Oceana. The pictures were valuable intelligence just like everything else on this ship that could point to the identity of the crew, but Dunstan felt vaguely dirty looking at the dead captain's cherished private moment, and he turned his head as soon as he was certain that his helmet optics had gotten a good scan.

The storage bin under the bunk was locked, secured with a biometric sensor that flashed red when he tried to unlock it.

"Robson, I'm in berth 3-2. There's a storage drawer in this berth that has a bio lock on it. Can you override that?"

"Give me a moment," Lieutenant Robson replied. *"Berth 3-2 storage . . . negative, sir. It's not on the network."*

"Figures." He pulled his sidearm from its holster and disengaged the safety. "Armer, heads up. I'm about to fire my weapon to bust a lock."

"Copy that," Armer sent.

Dunstan grabbed the safety strap draped across the bunk to keep himself in place in the zero-g environment. He pressed the muzzle of his weapon against the top of the lock and pulled the trigger. The propellant was formulated for low noise, but the sound of the shot still made his helmet's automatic hearing protection kick in. The drawer didn't budge when he tried it again, and he fired two more rounds on either side of the first bullet hole. The projectiles were designed to fragment when shot against a hard surface, to avoid punching holes into pressurized spaceship hulls, but they had more than enough punch at contact distance to demolish the locking mechanism. He holstered his gun again and grabbed the drawer's handle. It came open on the third pull, shedding bits and pieces of the broken lock as it slid out from its recess under the bunk.

The first thing Dunstan saw inside made him recoil from the open storage bin. The reflexive move sent him floating backward until the edge of the desk stopped him. When his adrenaline spike subsided and the world had not ended in white-hot oblivion, he pushed off from the desk and investigated the bin again. The contents inside were all secured with tie-downs, including the grenade in the center of the drawer. Against his instincts, Dunstan took a closer look. The safety cap was still on the fuse button, and the secondary safety was in place and unbroken. The markings on the cylindrical grenade body were in Oceanian, but he recognized the word for "incendiary." The device hadn't gone off when he had opened the drawer, and he didn't see any tripping mechanisms connected to the fuse cap.

Not an explosive trap, he thought. *That wasn't meant for me or anyone else.* Thermal grenades were not used for killing people, they were for destroying equipment and intelligence. Still, the rounds he had fired had passed maybe two hand breadths above the incendiary device. If it had gone off in the tight confines of the berth, it would have put him in a bad spot very quickly.

He took a deep breath to slow down his racing heart and looked at the other contents of the storage bin. There was a stack of civilian clothes and an assortment of freeze-dried snacks on top of a worn canvas travel bag. Dunstan gingerly moved the clothes and snack bags aside to go to the bag. It was an old-fashioned thing, leather handles and a zipper closure at the top, the sort of bag people used for short trips or weekend leave. The zipper was open, and he pulled the bag open carefully with two fingers. Inside was a small stack of paper notebooks that looked as out of time and place as the weekend bag that held them. Dunstan pulled the stack out to look at it. Each notebook was sealed in a plastic bag. He tucked the stack underneath one of the safety straps on the bed to keep the books from floating away while he checked the rest of the bag and the storage bin. The other contents were trivial—some more clothes, a small tool kit in a little carrying pouch, and a few other trinkets, nothing that seemed valuable or sensitive enough to justify the use of a thermal charge to destroy them in case of imminent capture. Once he was satisfied that he hadn't missed anything, he closed the storage bin and pulled one of the notebooks out of the stack. He slipped it out of its plastic bag and opened it to a random page. It contained columns of seemingly random letters and numbers, all in blocks of five, written by hand in a small and tidy script. Dunstan briefly leafed through the rest of the pages, which all had similar content.

The alarm he had set on his wrist computer went off with a silent vibration to remind him that ten minutes had passed since Lieutenant Hunter's warning. Dunstan closed the notebook in his hands and returned it to its bag. The notebooks were small enough to fit into the leg pockets of his vacsuit, so he split the stack and put half in each pocket, three notebooks per side.

He turned toward the compartment's open door and pushed off from the edge of the bunk. As he floated past the desk, he looked at the family picture on the wall again, the happy faces of a wife and children who would never see their husband and father again.

I'm sorry, he thought. *Not for you, but for them.*

—

When he descended into the airlock deck, Lieutenant Armer was already waiting for him. Robson opened the airlock for them, and they floated back to *Hecate* together in silence.

"I checked all the decks. It's a graveyard," Armer said when they were back on their own airlock deck. "They were running a lean crew. I counted thirty-three, not including the ones in CIC. Got a face scan of everyone. Shame we don't have time for more."

"That would take time and personnel we don't have right now. It'll have to do."

"Aye, sir. This was—pretty grim business."

"Yes, it was," Dunstan agreed. "I won't tell you that you'll shrug it off. But remember what the alternative could have been. These people murdered innocents for a living. None of them would have lost any sleep over killing us as well."

"I know," Armer replied. "Still."

"What we did to them was awful. We feel bad about it. But be glad that you do, Lieutenant. And hope the day never comes when you don't feel guilty for killing someone."

"Yes, sir." Armer removed his sidearm from the attachment point on his vacsuit and handed the holstered weapon to Dunstan, who took it and floated over to the arms locker. He pulled out his own pistol and cleared it in the safety funnel underneath the locker, then removed the ammunition block from Armer's gun and cleared it as well before returning both weapons to their spots on the small-arms rack. He closed the door and waited for the security bolts to lock into place, then turned to push himself up the ladderwell into the Ops deck above.

"I have the conn," he announced when he floated through the hatch opening and pushed off toward the command chair.

"Commander has the conn," Lieutenant Hunter confirmed. She unbuckled her harness and got out of the chair to make space for him.

"Retract the docking collar and cut us loose," Dunstan ordered while he buckled himself in. "What's the status on the contact?"

"They finished their deceleration burn five minutes ago. No ID on the hull yet. We've got about ten minutes before we need to start worrying about that corvette getting picked up on passive."

"Docking collar is retracted and stowed," Lieutenant Robson said. "Ready to maneuver."

"Get us a little bit of distance. Cold thrusters, push us apart a klick or two," Dunstan said.

"Aye, sir. Firing portside thrusters for separation."

Hecate started to open the gap between herself and the corvette. Behind Dunstan, Lieutenant Armer entered the Ops deck and launched himself toward his station with a quick flex of his knees.

"What are we going to do with that?" Lieutenant Hunter said with a nod at the sensor screen, where the corvette slowly shrank into the distance.

"I'd love to take her in tow and turn her back over to the Oceanians," Dunstan replied. "But there's no way we can stay stealthy while we are tied to that hull. And we can't risk letting her fall back into pirate hands. She's too dangerous."

"That's a shame," Hunter said. "But I concur. She hardly has a scratch on her. They'll hose her out and reload those launchers, and she'll be back in the raiding business in a few weeks."

Dunstan sat back in his chair with a tired little sigh.

Such a waste, he thought. *All these lives and all these ships. When are we going to be done with this business at last?*

"Tactical," he said. "Raise and energize the gun mount, load API. Target is Cerberus-class corvette off our portside, one thousand meters. Manual mode, no fire-control radar."

"Aye, sir," Armer replied. "Raising the gun mount."

On the lower half of *Hecate*'s hull, the ship's autocannon mount extended from its blister-shaped fairing. Armer turned on the optical targeting mode and opened a new screen above the tactical station that showed the view from the weapon's sensor cluster.

"Gun is energized. Loading armor-piercing incendiary. Target acquired visually, target ID confirmed," Armer reported. "I have manual fire control."

"Weapons free," Dunstan ordered. "Fire when ready."

The image on the screen flashed as the pair of 35 mm autocannons began pouring shells into the other ship's hull at a thousand rounds per minute. The corvette's hull armor was designed to stand up to missile shrapnel, not cannon fire, and the armor-piercing grenades ripped into it with ease, blowing deep holes into the ship's deck walls and bulkheads with a storm of penetrator rods. Armer had a steady hand on the controls. He rotated the turret to move his aiming reticle methodically along the length of the hull in a wide zigzag pattern that Dunstan knew would leave no compartment untouched. He briefly imagined the bodies on the command deck getting incinerated and blown to bits, and he shook off the thought before it could take up residence in his brain.

"Helm, aft thrusters. Swing us around for a circle strafe," Dunstan said.

Hecate began a slow orbit around the corvette as Armer kept firing the cannons in regular, measured bursts. The relentless stream of gunfire punched long rows of holes into the hull, tore loose shards of armor, and ripped away external sensors and antenna arrays until the other ship was clouded in debris. It felt like a slow execution, and Dunstan found it almost agonizing to watch. But there was something proper about it as well, a kind of funeral pyre for the people on board that had been killed by gravity instead of falling to an enemy's weapons. He didn't believe in the gods, but if there was an afterlife for warriors, the dead on that corvette now had a proper send-off.

There was no dramatic explosion, no fiery exclamation mark at the end of the pirate ship's life. It just fell apart bit by bit under the hailstorm of cannon rounds until it was a ruined shell, drifting in a cloud of its own mechanical entrails, beyond salvage or repair. When *Hecate* finished her orbit of the corvette and Armer ceased fire, there was silence on the command deck.

"Target destroyed," he reported in a quiet voice that carried no triumph. "Retracting and de-energizing gun mount."

Dunstan cleared his throat with some effort.

"Turn us away from the incoming ship's trajectory and throttle up for a one-g cold burn. Let's get out of here before they notice the fireworks."

"One-g cold burn, aye," Hunter acknowledged. "Laying in new course, 100 over 10."

Hecate silently accelerated away into the void again, leaving the ruined Oceanian warship in its wake.

Chapter 20

Solveig

When Solveig walked into the atrium at Ragnar Tower, Marten was standing in front of one of the reception stations. He was watching the foot traffic coming in from the street, monitoring the steady stream of employees arriving for work. From the way he straightened up when their eyes met, she knew he had been waiting for her. Marten had been the head of security for the company since before she was born, and she knew his body language as well as she knew her father's.

I bet I know what this is about, she thought as she crossed the atrium to where he was standing.

"Good morning, Miss Solveig," he said. "How is life at the new place?"

"Good morning, Marten. Life at the new place is good, thank you. How is Papa? I haven't spoken to him since I moved in."

"He's fine. I think he's a little grumpy that you didn't stay for the big party."

"How was the event?" she asked.

Marten shrugged. "Just like the old days. You know the crowd."

"I do," she said. "That's why I didn't stay."

The corners of his mouth briefly turned upward in the hint of a smile.

"Would you walk with me for a moment? I have something to ask you," he said.

"Of course," Solveig said.

They walked toward the skylift bank together. Even though Solveig was an adult now and higher up in the corporate hierarchy than Marten, she still felt a little like she had as a child whenever he had busted her for stealing treats from the kitchen or joyriding in one of the security scooters, and he was taking her to her father for summary judgment.

"Someone signed in with your biometrics after hours," he said. "At a building that's ten kilometers from here."

"That was me," she admitted. "I came across something odd when I was running an audit upstairs, and I decided to go over there and check it out."

"I can't tell you how to do your job, of course. But I am in charge of executive safety. It's not a good idea for you to be out in that part of the city by yourself at night. Never mind going into shuttered facilities with no on-site security."

"I had no idea it was shuttered until I went there," she replied.

"If you had let me know what you were doing, I could have sent someone with you. Please do me a favor and let me know the next time you go out exploring like that."

"I wasn't alone, Marten. Not that I need an escort everywhere I go."

His lack of surprise at her revelation told her that he already knew about it. If the building was on the network, so were the security sensors. She hadn't exactly tried to be inconspicuous—she had used her company credentials and biometrics to get inside, after all—but it was an unwelcome reminder that her father's right-hand man was still keeping a close eye on her whenever she was in sight of a Ragnar-controlled network camera.

They stepped onto the skylift platform together and started their ascent to the executive floor. Marten must have taken her silence as irritation because there was a softer tone in his voice when he spoke again.

"You are who you are, Solveig. Moving out of the estate and living by yourself doesn't change that. You know you'll never be just another employee here. If something happens to you that I could have prevented, I won't have a chance to fall on my sword before your father skins me with a salted peeler. So please, please, make my life and yours less stressful. Give me a bit of notice before you go somewhere that may not be safe so I can send someone along. All right?"

There it is, Solveig thought. *I just managed to slip the leash a little, and now he wants to put it back on me.* She wanted to argue with him, but something about the way he was leaning on her so quickly over such a minor risk felt wrong to her. Her instincts told her to retract the barbs for now and put him at ease, so she nodded with what she hoped was a mildly contrite expression.

"All right," she said. "Sorry I didn't think about that last night. I felt safe enough with the police detective who was with me."

Marten nodded.

"What exactly were you auditing that had you going out to the docklands after dark?" he asked.

The sense of wrongness was back, a little stronger this time. It was an innocuous-sounding question that wasn't out of place in their conversation, but she knew Marten too well to take it at face value. He was not a man who asked questions if he didn't have any professional interest in the answers. She had no desire to show her hand and tell him everything she had learned yesterday, but throwing him a little bit of meat could give him just enough to shake him off her trail for now. He would smell a lie instantly, but the truth didn't need to be served up all at once.

"I was going through some expenditures," she told him. "The power bill for that building didn't make sense. I went out there to see if I could figure out why the numbers were off."

"And did you?"

Solveig nodded. "It's a mothballed building. Nobody's been in it in years. But there's a pool in the basement they forgot to shut off and drain. It's been kept heated all this time. The whole place is full of mold. We need to send someone out there to take it off the grid and clean everything up."

"I'll take care of it," Marten said. "The caretaker maintenance section must have been asleep at the switch. Someone needs to lose their job over that."

The skylift platform came to a gentle stop, and the safety barrier slid open to admit them to the executive floor.

"Good job," Marten said as they walked off the platform. "Look at you. Two days back on the job, and you're out there plugging money drains. You really are your father's daughter."

Solveig smiled dutifully at the compliment.

"Thanks, Marten."

"Just remember," he said as he walked off. "No more solo adventures."

She watched him cross the executive lobby in his purposeful gait, a block of flint wrapped in a tailored suit, never wasting a step in a direction that wouldn't take him to his destination by the shortest route. People who crossed his path moved out of his way instinctively, as if they could sense the danger radiating from the coiled-up potential for violence at his core. Even after all these years, she still felt anxiety at the thought of making him upset with her. But allowing him—and by extension, her father—to put her back in a satin-lined showcase was not an option. She wasn't certain of much when it came to the insurgency that had almost claimed her life and Stefan's, but there were two facts she knew without a doubt. Whatever involvement her father had with the insurgency, it was worse than he had admitted to her. And Marten, his bagman, was just as deeply into it as he was.

He's worried, she realized. *And it's not really about my safety. What is it that you don't want me to see?*

—

Back at her desk, she had the AI restore her previous screen layout with all the data she had collected and compared before. For a moment down in the basement of the mothballed building, she thought she had followed a dead end, that the mismatch she had spotted in the data pattern was purely coincidental. But the numbers hadn't added up in her head, and they still didn't make sense when she ran them again on the network.

People lie but numbers don't, she thought. *Until they do.*

She told the AI to run a simulation of power usage for the building she had visited last night with Stefan. Then she repeated the simulation with different parameters, varying staffing levels, fluctuations in summer and winter. Some of the scenarios met or exceeded the recorded use, but only when she tweaked them so much as to be unrealistic, assuming full staffing levels and operations around the clock, with every device in the building running at full load. Nothing explained why the power use was consistently high for an empty building, not even with the heated pool added into the equation. These numbers definitely lied.

If it's technically impossible to rack up a bill that large, but the company pays it anyway for five years without complaint, there are only two likely explanations. Either the metering system is defective and accounting isn't paying attention, or we're paying the higher bills on purpose.

She looked at the screen that showed the out-of-range subsidiaries. *Five years are not a trend, they are a system,* she told herself. And six facilities overpaying for power were not an unlucky string of broken metering systems, they were an engineered cash flow leak.

And where does that cash flow?

Solveig looked up the provider for the building's power. Ragnar bought energy from a variety of vendors according to the local supply options and infrastructure circumstances. The company that held the contract for the mothballed training center in Sandvik's cargo district was called Caloris. A quick search on the Mnemosyne told her that

Caloris was an energy consortium on Hades. Solar power was the biggest export good of the planet, abundant and cheap as it was because of the photovoltaic arrays that blanketed large patches of its surface to siphon energy from the nearby system sun. The rate Ragnar paid per kilowatt was in line with the rest of the solar energy market. She went through the infrastructure expenses for the other five buildings on her suspect list again and looked up the providers. All of them were serviced by Caloris. When she ran all the energy contracts through a filter to only show her the facilities powered by Caloris energy, Solveig saw that those six locations were the only ones.

We have three dozen local and interplanetary providers, and the only ones that are under contract with this one company also happen to be the ones that have been overbilled for several years.

Going to the other five Ragnar properties to check them out in person would have been the logical next step to make the case airtight and prove the money leak without a doubt. But Marten had known about her nighttime excursion almost instantly, and now he would be keeping an even closer eye on her movements. If she started visiting each of the other places in turn, he would know that she had figured out the scheme. And right now she didn't know enough to connect all the dots. Someone was paying for energy the company wasn't using, but she didn't know the *who*, the *why*, or the entirety of the *how*.

Solveig looked at the screen again and adjusted the data fields until they were tiled across the display. The name CALORIS was the only similarity, but now that she had found that common thread, it stood out like a signal flare.

The Mnemosyne presence of the company was as generically corporate as the building she had visited last night, boilerplate language about mission statements and company culture. They had a business address on Hades, but no presence on Gretia. There were some showcase images of the vast fields of solar arrays on the surface of the planet. Solveig's brain had only one strong association with Hades—her mother, who had moved there eventually after leaving Papa. They talked infrequently, maybe once or twice a year, and the last time Solveig had seen her in person was the summer before she went to university. Thinking of her mother made her realize that they hadn't spoken since she started at Ragnar. Vigdis Jansen had dropped the Ragnar name when she left, and she had discarded most of her family ties with it. The loss of Aden to the maelstrom of war had frayed whatever tenuous regular connection they had maintained over the years to the displeasure of her father. Her mother was largely a stranger to her now, her presence in Solveig's life reduced to brief messages of congratulations on birthdays or the occasional two-minute vidcalls in which they had nothing of substance to say to each other.

I can't even tell her that Aden is still alive. Not over comtab messages or a vidcall where Marten or gods knows who else can listen in.

She turned toward the windows and leaned back in her chair to let her mind wander for a little while. It was raining again outside, one of the depressing winter showers that were a hallmark of Sandvik weather. To her right, the screens she had called up were silently floating above the surface of her desk, waiting for her input. The image of the solar arrays on the sun-scorched surface of Hades drew her attention again. Her knowledge of the planet was limited to what she had learned in school or read on the Mnemosyne. Aden had practically grown up on both Oceana and Gretia, and now that he was a spacer, he had probably been everywhere in the system. She had never even been off-world until her business trip to Acheron a few months ago.

I could go now, she thought. *I could fly out to Hades, or Oceana, or anywhere else. All by myself, without an escort or a minder. I don't have to ask for permission or money anymore.*

She tried to push the idea out of her head, but it kept taking over her thoughts even as she attempted to focus on numbers and financial transaction sheets again. Whatever was going on with the inflated energy bills, the money flow pointed to Hades. If she flew out there, she could follow the thread without Marten looking over her shoulder. She could see the planet and spend a few days exploring.

And I could visit Mama, she thought with a jolt. *Tell her that Aden is back.*

The sudden excitement she felt at the idea made her get out of her chair and walk over to the window. Thick raindrops were rolling down the Alon panel, blurring and distorting the city lights behind them. It was only morning, but the sky was so dark and glum that it looked like the sun was already setting. There was never any rain on Hades, she knew. The habitable zone of the planet was deep underground, a five-hundred-kilometer tunnel circling the planet just below its northern pole. It was a place with a reputation for easy living, an endless variety of amusements, and the best food and entertainment in the system. From what she had heard, there was nothing that couldn't be had on Hades, no tastes that couldn't be satisfied, no desires that couldn't be fulfilled. And she had a cover story to justify a visit, one that would be plausible even to Marten and Papa. Marten would fume at being sidestepped right after he had admonished her, but she had no desire to have one of his agents by her side to monitor her for the entire trip. Papa wouldn't care about her wanting to have a good time, but he'd be silently furious that she went to visit her mother because he would see it as an act of disloyalty. There would be fallout to endure from both, but Solveig found that she didn't really care. She wouldn't ask permission or seek forgiveness this time.

I'm an adult. I can go see my mother if I feel like it. And I can spend my own money on whatever I want.

She took out her comtab and sent a connection request to her mother's node address and slowly paced the space between the window and her desk while she waited for it to be accepted.

The woman that appeared on the screen was attractive, long dark hair framing a narrow face with high cheekbones that had a dusting of freckles across them. Her mother's eyes were a mélange of green and brown, one color fading into the other gradually. She was twenty years younger than her former husband, but unlike him, she hadn't undergone any surgical treatments to erase the traces and marks the passing years had left on her face.

"Solveig," Vigdis Jansen said. "This is a surprise."

"Is this a bad time? I should have checked your local time before I sent the request."

"It's never a bad time," her mother said. "Gods, it's been—what, six months since we talked?"

"Nine months," Solveig replied. "Sorry I didn't get in touch earlier. I was very busy. A lot has happened here since then."

"You look well. Different, somehow. Have you started your job yet?"

Solveig nodded. "Back in May. Take a look."

She flipped her comtab around so her mother could see her perspective, then panned the device in a semicircle to capture the room in front of her.

"That is a very nice office," Vigdis said. "Are you happy with the work?"

"It's fine. A little light on responsibilities for someone with an office like this. But you know why that is."

Her mother flashed a little smile. For some reason, even her expressions of amusement always carried a bit of sorrow, and that sorrow became slightly more pronounced whenever their conversations touched on Papa in any way.

"I've been watching the networks about the troubles you're all having right now. I hope you are staying safe in the middle of that mess."

Solveig stopped herself from reaching up and touching the scar underneath her rib cage where an armor-piercing rifle dart had exited her body after missing her spine by a few millimeters. There would be a time to tell her mother about the day she had almost lost her life, but it wasn't today.

"I have Marten and his people watching over me. You know how he is. If he could permanently encase me in a slab of Alon and store me in a safe, he would."

"I know how he is," her mother said, and the hint of a shadow darkened her face briefly.

"Listen," Solveig said. "I don't know if this is a good time for you. But I was thinking about coming out to Hades."

"You *are*? That would be wonderful. I told you, it's never a bad time. I mean it. I would love to host you and show you around. When are you thinking about coming?"

Solveig turned around and looked out over Principal Square. The cold wind was driving bands of rain across the plaza, and the sky was the color of dirty dishwater. On the screen projection at her desk, the Mnemosyne node of the energy company was cycling through a series of images showing one of the entertainment quarters in the habitation ring on Hades, a full-bore blast of lights and colorful laser displays that surpassed even the visual assault on the senses that was Acheron's Coriolis City.

I need a break, she thought. *Just a few days—in a place where no one is monitoring my steps, and nobody knows who I am.*

"As soon as I can get a flight," Solveig replied. "The spaceport is closed today because of the accident they had yesterday, but it'll reopen at midnight. I was going to try for a flight in the morning. If you are fine with the short notice."

Her mother chuckled softly.

"It's a four-day transfer from Gretia right now. I think I can manage to get the place clean before you get here. Are you bringing anyone with you?"

Solveig shook her head. "It'll just be me."

"That's wonderful. This is a lovely surprise, Solveig. I am very much looking forward to seeing you."

"I am looking forward to it was well," she replied. "Let me find a flight, and then I'll let you know the details."

"Of course. Safe travels. And thank you for this. You have no idea how much you have lifted up my week."

They said their goodbyes, and Solveig ended the comms, feeling vaguely guilty at her mother's excitement. Mama had been an afterthought, a plausible alibi for a trip to Hades. But after their exchange, she found that she did look forward to the visit. The black-and-white world of her childhood had been carefully curated by her father, and now that she was an adult and able to discern shades of gray, she was willing to revise her judgment. Almost everything she had come to believe about her mother was based on her father's side of the story. If there was no such thing as an objective point of view in such an acrimonious split, maybe she could come closer to a balanced one once she had heard her mother's perspective. This would be the first time they'd be able to talk freely, without Papa listening in some form.

I should have done this much earlier, she thought. *I still don't know if I can forgive her for going away and leaving Aden and me. But maybe I'll be able to understand why she did it.*

Back at her desk, Solveig swiped away all the data screens except for the one she had opened for the Mnemosyne query. She ran a search on flights to Hades. It was a popular destination for leisure trips, and there were several companies offering daily passenger services. She selected one of the available slots on a starliner due to depart tomorrow, the soonest flight on the list. If she was really going to skip out without telling anyone, she'd have to keep the window small in which Marten could find out. He would not be able to keep her from going, but he could make things complicated by sticking her with a personal protection detail, two or three of his minions to follow her everywhere and report back on where she was going and what she was doing.

No more solo adventures, Marten had admonished her. She had agreed to tell him if she was going to go somewhere that might not be safe, but Hades seemed like a safe place to her. There were no weapons allowed anywhere, and the violent crime rate was lower than Gretia's by an order of magnitude. She wasn't breaking her promise to Marten, technically speaking. She was merely interpreting the terms of the agreement to suit her preferences, something that Papa had taught her well by doing it frequently. It wasn't an *adventure*, just a family visit, a trip to one of the safest places in the system.

Just as she was about to confirm the reservation, she thought of asking Stefan to come along, but she dismissed the idea almost immediately. Even if he could clear his work schedule, and as tempting as she found the notion of having a few days alone with him in a place like Hades, it didn't feel right to bring him along on this trip. This would be the first time she'd meet her mother in person all by herself, and having Stefan with her would only complicate things. It was also the first time she would get to go off-planet alone, a new experience she didn't want to share, not even with company as handsome and pleasant to be with as Stefan.

Solveig touched the confirmation field on the reservation. One person, single-bunk suite, Apollo Starlines flight 601, departing Gretia One tomorrow at 1300 standard system time. A moment later, a confirmation message for the trip popped up on her comtab, along with a notification that the payment had been subtracted from her ledger balance.

She leaned back in her chair and let out a slow breath. Whatever happened next, it would happen because she had set it in motion, following no one's agenda but her own, and she would fully own the consequences of her choices. The thought was both exhilarating and terrifying, and for the first time since she had moved into this office, Solveig felt an impulse to go to the refreshments bar across the room and pour herself a healthy shot of something strong.

CHAPTER 21

ADEN

Aden had been to Vigard before, but he didn't recognize the succession of streets the pod was taking to their destination. It was a small town built around a large university that catered to well-to-do families, expensive lodging, and upscale clothing shops and eateries. The pod followed its preset course into the center, where they stopped in front of a restaurant that advertised fusion cuisine on its street-side advertising screens. He felt out of place as soon as they emerged from the transport pod. There was a park across the street, a tidy, tree-studded green that looked like a small version of the one on Civic Square in Sandvik, and everyone who was walking around here in the center of town seemed young and attractive, uni kids who were meeting up for after-class socializing.

The fusion eatery wasn't busy yet, but Bryn didn't claim one of the plentiful free tables for them. Instead, she led him to the back of the restaurant, past the kitchen and the bathrooms. There was a closed door at the end of the passage, and she knocked. A moment later, the door opened, and a man with a ruddy face and a buzz cut peeked through the gap.

"Evening, Master Sergeant," Bryn said. "I brought a new friend along."

"The more, the merrier," the man said and opened the door fully. "Good evening, Captain. Who's your companion?"

"Major Robertson, Blackguard Corps. Major, this is Master Sergeant Norum."

"Master Sergeant," Aden said with a curt nod.

"Good evening, Major," Norum replied. "Some high-ranking company tonight. Do come in."

He stepped aside to make space, and Aden followed Bryn into the room beyond. It was a large-function room, easily big enough to host a platoon-sized party. About a dozen people were in the room already, and Aden felt all eyes on him as he walked in.

"This is Major Robertson," Bryn announced. "He's going to stand the watch with us tonight."

She went through the room and introduced everyone, a flurry of ranks and names Aden did his best to commit to memory. The men and women in the room were cordial, but he could tell that most of them were on guard at his presence. Even if they trusted Bryn, he was an unknown quantity.

"Who'd you serve with, sir?" someone asked him.

"Blackguards," he replied. "Signals Intelligence."

Someone else let out a low whistle. "*Blackguard.* Hey, Stendahl. The major here is a Blackguard, too."

The man they had called out by name, a tall redhead with thinning hair, came forward and nodded at Aden.

"Which unit?" he asked.

"Signals Intelligence Company 300," Aden replied.

"Out of Oceana, right?"

"That's correct."

"Corporal Stendahl," he introduced himself. "Second Battalion, Fourth Blackguard. I had a friend in the 300th. Corporal Fiets. Did you know him?"

"I do," Aden replied. "He was one of my company supply clerks. Always tried for a beard when he went on leave. Never did manage to grow a proper one."

"That's Fiets," Corporal Stendahl said with a grin. "Do you know what happened to him, sir?"

"He was with us at the surrender," Aden said. "I don't know where he ended up after that. They broke up the company and sent us to different prison units."

"That's too bad," Stendahl said. "Haven't heard from him since I got back home."

"Sorry, Corporal. Wish I could tell you more."

"That's all right, sir. He'll turn up sooner or later, I'm sure. I'm just glad he's still alive."

The exchange with Stendahl had served to dissipate most of the tension Aden had felt in the room when he walked in. The group had been in the middle of going through equipment that was staged on two tables in the back of the room, and now most of them returned to that task. Bryn walked over to one of the tables and took a few items, then returned to Aden and handed one of them to him. It was a yellow warning vest with reflective panels, the kind that had been mandatory equipment in every military vehicle.

"It's our friend-or-foe identification system," she explained. "Makes you easy to sort in a scrum. We're not allowed to wear uniforms anymore, so we use those instead to look alike."

"That's not a bad idea," Aden said. He unfolded the vest and put it on, then closed the fasteners at the front. The smell and feel of the fabric were exactly as he remembered from the last time he wore a vest like this, when his unit had to load all their gear into cargo containers at the Blackguard base for transport to Oceana.

"All right. Listen up, everyone," Master Sergeant Norum said. "Most of you know the drill. For the new people, our mission is to link up with the rally organizers on the central green and keep the other side from disrupting the event. They'll make noise, but let them shout all they want. If they start putting hands on our people or their gear, the safeties come off and we'll engage in some corrective action. Remember your crowd-control training. Hold the line, cover your neighbor, listen to callouts, and don't let yourself get isolated. Now, let's get this done and regroup back here in time for dinner."

—

The central university green was a brisk five-minute march away. Their group didn't move in military formation, but Aden found himself falling into step with his companions out of long-ingrained habit even without anyone calling a marching cadence. People on their side of the street gave them wide berths as they walked by. The glances they afforded his group were not the same hostile ones he had received in his POW clothes at the spaceport on Rhodia, but it still felt uncomfortably similar, the sensation that he wasn't wanted where he was right now, an unwelcome intruder on someone else's turf.

The green was a large, open space in the middle of the town, an expanse of neatly trimmed grass crisscrossed by paved walkways. At the end of the green closest to the spot where Aden's group had arrived, there was a raised stage, a large stone structure that jutted out toward the center of the green like the prow of a ship. To Aden, it looked like the base of an unfinished monument. Someone had hung Gretian flags from the baluster that surrounded the back edge of the stage, and the green-and-silver cloth squares rippled in the cool wind that was gusting across the square. A few dozen people were up on the platform, unfurling more flags and banners. Out on the green, some smaller groups of people had gathered in the distance, obviously displeased with the activities on the stage.

Aden walked onto the green with his companions and followed them up the stone staircase at the back of the stage. When they were at the top, their formation spread out to take advantage of the space, and he walked over to the baluster at the edge to look down. The stage platform was maybe two meters above the grass of the square, and the baluster added another meter to its height. The front half of the stage had no barrier at the edge, presumably to keep the view from the square unobstructed. At the other end of the green, several police pods stood in a short line at the edge of the grass, and half a dozen Gretian police officers were standing in a little cluster of green-and-silver uniforms, observing the events from a distance.

"This is the stage for formal events," Bryn said. She had walked up next to him, and now she leaned on the baluster and crossed her arms. "Graduations, plays, that sort of thing. They won't be happy that we're running a flag rally up here. But it is public property, so tough shit."

"Isn't that just needling them at this point?"

"Oh, we're absolutely here to piss them off," Bryn replied. "But it is a little more than just that. Not everyone who goes to uni is a reefo. It's not even most of them. And the rest need to be reminded that there are other voices out there."

"So this is an educational event," Aden said.

"Precisely. We're here to dispense knowledge. What kind is entirely up to them."

"How often have you done this kind of thing?"

"Few dozen times. I lost count by now."

"Ever get hurt?" Aden asked.

She flashed a coy little smile.

"A few times. Kind of lost count of that, too, I guess."

Aden laughed. "Are you sure you aren't infantry? I've never met another supply troop so ready and willing to brawl."

"No, I'm definitely support branch," Bryn said. "Maybe that's why I'm happy to take the gloves off now. I feel like I didn't do enough while the real fighting was going on. I got to spend the entire war back home at the ammo depot. Counting pallets and signing forms while you were all out there putting your necks on the line."

"You put on the uniform, and you did your part," Aden replied. "There's no shame in that."

The look she gave him in return made clear that she didn't share that sentiment. But whatever reply she had on her tongue was cut short by a sharp whistle from the center of the stage.

"Protective squad to me," Sergeant Major Norum called out.

The security volunteers in the yellow vests gathered around the sergeant major in a loose semicircle, and Aden and Bryn walked over to join them.

"All right," Norum said when they were all assembled. "Some of you have been here before. Some more than once. It's hard to get up here without using the stairs at the back. Whoever comes up that way has only one spot at the top where they can get in. Four people on stair guard—Private Finn, Sergeant Kizer, Corporal Stendahl, Private Doren. The rest of you are mobile reserve. Back up the stair guard if they need help. Keep your eyes open and plug gaps when you see them. And keep the front of the stage clear. Any questions?"

He waited for a moment and nodded when nobody spoke up.

"Very good. Take your positions and commence the watch."

The four designated troopers went to the back of the stage and lined up at the gap in the baluster where the two staircases met. The others formed a loose line along the front of the stage, and Aden sorted himself into the formation next to Bryn. Since their arrival, the crowd on the green had grown slowly but steadily as people came out of the surrounding streets and onto the square individually and in small groups that gradually coalesced into bigger ones as if pulled toward each other by a kind of social gravity. On the stage behind Aden, the rally had kicked off with music, interspersed with short speeches about the sorry state of affairs on Gretia, detailing the numerous ways in which the planet was going to all the hells under the exploitative rule of the Alliance occupation authorities. The speakers had various degrees of oratory talent, but most of them preferred simple, repetitive phrases and sheer volume over nuanced arguments, and Aden stopped paying attention after a while.

It didn't take long for the first people out on the green to pick up the challenge. The groups that gathered in front of the stage started counterchants whenever a new speaker took over the sound projector behind Aden and launched into a fresh monologue. It didn't look like a large crowd yet, but it already outnumbered the rally attendants on the stage, and more people kept crossing from the periphery of the park to join the gathering. Aden looked over the small sea of young people staring back at him from below. Most of them were more amused than agitated, but there was hostility in a lot of those faces as well. He was an unwelcome intruder, part of a noisy gang of outsiders that had taken over the center of their community, their place of celebration and enjoyment. The thought made him uncomfortable in a way he hadn't experienced since the first days of occupation duty on Oceana.

Thirty minutes into the rally, the crowd had grown large enough for the noise of their counterchants to compete with the volume of the sound projectors on the stage. Some of the newcomers had brought their own handheld voice amplifiers, and the reformer flags that had started to dot the green earlier were now more numerous than the loyalist ones flying on the dais. The gestures were more aggressive now, and the expressions of dismissive amusement he had seen earlier had mostly given way to the sort of focused anger he knew all too well from the anti-occupation demonstrations on Oceana during the war. A crowd of this size had mood dynamics that could shift as quickly as springtime weather in Sandvik. For all the increased noise and activity, the police presence hadn't changed much in response. A few more patrol pods had shown up, but the newly arrived officers were only watching the event from the periphery of the park, dressed in their regular jumpsuits instead of riot gear. A light drizzle had started since Aden's group arrived, and the rainwater was pooling on the marble floor of the stage in some spots, reflecting the lights from the nearby buildings.

"Hey there. *Hey,*" someone shouted to his left. Aden turned his head to see one of the soldiers in his group over at the baluster, pulling at one of the flags that were hanging over the top rail. Someone had jumped up from below and grabbed the bottom of the flag, and now the veteran and the counterprotester were engaging in a tugging match. Finally, the soldier won the contest with his two-handed hold on the cloth, and he jerked the flag up and out of reach of the crowd below. Then another flag started to move as someone was pulling it down from below. The soldier who had rescued the first flag dashed toward the new target, but he was a step or two too late, and the Gretian flag slid off the baluster and disappeared below the edge of the stage.

"They're grabbing our flags," someone shouted behind Aden. *"Pull 'em up, pull 'em up."*

The protective line dispersed as everyone rushed to the sides of the stage to rescue the flags that were still draped over the baluster rail. Aden reached the one closest to him and hoisted it up, out of the reach of a university kid below who was trying to climb the side of the stage to reach for it. The marble was wet now and difficult to climb, and as Aden pulled the flag away, the kid reached into thin air and fell back onto the grass.

They managed to secure most of the flags, but there were more people jumping for them now than vets rushing to save them, and several ended up as trophies for the crowd below, tossed and waved around to loud jeers. The partial success of their first physical contest with the rally goers fired up the counterprotesters closest to the stage, a mood shift Aden could see rippling through the crowd like a wave. Now they began to push forward and against the stage from all sides, shouting insults that grew coarser and louder with every passing moment. Then the first drink container flew up at Aden and his group. It missed them and hit the stage floor behind Bryn, spilling its contents as it bounced across the marble. Within seconds, another followed, then a third that would have hit Aden's shoulder if he hadn't reflexively swatted it aside and sent it back over the edge of the baluster.

"Contact front," Master Sergeant Norum bellowed behind them. *"Re-form the line, re-form the line!"*

At the prow of the stage, several pairs of hands had appeared at the edge, people trying to pull themselves up onto the dais. One of Aden's new comrades rushed forward and pushed the fingers off with the side of his boot to a new swell of angry shouts from the crowd below. Then someone threw something small and hard that hit the soldier square in the face and knocked him to the ground. The shouts from the crowd in his vicinity turned to jeering, and more hands started to come up over the edge of the stage. The soldier they had knocked down was holding his face with both hands. Aden's stomach churned a little when he saw the blood leaking out between the soldier's fingers.

This is not going to end well, he thought.

To his left, Bryn was stepping on fingers to dislodge their owners from the edge of the stage. The others in the line did likewise, and Aden joined in. There was no lack of targets now. When he was at the edge, he saw that people had started to form human siege ladders, boosting up their friends to reach the top more easily. For every pair of hands he sent back from the rim of the marble dais, two or three more popped up somewhere else. The fiery speeches had ceased behind them, replaced by more yelling and shouting. When he glanced toward the back of the stage, he saw that the team blocking the stairs was engaged with another group of counterprotesters that were coming up the staircases on both sides. In full riot armor, with stun sticks and force shields, they would have been able to hold the gap easily. With just their bodies to block the flood of people surging up from below, Aden knew that the outcome was a foregone conclusion.

He looked around for allies to rally as reinforcements, but now the first climbers had made it onto the prow of the stage in front of him, and he rushed to push them off. The drizzle had turned into a light shower, and the marble under his feet was slick with rainwater. He shoved one of the climbers off the prow, but he slipped and fell on his ass, and his own momentum almost carried him over the edge as well. Several pairs of hands were grabbing for his legs to pull him down, but he kicked out with both feet to free himself.

Aden retreated from the edge, his heart pounding. Someone pulled him by the back of his vest and helped him to his feet. He turned his head to see Bryn's face, pinched with focus and determination. Behind her, the line blocking the crowd at the stairs was faltering against the volume of bodies pressing in on it. A small group of counterprotesters had made it up the front of the stage, this time uncontested, and they were quickly pulling more of their friends up from the crowd below. One of the veterans ran past Aden with a flag on a pole in his hands. He swung it at the group and knocked one of them to the ground with the metal flagpole before the others seized the pole and tried to yank it away from the soldier. Someone slipped and fell on the slick marble floor, and the entire group stumbled and went down one by one as they struggled for control of the pole. Out of the corner of his left eye Aden saw quick movement, and he raised his arm and ducked just in time to block a fist directed at the side of his head. He threw a return punch that connected with a face and made his attacker shout out in pain and stumble back a few steps. Aden helped him along with a kick that sent the other man careening backward and falling over the group that was still fighting over the flagpole on the ground.

The familiar two-tone warbling of police sirens was cutting through the noise now, but it sounded distant to Aden. He looked around for the source of the sound. The police officers had finally started to make their way through the crowd, but they were still at the edge of the massive scrum the rally had become, and there weren't nearly enough of them to have any hope of separating the belligerents now. The team holding the staircase was scattered. All Aden saw of them at the back of the stage were glimpses of yellow vests and reflective strips in the general mayhem. Several counterprotesters were kicking and stomping the sound projectors that had fallen silent. As if to send a commentary from the gods, the rain shower had turned into a downpour, drenching the stage and everyone on it and making it hard to find solid footing on the marble floor. The rally had gone from noise to all-out violence in just a few moments. A rock hitting a face and drawing blood had been all that was needed to light a spark and ignite the volatile atmosphere like fumes from an empty fuel tank.

Someone pulled on his vest from behind. He turned around with his hands up, ready to fight, but he dropped them when he saw Bryn's face again. She had blood coming from her nose that had flecked the front of her vest with big splotches of red. She reached up and opened the fasteners of the vest, then shrugged it off and let it drop to the ground.

"*Take that shit off,*" she shouted at him and yanked on the collar of his safety vest. He did as she had done and peeled off the vest. She took it from him and threw it aside.

"Let's go," she told him and took his hand. She pulled him toward the edge of the stage, where people were still climbing up to join the fracas. Before he could voice any dissent, she stepped over the edge, still holding his hand, and pulled him along as she jumped off. They landed in the soggy grass at the bottom, and she dragged him to the ground with her.

"We have to go," she said.

"You're going to leave the others on their own?"

"We get overrun, we scatter and regroup at the rallying point. And we just got overrun. Now let's move it. Unless you want to end up in jail or in the hospital tonight."

Bryn got to her feet and pulled him up. There were counterprotesters all around them, but they were focused on getting up onto the stage and into the fight, tunnel vision induced by hunting fever. Aden followed Bryn as she started to make her way through the crowd against the stream of people. In the darkening sky above the park, the police finally made their presence known in force. A pair of gyrofoils descended out of the clouds and took up position overhead. High-powered searchlights cut through the downpour and illuminated the stage and the area around it. Ahead of Aden and Bryn, more police pods appeared at the edge of the park, and she nudged him to the right and away from the patrol vehicles. Some people in the crowd gave them suspicious looks as they passed, but Bryn forged ahead without paying them any mind. Then someone shouted behind them, and Aden turned his head to see a few protesters following them through the crowd.

"Move it, Major," she said and started running. He followed suit. His clothes were drenched, and the shoes he was wearing were not made for sprints, but the certainty of being chased gave him an adrenaline jolt that let him catch up with his companion and keep pace with her. They were in the center of the green now, and the crowd was much thinner out here, smaller clusters of people that were easier to avoid. He dared to look over his shoulder to see that the small group in pursuit was falling behind a little, and he willed his legs to find some extra strength to widen the gap.

Finally, they were off the green and racing down a street, dodging pedestrians as they went. When Aden looked over his shoulder again, their pursuers had given up the chase and turned around just short of the edge of the park.

"We're clear," he shouted. The effort used up what little air he had left in his lungs, and he slowed down to a trot. Bryn stopped to let him catch up.

"Well, that went to all the hells in a hurry," she panted. When he was next to her, she bent over with her hands on her thighs to catch her breath. A few drops of blood fell from her nose and dripped onto the pavement. She wiped her face with the back of her hand, which only resulted in smearing a red streak across her cheek.

"You're leaking," he said. "We tossed the first aid packs along with the vests."

"Don't worry about it," she replied. She turned toward the nearest storefront and checked her reflection in the windows, then used the sleeve of her utility jacket to clean off her face. "This isn't my first dance with these people."

"Ever had your nose broken?"

"Not yet," she said. "Despite my best efforts. Turns out a lot of people are squeamish about punching women in the face. This was from a stray elbow, I think. Didn't even get to return the favor."

"Setting up on that stage was a mistake," Aden said. "Elevated position, but no route for a retreat. Too easy to surround."

"I guess they didn't expect the reefos to come out in such numbers. Or be so fired up." She gave Aden a quick head-to-toe muster. "You did all right for a first timer. Are you sure you've never done this before?"

"Not until now. I usually try to stay away from big crowds."

"I should be that smart. But I can't help it. Makes me feel good to know that I am out there risking something. I kind of love it, to be honest."

There was a new swell of noise from the direction of the green, more police sirens and amplified voices shouting commands. Above their heads, another gyrofoil soared toward the park, low enough that Aden could read the safety markings on the side of the cockpit.

"Let's try to circle around and get to the rally point from the other side," Bryn suggested. "That square is going to be a wasp nest for a while."

They walked away from the central green for a few blocks. Aden took the lead and made a series of random turns to see if anyone was still trailing them. When he was satisfied that they didn't have a tail, he checked his comtab's map and memorized a route that would lead them around the park and back to the restaurant their group had been using as a staging ground. The rain hadn't let up, and he felt like every single fiber strand of his new wardrobe was now thoroughly soaked. Even without consulting the map again, it was easy to tell the direction of the green just from the continued sounds of sirens and crowd noise.

Aden's plan had been to move down the side streets parallel to the eastern edge of the park, but the first southbound street they tried was blocked by a row of police pods and mobile barriers in the distance. As they got closer, they saw that the local police had set up a checkpoint at the corner of the next block. He took a left turn to cut across to the next southbound route, but that one was blocked off as well. However lackluster the police presence had been at the start of the rally, they had finally responded in force. Half an hour of walking later, it was clear to Aden that the police had set up a wide perimeter around the park that covered every key intersection between them and the rallying point, checking everyone who left the area and letting nobody back in.

"I think we may have really pissed them off," Bryn said when they spotted yet another roadblock. It was dark now, and they were both cold, wet, and aching. On a normal day, that confluence of conditions would have made Aden miserable, but somehow he felt energized instead, his senses heightened even as his body was tiring. He realized that he hadn't felt firmly in the present like this since he'd been on *Zephyr* on the day they'd made a suicidal run at the pirate gun cruiser, with rail-gun slugs coming their way and Maya steering the ship through the storm with a skill and focus that bordered on the supernatural.

"We're lucky that we're on this side of the perimeter," Aden said.

"Yeah. I don't think there'll be any regrouping going on tonight."

"I'm guessing that means we won't get a free dinner," he said, and she laughed. To his complete surprise, she stepped close to him and kissed him, a brief but intense kiss that left his nervous system tingling when she pulled away again.

"Sorry," she said. "I'm taking some pretty bold liberties here."

"Not at all," Aden replied.

"It's just that these things get me spun up a little. And I don't usually have a good-looking man around who also happens to outrank me."

Aden laughed. "You don't start anything with noncoms?"

She shook her head firmly. "Shacking up with subordinate ranks, that just leads to all kinds of complications."

"So how long has it been since you ran into a good-looking man who happened to outrank you?" he asked.

She flashed a little grin. "It's been a while. Handsome field-grade officers who can hold their own in a tussle? Those are a rare commodity around here."

She's either a little bit nuts, or I am a big idiot, Aden thought. Of course, there was always the possibility that both of those options were true.

"I think we can get our own dinner," he said. "I'm willing to chalk this whole mess up to community service."

"That's a great idea," Bryn replied. She pulled out her comtab and flicked open a screen projection. "How about we hail a pod and get the hells out of here?"

"Best suggestion I've heard all day."

She checked her screen for a few moments and looked up with a frown.

"*Shit.* They've disabled public pod access for the entire inner city."

"How far of a walk to where we can hail a pod?"

"Six and a half klicks," she said.

Aden looked around with a sigh. The rain was still coming down steadily. Six and a half kilometers would take them a good hour of brisk walking while tired and soaked to the bones before they could get a pod to go home, and that was assuming the police wouldn't simply widen the block zone while they were on the way. He pulled out his own comtab and pinched a screen into existence above the device.

"There are plenty of hotels around," he said. "We can get dry, order some food, and wait out the block. I'm sure they'll have it lifted by morning, or they'll have a commuter riot on their hands. What do you say?"

Bryn closed her screen and shoved her comtab back into her pocket.

"Who am I to argue with a Blackguard major?" she said. "You lead, I'll follow."

Chapter 22

Dunstan

When the engineering officer came up the ladder and stepped off into the galley, Dunstan was glad for the excuse to push his half-eaten meal aside. They had run out of fresh ingredients days ago, and until they docked at Rhodia again, the cooking in the galley kitchen would be limited to heating up pre-packaged meal trays. Most of the remaining supply seemed to be all the stuff he didn't like, and he resolved to have a word about the selection allotments with the navy yard's supply quartermaster when they got back home.

"Lieutenant Fields," he said to the newcomer. "Have a seat. I'm hoping for some good news because this noodle tray just made me sad."

"Do not saddle me with *that* kind of responsibility, sir," Fields said as he went over to the coffee dispenser to fill a mug for himself. He carried it to Dunstan's nook and sat down, then placed both the coffee and the engineering compad he was carrying on the table in front of him.

"For what it's worth, we got off easy," he said. "Relatively speaking, of course. The one hit they did get in is going to end up being expensive, though."

He brought up a schematic on the compad and rotated the screen so Dunstan could see it.

"We got a cannon shell right on the nose, dead center on the armor. It broke up the shell, but a bunch of the shrapnel deflected off the armor slope and into the bow sensor cluster. One of the two long-range optics mounts is wrecked. That's not so terrible because we have a backup. But the solid-state array got torn up as well, and that isn't so good. We have no long-range radar."

"How bad is it? Anything you can patch up provisionally?"

Lieutenant Fields shook his head.

"Even if I had a bunch of spare emitter segments sitting around, we can't rebuild the whole array and then calibrate it again by ourselves. Not out here. That's a job for a fleet dry dock."

"Fantastic." Dunstan took a sip of his own coffee. "They let us take out the navy's most expensive ship, and we're bringing it back broken."

"Like I said, we got off easy, sir. It's just a sensor array. And we caused a whole lot more damage than we took."

"When we get back, the admiral is either going to give me a medal or a disciplinary hearing," Dunstan said. "Maybe both at the same time."

"That's well above my pay grade. I just spin wrenches and move levers," Fields replied with a little smile.

"You've been the head of engineering since she went out for the first time. Give me your honest opinion of this ship, Lieutenant."

Fields sat back and took a slow sip of his coffee while he was thinking about his reply.

"She's like nothing else out there, you know that. She's nimble, she's stealthy, and that AI core is like someone stuffed the brain of one of the old gods into the hull. But I think she has a few design flaws."

"Go on," Dunstan said.

"She's too slow. The stealth nozzles limit the output too much. They're amazing for staying stealthy, but stealth isn't everything. Sometimes you need acceleration, and she doesn't have enough of it. Not for our size and power output."

"All right." Dunstan nodded slowly. "What else?"

"She's just too small. She doesn't have enough firepower because they couldn't fit more weapons into the hull. It's like whoever designed her got so excited about the stealth and the AI that they forgot she's supposed to be a warship. We can go and sneak into places nobody else can reach undetected. But once we're there, we can't do much other than watch and listen. And she doesn't have the endurance for long deployments because we can't bring enough supplies to sustain us for more than a few weeks."

"Thank you for the honest assessment, Lieutenant. I'll bring up your points with the admiral once we get back."

"Don't get me wrong—I love this ship," Fields said with a shrug. "We've done things with her that no other ship could have done. She'd just be better if she was a few hundred tons bigger."

Dunstan nodded again.

"That's the problem with experimental designs. You never know how well the design theory translates into practice until you take them out into the void," he said.

"That said, sir—she's had an amazing trial run, hasn't she?" Fields smiled.

"That she has, Lieutenant," Dunstan agreed. "That she has, indeed."

Hecate was back near the regular transfer lanes, and the comms chatter from nearby merchants and warships was a welcome low-key background noise on the Ops deck again after two weeks of radio silence. Near the edge of the tactical plot, a cluster of blue icons was moving steadily off into the distance toward the outer rim, the ad-hoc task force the navy had assembled to rush to the coordinates *Hecate* had sent with her report on the pirate station. Even at their standard three-g fast transit burn, the trip would take them days. Dunstan was certain the three frigates and two cruisers rushing out to the wrecked pirate station would find little more than scuttled hulls and empty life pods after all the time that had passed since the station had gone down.

He had just started his watch ten minutes ago, and there was a cup of double-strength fleet coffee in the cup holder on his chair's armrest, but Dunstan felt like he had barely gotten any rest in the six hours he had spent in his berth. He lifted the cup for a sip but had to pause the movement because he felt a yawn coming on that resisted his attempt at suppressing it.

"Oh, now you've done it," Lieutenant Hunter said. A moment later, she let out a hearty yawn of her own.

"I have the conn, Number One. What are you still doing in Ops? Go and get some sleep. I don't want to see you back up here until 1400 at the earliest."

"Aye, sir." Hunter didn't look like she had any desire to argue. "Just tying up some end-of-watch stuff. It was a quiet one. I have no idea why I'm dragging so hard."

"It's strange, you know. We've only been out for a little more than three weeks. But it feels like we're coming back from a six-month deployment."

"It's that special blend of long periods of boredom interspersed with moments of pure terror," Hunter replied.

"Have you notified *Zephyr* that we won't be able to meet them at Oceana after all?"

The first officer nodded.

"We've sent out three back-channel messages since we got back into the regular comms network. No reply yet."

"Let's hope they're just busy running a juicy new contract."

"Or they're down on Adrasteia for some extended R & R while they're waiting for us to catch up with them."

"That would be a smart thing to do. Now haul yourself out of that chair and hit the rack, Number One. Before I call the master-at-arms to lead you to your bunk at gunpoint."

Hunter raised her arms in mock surrender.

"Fine, fine. Let's not blemish a perfect disciplinary record."

She unbuckled her harness and got out of her seat.

"It does feel that way, though, doesn't it?" she said to Dunstan. "Like we just came back in from a hot wartime patrol."

"That's because we did," he replied. "We're in the middle of a shooting war. Whether anyone declared it or not."

—

A few ten thousand kilometers ahead of *Hecate*, the current transfer lane between Rhodia and Pallas was evident by the line of civilian ship icons that crossed the tactical map like a slow-moving river, dozens of commercial and private vessels that were broadcasting their transponder IDs and keeping their safe transit intervals. Back in the war, the Rhodian Navy had tried to use convoy tactics, sending half a dozen ships through the lane at the same time with a warship as escort, but there had never been enough available to handle the volume of trade that crossed the system even in wartime, and the larger clusters of ships had attracted pirate attacks instead of deterring them. Now and then, the best chance a ship had was to make the run alone and roll the dice. It was impossible to know for sure, but the odds almost guaranteed that *Hecate* had saved some of the ships currently on the tactical display from a future attack by thinning out the pirate fleet.

Maybe we finally put a stop to it all, Dunstan thought. *If that was their main supply hub, there's no place for them to rearm and refuel.*

"We're on a shortest-distance approach to Rhodia One," Lieutenant Armer reported. "We have a priority vector for docking in the navy yard. Time to arrival is fourteen hours, twenty minutes."

"I wonder how long it will take them to patch us up and send us back out," Lieutenant Robson said.

"I'm not a subject-matter expert on phased sensor arrays," Dunstan replied. "But our chief engineer says it'll be a few weeks at least. Don't worry. We'll all get our shore leave after this."

"Commander?" a familiar voice called out behind him.

Dunstan turned in his chair to see Lieutenant Hunter on the ladder, poking her head into the Ops deck from above.

"I thought I ordered you to your bunk half an hour ago, Lieutenant."

"Yes, sir," Hunter acknowledged. "I was held up with something on the way. Could you come up to AI Core Control for a minute, please?"

"Another crisis?" Dunstan reached for the buckle of his safety harness.

"Not a crisis, sir. But it is kind of a big deal."

"Well, then." He got out of his chair and stretched his back for a moment. "Lieutenant Armer, you have the conn."

"I have the conn," Armer confirmed.

Dunstan walked over to the ladderwell and nodded at Hunter.

"Lead the way, Lieutenant."

—

The AI Core Control compartment was the topmost deck of the ship, only accessible to Dunstan, his first officer, and Lieutenant Robson as the electronic warfare officer. Lieutenant Hunter stepped off the ladder and walked over to the central console. She authenticated herself on the system, and a screen projection opened in front of her. Dunstan walked up behind her to look at the contents.

"I ran the notebooks you retrieved through the AI," Hunter said. "The hardest part was scanning all the pages individually. That took a few days."

"You've done scans of every page in four notebooks?"

"Yes, 192 pages per book, 768 pages total," Hunter said. "There's a reason why nobody uses paper notebooks for anything anymore. I can't believe they used to run entire civilizations on stuff like that."

"Analog records still have their place. Especially for sneaky stuff. You can't hack into a paper notebook. And it's easy to destroy if it gets compromised."

"Oh, I know all of that. It's just so inefficient."

She enlarged one of the data fields on the screen in front of her and slowly scrolled through it.

"Once I had everything digitized, I had the ship's AI take a swing at it. It's a simple encryption cipher. Of course, it wasn't meant to stand up to quantum computing decryption. Just prying eyes."

"I'm going to assume that I didn't risk my neck just to recover the captain's personal journals," Dunstan said.

"His gambling ledger," Hunter said. "He was betting heavily on socaball league matches." She chuckled when he made a sour face. "No, it's nothing personal. Unless he was really into numbers. It's an algorithm. The AI had it figured out in a few seconds. They're times and coordinates."

"Makes sense. They had to have a way to know when and where to meet without putting it out into the network for us to find. I bet every one of those pirate ships has a stack of books like that in the captain's bunk drawer."

"That's a fair assumption. We've just never captured a ship intact without giving the crew time to light up the analog evidence," Hunter said. "But that's not the best part, sir."

"Go on," Dunstan said.

"There are multiple spots where the entries are mutually exclusive. The time overlaps but the coordinates don't."

"Alternate meeting points, maybe?" he asked.

"That was my thought, too. But the AI doesn't think so. If they are alternate coordinates, the sequence doesn't make much sense. Unless they have ships that can fly across half the system in a day."

"So there may be more than one of those replenishment points out there," Dunstan said.

Lieutenant Hunter nodded.

"Cassandra here says there's a ninety-seven percent likelihood that there are two more. One is in the outer reaches between Hades and Acheron, and the other is going back and forth between the outer rift and the edge of Palladian space."

Dunstan laughed and shook his head.

"Are you positive about this?"

"Cassandra is," Hunter said. "You know she's been right on the marker so far whenever we've relied on her predictive algorithm."

"I'd say that was worth the little field trip. When we turn that over to fleet intelligence, they may even forgive us for denting the ship."

"It could still be a ruse," she replied. "If you're looking for a possible fly in the soup. Just because we have times and coordinates doesn't mean they have to be real."

"Planting fake codebooks for us to find so we start chasing ghosts in the outer rim?"

Lieutenant Hunter shrugged. "It wouldn't be a terrible idea. We're stretched thin as it is. Nobody's going to go out there with less than a small task force. That would pull available units away from the transfer lanes."

"I don't know, Number One. They could have sacrificed one of their welding shop specials for that. Not a good warship with a capable crew."

He straightened his back with a little groan.

"But that's for the intelligence division to figure out. We're just the muscle," he said.

"We took a lot of ships off the board," Hunter said. "And now we may know where and when to find the rest of them. This whole thing could be over in another month."

Dunstan felt a little rush at the notion. With the piracy problem solved, the navy could return to peacetime operations. They would no longer have a shortage of warships, and the operational tempo could be throttled back to the point where the crews could have sane deployment rotations again, only going out a few months out of the year rather than being kept out on patrol for as long as people and machines could bear it. He could go home for more than just a week or two at a time and get to spend more time with his family before his daughters were all grown up and busy with their own lives, remembering their father mostly from shore leaves and occasional vidcalls that had to be cut short half the time. But hope was a fragile thing in the military, and the fates tended to home in on it wherever it cropped up.

"I won't shed any tears if they've mopped up the mess before we can get back into action, Lieutenant. But I've been in the navy too long to wager any money on the possibility. We'll be back in the thick of it before we know it."

His first officer smiled without humor.

"I'd love to disagree with you, but I can't," she said.

"That's the attitude," Dunstan replied. "Now you're ready for your own command."

He walked back to the ladderwell and started his descent back to the Ops deck. Just before his head dipped below the hatch collar, Lieutenant Hunter called after him.

"Oh, Commander?"

Dunstan paused his climb. "Yes, Lieutenant?"

"We're back in Mnemosyne range, so I checked the dockmaster's logs at Oceana a little while ago. *Zephyr* never made it. There's no record of them docking there since their last visit three months ago."

He pursed his lips and exhaled slowly.

"I hope they just decided to drop off the grid again and stay low for a little while," he said. "Because it looks like it may be some time before we can go out and search for them."

Chapter 23
Solveig

The cabin on the starliner was small, the fabric covers on the furniture worn and faded from many years of constant use, and the bathroom was just a nook next to the bed that had a toilet and a sink below a label warning Do Not Use In Zero Gravity. The accommodations on the Ragnar corporate shuttle, the only other starship she had ever taken, were far superior in every respect, but Solveig was utterly content. As small and dingy as it was, her cabin was private, and there was nobody on the ship who knew or cared who she was. There was no assistant to hover over her shoulder and try to predict her needs and desires, and no Gisbert sitting across the cabin from her, pounding drinks and attempting to engage her in conversation. She was truly by herself for what felt like the first time in her life, and she loved it.

Apollo 601 had left Gretia's spin station an hour ago, and they had just settled into the transfer lane at the standard economical one g of cruise acceleration. The spaceport had been exciting but also a little anxiety inducing because there was still a chance Marten or one of his security minions could catch up with her and either try to strong-arm her home or simply come along. But once the starliner had closed its airlock hatch and detached from the station, the anxiety had fallen away from her along with the pull of gravity. Now she was humming softly as she was settling in and stowing the contents of her travel bag in the drawer underneath her bunk.

It didn't take long to put away the few things she had brought, comfortable clothes to last her for the journey and some items from the shops at the spaceport. When she was finished, she closed the drawer and made herself comfortable on the recliner chair that took up most of the rest of the cabin.

I'm skipping work for the first time in my life, Solveig thought. Anja *probably* wouldn't have snitched on her, but that was a risk she had been unwilling to take, so she had not informed her assistant she wouldn't be coming in today. Now that she was safely and irrevocably in space, she got out her comtab to send an update. When she turned on the device, she saw that Anja had already sent her five comms requests this morning.

Solveig sent a request in turn, which was accepted almost as soon as she had tapped the send field.

"Miss Solveig," Anja said. "Are you all right? I was about to send someone from security over to check on you."

"I'm fine, Anja. Sorry I didn't let you know ahead of time, but I need to take a little bit of time off for some unexpected family business."

Even on the small screen projection from her comtab, Solveig could tell that Anja was subtly trying to make out the background to deduce where she was.

"I understand, Miss Solveig. I hope it's nothing bad. How long would you like me to block off your schedule?"

"Make it two weeks for now, please. If anything changes and I need to stay away longer, I'll be sure to let you know."

"Of course. Safe travels, and do not hesitate to contact me if I can be of any assistance."

"Thank you, Anja. I'll see you back in the office in two weeks."

Solveig ended the vidcall and turned her comtab off again. It was only a question of time before Marten, and by extension Papa, would know that she was out in the world and traveling by herself, without a safety net or a chaperone, and she didn't want to have to decline the flurry of comms requests that would inevitably follow. There would be much sound and fury when she returned, but there was no reason for her to listen to the speeches early and spoil the trip.

There was a compad on the little table next to her chair that controlled the room's functions and the entertainment options, and she picked it up to look at the offerings. A screen projection opened in front of the bulkhead above the bed, showing a system chart with the current transfer lanes between the planets. The starliner's position was marked with a small graphic representation of the ship, accelerating along the transfer lane to Hades. Another data field showed the current velocity of the ship, climbing steadily at 9.81 meters per second squared, and the time left to the destination, 89 hours and 14 minutes.

Now that she was underway, Solveig felt the morning's hectic schedule catching up with her. She'd had to get up early to make her orbital connection from the Sandvik spaceport, and she had gone there the roundabout way, via public pod and then a loop train detour via Civic Square, to ditch any security escorts Marten may have tasked with following her. She had been awake for six hours already, all of which she had spent on the go and in a constant state of anxious vigilance. Now that she could relax, her body reasserted its need for some rest. She moved over to the bunk and lay down on it, fastening the safety belt as instructed by the warning sign on the bulkhead above the bed so a sudden loss of gravity wouldn't send her to the ceiling in her sleep. The mattress was thin but comfortable, and she closed her eyes to drift off to the soothing low background rumbling of the ship's fusion drive.

"Attention, attention. This is the dinner announcement. Meals will be served in the dining section on deck five for the next ninety minutes. I repeat, meals will be served on deck five for the next ninety minutes. Announcement ends."

The dinner call woke Solveig from her sleep just in time for her to catch the repeat of the message. She tried to sit up and felt a brief surge of panic when she couldn't, until she remembered the safety belt and reached for the buckle to unfasten it.

The Ragnar corporate shuttle had a lovely bulkhead projection that went through the day and night cycle for standard time on Gretia, but this starliner didn't have that kind of luxury feature, and she looked at the screen projection above her bunk for a time reference instead. The little ship graphic had moved along the track to Hades a very small amount, but there was now a tiny gap between it and the bigger orb representing Gretia, and the time-to-destination counter currently showed 86 hours and 55 minutes.

That was a three-hour nap, she thought as she slipped on her boots. *I must have been more tired than I thought.*

The starliner wasn't a huge cruise ship, but it was much larger than the company shuttle she had taken to Acheron, and the decks were more than twice as wide across. The galley on deck five looked a lot like the canteen back at the old police headquarters where she had eaten lunch with Stefan just before the insurgent attack, a simple but clean utilitarian space with enough seating for two dozen passengers if they didn't mind rubbing elbows.

The food on offer was as basic as the ship, but it had come out of pots and pans in the galley instead of a prepackaged tray. Solveig filled her tray with greens and some fish and sat down at one of the tables to eat. The other passengers on the mess deck were a mixed bunch of mostly older people, all Gretians from the sound of their conversations, with a few young faces scattered throughout the group. To her, it looked like she was the youngest passenger on the ship by ten years.

She was used to men staring at her from time to time, and when she briefly caught the gaze of another passenger on the other side of the dining room, he smoothly averted his eyes. She usually would have shrugged it off as some guy sneaking a few glances at a face he found pretty. But today had started with the stress and subterfuge of her trip to the spaceport, and Solveig was still a little bit on edge despite the earlier rest. Over the years, she had developed a sort of sixth sense for being followed or watched. Something about her observer set off that sense now. His look in her direction hadn't been the usual male gaze, and the way he had avoided her eyes had been entirely too smooth and casual. Now he was concentrating on his own meal and looking at his comtab, but his eyes were not focused on the screen like they should if he was just scrolling through messages or reading news. Something about his face triggered a faint recognition in her brain, as if she had seen him once or twice before. He wasn't one of Marten's estate team or the executive protection group, but she knew that if he had sent someone to shadow her on this trip, he wouldn't have picked a face she knew well. Now he was studiously avoiding looks in her direction, which was suspicious. She turned her head and resumed her meal. If he was one of Marten's people, she didn't want him to know that she was aware of his presence. For a few moments, however, she was tempted to pick up her tray and walk over to his table to put him on the spot.

Marten, she thought. *I need to stop underestimating him.* He had figured out where she was going, and all the sneaking around and changing modes of transportation this morning had been for nothing. While she had been looking over her shoulder for a tail, he had somehow managed to discover the secure data link she had used for booking her trip and simply booked one of his men onto the starliner as well.

Maybe I am being overly cautious again, she told herself. *It's probably just some awkward loner looking at the only young woman on the entire ship.*

There were days when she would have concluded just that, when she would have let go of her suspicions and assumed the simplest explanation was the correct one. But those days had been long ago, before she had even been out of university. After everything that had happened in the last year, she knew that suppressing the little alarm bells in her head never worked out in her favor.

Nice move, Marten, she thought with grudging admiration. *Now let's see how well your man can keep up with me once we land on Hades.*

On the way back to her cabin, Solveig pulled out her comtab and turned it on. As expected, there was a long list of connection requests. It seemed like everyone who knew her had tried to contact her while she had been asleep. There were too many requests to address them all individually without spending the next three hours on vidcalls, so she composed a status update and sent it out to the people on the list.

> I'm on a personal trip and will check in with you when I return.

She turned the comtab off again before the next request could come in and tempt her to answer it directly. Her problems would still be there when she returned.

If *I return,* she thought. *I could just stay on Hades with Mama. Or skip around between the planets like Aden.*

The thought of Aden reminded her of the purchase she had made at the spaceport before her departure. Back in her cabin, she closed and latched the door behind her. Then she knelt in front of the bunk and opened the drawer to reach into her travel bag and pull out the new comtab she had bought at one of the shops in the central concourse. It was a basic model that wasn't half as capable as the one she already owned, but it wasn't registered to her ID pass. Without a personal ID link, it wouldn't work on Gretia, but out in space, the interplanetary quantum relays forwarded the traffic from any active node regardless of its registration status. It was a loophole intended for emergency comms, but while she was in the transit lane, she could use it to send messages without using her own device.

Solveig unwrapped the comtab and activated it. Without a linked ID, it was almost useless, but it could access the Mnemosyne and send quantum-band messages. She had memorized the node ID of Aden's comtab since she had met up with him on Acheron, and she hadn't forgotten it despite everything that had happened in the meantime. It had been three months or more since they'd exchanged a message, and the prospect of having a longer conversation with him again without needing to look over her shoulder made her hands shake a little with anticipation.

Hey you, she wrote. This is Shorty. I am on the way to Hades, if you can believe it. Can you come?

She sent the message into the quantum network. Almost immediately, her burner comtab chirped with the notification of an incoming reply. Solveig opened the screen and held her breath for a moment.

Delivery failure: Not a valid node, the reply read, and her heart sank.

I messed up the address, she thought. But when she entered it again and sent the message out, the reply came back the same way. Delivery failure: Not a valid node.

The sudden disappointment left a bitter taste in her mouth. She put the comtab on the bed and stared at it for a few moments, trying to will it to deliver a reply from Aden. When it didn't, she stood up and paced her little cabin with her hands on her head, taking deep breaths to slow down her racing pulse.

Where are you, Aden? she thought. *Please don't disappear again. Not now. Not when I just found you.*

Epilogue

Aden

Aden woke to sunlight warming his face.

He blinked a few times to let his eyes adjust to the brightness of the room. It was a small hotel suite, and the clothes scattered on the floor and the empty glasses on the table by the window helped him with the reconstruction of the events of last night. Bryn was sleeping next to him, breathing deeply and evenly, one shapely leg on top of her cover. The only thing she was wearing was the chain around her neck with her military ID tag, which made her slightly more dressed than he was.

He slipped out from under his own cover and got out of bed slowly and gingerly, aided in his effort by the fact that the bed had two separate mattresses and split covers in the old-fashioned Gretian style. His clothes on the floor were intermingled with Bryn's and scattered in a path that made it easy to retrace the sequence of their mutual undressing. Aden picked up her clothes and straightened them out over one of the chairs, then did the same with his own before going to the bathroom and closing the door as quietly as he could.

When he came out again, Bryn was in the same position, lying on her side with her right leg wrapped around her cover, but her eyes were open, and she smiled groggily when she saw him.

"Good morning," he said. "How are you feeling?"

"A little worn out," she replied. "But the good kind."

"I'm glad to hear that."

She stretched with a little groan and sat up. "What time is it?"

"Already 1020," he said. "We're way late for morning orders."

Bryn chuckled softly. "We're officers. We don't show up for morning orders. That's why the gods made company sergeants."

She threw off her covers and got out of bed. When she was on her feet, she stretched again, a slow and languid move that seemed perfectly executed to let the sunlight emphasize the geometry of her curves. Aden shifted his gaze with some effort and walked over to the window. Outside, the rainy and dreary weather of last night had given way to clear blue skies. When he opened the window, a cool and pleasant breeze blew into the room, and he closed his eyes for a moment to enjoy the sensation. Behind him, Bryn walked to the bathroom and turned on the water.

"Look, if I was a little too forward last night, let me know. I'm not usually that assertive. But getting into a good tussle gets me firing on all engines. And the drinks did the rest," she said through the open door over the sound of the running faucet.

"Let the record show that I am not complaining in the least," he replied. "I'm pretty sure I was an active participant."

"Very active," she confirmed.

"What's next?"

"You mean today, or with us?"

"Both, I guess," he said.

She came out of the bathroom, rubbing her face with a towel.

"Here's the thing. I don't bed subordinates. That's nothing but trouble. People get all wound up about taking orders from somebody they've slept with. But captains and majors are hard to find around here. Especially attractive ones. So I am okay with letting things run and finding out what's next if you are okay with that, too."

"I am," he said.

"Good. I was worried things would get awkward," Bryn said. "As for today, I'd suggest we get dressed and find some breakfast, then hail a pod to take us back to Sandvik."

"No objections," Aden said. "Proceed as suggested, Captain."

She smiled and flicked a little mock salute in his direction.

This assignment is going in ways I didn't anticipate, he thought as they got dressed. Being an intelligence operative meant having to go with the flow, to compartmentalize the things one did on the job, to disengage the self. He wasn't the one who elbowed the reefo protester in the face and broke his nose, it was Aden Robertson, the proud Blackguard. But as much as he tried to write off last night to Aden Robertson's desires instead of his own, it didn't serve to numb the sting of guilt he felt when he thought about Tess. Before last night, he had been able to tell himself that he was playing a part, that he was being a savvy and skilled operative who was merely doing what he had to do, but now he wasn't so sure anymore.

When they were both dressed and cleaned up, they picked up their detritus from last night, empty bottles of cellar ale and containers of late-night food-stand meals. Aden went out into the hallway and dumped the refuse in the recycler chute. In the room, Bryn turned on the viewscreen, and the chatter of network news streams reached Aden's ears at the end of the hallway. When he returned, she wasn't looking at the viewscreen. She was sitting on the bed with her comtab in her hand and a troubled expression. She didn't look up at him when he was back in the room. Instead, she was focused on the device, and the concern on her face seemed to grow with every flick of her thumb. Finally, she looked up and noticed him.

"Bad news?" Aden asked.

"Fuck," Bryn replied. She stood up and began to pace the room. "Fuck, fuck, *fuck*."

She tossed her comtab onto the bed and looked at Aden.

"That was Lars. The bastards got Helge. He was working his shift at the spaceport when that shuttle went up. Lars went to check on him this morning. He says there's Alliance all over his building."

"Shit." Aden ran his hands through his hair. "That's not good."

"That's very not fucking good at all," Bryn said. "If they nabbed Helge, they're going to come looking for us as well."

"We didn't blow up that shuttle," Aden replied.

"Doesn't matter." She looked up at him. "They'll go down the list of his known associates. Especially the ones with expertise in munitions. I spent three days in interrogation lockup after the Principal Square bombing. I do not care for another round of that."

Why would they go after Helge? Aden thought. *They don't just pick people off the street at random. What did he do that warranted a raid team? And did you know about it?*

He could sense that she wasn't telling him everything, but the fear that had crept into her eyes was genuine, and the way her eyes had started to scan the room at every new sound from the outside was the kind of prey reaction that was difficult to act.

Aden walked over to the window. Outside, the streets looked like they had when he had opened the window just a little while ago, but Bryn's anxiety was starting to rub off on him, and the knowledge of their new peril made everything look suspicious to his mind. Was there too little traffic on the street suddenly, too few pedestrians on the sidewalks? In his mind, he saw Alliance roadblocks being set up at the nearby intersections, and a tactical team moving in through a side street, armed to the teeth and afflicted with itchy trigger fingers. If he and Bryn came across a commando squad out to find them, he knew they wouldn't be interested in talking. More than a hundred of their comrades were dead, and they'd be out for blood.

Outside, a military gyrofoil flew low over Vigard, close enough to their hotel to make the leaves on the trees in front of the hotel sway in the breeze of the rotor downwash. Aden closed the open window panel to dim the noise.

"We need to get the hells out of here," he said.

"We can't go back to Sandvik," Bryn replied. "Not while they are kicking down doors and hauling in anyone Helge's ever met."

"All right," he said. "We don't go back to Sandvik. Where are we going instead?"

"I have friends down in Arendal. One of them has a place on the coast he lets us use when things get a little hot. It's a bit of a dump. But we won't need to check in with ID passes to stay there."

She put her comtab away and stood up. "Sorry for dragging you into this. Are you sure you want to come with me? You still have a clean slate with them."

"I'm a Blackguard," he replied. "I never had a clean slate with them. Of course I am coming with you."

"All right," she said with a little smile. "Then let's go. Time to go into hiding for a while."

They made one last sweep of the room to make sure they'd leave nothing behind. Before they walked out, Bryn pulled him close and kissed him, a hungry and urgent kiss that made his head swim for a moment.

"Thank you," she said when she pulled back. "I'm really fucking glad you're a major, by the way."

"That makes two of us," he said.

They left the hotel at a measured pace and turned right onto the street, toward the public pod corral at the end of the block. Nobody came out of the shadows to shout a challenge at gunpoint. Aden took a deep breath of the cool morning air and recited his covert mission mantra in his head as he walked ahead of Bryn.

I'm Major Aden Robertson. I am a proud Blackguard and a patriot of Gretia. I hate the boot of the Alliance on my neck, and I will do what it takes to pry it off. It was still a lie, all of it from beginning to end. But every time he said or thought the words, they came a little bit easier.

Acknowledgments

This novel is the fourth in the Palladium Wars series and my thirteenth published novel since 2013. Thirteen is usually considered an unlucky number, but it's a good number in this household: Robin and I got married on a Friday the thirteenth, and we celebrate our anniversary not on the date we got married but on every Friday the thirteenth, which means we got a lot of bonus anniversary dinners in over the years. "Lucky Thirteen" was also the name of a Frontlines short story that made it all the way onto Netflix as the source for an episode of *Love, Death + Robots* a few years back, so the number thirteen has brought good luck for me.

After thirteen novels with largely the same people to thank, acknowledgments sometimes feel like I'm writing the same thing over and over again at the end of each book, but they're important because those thanks are owed every single time. The novels simply wouldn't exist without all the people who work on getting them out into the world.

First on the list is always Robin, my first reader and editor, who has spent as much time on this story as I have. Thanks are due to Evan, my agent, and my editor Adrienne and the crew at 47North, as well as Andrea, my developmental editor. (Edits are a lot of work for everyone involved, but they never fail to improve the final product a great deal.)

Thank you to my friends: Tracie, Stacy, Monica, Tamara, and Paul. I'm glad to have you in my life, and I still hope to contribute that private jet to our retirement compound one day.

Thank you to my writer friends for your friendship and continued support: Delilah S. Dawson, Chuck Wendig, Kevin Hearne, John Scalzi, George R.R. Martin and the entire Wild Cards consortium, my magic collaboration partner Kris Herndon, and Claire, Kat, Julie, Chang, and the Viable Paradise gang.

And the last and most important item on the list: a heartfelt thank you to my readers. You continue to buy my books and spread the word, and because of that, I get to keep making stuff up and writing it down. I am grateful beyond measure that I get to live this life and do what I do for a living.

About the Author

Photo © 2018 Robin Kloos

Marko Kloos is the author of two military science fiction series: The Palladium Wars, which includes *Aftershocks*, *Ballistic*, *Citadel*, and *Descent*, and the Frontlines series, which includes, most recently, *Centers of Gravity*. Born in Germany and raised in and around the city of Münster, Marko was previously a soldier, bookseller, freight dockworker, and corporate IT administrator before deciding that he wasn't cut out for anything except making stuff up for fun and profit. A member of George R.R. Martin's Wild Cards consortium, Marko writes primarily science fiction and fantasy—his first genre loves ever since his youth, when he spent his allowance on German SF pulp serials. He likes bookstores, kind people, October in New England, fountain pens, and wristwatches. Marko resides at Castle Frostbite in New Hampshire with his wife, two children, and roving pack of voracious dachshunds. For more information visit markokloos.com.